SOFTLY CRIES THE CURLEW

PART TWO OF

'Jack Tucker of Exmoor'
A Family Saga 1815-1875

Paddy King-Fretts

ryelands

First published in Great Britain in 2008

Copyright © 2008 Paddy King-Fretts

British Library Cataloguing-in-Publication Data
A CIP record for this title is available from the British Library

ISBN 978 1 906551 07 0

RYELANDS
Halsgrove House
Ryelands Industrial Estate, Bagley Road,
Wellington, Somerset TA21 9PZ
Tel: 01823 653777
Fax: 01823 216796
email: sales@halsgrove.com
website: www.halsgrove.com

Printed and bound in Great Britain by Short Run Press Ltd, Exeter

Front cover illustration
Landacre bridge **by Jack Hoar**
Tel: 01769 572131 e-mail: jackhoar@hotmail.com

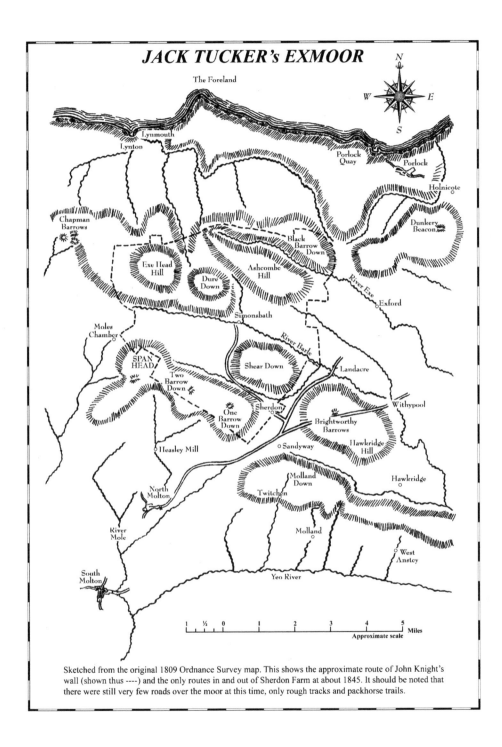

JACK TUCKER's EXMOOR

Sketched from the original 1809 Ordnance Survey map. This shows the approximate route of John Knight's wall (shown thus ----) and the only routes in and out of Sherdon Farm at about 1845. It should be noted that there were still very few roads over the moor at this time, only rough tracks and packhorse trails.

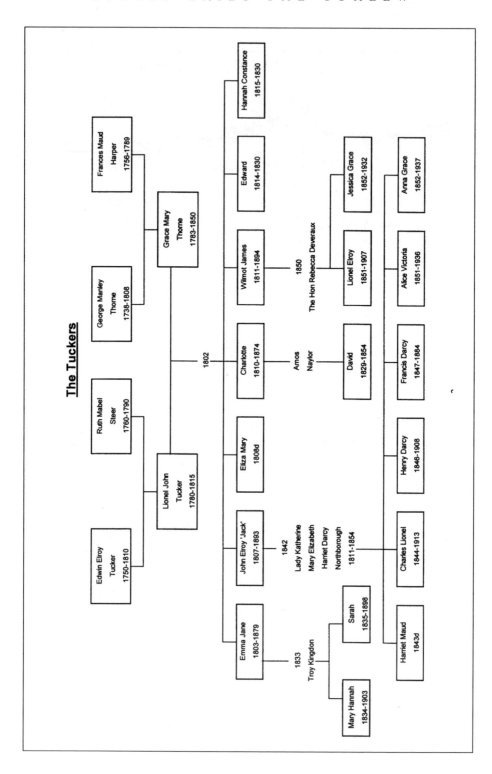

The Tuckers

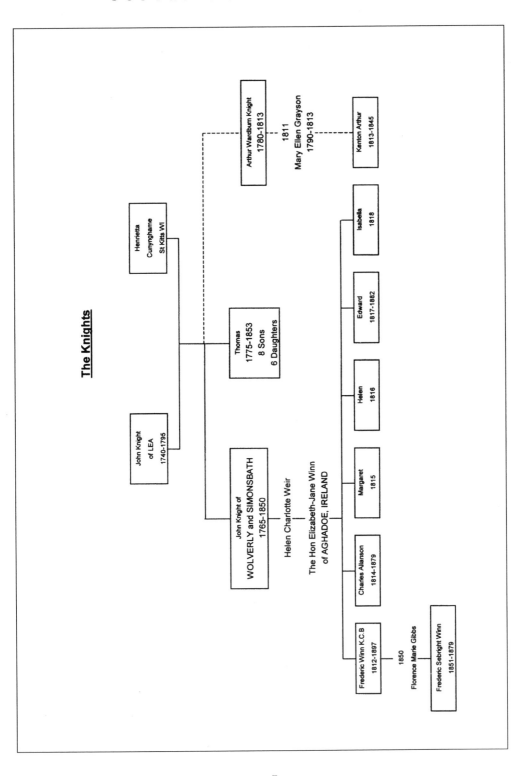

The Knights

John Knight of LEA 1740-1795

Henrietta Cunynghame St Kitts WI

Arthur Wardburn Knight 1780-1813

1811

Mary Ellen Grayson 1790-1813

Kenton Arthur 1813-1845

John Knight of WOLVERLY and SIMONSBATH 1765-1850

Helen Charlotte Weir

The Hon Elizabeth-Jane Winn of AGHADOE, IRELAND

Thomas 1775-1853 8 Sons 6 Daughters

Frederic Winn K.C.B 1812-1897

1850

Florence Marie Gibbs

Frederic Sebright Winn 1851-1879

Charles Allanson 1814-1879

Margaret 1815

Helen 1816

Edward 1817-1882

Isabella 1818

Principal Characters

(less those covered by the two family trees)

Acland, Sir Thomas. 10th Baronet, landowner and M.P. Lady Acland, Lt Charles RN and James.

Bawden, Stan. Labourer at Sherdon.

Benson, 'Benny'. Head gardener at Blagdon Park.

Burge, Davey. A Brendon farmer and part-time smuggler.

Burgess, William. A notorious Exmoor murderer who killed his daughter, Anna, aged six.

Chanter, Oliver. The builder who built Sherdon.

Chapple, Miss Enid. Governess to the Knight children.

Cockram, Hardy. Landlord of The Sportsman's Inn, Sandyway and father of Bess.

Collyns, Dr Charles Palk. A well known doctor and benefactor from Dulverton.

Coward, Hector. Frederic Knight's groom and a friend of Jack Tucker. Husband of Nancy.

Daniels, Private Billy. Soldier of The North Devon Militia and wrestler.

Deveraux, Mr Piers and The Hon Mrs. Shipping magnate and parents of Rebecca and Susannah.

Fisher, Harry, Gwen and Gaile. Farmers from Ferny Ball.

Froude, The Rev John. Vicar of Knowstone and Molland.

Gale, Sir George. Magistrate and Chairman of The North Devon Bench.

Grant, Leonard. Gardener/groom to the Knights and a friend of Jack Tucker.

Grayson, Mr Varney. Frederic Knight's Land Agent.

Hannaford, Rob. Special Constable from Lynton.

Harper, Luke. Smuggler and swordsman and uncle of Jasper, a highwayman.

Hawkins, Jason. A shepherd from Molland.

Heard, Bamber and family. Farmers from Withypool.

Luttrell, John. Bachelor and Master of Dunster Castle.

Mason, Edgar. Friend of Kenton Knight.

Morgan, Mr Durnford. Merchant banker from Esdaile's Bank, Lombard St.

Naylor, Amos. Foreman at Heathcoat's factory, Tiverton.

Northborough, The Duke and Duchess. Friends of John Knight.

O'Hara, Declan. Irish labourer who worked for Jack Tucker at Sherdon.

Parker, Mr Bernard. John Knight's head butler.

Preston, Lord Herbert. Heir to The Duke of Northborough and friend of Kenton Knight.

Rawle, Kitty and Gillan. Neighbours of the Tuckers at Sherdon.

Rudd, Ralph. Relative of the Tuckers who worked at Sherdon.

Russell, Parson Jack. The famous hunting parson.

Shaddick, 'Devil'. Public hangman at Taunton gaol.

Slocombe, Joshua. Tenant farmer at West Lyn Farm, Barbrook.

Swain, Jethro. Master-at-Arms, The Royal North Devon Hussars.

Tennyson, Alfred Lord. Poet Laureate.

Tucker, Davey. Son of Charlotte, Jack's sister.

Webber, Dan. Groom to Frederic Knight and friend of Jack Tucker.

Westcott, Billy. Young relative of Jack's and great friend of Davey Tucker.

PART ONE
Tempered Steel
Summer 1838

Chapter One

Conversation had been difficult and Lady Katherine Darcy was nervous. Having moved slightly apart from the others she stood looking out of one of the hall windows and onto the forecourt. She had been to Dunster Castle before but this time, as soon as the visit had been arranged, she had become increasingly apprehensive. Even now as she surveyed the scene, Francis Luttrell, her host, stepped forward to greet the coach, pulled by four heavy bays, as it swept around the wide, gravelled concourse. John Knight and his wife, Elizabeth-Jane, also guests at today's luncheon party, had arrived. Katherine looked on anxiously.

It had been over two years since the terrible day at their Simonsbath home, yet only recently had the storm subsided. Elizabeth-Jane had written, assuring her that she would always be most welcome, nevertheless it had been a year before Katherine had summoned the courage to visit and a further six months before she and her sister, Lizzie, had gone to stay. Elizabeth-Jane had been the easier by far, each time taking pains to convince her that the matter was over until, at long last, the subject appeared to have been forgotten. Her husband, however, had been more difficult, distancing himself from the two sisters until he had stayed with their father, the Duke, at Blagdon Park.

Unaware of those nearby, Katherine moved closer to the window and craned her neck to see better. Luttrell, gaunt, balding and looking all of his fifty years, lived alone in the castle, relying heavily on other members of the family to help entertain. As soon as the footman had lowered the folding step and opened the coach door he stepped forward. The figure that emerged presented itself backwards, very slowly and with its head bent low to avoid the doorframe. Katherine watched fascinated as John Knight arrived step by heavy step until both feet were on the ground. Only then did he turn, flushed and squinting in the noonday light.

"Welcome to Dunster, sir." Francis Luttrell took his hand. "Delighted to see you again. And, if I might say so, you're looking in rare good health." John Knight, Master of Exmoor and now over seventy, inclined his head stiffly before both men turned and looked on in silence as Elizabeth-Jane was helped from the coach. Once more Luttrell stepped forward, this time to accept the proffered and gloved hand. "A great pleasure, madam, as always…and a joy to have your company once again."

"Aah, John, my thanks. How kind." Elizabeth-Jane paused to take in the surroundings. "It's lovely to be back, really it is." Although she enjoyed her host's generous hospitality she was never quite able to relax in his company. Most likely it was a figment of her imagination but something about him made her uneasy. He was clever and austere but never a woman's man and would forever remain a bachelor. Of that she was sure. Gesturing for their coats to be taken, Luttrell lead the way to the Inner Hall where the party had assembled. As soon as she heard their voices Katherine tensed, offering a silent prayer that the Knight's stepson, the cause of all her troubles, would not be following them. Her smile in response to John Knight's wave of acknowledgement was more one of relief than endearment.

✳

After luncheon in the Great Parlour the guests moved to the drawing room. At first they stood chatting amicably, the ages mixing easily, everybody pleased to talk with those they had missed at the table. But gradually, and encouraged by their host who fussed about anxiously as the footmen pulled chairs together, each gathered in their own group. The older men, now bent on matters of more immediate concern, eased towards one another while the ladies collected expectantly, their eyes alive with the promise of gossip. As tailcoats were lifted, dresses arranged and backsides parked squarely on seats, the younger generation watched patiently before making their move.

Henry King, tall and well built, with his brown curls tumbling over his high-winged white service collar, lifted his chin and winked. He had come in uniform, the Prussian blue frock coat with its long white lapels and two rows of brass buttons cutting a dash against the grey stonework and faded tapestries. He was a first lieutenant and wore the patterned insignia at his throat attached to the dark blue cravat. Home on shore leave before *H.M.S. Cornwallis* sailed, he and Lizzie, Katherine's sister, had announced their engagement then driven down to join their friends at nearby Holnicote. On hearing the news, John Luttrell had arranged today's lunch party in their honour.

King moved quickly, even before the footmen had left, taking his fiancée by her arm and gesturing to the others. The garden it was to be, the Green Court beyond the keep. The Aclands rose first, Lord Herbert Preston and others also but Katherine declined, preferring instead her own quiet company. Happy to be on her own, she was bored with the idle chatter of the young yet had no interest in joining her mother and her friends whose endless tittle-tattle drove her to distraction. The spot she had spied by the tall window curtains on the first floor gallery was comfortable. The deep, high-backed library chair had been set perfectly to look across the great sweep of the deer park that ran down to the salt marshes, across which the afternoon tide was flooding.

As she settled so the conversation behind her burbled gently on, broken occasionally by an abrupt burst of laughter or short silence as some piece of news was digested. She half listened but was not really concentrating. John Knight's voice took her back to Simonsbath, to the rose garden last summer when, in a gesture of reconciliation, he showed her the new beds he had created. Perhaps he really had forgiven her after all.

Her eyes closed but she could still hear him. He was always there somewhere, sometimes holding forth, sometimes leading the laughter. She heard that more parties at Simonsbath Manor were to be arranged then she heard him call across to her mother and to Elizabeth-Jane. But it was not to be; things *had* changed, of that there was no doubt. Through Kenton Knight's treacherous exposure of her affair, John Knight knew too much and any future visits to his Exmoor home would never be quite the same.

Now they were discussing hunting again, then falconry. She turned her head to listen more clearly and, as she did so, the warm April sun fell across her face forcing her to shield her eyes. Her father was still talking, then Sir Thomas Acland. Moments later her mother laughed in her high-pitched, gulping way. Katherine allowed her head to loll back against the deep cushions. Nearby a bluebottle buzzed against the windowpane, brought to life by the sudden warmth. It kept starting and stopping as though changing its mind about what to do. Somewhere, in the far distance, she could hear the sound of horses, then men's voices calling out to each other. Next it was the stables with that earthy tang of the animals mixed with the scent of oiled leather in the harness room.

Gradually the figure looking her way took shape. It was *him*, Jack, of that she was certain. She could see the open, light brown shirt that he always wore. He was staring with his head on one side like he did with those grey-blue eyes of his looking straight into hers. Then he began to walk towards her, smiling in that shy, boyish way of his while his hands reached up and brushed back the long, straw-blond hair, catching it behind to tie the ribbon. Her heart was beating faster. He was saying something and she strained to catch his words but somebody nearby was talking as well. Then she started. "Lady Katherine. Lady *Katherine*." The voice was louder. "Wake up, you nearly fell."

Margaret and Caroline, John Luttrells two nieces, were standing in front of her laughing shyly. "You jumped," Margaret giggled. "You were dreaming weren't you? And talking…in your sleep…what was it about?"

"Mmm?" Katherine blinked and sat up. "Oh, I can't remember. I was miles away." She rubbed her face and tasted her mouth. "Miles and miles away…oh dear, I'm sorry about that."

"Let me guess." Caroline swung from the arm of her chair. "I *think*…" the nine year old paused rolling her eyes as she deliberated. "I *think*…it was about…"

"Oh, come on, Caro," Margaret pulled the younger girl away. "Uncle John has sent us to find you, Lady Katherine. To bring you down…and to come and join the others so he said." Katherine laughed at their prattle and rose eagerly, glad to be back from the bright sunlight and it was indeed time to rejoin the guests. At the top of the wide, oak staircase she paused before beginning her descent. Half way down she caught her balance, held on to the balustrade to re-adjust her shoe and looked up. And there she paused, staring in horror. Below her, in the hall and talking to her brother with his back towards her, was Kenton Knight. The man must have arrived while she was upstairs.

"Ah, *there* you are." Her brother, Lord Herbert Preston looked up and raised his hand. "We'd all been wondering where you'd got to." In the sudden hush, heads were turning her way. Nobody moved until Kenton Knight started to walk towards her.

"Hullo, Katherine." She saw him glance at her brother before looking back up at her. "How *lovely* to see you again," he smiled disarmingly but she ignored it. "It's been a very long time…you're looking more beautiful than ever."

"Stay where you are," she hissed, suddenly breathing hard. "How dare you talk to me like that. How *dare* you." She could feel herself glaring defiantly at the man who had betrayed her.

"But Katherine, come…."

"Stop it." Her voice crackled. "Don't even think of talking to me. I don't want to hear your voice…neither do I wish to have anything to do with you. Not now…not ever."

"But surely…."

"*Stop! Enough!*" Her voice carried across the room.

Francis Luttrell rose nervously from the window table where he had been talking to the Duke and Sir Thomas Acland. He had been warned about the situation but Kenton Knight had not been expected and he had thought no more of it. This was dreadful and he half tripped in his haste. "I say, nothing wrong, I trust?" He was hurrying now, glancing around anxiously. "Katherine, dear lady, is there anything I…."

"Thank you, sir. I'm quite well, really I am." But her eyes remained on the new arrival. "I'm fine however I fear that there's somebody here whose presence I am unable to accept. It is *him*," she gestured. "No doubt he will be able to explain himself. But thank you again, sir. Should I have interrupted you all…I do beg your pardon." She returned his look. "I must ask you to excuse me, sir…I think it best if I retire. Perhaps you would be kind enough to send somebody when my family takes their leave…or when this man has left." She turned, as if to go back up the stairs.

"Come down *here.*" The Duke of Northborough's voice echoed around the hall. "*Katherine*, come here at once. *At once*, I say."

She stopped, hesitated then turned and looked at the upturned faces. Slowly and almost imperceptibly she shook her head. "Father dear, there's no need to raise your voice in such a manner. I can hear you quite well enough...as can we all. I'm not a child any more and I know my own mind. Thank you, sir." She turned back and continued her lonely walk.

2

Amos Naylor's new front room seemed crowded yet there were only three others. Zac and Reg sat together on the roughly hewn pine bench over by the bread oven. The visitors chose to keep their distance for the big man could be awkward and they could see the news they brought had upset him. The table with the broken leg had been pushed to one side making way for the fourth man who sat on a box. Mort Newbold had heard that Naylor could be difficult and was happy enough to be where he was, leaning against the far wall and watching carefully.

"Wha'dya mean by that?" Naylor held a finger against his nose, blew hard into the fire then looked at his hand before wiping it. "They ain't the guts to do nuthin' like that...and anyway they wanna keep their jobs. First sign an' I'll be on to 'em...you watch." When he first heard of trouble at the factory it had scared him and he spent most of the day on his guard. He knew the ringleaders and watched them but he overdid it and they became suspicious. That only made it worse. But the factory had seemed quiet enough. There was no laughter or banter as there used to be but that was right and proper. He, Amos Naylor, had brought order to the place.

"No, no, they won't be doin' it like that, Amos." Zac Hamer, his slate-grey head, shaven like a cannon ball, leant forward earnestly. "They won't come for yer face to face, like. They'll go fer yer house...torch it like they did up Bristol way. Most likely keep yer woman an' kid inside an' all."As the four contemplated the prospect, Hamer opened his collarless shirt and scratched.

"They're clever, mind." Reg Carver refilled his tankard. "They brought this bloke down to Exeter. Blackens up his face an' only comes out ni'times for meetings." Reg always managed to hear things first. Tonight his red, swept back, crinkly hair and pointed nose made him look more like a fox than ever. He was cunning also and Naylor watched him. "Tells 'em what's to be done and who's to do it. S'posed to come from up country, so 'e is...Lancashire or some place like that. Runs the union up there like the military."

"Well, they're not runnin' me like no military. Right?" Naylor glared. The news made him uncomfortable again; he could feel it deep down. "If my lot don't like me that's their 'ard luck. They don't worry me, friend. And anyways," Naylor turned towards Hamer and nudged the smaller man with his foot. "It's all that new machinery in your place you want to be watching, Hamer...them new power looms an' that you've got down there. *That's* what scares 'em. Gets 'em going...thinks they'll be losing their jobs. That's what gets them fighting mad."

11

"P'raps." Hamer examined his fingernails. "P'raps that's so...but at least they aren't after our blood, Naylor...*you're* the one they're after. Your name's bin mentioned more than once, an' all. You wanna be on yer toes."

"Stuff the bastards." Naylor feigned indifference. "Touch me...just one finger an' I'll 'ave their guts."

"So what about your missus and the lad?" Mort Newbold, Naylor's understudy at the cotton mill, had been sitting quietly. Newbold was another clever one, and smart at that. His frock coat and cravat might not have been new, in fact they were old and ill fitting like his brown boots, but they impressed Naylor, as did his dark, tidy hair that he pomaded whenever he could find enough powder.

Amos Naylor kicked out to stretch his leg but Newbold pressed his point. "She's on her own, y'know, an' there's plenty that don't care for her...seein' she's just walked into your new place like that."

"Sod 'er." Naylor tipped his head back and gulped. "That's 'er look out. Bloody cow." The moustache of froth remained on his top lip. "Nort I can do about that. Anyways, if the crowd want her," he jerked his thumb towards the ceiling. "That's up to them...nort I can do about it."

✳

At first Charlotte thought the horse was going past the window but it stopped and the rider alighted, shutting out most of the light. Jack Tucker's sister, and now kept by Amos Naylor, moved further into the shadows, one hand on the blackened stair rail but it was the voice calling her name that made her change her mind and she hesitated.

"Just on my way back from Exeter." Parson Jack Russell took both her hands in his. "There we are, there we are...I'll be seeing them all in Molland tomorrow. So how are you?" He could see immediately. Her eyes were puffed, whether through tears or blows to the face it was difficult to tell. And she had lost weight, the same cotton smock he remembered was hanging in loose folds.

"Oh, vicar...'tis a nice surprise." Charlotte looked away in embarrassment. "Bit of a mess, I'm afraid...an' not much 'ere to offer you." Turning away, she raised her eyebrows and sighed, now less sure of herself. "Spot of alder p'raps? Luckworthy wine. Mother's...made it from the two trees by the farm gate." She smiled self-consciously but was relieved when he waved away her offer for the jar had lost its stopper and the wine was old.

"Thank you but no, Charlotte." Russell smiled but he was watching her closely. Her mother, Grace, had been right, the girl was miserable. He patted the other half of the bench for her to sit but she stood back, wary and nervous like a stray dog. "*So*...how are you faring?" The answer was obvious. He could see for himself but he wanted her to talk.

"Oh, Amos and I manage." She shrugged and stood with her back to the cold, black fireplace where the rubbish was piled. Russell waited but she remained silent with her head bowed.

"And the lad?" She shrugged again. "They're worried at Molland, you know." He saw her startled look. Whether it was because of what he said or the speed he moved she couldn't tell but he was too quick for her. Even as she shrank back, his hand pulled the smock from around her neck.

"No," she cried but froze, cowering away from his touch. The weals, yellow and mauve, were plain to see. His other hand lifted the sleeve and he turned her arm to expose the cuts where the cane must have fallen as she tried to protect herself. The blood had dried but the marks were still angry, worse than Collyns had described to him. She remained still, staring at the floor.

"How long?" he murmured, adjusting her collar. "Mmm? Charlotte? How long's all this been going on...d'you want to tell me?" He paused but she stayed silent. "It's what we'd been hearing, my dear, and I had to be sure." Russell turned her round, easing her back towards the bench and steadied her as she sat. She was helpless, not having the strength even to hide her shame and there would be more violence to come. There always was, it was the way the brutes like Naylor satisfied themselves.

"Go," she whispered. The tears fell silently onto her clenched hands. "Please go. Don't worry about me...I'll manage." The shoe made them start as it rolled and bumped down the stairs. The little boy must have dislodged it as he crept forward to the edge of the railings to see who it was. Russell caught sight of the staring face but already Charlotte had moved.

"Don't worry, dear...'tis all right. Just the vicar come to see us." He listened as she reassured her child, settling him back in his room or wherever. It was a soft voice, gentle and calm. Somehow the mother's love had prevailed through the pain and fear, and the filth of this black den. She had found life from somewhere but he would have to get them out.

"Shall I speak to your brothers? They'd help, I'm sure...help you to move." As soon as he spoke he knew it was wrong.

"No, no, in God's name no." She took his arm, looking at him for the first time. The very idea had horrified her. "No, vicar. Don't say nuthin...please. I beg yer, don't say nuthin." Russell turned away. He tried to imagine what it must be like to sit trapped week after week with the family so close yet she was still here, ensnared and hidden away from life. "Honest, vicar, I'll be fine." There was a hint of a faint smile. "'Tis better than it was...not so bad now. Don'ee go worrying."

13

"But the boy, Charlotte? What about the little lad? We can't let him grow up in...here." Russell waved his hand. "He needs to be away from it all...same as you." She was silent again. He could see she knew he was right yet still she hung back. "We'll think...the two of us. We'll think of a way out of this mess." The parson took her hands again. "I'll be on my way, but I'll be back and we'll talk again."

"Don't say nuthin', will you, vicar," she pleaded, hanging back from the open door. "Couldn't bear mother to know, nor Jack."

"I'll say nothing." Russell took her hand. Grace was already worried and would be anxious to know what he had found. He had promised he would come and find out but what could he say. "Think what I said, Lottie." She smiled at the use of her name. "I'll be back and we'll talk. Take care, now."

*

The parson waited as the cattle, with their heads low, crossed the ford in front of him snorting suspiciously as they picked their way with the water splashing only as high as their knees. The River Exe was low.

Jack should be told, and Wilmot, too. They would feel obliged to come and see for themselves, yet he had given her his word. Perhaps he could suggest she was missing their company, then they would have no option. But that would take time and the girl had to be moved soon for these things only got worse, not better like she said.

3

"Listen, the band...over there, look." Durnford Morgan, sitting next to Elizabeth-Jane, rubbed his hands in anticipation and craned his neck but the regiment, drawn up behind its colours, was still hidden by the trees on the far side of the meadow. He had met her earlier in the hall as agreed and had watched admiringly as she descended the main staircase. Her jade-green, silk open gown with its closefitting bodice and flared sleeves had come from Addison's of Mayfair two weeks ago. Her jewellery, amongst which was the magnificent set of sapphires and amethysts, had been collected from her husband's safe in the bank by two of their footmen.

Her smile on greeting him again had been the same, as was her perfume and the warmth of her touch as he raised her hand to his lips before offering his arm. It was wonderful to see her once more and his heart had leapt but they had long ago left it like that. Nothing had been said for it was not necessary. Their relationship was something precious, like a piece of fine crystal that was delicately balanced and which would have been shattered had he pressed her further. Both knew each other's thoughts and that's how it was left.

14

Elizabeth-Jane had been sitting quietly on his right wondering what her husband and the others would be doing in London. The young queen's corona- tion service had been at noon but there had been more, much more, even after the reception at the Mansion House and the dinner at the Palace of Westminster. Thomas Acland had gone with him, as had Geoffrey Frobisher together with all the other Members for Devon, even John Chichester.

Caroline, Chichister's wife and mistress of Arlington Court, had been outraged. "*Right*," she cried when John told her he had to be in town for the whole week as Parliament was still sitting. "In that case we'll celebrate here at Arlington on our own without you, and you can stay away as long as you like. *Honestly*, this *Poor* Law or whatever it is you find so important. Really…it's too much."

So Elizabeth-Jane had been co-opted as had Georgina Frobisher, Lydia Acland and Flossie Westham. No sooner had the Yeomanry become involved than Colonel the Lord Rolle nominated Major Arthur Shirwell and Ensign Frederic Knight to liaise with what had now become a formidable pageant committee. Gradually, as spring turned to summer, the Coronation Ball began to emerge from its chrysalis.

Week by week plans became more elaborate and thus more complicated. The military ride grew into a tattoo, the few, modest fireworks into a spectacular. Tickets, difficult to acquire from the outset, became ever more so until finally they were impossible to find. Now, at nine-thirty in the evening, on Saturday the twenty-eighth of June, eighteen thirty-eight, the drums began to roll. Two hundred miles away, a diminutive and softly spoken teenage girl had just succeeded her uncle to become Queen of the United Kingdom of Great Britain and Ireland and Empress of India. The age of Victoria had begun.

✳

Caroline Chichester, sitting at the front and in the middle of the dais, sat back to watch. Others did likewise, but many more leant forward eagerly as the columns of Redcoats marched on to the field with bayonets fixed and colours flying followed by two squadrons of The Royal North Devon Hussars.

All day the crowds had been growing, many camping out to enjoy the funfair between the ornamental lake and long avenue of limes stretching away to the main gates. They had walked and ridden for miles, some from as far as Ilfracombe and Barnstaple, a few from Exeter and the gypsy fortune-tellers, so the gardeners said, had come from Bodmin. Now they hobbled, walked, skipped and ran to the sound of music, crowding along the wooden railings and cheer- ing loudly.

"I wish you were out there with them, Freddy." Elizabeth-Jane glanced briefly behind her at his sword then up to his face, half hidden under his helmet and plume.

"Sorry, mother…duty calls." He smiled back down at her. "Behold, your gallant Duty Officer."

"Not now, surely?" Durnford Morgan half turned. "Really? Today of all days…that cannot be right."

"Well, that is what has been decreed. Ilfracombe, Torrington and Tiverton…they're all likely trouble spots." Frederic eased forward, pulling on his folding chair until his head was between his mother's and Morgan's. "Exeter as well, they say. There were riots there twice last week…we've been told to keep three troops ready, so here we are. I'm lucky in fact…the others back at Ebberley Lawn are kept just sitting around and waiting for something to happen." They paused, watching the parade, then applauded as both the band and orchestra struck up the fanfare. The infantry had formed line and the musical ride had begun, many of those sitting near them standing and clapping in time to the drumbeat.

"Did you say Leonard's out there somewhere?"

"Yes, and Hector…Dan Webber as well. Leonard's here look, the column coming past now…there, the light bay with two white socks." Frederic grinned. "Can't miss him." Even in his hussar patrols and shako, their burly groom cut an unmistakable figure.

"Oh yes," Elizabeth-Jane laughed delightedly. "Oh…*dear* Leonard. Well…I think he looks very smart and I shall take it upon myself to tell him just that." She turned and shook her head politely at the periwigged footman in the ochre and dark brown Chichester livery. He bowed and moved on to Morgan who took a flute of champagne from the silver tray.

By the time the lone petard whooshed high into the sky dusk had fallen. Those on the platform had risen to leave but paused to turn and watch the first flicker of light from the beacon next to the obelisk in the high field beyond the rhododendrons. It would burn all night, fuelled by timber from the estate as the flames of Arlington pledged their loyalty with thousands of others across the land.

✳

"Well, m'dear, you dance like an angel." Sir George Gale bowed then waited for Elizabeth-Jane to take his arm. "'Tis a mercy John's away in town doing his bit…gives us lesser mortals a chance."

"Come George, you were skipping and turning like a youngster yourself…and beautifully too, like a boy half your age," she added and they both laughed. Gale nodded to the footman who held out his partner's chair. "But listen, George…seriously now, I want you to tell me something." She tried to move closer but the hoops under her dress prevented her. "Here," she beckoned him forward and spoke quietly. "Why're Freddy and the others on stand-by like this?

Can it *really* be that trouble's likely…trouble enough for the army at a time like this?"

Sir George Gale, thickset and heavy jowled, wrinkled his nose. He was far older than her, not as old as John but well into his sixties and had been on the Bench for more than twenty years before becoming North Devon's Chief Magistrate. "It's difficult to say." Aware that other eyes at the table were on him, he shuffled forward in his chair, his craggy features puckered in concentration. "Things aren't easy, y'know, m'dear. Probably won't come to much though, and we don't like committing the Yeomanry anyway."

"But *commiting* them and to *what*? Not down in this part of the country? Things aren't that bad are they?"

"Well, they're not *good*…it's all bubbling away."

"Mmm." Elizabeth-Jane looked at him. His eyes were kind but they were also wise. "Just me being a silly old mother, I s'pose." She sat back and watched as the dancers were taking to the floor.

"Not at all, m'dear." Gale patted her hand. "Everyone's a mite concerned. This week's helped us to forget it all for a while but it's not gone away. Freddy'll be fine, you'll see. He's a grand lad…an' doing well so John Rolle tell's me."

"Talking of him, who's he with now? Over there, look, by the red curtains near the pillar. They're not officers…one of the footmen brought them in."

"Oh yes…not sure," he lied. Gale knew at once that they were messengers, most likely from Ebberley Lawn. Even as they watched, a senior officer joined them. Elizabeth-Jane's eyes followed Frederic as he summoned a footman to his side.

"What's going on George?"

"I don't know, m'dear. Can't really see. It can't be much or they'd be outside by now. Military business has to go on y'know, coronations or not. We'll know soon enough." As the band struck up again, he half rose and offered his arm. "Perhaps you'll allow me?"

*

But the news was *not* good. Three days earlier there had been riots in Bristol, followed by unrest in Taunton and Bridgewater. The Chartist movement, the union of workers who feared for their livelihood, was growing and moving south. The messengers had not been from Ebberley Lawn rather they had come from Western Command in Exeter. Orders had gone out for the military to work in conjunction with the civil authorities and to deal with any unrest as they saw fit.

4

John Knight moved his head to see better, glowering darkly as he skewered the end of his ivory-handled paper knife under his left thumb nail. He then bent to gnaw at the piece of hard skin he had managed to detach. It had been almost three months since his butler had come to him yet, even now, he could scarcely believe it.

Parker's resignation had been simple enough but then had come the first of the thunderclaps...America...the *New World*. After making the announcement, the man had just stood there with his hair slicked back and his face that same waxed, expressionless mask it always was when there was drama in the wind. Knight remembered finding himself staring in disbelief. Why America? Why not back up to the Midlands or some steady retirement job in Devon? But...*America*.

Then came the second broadside...Miss *Chapple*, the governess. Dear God alive. He had heard word of a little 'affaire de coeur' but this was something else. "And *what?*" Even now he could see the look on Parker's face as he had leapt to his feet. "*Marriage*," Knight had gasped. "*Marriage?*" It had all been too much and he had had to sit down again. Now, smiling wryly to himself, he returned to the business of dealing with whatever was under his nails.

Elizabeth-Jane seemed to understand better and it had been her contacts that had secured Parker's interview. Apparently it had gone well and they had been asked back for a second. Knight fumbled for his fob watch and checked it against the bracket clock – the three of them were due in ten minutes or so. Thank goodness for his wife.

He knew the Astors well enough but Elizabeth-Jane had picked up news of the position through the Curzons of Sloane Street. Jacob Astor's brother, John Waldorf Astor, had been over from New York. Their daughter, Clarissa, a stupid, empty-headed girl according to Elizabeth-Jane, was getting married and it was them, the young things, who wanted an English butler and housekeeper. Heaven only knew why.

Albany, at least an overnight journey up the Hudson River from New York, even in one of those new-fangled steam paddle boats, would be like the moon to Mr and Mrs Parker, or anyone else straight from England. They would be lost, wouldn't know which way to turn, where to go for help or who to ask for this or that. It would be hopeless. But, no, an English couple it had to be. John Knight sat back with his legs outstretched and his hands locked together behind his head.

But then, on the other hand, it *could* work yet the very thought of it made Knight look as though something bad had just passed under his nose. Parker was good, no doubt about it and the house staff would be kept up to the mark but she was an oozy, grovelling little woman. His face contorted at the memory of her sitting perched on the edge of her chair at his dining table, nibbling away at her food like a squirrel and twittering on about all sorts of nonsense. She had brains enough and knew her literature but that was all.

A man needed more than that on a cold night. What, he wondered, would the parlour maids out there make of the new English butler, and he of them? The old dog had a few 'affaires' left in him yet. Knight smiled, got up and checked himself in the mirror. The oval Regency was his favourite and he blew gently onto the veneered and gilt frame then ran his finger around the carved trailing fruit before checking absentmindedly for dust. "Oh dear, poor old Parker," he sighed, then turned as the door opened.

✳

"Very well indeed, thank you Mr Knight." Enid Chapple strode assuredly across the study floor offering her hand in reply to his question. Elizabeth-Jane had warned him that the governess appeared to have changed, and she had.

The simpering creature he remembered had gone and he watched in amazement as she flicked through the pages of her leather-bound book with a confidence he had not seen before. The mousiness had disappeared as well, rouge and pomade had been put to work on the most redeemable features. The clothes were better and the thin filigree chain round her neck suited her. Knight caught Parker's glance but the man looked away too quickly for him to signal his approval.

"Now then...let me see. Greyways, that's the name of the house," she announced tartly. "It's new or newish...built after that war of theirs, and it's set back on the east side of the river. Lovely views to the west apparently. We saw some pictures, didn't we Bernard? They've quite the nicest buildings up there, so Mr Waldorf says...only *the* most important live there, and they come and go by the river...very smart."

Knight was staring. The wretched female was insufferable; preening herself at the thought of it all. "Spacious, of course, so they'll be plenty to do and about twenty staff...and that's just in the house, of course." The woman in front of him was making statements and pronouncing judgement as though she owned the place. "Bernard liked him, didn't you dear." Knight saw his butler look up. "Mr Waldorf," she prompted. "Yes, that's right...we both liked him. Very nice he was."

"And they're going to look after you very well so I hear, Miss Chapple?" Elizabeth-Jane had been astonished to hear the terms they had been offered. She could see her husband was agog for his jaw had dropped again.

"Quite comfortable, thank you Mrs Knight." Her chin rose. "Yes...comfortable but no more than that." Knight chose to stare at his hands.

"So, Parker." Eventually he looked up and turned to his butler, relieved to find a face he could understand. Quite obviously the woman had got hold of him. He was dominated, poor chap. Doomed most likely. "What did we say about dates."

"Sir?"

"*Dates*, Parker. What *dates* were we talking about when we spoke last?"

"Very good, sir. Er…well." Parker straightened his cuffs. "We've had a slight change, sir…only a couple of months or so but, and that's if it pleases you but I'd like to remain here for a few months longer. If it's not inconvenient that is, sir. You see," he looked at Elizabeth-Jane for help.

"It's all right, Bernard. I'll explain." Edith Chapple silenced him with her hand. "We, rather I'm expecting, Mr Knight. I'm expecting in January and we're to be married in a month's time, in Barnstaple."

"Just a few months delay, sir," Parker broke in. "*Sir*…Mr Knight, sir…excuse me." The butler leant forward. "Mr *Knight*, sir." The master was staring as though he had just seen a ghost. "Say six months, sir. Then Enid, Miss Chapple that is, has been making enquiries at the Coastline Transportation Company…it's an American line, sir. They sail from Gloucester but call at Ilfracombe and we're planning to sail from there."

5

If anyone had looked closely they would have been surprised for the two farmers were shabbily dressed. They were dirty and they were unkempt however they were clean-shaven and their horses were fine animals, the leather oiled and well polished. "That's var enough, buiy…us'll be right on top o'they, else." The accent was rich, if a mite too thick.

"Yazzur." Corporal Buckingham pulled alongside Frederic and the two sat together watching the scene in front of them.

✳

The large crowd at the junction of Wellbrook and Church Street had been waiting since dusk, but the light drizzle had neither dampened their spirits nor doused the flames of their torches. More and more were joining, pouring out of the many inns and taverns nearby. Those who arrived late were pressing forward and calling noisily for the speakers. Every labourer and factory worker within miles of Tiverton had gathered to hear the Chartist leaders. Windows and balconies along the streets were full. Others had climbed trees for a better view. Still more had clambered onto rooftops, sitting precariously with sacks and coats over their heads in an attempt to keep dry. The air was filled with noisy banter, but the speakers were late and the crowd was becoming restless.

Then suddenly, without any signal and after a deep sigh of recognition had rustled across the square, a silence fell. Heads turned and necks craned forward, all eyes now on the first floor balcony of the tall, half-timbered corner shop. Those at the back pressed forward, this time more urgently, pushing and jostling each other for a place where they could hear.

He was difficult to see clearly and the crowd stood hushed like a congregation awaiting the sermon. For some time he stood motionless, merely surveying the host of expectant and upturned faces. Apart from the odd drunken shout and the distant barking of dogs, there was nothing.

When at last he spoke, his thin, high-pitched voice carried clearly to those standing in doorways and others near the back of the crowd. Benjamin 'Caesar' Wilson, the Halifax and Methodist Chartist, spoke skilfully, gradually lifting the crowd. He had been doing it for years and he knew his craft. Wherever he went they listened. Parliament, Caesar told them, was beginning to take note but nothing had been done…nothing at all. The fight, he urged, would have to go on and he asked them to join him. They would fight together.

The crowd had loved it and roared their approval but now they were splitting. Many, right at the back and unable to hear clearly, had become angry and were moving away on some mission of their own, while the ones in front stood urging their man on, not caring about those behind. The mill, so the word went, was to go up that night.

"You with us, boys?" a dozen agitators surrounded the two riders. "Best leave yer 'orses out of it." A thin, mouse haired man approached and caught hold of Frederic's bridle. "Aye, leave 'em behind an' pass the word. Talkin's finished now," the man growled. "'Tis time for justice."

"Oh, argh." Frederic nodded thoughtfully. Buckingham finished his apple. "Us'll be giddin on over…drop 'em orf, way back." He drawled. "'Ere, Jan…us best be gwin on." The officer and his corporal swung away and pressed hurriedly through the throng. Once clear they dug in their spurs.

*

"Filthy, 'eathen swine. Oi bloody hates them I do." Sergeant Fanshawe adjusted his charger's curb chain and throat lash. "A bleedin' good 'iding that's what they need. Once we get down there, lads, you listen to me…do as I say. Right?" He jabbed his chest. "Mr Knight's not a bad young 'un, not bad at all, but 'e don't know nuthin' about real soldiering. Can't 'ave this lot of savages climbing all over 'im…no way."

Frederic and Daly rode hard from the town. By the time they reached the troop, the men had settled themselves on the low bank in front of Fanshawe. Frederic reined in first. "It looks as though they're going for Heathcoat's, the new factory." He thought it best to break the fresh news at once. "And they seem hell bent on the idea as well."

"A bloody good 'iding," Fanshawe looked at the three corporals. "That's what they need, Mr Knight, sir. A touch of the sabre and no messin'". Knight could see the men watching him. His sergeant was wrong and they knew it. It couldn't be done that way but the man was challenging his authority and they were waiting to see who would give way. Two of his corporals glanced at each other.

The meeting at the Tiverton courthouse earlier that day had not gone well. For more than an hour he and the others had waited while the magistrate dithered. His Special Constables had been unable to control the crowd and had withdrawn; now a second mob was rumoured to be approaching from Exeter. Tiverton was out of control and it was only when Major Shirwell beat the hilt of his sword on the table that the man made his formal request for help.

Shirwell acted quickly, sending a galloper to Barnstaple with the news, then commandeering the courthouse for use as his headquarters. Two sections of hussars were sent to block the Exeter road, another left to protect the courthouse. It was then that he had turned to Frederic. "Take the remainder to protect the mill," he ordered. "Go steady, mind...remember who they are. No bloodbaths tonight but I want the place secured, Mr Knight." It was then that Frederic had decided to go and see for himself.

On his way back from the crowd, Frederic had to think quickly. How, he wondered, would Fanshawe react to such caution? He needed the man's help and advice. How was he going to place out his men? Who should do what and how, and when should he address the crowd? Fanshawe was going to be difficult. He could go either way.

＊

"Thank you, Sergeant Fanshawe." The men had placed a number of torches in the ground where they were sitting and Frederic could see their faces in the pale light. "Thank you for that, but I've had my instructions and we'll be doing it my way."

"Suggest I take in the lead section then, sir." Fanshawe was persistent. "I know what these ruffians need. Corporal Bond'n I'll handle that lot. No problem, eh Corporal?" Bond nodded, the others barely looked on.

For a moment nobody spoke. Frederic saw his sergeant grin. "Listen...all of you." He raised a hand. "I've *seen* them. Right? Corporal Buckingham and I have been over there and talked to them. They're *not* the French, for Heaven's sake, and they're *not* convicts either. They're good men of Devon like you and me but who're frightened and worried for their jobs." Knight raised his voice. "We're *not* going to attack them and beat them down, not at all...unless there's no other choice." Heads nodded and in the silence that followed, Fanshawe moved.

The sergeant drew himself up and pulled the creases from his jacket. "Very well, sir," he nodded supportingly. "Just as you say then. We'll best try it softly first, like. But any nonsense, sir," he added hurriedly. "Any nonsense at all from that bleedin' rabble and that's it. Can't 'ave you being messed about by a mob of savages like them lot...disregarding the Queen's orders an' that." Fanshawe preened himself and rolled his shoulders. "Never fear, sir. We'll be right behind you, but any trouble an' we're right in among 'em."

"Here, sir. Over there, look." Corporal Buckingham was pointing eagerly. "Looks like they've split an' one lot's on the move, just as they said they would...over there. Be'ind them trees. All them torches...the very devil but there's scores of 'em."

They could see the torchlight column moving away from the main body of the crowd. Behind them a fire appeared to have broken out among the timbered houses in the old quarter beyond the square. Frederic nodded to Fanshawe. It was time for him to change back into uniform and for the troop to be moving out.

Chapter Two

"Into half sections, at the trot...march." Frederic watched critically while his cavalrymen changed formation with legs thumping and tongues clicking as the plumes on their shakos swayed rhythmically. Here and there a trooper muttered quietly to his mount, while a number of animals tossed their heads impatiently, glad to be underway at last. They had been well drilled for even in the dark everybody knew where to go and what to do.

Sergeant Fanshawe rode out to join him. Frederic was still not sure about the man and remained suspicious of how he had tried to hold sway over the troop. It had been close and he remembered that last long silence until the sergeant had accepted his plan. The man was canny but he was glad to have him alongside nonetheless for the situation could well deteriorate further.

"Number one section...draw muskets...and check weapons." Knight watched closely as they unfastened the leather hold-strap then lowered their heads to check the firing mechanisms. "Weapon loaded and primed, sir." One by one they gave their report.

"Wha' d'ya reckon, sah?" He had come up close and their boots brushed. "Take 'em from behind, shall we?"

"Yes, but quietly." He saw Fanshawe frown. "Yes...we'll get as close as we can, then I want to talk to them."

"You *what*, sah? Talk to them bleedin' lot?" Fanshawe stared. "Best if I come along with you then." The sergeant's charger backed away but he dug him forward again. "Can't 'ave you facin' that mob on yer own, y'know."

"No...my thanks, but I'll go alone. Any more and it might panic them...they'll be scared stiff anyway." He never caught Fanshawe's reply but the man was alongside him again.

"But don't go having no truck from 'em, sah. And no back chat neither. You just tell 'em."

"That's right. Now get the troop ready, if you please." Frederic raised his head to adjust his chinstrap then pulled ahead into the shadows of a thorn thicket where the ground was wet, listening as the troop went through their drills. The leading section had drawn muskets, now the remainder drew sabres; Fanshawe was doing his stuff. The sound of his stifled commands, the quick movements in response and the rasp of metal were reassuring. Pray God it would work.

✳

24

By the time the three elderly men at the back of the crowd noticed the hussars behind them, the troop had halted. Frederic rode on alone. "Hullo there," he called. "Who's leading you?" Several in the crowd now turned towards him. "Who's your leader, and where is he?" He paused then asked again, this time shouting over the heads.

"What's it with you?" The crowd parted as two men pushed their way forward. "Why don't you clear off and leave us to it."

"Nothing but lackeys, you are," another shouted. The voices grew into a chorus. Several stones thumped into the grass, then a stick. His horse shied as a heavy clod of earth fell nearby.

*

"Get back 'ere, sir...get back out o' the way." Fanshawe's voice was loud enough but Frederic had already turned and trotted to one side. He stopped, turned to face his troop and cleared his throat.

"Number one section...cock muskets." His words of command drew an instant reaction. "In the shoulder...*ready.*" The demonstrators nearest them stopped now unsure of themselves. "On my command...*fire!*" As the crash of musketry sent the first volley high into the air, two horses leapt forward. Fanshawe shouted. Then silence again as the thick, bitter smoke drifted away.

Many in the crowd spun round anxiously. For a moment nobody moved then those furthest away began to push closer in order to see better while those nearer began to press back. Slowly at first, then more urgently as if they feared something worse was to come, most began to force themselves away from the hussars. Some moved quietly, trying to worm their way between the figures around them, others began to push and shove. Within seconds a number had fallen to the ground and, suddenly, there was a great melee of struggling bodies. Frederic rode forward again.

"*Stop, sir.*" It was Fanshawe. "Not going out there again are you, for gawd's sake? There'll be trouble, y'know. Them lot 'ave had their chance. You've given 'em that...more'n a fair one as well." Frederic raised a hand in acknowledgement but rode on. Those nearest seemed reasonable enough but what of the others...where the stones had come from, for instance? By now he was committed and had to go on. The troop was some way off but Fanshawe was still there, thank goodness.

"No...we're going on," he replied. "We've got to try again."

"Then I'm with you, sah. Can't 'ear nuthin' back there anyways." Fanshawe urged his horse forward.

*

"*Stop.* " This time Frederic's right arm was lifted high. "Stop and listen...*listen.*" Now he was standing in the saddle. "Stand still and listen, will you. *Hold hard there.*" He could see that the shots had frightened them. "Listen to me," he appealed. "We have our orders from the magistrates to disperse you. This assembly has been declared unlawful. You must disperse... you have to go. Go on your way now...back to your homes."

"Why don't you lot leave us alone?" The tall, unshaven man standing in front of him looked bolder than the others. He had wriggled his way through the crowd and now stood in front of them. "Why're you telling us what to do?" he cried. "We've no argument with the military...nothing against you lot."

"Listen, friend," Frederic spoke loudly enough for those around him to hear. "You can't be doing this, y'know. We've had our orders to see you away from here...an' that's what we must do. We've not come to harm you...really we haven't. Forget what you've heard about the yeomanry. We're men from Devon...the same as you." But then he stopped.

A trooper was racing towards them, shouting to make himself heard above his horse's galloping hooves. Everybody turned. Frederic knew his moment had gone and reined himself back. The spell, that rapport between himself and the crowd, was broken and he cursed. He could feel the suspicion and aggression returning at this sudden intrusion. It had been there the whole time but only smouldering and he had been able to deal with it. Now it had flared up again.

"Mr Knight, sir...Mr Knight." Horse and rider were breathless. "There's another lot attacking two houses across the water. The major said for you to make them safe, sir." The galloper caught his breath. "Passed 'em on the way. Don't look too good, sir. Best to hurry."

✳

Amos Naylor had his arm round her throat. Much shorter than him, Charlotte was having to stand on tiptoe and was pulling desperately against his arm. Her breathing was coming in gasps. "Shut up, you crabby bitch." The words were hissed but the voice was faltering. The strength of his forearm was choking her. "Shut up an' do as you're told."

He turned at the sound of the voice behind him. "*What's that?*" he shouted, dragging her along with him like a sack. Then a window smashed and he cried out again, this time in fear. Charlotte could smell the mutton fat on the burning rags they had just thrown in. Already the rush matting by his chair had caught and she pulled at his arm frantically as he tried to stamp out the flames. "Well *drag 'im out* then, for Christ's sake," he yelled back at the voice upstairs. "And get 'im down 'ere quick."

She knew he was afraid for the anger had gone from his voice. "Come on, *hurry*, for Christ's sake." Amos Naylor was trapped; they had come for him just as Hamer said they would. He could hear them shouting outside and he cringed at the sound of the something heavy being driven against the door. They were coming. "Jesus," he whimpered. "Come on, come on. Get the bloody boy down here."

Zac Hamer reached down and grabbed the thin bare feet, dragging the screaming child out from under the bed and into the room.

*

"*Ready?*" Now Naylor's eyes were wide with fear. "Right...open it up , *now.*" The circle of tightly pressed bodies outside the door moved slightly, just enough to make room for the terrified mother and child that had been thrust into their midst.

"*Shut it,*" he yelled and the two men threw themselves against the door then forced the bar back into place. Immediately the heavy blows fell again, more furiously than ever. All of a sudden and even as they watched, the wood began to splinter. "Come on, man...out the back, there's still time." As he ran, Naylor snatched up the kitchen knife.

"Beelzeebub, the crowd're going in after them...by the door. Look at them all." Corporal Stapleton stopped his section. "Fighting bloody mad, they are." He looked round quickly. "Here, Thorne, get back to Mr Knight...tell him to get here, *fast*...right here with the whole troop." He wiped his mouth. "Tell 'im it's gone real nasty."

"*Grant,*" he yelled. "You and Coward get up 'ere bareback behind me and Solly. *Fraser*, you come along as well. *Stephens,*" he looked round again, this time urgently. "Here...take their horses. We're going in for the woman an' child. Right...soon as we're there, grab 'em. We'll keep 'em off. Move yourselves. *Move!*"

They rode straight into the crowd outside the door, the horses throwing their heads from side to side in their attempts to avoid anything in the way. Stapleton had drawn his sabre and was yelling. Men were screaming at them. Most got out of their way but some, a few, fell under the chargers' hooves. Hector slashed at a hand that grabbed for him. Leonard, by now bareheaded, cut hard at two more.

Hector reached her first. "Come on, love," he put an arm around her and pushed her along the front of the house.

"My boy, my boy," she shrieked. "Oh God, where is he?" Davey was against the wall, his eyes staring wildly at the angry mob. It was Leonard who bent and scooped him up with one arm, the child's thin body dangling like a fish in the air before he caught hold of him properly. The crowd were all round them; some were trying to hold back, others pressing forward shouting. Everywhere the troopers looked, arms were raised against them.

*

Frederic had taken his fourth and last section to the back of the house. Some of the troop had got there before him and were trying to keep the crowd back but, by now, the fire had taken hold of the building. Flames were flickering at the windows while showers of sparks were shooting high from where the roof was ablaze. Even as the troopers were forcing their way to the back door, a heavy beam, alight and flaming from end to end, crashed to the ground.

Those nearest saw the back door open and watched as the figure in the doorway crouched low before rising suddenly with one arm raised high. Metal glinted, a trooper ducked then a sabre flashed and swung again. *"Yaaaaah…*dirty, 'eathen vermin." Sergeant Fanshawe stood over the body, watching carefully as it bucked and twitched on the steps, then he swung back to face the crowd. "Get back, you goddamned savages," he yelled, jumping forward with his sword raised. "Get back…go on…back or I'll 'ave another of yer. Get back, yer bloody animals."

As they dragged the body away from the flames, Frederic spurred his horse forward. He dismounted and came over to join his sergeant and the men around him. "'Ad to be done that way, sah." Sergeant Fanshawe was wiping his sabre. "No good 'aving them animals going for our lads with meat cleavers an' that. Can't 'ave nuthin like that." Frederic looked up and nodded.

"Anyway, sir, we got the girl out…got her an' the youngster away safe. Men say she's called Tucker…yes, that's right, Tucker, from a place called Molland or summat."

2

Joshua Slocombe peered closely to make sure he remembered his place then gently closed the heavy, leather-bound bible. The eyes, little more than sunken hollows, then shut and his thin, gaunt face bent over the table. "Let us pray for the sick and for those who are afflicted."

As he leant forward and clasped his hands, his locks of greying, dark brown hair fell past his sideburns, leaving the high dome of his head to gleam in the dim light. Last Sunday had been his fiftieth birthday when he and his three elder sisters had devoted the day to one of prayer and thanksgiving. Today, as with every other at West Lyn farm, work stopped so they might hear the voice of the Lord. "Remember not, O God, our iniquities, nor the iniquities of our forefathers." His face was screwed tight in concentration. "Spare us, good Lord, spare thy people whom thou hast redeemed with thy most precious blood, and be not angry with us for ever. Amen."

"Spare us, good Lord." Gwen Slocombe's thin hand crossed herself before she glanced up at the sound of the door opening. She was an anxious-looking woman with a long, sad face, short-cropped hair and a wart on the side of her chin.

"Where's Dak?" The moon-like face stared blankly. Winnie, now fourteen had stopped growing when she was nine. Her body had thickened but long before, when she could barely walk, her parents knew she was wrong. The small, close-set eyes flitted from one to the other expectantly. "Ma-ma, where's Dak?" she asked again.

"Come here, dear." The child, for that is what she still was, shuffled across the room, clutching her rag doll. "Jack's away ploughing, dear…the field up by the summer house. He's up there with the two big horses you like…Prince and the other one, the two white ones." Winnie, with her mouth open and tongue lolling, gaped vacantly out of the window as Gwen wiped the dribble from her mouth.

Joshua rubbed his chin thoughtfully and stretched. He was tired, but these days he always was. John Knight had bought the farm when he moved to Lynton, keeping himself on as manager. How he ever coped with the workload before Jack Tucker was sent to him he would never know, even so life remained hard. The steep ground and poor soil were fine for the stock but had been difficult to work with the horses. He yawned and continued to caress his chin. Tucker had changed their lives, of that there was no doubt. He remembered the day he arrived, shortly after the young Mr Knight had come to explain.

✳

Gwen had heard the cart first and the two of them stood looking together through the parlour window. The tall young man in a bottle-green waistcoat and brown working breeches, with his fair hair tied back, lifted his things from the cart then stood surveying his new home. It was raining and the wind swept a lock of loose hair across his forehead.

He had said little at the door, just took their hands as he ducked under the porch beam. It was Winnie who caught his eye, just when he turned to pull in the last of his boxes. For weeks they had been worried about her, about how she would react to a strange man in the house and how he would feel on seeing the young girl the Lord had visited as he had. But it was to her that the newcomer had spoken first, dropping to one knee and holding out his hands.

"Hullo, Winnie," he said. "I've heard about you…lots. Mr Knight told me. We're going to be friends, and he told me that as well." It was odd in a way; most people ignored the child, feeling awkward in her presence but the young man spoke softly, his eyes level with hers. "I've come here to work, I have, and you're going to help me. Eh? That's what Mr Knight said an' I hope you will…I hope so."

The girl had shrunk back, holding on to her mother's skirts, but then came forward again warily with one hand to her mouth. The other she held out. She smiled, a faint, coy smile of friendship, watching fascinated as he reached out to touch her hand. He took hold of her wet fingers, held them for a moment then shook them and smiled back. The girl's mouth had opened and she looked up in wonderment, her eyes moving from one face to another before returning to the man in front of her. He remained quite still, watching her quietly as she reached out further to touch his shoulder before catching hold of his hand. Her fingers were still wet but he held on to them gently, waiting for them to curl around his.

Nothing more had been said but from that moment the child followed him everywhere, calling out his name and laughing happily whenever she caught up with him. 'Dak,' she would cry, 'Dak.' It was the nearest she could manage but the two of them would laugh about it together. She wouldn't leave him and he would be forced to come to the door of his room when she sat outside calling his name. He would crouch beside her talking quietly before bringing her back down the stairs.

*

The boy was blessed, Joshua could see, and for that they were grateful, yet he had much to learn about the Greater Life and seemed uninterested in the word of the Lord. Gwen had prevailed upon him to bide his time with the newcomer, but women did not understand these things and Joshua had taken it upon himself to instruct the boy. He had been pleased enough to take his food at their table and to bask in the warmth of their home yet had never paused to give thanks to Him, the one who provided. It hurt Joshua to see such a spirit taking so much but not giving in return. "Have you no wish to hear the gospel of Christ, Jack? To rejoice in the company of our Lord with others?" he asked.

Jack knew he was referring to the new chapel next to the mill at Barbrook. "No, Joshua, I'm not for that…I've no wish to become involved with anyone else," he replied as he had on countless occasions. "Come the Sabbath an' we've enough to do as it is without walking miles to pray." He longed for the peace and quiet of the seventh day when he could wash and mend his clothes before taking what little time he had to ride out with his friends when they came.

The older man had struggled with his reply. For what seemed an age the farmer sat with his thin, pointed chin resting on his clenched hands, moving only when he felt the need to rub the crown of his head. "You're heart remains hardened, Jack." Joshua's sorrowful eyes looked him up and down. "You well know it's written that God must first wither our gourd and blast the flower of proud hope." He rose and pointed a warning finger. "Only then can the sinner be brought to the foot of the Cross." Jack bridled, his jaw set. He had heard this many times as well but the constant accusation of perpetual sinning, made by those who claimed to have found salvation, irritated him.

He had heard it from the preacher O'Bryan as well and their arrogance angered him. They had come to him initially after Joshua had found him walking hand in hand with Katherine over a year ago. Now they kept on at him every time she came; they never let go. Who were they to claim such moral superiority that they should try to get him to beg God's forgiveness in front of them all; to confess his transgressions in public at their place of worship? What sort of twisted minds thought like that?

"My heart's not hardened against anything, Joshua," Jack could feel his frustration building. Once Joshua got into one of his persuasive moods it was difficult to escape and he wanted none of it. Enough was enough. "It's not that at all. Why should I be better off praying and begging forgiveness from everyone else? 'Til you or anyone can answer that, I'll not consider it…not even stop to think about it, sir." He saw Joshua's sharp glance. "And that's no offence, mind." Jack held up his hand. "No offence at all but you must learn to leave me be. Right? I'll do things my own way…just as you asked. Remember?"

Yes, Joshua remembered it all so well and he raised his eyebrows, nodding sagely. The boy was right. Time and again he had called upon Jack to consider his Creator as he went about his work. But he could see the young man had yet to be convinced, and there were times when he, Joshua, began to fear he might be versed in Hell's Black Grammar. In return Jack had fought against Joshua's persistence as though the very last vestige of his freedom was at stake.

The deep humiliation of leaving Simonsbath had marked him, the cut to his wages and freedom had hurt. But it was the cruel loss of friendship and laughter he missed most. The miserable loneliness, aggravated further by the long, pensive silences in the household, broken only by prayer and readings from the Good Book, bore heavily. It was not as though he did not believe; rather it was his pride that made him stand fast, that and his refusal to bow down and surrender to a life of interminable solemnity.

✳

But in Winnie, he saw brightness. Her mind, uncluttered by the greater mysteries of life, looked out on a simple, innocent world where little things brought happiness and laughter. Time and again when he was wrestling with his melancholy, she would come to him, presenting him with a posy of flowers from the hedgerow, by then half crushed in her clumsy hand, or birds' feathers she had found in the rickyard or pebbles from the stream. They would talk together, examining her gifts, her joyous simplicity sweeping away his black despair and bringing a freshness and purity into the day. Her laughter and gaiety brought him back to reality and he welcomed her company, often longing to hear her chatter.

Joshua sighed and looked at his daughter. "Run along and help Jack, then." He got up and took the girl's hand. "Ask him to show you your sheep. Remember to count them carefully, mind."

✳

Less than an hour earlier Jack had reached the headland. Pressing down on the plough handles, he watched closely as the beam lifted the gleaming shear-tip

31

from the furrow. He worked both horses together using the rope lines, turning them away and on to the stubble. Once he had unhitched the chains he walked the two animals clear to let them pick at foliage in the hedgerow.

For a few minutes he stood talking to them quietly, running his hands over their great muscular shoulders, now steaming wet and thick with foam where the harness had lain, pausing to study the clouds of gulls and rooks that had gathered to search for food in the freshly turned earth. As he adjusted the bridles, he whistled quietly to himself listening as they mouthed their bits and to the jangle of the brasses when they threw up their heads. The two big greys were tired but the day's work was done.

He stretched leisurely and bent to rub his limbs before putting on the faded, green waistcoat. Only two of the buttons with the Knight motif remained but Nancy Coward had sewn on whatever she could find to replace those that were lost. He walked slowly across to the old summerhouse, leant against the ivy-covered wall and stooped to scrape at the mud on his boots. He loved it there, and now in the evening light the view held his gaze. Far below, the houses of Lynton lay huddled together at the neck of the long valley before it fell away to the sea, each one clinging as best it could to the sides of the steep ground. Castle Heights, his home for so long, stood out clearly, perched high on the cliff tops at the far edge of the town. Even from where he was he could pick out the stables and see signs of movement; Dan perhaps or Leonard. His eye followed the thread of the path down to the forge where the grey smoke showed that Ruben was still at his anvil.

Then way, way beneath him, almost as if he was a high-soaring bird, lay Lynmouth, hundreds of feet further down again. The harbour, now more than half full of sailing vessels, was ringed by the fishermen's cottages he knew so well. From where he sat they looked tiny, no larger than a child's toy bricks, their thin trails of coal smoke drifting away on the breeze together. The whole of the great valley floor beneath him lay in deep evening shadow, even so he could still see people moving about, most of them attending to the boats moored along the quayside. He listened quietly but no sound came up to him. He was too high: for him there was just the cry of seabirds and the distant soughing of the sea.

✳

Pushing himself away from the building, he walked down to the boundary hedge and leant over the gate where the rusty hinges were still loose. Even now he was shaken by the news Hector and Leonard had brought when they called and told him about Tiverton. He had been mortified to think they had gone without him and still felt the anger that had boiled when they told him about Lottie and Davey. Naylor was dead and gone and that was good. He would liked to have seen that, but their visit had left him shocked and bewildered.

That was more than a week ago, before Frederic had ridden out to the farm with two troopers to find out why he had failed to respond to the regiment's call to arms. Knight explained that he had been ordered to come and find out then, if necessary, to arrest him. It had been a black moment, the more so when he had protested his innocence and saw the disbelief on the soldiers' faces.

"If you say you never received the message then you're going to have to explain how," Frederic had warned. "Redman, here, swears blind he brought it. Unless you can give us a satisfactory explanation, I've been told to take you in. So what *do* you have to say for yourself," he urged. "For God's sake...it's serious, you know, and carries a stiff penalty."

Almost when he had resigned himself to the consequences, Trooper Redman, the one who had brought the message, caught sight of Winnie. "'Ere," he cried, pointing. "That's 'er, the one I gave it to. Over there look...that funny one. I remember now. That's 'er." Jack, stung by the man's callousness, ran to her then took her indoors. There, he and Gwen had taken time to coax the story from the girl. Eventually she had gone to her bedroom and retrieved the document, bringing it proudly into the kitchen, still sealed.

Easing his arms on the gate he smiled, remembering how they had laughed with relief.

*

If it was Winnie who had given him strength, it was Frederic who gave him hope. Ever since he had been banished to the farm, the young master had demonstrated his loyalty, lending him two horses and paying the difference in his wages. There were times when he wanted none of it. Fate was forcing him to see out his penance as he was and that was the way it should be, with Joshua's words about purging the soul tormenting his conscience. Soon after his visit with the soldiers Frederic came again, this time alone and it was then that he and Jack had talked.

"Don't be such a damn fool, man." Frederic's laughter made him feel just that and he looked away until the man caught his breath. "That's nonsense...all this penance business and these days and nights in the wilderness. Really, it's mad." The two were sitting together on the grass mound by the ruins of the summer-house. "Honestly Jack...had father wanted to hang you from on high he would have banished you for ever, driven you out, dismissed you. *That* would have hurt and you would have been sunk."

"But then why this all kindness of yours, Master Frederic? 'Tis almost as if you're working agin your father. Were he ever to know we're here like this...there'd be hell to pay, for you as well as for me."

"I daresay he does know."

"*What?* How come, sir? Can't be so...can it?" Frederic eased his seat but made no reply. "D'you really think your father knows?" he persisted.

Frederic shrugged. "There's not much he doesn't know...but he knows for certain that we've been together for more than twenty years and that our friendship is well known across the moor, so I daresay he has a fair idea. Oh yes...if he had it in mind to make you really pay, then he would have tried to put a stop to my coming here. Not that he could, of course."

"How so?" Jack stared at the ground between his feet, suddenly aware of what was being said.

"'Cos our friendship's stronger than all that nonsense at Simonsbath. And because I've witnessed with my own eyes how you and Katherine will see this through whatever happens...and...well, because it's my desire to see you out of here just as soon as I can."

"But how?"

"Because I need you, my friend. I'll need every good man I can get, but those I know and trust most I'll need more than anyone. Father's ageing fast...he'll not be here for many years more then Exmoor'll be mine." Frederic took a deep breath. "And when that day comes, whenever it is, I'll have to run the place...and I'll be needing you, Jack. There's work to be done and I've a place for you in my plans." He checked himself again. "But there's something else...another thing." This time Jack turned and met his look. "It's you and your own future that concerns me."

He tried, in his own way, to thank him but the words never came, Frederic brushing aside even the best of his efforts. When time came for him to ride away the two of them were laughing together once more. Jack's visitor had gone but he had left his friendship, its strength now deeper than ever. Even so, and in spite of his generosity, money remained tight and he found it difficult to put any to one side. His clothes from Simonsbath were all but spent and he had to replace them out of his own pocket. He paid Gwen for his food and lamp oil then sent what was left home to his mother. Now Lottie and Davey were with her he would have to find more and it troubled him.

✳

But life was not all worry. He had his friends and, more than that, there was Katherine. That, too, had been due to Frederic. He, the Aclands and Lizzie Darcy had conspired to pass their letters between them and, when she was staying nearby, they helped her to visit West Lyn or for the two of them to meet on the moors. As soon as he knew the date of her next visit he would make a chart of the weeks, marking off each day, willing them all to speed by.

Only last month they had arranged for her to stay with Hector in the gardener's cottage and he had brought her up to see him. She was dressed as a boy, riding up the cliff path astride one of the packponies scarcely bigger than the donkeys that worked in the harbour. It had been a wonderful moment and they had later spent the evening together, sitting on the bracken-covered slope at the end of Hector's garden.

He had watched her searching for wild flowers among the heather and broom, turning every now and then to show him what she had found. Some he took from her, placing them in her hair as she lay beside him. The tiny, pink bloom she had stolen from the rosebed by the cottage window he kept for himself, determined to press it dry then tie it to the rail above his cot. Later that evening as they lay on the mattress by the hearth, they had made love, gently and tenderly, the light of the fire playing across her face as she looked up before pulling him down and wrapping her arms around his neck.

Long before dawn, when it was time for him to go, she had clung to him tearfully, her soft, warm body pressed against his until the very last moment. He remembered how she had turned away, burying herself under the blankets in anguish. He had scooped her body into his, wrapping himself around her protectively like a shell, his face nuzzling against the back of her neck. The last tender kiss had been cruel and they had let their lips linger before he slipped from the cottage and raced up the same cliff path they always used, his thighs aching and lungs gasping for breath.

*

"Da-ak, Da-ak." It had to be Winnie and it was: she was standing by the horses waiting for him. He had no idea how long he had been leaning over the gate but the sun had gone and the evening breeze off the sea had chilled his bare arms. She had come out to meet him so she could drive the horses back past the farmhouse to the stone trough where the lane joined the Lynton road. He gave her the plough-lines then held them behind her as they walked, letting the girl believe it was she that was guiding the big shires up the narrow, high-banked lane.

Later, once the horses had been turned out, he took her to check the sheep. His shrill whistle sent the two dogs racing one another in a wide arc around the flock before they turned and worked the animals towards them. She took his hand and they followed the sheep until they were cornered where the two hedges met the broken gate. Once trapped, he let them run back to the field one at a time so he could check each one.

"There, Winnie. Two of yours, look…and another…and there's the fourth. That's the lot. All yours." Jack had marked hers with a red cloth dye.

"Next lambing, more," she chortled, clapping her hands in delight before clasping hold of his once again. "Lots more."

"Aye, seven or eight, maybe," he held up his fingers counting with her as she skipped beside him. "Here, Winnie, count. Come on, count…that's right." Neither of them noticed her mother watching from the kitchen as he crouched beside the girl to shake the stone from one of her clogs before wiping her mouth with the hem of her dress.

3

But Jack's worries remained. In spite of Frederic's help, he needed a new pair of farm shoes and his black riding boots, almost worn through, required patching where they had split. Ben Jones, the fat, bearded cobbler in Barbrook, had refused to extend his credit until he had worked on his vegetable garden for two Sundays. Then Paulus Baker, the tailor on the corner of the Lynton road, a miserly man with the noisy wife, had asked too much for his cord breeches and cloth shirts. His funds were exhausted. Luke Harper was his only hope.

"There's a run coming in two weeks, but I've got my crew." The black eyes stared back as he shrugged glumly. Luke was older, more leathery and gnarled than Jack remembered. The face looked drawn but perhaps that was because the hair had receded, seemingly pulling his face back with it. There was little greyness though, very little, just a touch on the beard and under the ears but no more. The beetling, glowering eyebrows were the same, as were the creases on his brow although one, perhaps two, might have been scars.

"Davey Burge's doing the ponies…along with Ned Hawkins and his lot from Brendon. Sorry, Jack, there's nort to be done…not now, anyways. Next time p'raps." Jack's head dropped. It hadn't been easy to ask like that but money had forced his hand. Luke, however, had nothing to offer.

His heart sank and he rode the pony home, saddened and hurt with his head down and the reins loose. But then, and it was a thought that came slowly, perhaps it was just as well. After all he would get by somehow. His clothes would have to wear a little longer as would his boots. He would manage and, anyway, he would have nothing to hide. His conscience would be clear and he could look the world in the eye. There was much in life to be looking forward to and better by far to be like that than to be branded a smuggler for life.

✳

Ten days later Luke sent word for him. He was worried and pressed for time. "Thing's 'ave changed, Jack…they fellas at Exford have let me down. Only want half the goods and I told 'em 'twas all or nothing. Wouldn't have it so I've switched to Mole's Chamber…The Acland Arms. Can yer make it?" Luke's eyes left the stone his boot had been scuffing while he spoke. "What d'ya think, man?" he searched Jack's face.

"The Chamber," Jack whistled and shook his head. "That's a devil of a long run

36

from here. And by Judas himself 'tis one hell of a rough place. You get 'em all up there…gypsies, footpads, miners…road gangs, the lot. That Irish crowd of the Knights as well."

"Aye…all of that and more," Luke pulled one of his faces. "But the customs men keep well clear. It's too far out for the Redcoats and the last lot there took a right beating. 'Tain't a bad spot…quiet like and the buyers come in from miles." He was scowling again. No man of words he was searching for something more to say. "Landlord Jim reckons he can shift the goods in a coupla days or less an' Davey's running the packtrain. I could do with yer, Jack." He pulled gently on his earring and cocked his head. "You know the moor up there better than any. An' I'll pay yer well, you know that."

"What's in it for me, then?" That was it. No sooner were the words out than he was pledged. He was in. To stammer or stutter or fiddle about now was out of the question. He had not even stopped to think, not given himself a second. The words came straight from his heart. His head had been empty but his soul had been bought. He felt Luke's hand on his shoulder.

✳

Jack met the packtrain at the bridge over the Lyn in Barbrook. The night was black. More than that a heavy drizzle and thick mist rolled down from the moors above them.

For three hours they climbed, leaving the last of the trees behind at the bend in the river where it fell, tumbling and roaring over the rocks and into the deep pool. The higher they rose, the wilder the night became, until the wind was a full gale, lashing furiously across the open moor, shards of hail and sleet driving into the faces of men and ponies as they forced their way against the elements. When they turned it was into the teeth of the weather. Then they climbed again, slipping and floundering in the thick sedge until the land levelled out before dropping down to the Simonsbath road.

"Two more miles at least, I'm afraid." Jack huddled next to the two in the ditch where the water rose above their bootlaces. All thoughts of what was at stake had gone from his mind. He had a job to do and they were looking to him, all of them, old and young alike. He had to get them there. There was no choice. The three crouched together for warmth, blowing on their hands with their bodies soaked and frozen.

"Black as a curse, here," Davey Burge gasped. "Don't go leading us all about the place up 'ere, boy. Press on an' let's get it done, then back down again." Even the Brendon farmer was shaking with cold.

"How long, Jack?" Luke peered into the darkness. "By Jees it's freezing."

"More than an hour yet…and that's if I can find the Sloley Stone and the top of Lew Coombe." Jack could feel his teeth clattering together. Rainwater was running down his face and into his mouth. "I'll do my best…"

"Just bloody get us there." Davey Burge turned his back on him.

*

They stopped finally where the track dropped and turned sharply. It had gone midnight. The inn was quiet, none of the usual light and bustle. Behind the unlit buildings a tall beech hedge swayed and tossed as the tempest roared angrily through the branches. Beneath the trees the stream, usually no more than a tinkle of clear water, tumbled and foamed. Only the mad would be out on a night like this.

Jack watched as Luke and Davey Burge crept forward. Luke had his cutlass, Burge a club. Suddenly he was afraid. There was no denying it, he could feel his heart racing. These men were going in prepared to fight, to strike out at those in the building, to wound and murder if needs be. He and the others were in it and there was no escape. Just pray to God he could do his bit and not let them down.

He heard them hammer on the door then saw a chink of light. It was only minutes, yet it seemed an hour before they returned to guide the packponies through the narrow entrance to the stable yard at the back. Hewett, the landlord, and another, a wild brute of a man, met them with a storm lantern that swung in his hand, then watched and counted as the kegs were hidden under the hay. It looked simple enough, so where was the danger? Where was the battle they had been talking about? Cheered and relaxed, he stood and rubbed his bones.

Burge left two on watch and took the others into one of the open stables. He had a bottle and, with the lantern turned up, the men began to relax. Clothes were rung out, arms were beaten together and feet stamped to bring life back into frozen limbs.

But they had forgotten themselves and dropped their guard. It was a terrible mistake.

*

Jack saw Luke turn. "*Davey*, come with me," he called quietly. "And you, *Jack*. Quick…come on but stay back while I go in and settle up. Ned, you and Jasper take t'other side." He looked at the others. "I'll only be gone a few minutes…soon as I'm back we're away." He should have cared more, of course, and now he was taking a chance. Jack's heart was pounding again. He moved to follow Luke but the smuggler waved him back and he stopped, crouching warily by the low bank set back from the door. Luke could look after himself.

The moment the door slammed he knew it was too late. They heard the shout and the two of them charged but the door had been barred. Luke was in trouble, desperate trouble.

"Quick the back." Burge ran, Jack just behind him. They could see a lantern but that door had been barred as well. Three of them charged and it gave suddenly, all of them stumbling and tripping as they crashed inside. Luke was on the taproom floor, his body curled tight into a ball to protect himself. Two had fallen with him but others were shouting, stamping and kicking at the trapped body. Davey leapt at them, Jack too. More men appeared.

The Irish had heard about the smuggling run and held Mary Hewett captive while the contraband was hidden away. As soon as Luke had come for the money they pounced. The miners and roadmen from Cork were fighting fiercely, hurling bottles and furniture, using staves and chairs as clubs. They battled grimly and desperately with everything to gain and everything to lose.

Jack threw one man aside, kicked him and was grappling with a foul-smelling savage when the club crashed down. He was on the floor, blood streaming from the wound, his eyes no longer able to focus on the trampling, stomping feet in front of him. A boot caught him full in the face. Davey Burge brought down two before a group of screaming celts leapt on him, beating his head and body until he could no longer breathe. Jasper Watts backed into a corner, fought hard but he, too, was clubbed to the ground.

In seconds it was over. They had gone, windows and doors left banging in the night, the flickering lantern just enough to see. For some time no one spoke. "Where's Luke?" Jack tried to stand but fell back across the table as his legs collapsed like broken twigs.

"*Jack…Jack,*" Ned Hawkins was shaking him. "Come on, drink this…drink, man, for God's sake." Jack swallowed and coughed, then spluttered and coughed again.

"'Tis bad, Jack…Luke's hurt bad, two wounds and one of them's deep. Jasper's arm's broken and Arthur took a right hiding when he tried to save the ponies." Once more Jack tried to stand, this time swaying and clutching for the wall. He could taste blood and one eye was closing. He reached up for his nose and yelped like a child as the bone grated.

"You there, lad?" Burge held his head and peered, feeling his face. "Looks like yer nose has gone but nothing worse. We'd best be getting back with what us've got left." He shook his head. "Sweet Jesus, what a mess…never slipped like this before. The devils 'ave got the lot…the money, the goods and half the damned ponies. We nailed a few of 'em though, and one's a gonner. Over there, see."

✳

Someone had drawn the curtain. The light that woke him shone through the window and onto his cot. He knew where he was by the hole in the ceiling where the plaster had fallen from the lattice, but no more than that and he flinched at the damp cloth that was bathing his brow. "That's better. At least we know you're alive." He turned at the sound of his mother's voice then frowned and tried to focus. She was looking down at him, smiling like she used to and he smiled back, taking her hand.

"Mother," he murmured. "What brought you up here then?"

"Shhh, Jack. It's me, Emma, your sister. I've been here three days now watching you slip back and forth. You took a terrible beating and Hector came for me. Dr Collyns has been here, too. He patched your face and set your nose. And Master Frederic's bin also…you can't remember can you."

Jack closed his eyes. He could remember voices, faces peering down out of the dark as they discussed him. Two had come back a second time and stood over him nodding sagely. Just then Scamp crept up to his face, belly down and tail wagging, guilty at getting so close. Jack lifted his little dog, turned him on his back and rested a hand on the soft, warm tummy.

"Troy told me to come up for you. Mother's worried stiff but we calmed her." Emma mopped his brow again. "What the devil were you up to out there? That Mole's Chamber's a terrible place." He coughed and winced as the pain knifed through his head.

"I know, Emms. I know," he muttered, his mind clouding. "That's why we were there…just part of the great game. Everyone does it…have to…there's nothing else."

"But that's *wicked*, Jack. Terrible…really. You know what they do if they catch you," Emma smoothed his hair.

"We all know…"

"Shush," she scolded. "Listen…don't say anything to anyone about it. *Anyone* and I mean it. They're saying you fell from the bridge in Barbrook. D'you hear? You fell from the bridge in Barbrook…right? That's what you did and that's all we know…so say nuthin, *nuthin*."

It took a week but time mended him. Davey Burge came and together they discussed the disaster. "Can't blame it all on Luke," the big man muttered. "Should've been on our toes, all of us, not blathering away in the barn like that. Should've seen 'twas too quiet…even on a night like that."

"And Luke?" Jack remembered the wounds.

"Oh, he'll live. One went deep but the man's tough." Burge's body shook as he laughed, scratching his beard. "Blames himself, of course...but that Dr Collyns, the one young Knight brought along, he's seen him twice...says he's lucky. The knife or whatever 'twas, missed his heart but not much else." Burge paused. "Wants another run, so 'e does but we told him to wait...wait till the weather's better."

"You want to go back?"

"No choice, is there?" the farmer shrugged. "It's do the runs or starve...that's it. You must see that now you're living the same as the rest of us. How else's a man s'posed to live?" Jack felt his nose. He had been lucky to escape with his life, that was for sure but the night had cost him dear for his coat had been slashed and his wages stopped.

4

John Knight decided to leave Holnicote soon after the reception. The Memorial service for Charles Acland had been a harrowing affair; the bright, vivacious naval lieutenant had gone. Both John and Frederic had fond memories; to Frederic he had been a dear friend also.

They had seen him last at Dunster just before he and Henry King sailed. *H.M.S Cornwallis* had been ordered to the East Africa station for anti-slavery duties and had put into Mombasa where blackwater fever was rife. Charles, ashore on a victualling patrol, had caught the disease along with several others and those that had perished were buried at sea. A service of thanksgiving had been held in Exeter Cathedral but the family decided to hold another in West Somerset to make it easier for those who lived locally.

Knight had seen that Sir Thomas Acland, now Member for North Devon with Lord Eglington, had taken the loss badly. James Acland had asked Frederic to sit with him during the service. Many had been moved deeply. Katherine and Lizzie Darcy had been there with their father, the Duke, as had the Luttrells and the Frobishers, the Chichesters, the Bamfyldes and many others. Admiral The Lord Effingham gave the address. Lady Acland had asked many of the villagers and estate workers to join them and it was one of those rare moments when the world came together. In its own sad way it had been a grand occasion.

✳

Frederic Knight sat looking at his father. The light travelling coach was rolling from side to side as the postilion urged the two extra heavy horses towards the fearsome Porlock Hill. The old man looked drained of energy and his head nodded against the damask cushions. Over the last two years he had aged noticeably; the fire that had driven his enterprises so ruthlessly had started to fade. There had been moments of success as well as the bitter taste of failure and now, at well over seventy, he had been considering the future. They had talked already, several times in fact.

A sudden jolt and the shouts of the two servants behind them made him struggle to sit. "You know, Freddy." Knight gazed out of the window, coughed and cleared his throat. "I reckon the time'll soon be right for a change. Still so much to do but not enough time for these old bones," he gave a little laugh. "It'll all be coming your way soon, you know…soon enough." He nodded at the thought, looking back at the coach that passed the other way. "But I've been worrying y'know, worrying that you won't be able to handle it all…cope with everything else you've taken on." He checked himself again, looking his son up and down then yawned and stretched. "It's a lot you've got on, y'know."

Both he and Elizabeth-Jane had been watching with mounting concern as their son had struggled to force his way into West Worcestershire's politics, dashing across the country to Wolverley or up to Portland Place in Westminster. But there had been little sign of progress to date. It would have been hard enough from the county itself, but a single round trip from Exmoor was more than four hundred miles and the boy's life was already full.

"I'll manage, father." Frederic nodded confidently.

"But what of the moor and all that's been done here? It'll need a firm hand, y'know, there's so many pieces to fit together…and then there're the mines. The place's the devil's own distance from London…and that's when the roads're good." He scratched at his snow-white mane. "Running as a Member is one thing…doing that *and* running Exmoor as well's quite something else."

"My run for Worcestershire's going to take a while," he countered. "Something I'm not going to rush. I can't anyway. Lord Melbourne and his Whigs look set for a spell, Thomas Acland's certain of that. And Sir Robert Peel's biding his time, three years so I hear…that's according to Bayswater who got it from Lord Derby himself. It'll give me a chance to get things straight down here…there's time enough."

"Unless there's a snap election, of course." Knight frowned. "These things happen y'know and you wouldn't want to be wrong footed there."

It would indeed be hard, not just the tasks he had set himself but harder still succeeding his father. For years, as long as any of them could remember, the Master had seemed indestructible, his name held in awe wherever they had gone. But since the scare over his heart he had decided to step down and he, Frederic, would have to try and fill the void the old man's absence would leave. Had he, he wondered, inherited enough of his father's wisdom? Had he got his father's strength? Could he command his absolute authority?

"And you've got the Yeomanry, too." Knight turned suddenly as if the thought had just come to him. "We're proud of that, Freddy, very proud. John Rolle's told me how pleased he is...all that Tiverton business. But," Knight faltered for a moment. "It's an awesome challenge you've set yourself...one hell of a lot. You can see why I feel like I do. Eh?"

"Oh, indeed, sir, yes." He glanced at his father knowing he was going to have to spell it out. Then he leant forward to catch the old man's eye. "I've *got* to give it a try, father...all of it. If it does turn out to be too much then things'll have to go. The Yeomanry for instance: it's fun and I've the time right now but it's not essential, I can live without it. Even going for Parliament...I admit I fancy my chances and Sir Thomas's been a great help but that could go too. It's an ambition, no more'n that." His father's eyes were half shut but he was looking his way, and nodding benignly. A shock of white hair flopped over his face and Frederic allowed himself a smile. He may have looked asleep, half asleep even, but he wasn't. He was listening to every word and taking it all in.

"And that leaves the moor." Frederic sat back. "Well, you know about that...I *can* manage. Hard work to be sure, but there's nothing that can't be done."

"Ah...well." The old man yawned again, louder this time. "Another year or so then enough's enough." He turned to peer at a wagonette easing its way past them on its way down the steep slope. The three passengers were walking behind, leaning back on ropes to relieve the pressure on the horse. Two boys were moving alongside, crouching ready to place blocks of wood under the front wheels should the driver call for assistance. Their own climb had just begun.

Chapter Three

Elizabeth-Jane bent slightly to check her satin ankle boots, then straightened herself and smiled. She was delighted to see Durnford Morgan again in spite of the somewhat formal, office surroundings, but it was the melodic chimes of the French boulle clock behind his pedestal desk that reminded her how much of the day had already gone. It had been more than eight hours since she and Frederic were standing at the end of Ilfracombe's windswept wooden pier.

＊

They had watched quietly and waved to the two figures standing forlornly at the stern of the 'Camerole' as she manoeuvred quietly out of the harbour. Her patched, buff-coloured lower foresail flapped noisily as she caught what breeze there was, for the captain preferred to let the strong-running spring tide carry her past the shallows. Only after she had cleared the Benricks did she set more sail, her pace quickening when the sou'wester caused her to heel suddenly as she hardened up on a course to clear Beacon Point.

Elizabeth-Jane had been determined to see them off, as had John until Collyns confined him to bed with a severe warning. Frederic had come instead and she had watched proudly as he pressed her husband's letter into Parker's hand.

The promissory note together with its letter of authority to draw one hundred guineas against Esdaile's had been signed by Sir James himself, having assured Frederic that Solomon's of Albany, New York would honour the agreement. For years, he announced, business between the two banks had been secure; ever since that place across the Atlantic had demanded its independance.

But the parting had been difficult. When time had come for the couple to go on board, Parker had taken both her hands in his, clasping them tightly with his voice strangely thin as he professed his devotion to the family. Then, in a sudden gesture of affection, he had raised both her hands to his lips. She had seen the tears in his red-rimmed eyes, the same eyes that had watched over them for so long.

And she had been tearful too, when she looked on as Freddy and Parker embraced each other, both knowing well it would be the last time they would meet. Edith, however, had been her same, distant self, constantly chivvying her husband about this and that, even as she followed him up the narrow, rickety gangway. They had all worried about poor Parker but now it was too late.

＊

"Tea would be lovely, Durnford...where do you recommend?" she asked as she tidied the line of her striped green dress. She could see he approved for she had caught his eyes straying even as they had been discussing the farms. "But wait…Freddy, dear, we can't be too long, can we?"

Frederic checked his watch against the wall clock. "No immediate hurry, perhaps an hour…but little more." He glanced at Morgan.

"Wonderful…that's plenty of time." Morgan rose and rang the ornamental brass hand bell on his desk. "The Old Coffee House in Church Lane's just a five minute stroll. Bear with me a moment, would you, while I clear these things." Then he lifted a finger. "Look, better still, why not go on ahead…I'll be five minutes at the most. I hoped you'd agree to my suggestion and took the liberty of booking a table…we shall be on the first floor, in the back room."

✳

Frederic had found lunch and the earlier meeting with Morgan easier than he expected. His father had told him to go to the Barnstaple bank and acquaint himself with the estate books. There were no horrors, he had assured him, nonetheless the figures for the now defunct mining exploration had not made for pleasant reading. While his mother had shopped with her maid, the two of them sat in the deep bow window overlooking the High Street where they poured over the ledgers. Frederic's intention of further surveying the moor had been discussed already.

Maxwell had been unable to join them but had verified the farming figures and dates a week before. "Four farms with tenants will keep things even." Morgan had double-checked the statements. "Six would be better and eight would make it all a deal more comfortable…but even that won't leave us with anything for any new mining adventures," he warned. "That would require the maximum income from a further six homesteads, at least." Frederic's mouth rested on the tips of his fingers and his eyes were lowered as he listened to the banker's deliberations. "We can do the roads with what we've got," he continued, "But they're not cheap, you know…neither are the walls. But it's these damned labourers." Morgan tapped the page. "Look at them…over two hundred and fifty for Heaven's sake."

"Not for much longer." Frederic scratched his head.

"No, but long enough. Especially if we want to get these new steam ploughs and so forth in to start breaking the land." Morgan reached across the mahogany table. "Here, look. Maxwell's notes." He licked his fingers and flicked through the pages. "He insists that we get the land broken then put it to roots and grass as soon as we can…and that'll take two years at least…three he says here."

"Well, it makes sense." Frederic sat back. "The tenants won't make much of a living until they've got grass for the stock…and until then they won't be able to pay the rent," he added with a laugh. "Or that's what they'll be telling us, and they'd be right." Morgan could see that son and heir had a firm grasp of economics and knew what was required, more so than his father who had simply thrown money at everything. But the second heart attack had laid the old man low and things were now very different.

"Father'll hang on as long as he can." The statement had come as a matter of fact but Morgan could see he was worried. "They've told him he's got to ease up but you know him as well as any of us." Morgan nodded. He did indeed, as long as there was breath in the man, he would continue to drive himself.

"And are there plans...I mean for the long term?" Morgan had often wondered what the outcome would be were anything to happen suddenly to Knight. For years the thought that Elizabeth-Jane was but a lone heartbeat from being on her own, partnerless and vulnerable, had filled him with the most uncharitable sentiments. The idea excited him yet shamed him at the same time. Such intimations about one he liked and respected so much were callous and such dreams no more than pure fantasy. Yet they had persisted for it was something over which he had no control. Would she, he wondered, go back to Ireland, or leave Exmoor for London? Or would she stay on, struggling to fulfil her husband's vision? Such thoughts always stirred him.

Frederic shrugged. "Who knows? Just now we're having to take things day by day. They've certainly muttered about getting well away when the time comes...abroad even, yet I can't see it. Mother loves it here...and everything about the place

＊

Tea was late. Elizabeth-Jane had forgotten to go back to her dressmaker and Frederic had to run to catch the jewellers before they closed. In the end they had but half an hour together making small talk while waiting for the coach. By the time they came to leave, the weak March sun had given way to an evening chill that descended slowly, bringing down with it the hazy smoke of countless household fires. Mother and son rode inside together, the maid, muffled and shawled, up top with the coachman. As they passed through the narrow cobbled streets of Marwood and the gypsy camp at Raleigh, Leonard Grant, brought along as an outrider, stayed close by the coach.

"Goin' to press on up the hill now, ma'am." Grant bent further down, his head half way through the open window. As he did so, Elizabeth-Jane sat back to avoid the blast of his raised voice. "Two or three riders up front, Master Frederic, sir. Don't s'pect 'tis nort to worry about but's best to gid on an' check."

"Leonard's a dear." Elizabeth-Jane watched as their guardian kicked on ahead.

"Brave as a lion, too." Frederic laughed suddenly. "And strong, my goodness. You should see him teaching the boys to wrestle. They love it but I've never seen him really trying...he'd break them in half."

She watched fascinated then pulled her son across to witness the sight of the burly, round shouldered figure trotting away, his arms flapping to balance the heavy body which bounced precariously on the saddle. They looked at each other then burst out laughing together.

2

Lambing at West Lyn began during the last week in March. Any earlier, so Joshua decreed, and the young lambs would be caught by the weather.

Most of the land lay over eight hundred feet and March on the moor was well known for its harshness, even heavy snowfalls. They never lasted long but were enough to kill off any newborn lambs that were caught in the open. If they started later the youngsters were behind for the rest of the year. Come the autumn sheep fairs and any pens of lambs that looked smaller than the rest rarely sold well. So the end of March it had to be.

*

Hector's wife, Nancy, came and helped then, later, she returned for the shearing and haymaking, bringing with her stories of life at Castle Heights. Jack had known the neat, trim sandy-haired girl since he and the others were stable lads when they used to meet the village children at the forge. She was younger than him and he had ignored her at first, until the day they met at the saddlers when he rode down from Simonsbath.

The shy, grubby little Nancy Mathews, he remembered, had changed in the time he had been away. Now the eyes, half hidden by curls, danced naughtily and the rosebud mouth pouted as she chatted away merrily while he chose the new saddle and stirrup leathers. But she was Hector's; he had heard word of their courtship and had been there at St Mary's in Lynton when they were married.

"Listen to the maid," Joshua warned. "Listen well and learn. 'Er has a way with stock and's a proper shepherd's lass." It was strange at first, difficult almost, kneeling behind an animal as it gave birth, witnessing nature at work while listening to a young woman he had known since she was a girl. She saw his reserve and laughed it off, just as she laughed as a child.

"Don't be daft, Jack...'tis nat'ral, the most nat'ral thing of all." He had wavered, unsure if it was because of the presence of the girl herself or what they were having to do together. But he watched closely, marvelling at the way she worked, and at her patience and gentleness. Joshua had put it in his own way. "Fear not the work of the Lord, neither be ashamed. Life on a farm is none other than the witness of creation in the blood and in the soil as the Almighty had decreed...not as the ignorance and wickedness of man perceives it to be."

"Turn her gently, like so." Jack watched as she held the ewe by one horn, reached underneath for the far hind leg then, half lifting, tipped her carefully on to one side.

"Until the lamb's ready and she's lying still, you've only got one hand to work with." Nancy bent down and pulled the wool back from the ewe's hindquarters. "There look. There's the nose and two feet, see? 'Er's coming on well. No problem there." She helped the ewe to her feet and watched as she walked clumsily to the hedgerow, calling softly and sniffing the ground. "Be a few minutes yet, bit more maybe." Nancy wiped her hands on the grass then stood. "Could be twins there…us'll have to see."

*

For the first year Jack followed her, learning the ways of lambing and the multitude of problems that might arise. He learned quickly but there was always something new. Now, three years on, he took the night watch, rising every hour to check those due to give birth. Rather than retiring to his cot, he pulled the kitchen chair close to the fire and snatched what sleep he could, tucked under one of Frederic's old frock coats. Sometimes his visit to the lambing pen took no more than a few minutes, on other occasions he was out for hours on end. Tonight it looked like being a long night.

Two ewes had lambed quietly and he checked that all was well before moving one into a more sheltered position under the hedge. Lifting the still wet lamb by its front legs, he walked backwards calling to the mother who followed bleating reassuringly with her nose never far from her lamb. As soon as he put it down, the lamb rose up, tottering and calling. He stepped back and watched as the ewe cleaned the lamb then nursed it, the youngster's tail wriggling as it took the warm milk.

By the light of his storm lantern he saw that the tail of a lamb was showing behind another ewe: it was coming breeched. He caught the ewe and turned her gently. "They're the very devil," Nancy had warned. "'Tis a terrible strain on the ewe and either she dies or the lamb's born half dead with its ribs crushed. Only way's to try an' turn 'im…if you can, that is." Holding her still with his knee, Jack felt behind her. He could see she was contracting and there was little time.

Nancy had taught him how to feel with his fingers and how to ease his hand inside. Hers was tiny but his were large with broad, wide knuckles and he never failed to be aware of the pain such an intrusion caused. He winced at the ewe's loud bleats, but gradually managed to push the lamb back towards the womb. Bending down, he reached further, now up to his forearm and felt for the head. Using just his fingertips he began to ease it towards him as the ewe panted and called hoarsely.

"Come on, come on," he whispered to himself, straining to turn the unborn lamb. When eventually it arrived, he cleaned the mucus from its face, opened the mouth and blew into the lungs. There was little sign of life so he massaged the chest, careful not to press hard on the tiny rib cage and used his own body to shield the lamb from the wind. When he had all but given up, the lamb raised its head and shook itself so he kept the mother down, held the lamb's head against her warm udder and squeezed the first milk into its mouth.

Dawn came and still Jack was in the pen. Six lambs had been born and another ewe had begun. He was muddy and tired, his hands and clothes filthy with blood but he felt a deep sense of wonder and fulfilment. Some great, mysterious force, quite beyond his comprehension, was moving nature to bring new life into the world. He had seen it at work and, in his own small way, had been able to help. He needed no convincing that his Maker, the Creator of all things, was at work. It was impossible not to believe. He sat back in the lee of the hedge, listening to the morning birds as light from the east flooded across the countryside reaching down into the darkest hollows to bring in a fresh, young day. The wonder of it all humbled him and he was happy to give thanks. Joshua had been right but he would do this by himself and in his own time.

It was time to go in but he stayed on, allowing himself a few moments more to take in the sights and sounds of the new day. Nancy was due and he decided to wait. He saw little enough of her at times like this, Hector also, and he treasured their few moments together. She was his bridge to the world beyond West Lyn and the two of them guardians of his secret life with Katherine.

✳

"She's real lovely, Jack. Honest to God she is." Nancy smiled as she took his arm. "We love 'aving her to stay. Gets better every time, y'know. Us knows she's real fancy, a lady an' all, but she's like one of us…really she is. Talks an' laughs away, 'appy as they come. Do anything for us, she would…not much good with 'er hands though. Be no good up 'ere just now." She laughed and paused, tightening her grip on his arm. "She loves yer, Jack, dear…real loves yer, she does."

"I know, Nan." Jack brushed a hand through his hair and looked away. Katherine had told him so herself, swearing to give up everything she had. He should have been proud, overjoyed yet what Nancy said disturbed him. He had nothing to give in return, no sacrifices to make in exchange for her love. She was giving everything but could take it all back whenever she wanted, just like that. "I know but what can I do?" he looked at her helplessly then turned away again, cheered yet afraid of the truth in her words. "Just look at me, for God's sake, Nan. Covered in muck and slime. No home…no money…no nuthin. Can't even mend my own clothes…I've *nothing* to give. It's on my mind every day of my life but I'm stuck…what hope've I got?" He paused. As his head dropped wearily she reached up and stroked his cheek.

"'Tis just as well really, I s'pose," he muttered eventually. "Nothing'll come of it…nothing ever could. How could it now?" His voice faltered. "She'll see sense one day. Wake up one morning and see her madness and that'll be that. Honest, Nan."

"Oh come on, Jack," She ruffled his hair and pulled him towards her. "Don't get like that, love. She'll not change, I know she won't…gone too far, she 'as. Summat'll come of it. Listen, you're tired…worn through. It's bin a long night and anyone'd feel the same. Gid on in, 'ave a wash, get summat to eat then get t'yer cot." She squeezed his arm. "Summat'll work out…you'll see."

49

*

Hector came just as Jack finished filling the gap in the hedge made by the lambs, bringing with him the notice about the forthcoming fair at Barbrook.

"'Ere, Jack," he cried dismounting in the yard. "Take a look at this. Leonard said to bring it up. See this 'ere…wrestling at the fair." The two men studied the paper together. "*Wrestling contest,*" Hector, his brow furrowed in concentration, pointed with his finger, stumbling through the words. "*Grand competition. Open and Novices. All day. Evening finals. No gouging, No fisticuffs, No kicking. To the winners Ten Guineas, Second man five.*

"That's Leonard and you, Jack," he nudged his friend. "Len told me to ask yer to help 'im…for you to be his man, his second as they say. 'Es going in for the Open…says 'e needs your help. You'll get paid mind, if 'e wins."

"No, I couldn't do that, Hector." Jack thrust back the notice and shouldered his tools. "I couldn't go taking no money off Len. Not for that…wouldn't be right. Not when 'es done all the work an' I've just sat there by the ropes."

"No, no…'tis in the rules, Jack. Honest…Leonard said to tell you. In the Open, the winner's to pay the helper. He'll get two guineas if he wins and one if he's second. That 'bain't bad…and you could do with that, couldn't you?"

"Dunno 'bout that." He hunched one shoulder to steady his load and reached out for the notice, this time studying it carefully. "Tell Len, I'll think on it. I'm not sure whether 'tis me or no."

"Don't be daft, man. He's asked for yer…he's yer friend and needs yer help. You can't say no…'twouldn't be right."

3

Blagdon Park basked in the early spring sunshine. Anyone passing along the main road between Winchester and Romsey could see why the house remained one of Hampshire's finest examples of Georgian architecture.

Designed in 1750 by Holland, Blagdon retained most of its original features, in particular those of the interior created by Robert Adam. Whatever had been lost or damaged by the fire in 1812 had been restored in the following years by the architect Nash. Built to the orders of Arthur, the second Duke of Northborough, Blagdon was inherited by his son, Henry, before passing to George, the fourth and present duke, on his death in 1810. A sizeable part of the immense family cotton and wool fortune had been spent in restoring the family seat to its original glory.

*

Katherine sat humming to herself. Just an hour ago she had returned from her morning ride with Lizzie and now, while she waited for the gong to summon the family to lunch, she sat at her black Venetian dressing table. It was a present from her father, always reminding her of him and she treasured it, even now as she sat attending her face and stopping only to answer the knock on her door.

"Beg pardon, m'lady," Sarah curtsied in the doorway. "Mr Evans's compliments ma'am, but he says that His Grace is waiting for you in the library."

"In the *library*?" Katherine turned looking puzzled. "Why there?" she never could understand why the new butler sent the staff running around with such messages. It was his job, not that of her lady's maid; perhaps it was the Welsh in the man.

"So." She cocked an eye, got up and walked frowning to her mirror stand where she turned slowly to check herself. The dark Hussar jacket with braid and fur decorations, over her long, olive-beige silk gown was *parfait pour le printemps* so Madam Corellier had insisted. The Bruton Street seamstress had made it especially for her tall, full figure and it fitted perfectly.

"Goodness, Sarah…whatever's the matter?" She peered at the pale girl holding the door. "You look as though you've just seen a ghost."

"Thank you ma'am." The young maid glanced down shyly, bobbing a curtsey as Katherine left the room. As she went she sang to herself, tripping lightly down the stairs and, still humming cheerfully, swept through the open library doors. The moment she saw them she knew something was wrong.

The three of them were there together. Her mother and brother, looking tense and nervous, stood behind her father who was sitting at his favourite rosewood table. As soon as they saw her, all three started. Her mother looked distraught, her father black and foul tempered. He rose heavily before she had time to ask what was amiss. "Shut the door, Herbert." Her brother jumped. "Be quick and return to your mother's side."

"What on earth's the matter with everyone?" Katherine looked from one to another incredulously. Deep inside, her body was freezing. "What's happened for goodness sake?" Neither Herbert nor their mother met her gaze.

"You know well enough." The duke's face had reddened. "In fact you know perfectly well so just listen to me. Wherever I go these days, I hear nothing but talk of your exploits on Exmoor. The Westhovers asked me about it in London the other day, the Havershams…and the Mailsoms." Katherine swallowed but her eyes, troubled yet defiant, remained fixed on her father's.

"And if all that's not enough I've had a letter from Lady Acland's cousin. The whole world's giggling and sniggering about it and I want it out *here and now*." He paused. "What the hell's going on down there? Eh?"

51

Katherine took a quick breath. She could feel her heart racing. For a moment she said nothing then, clasping her hands behind her back, she raised her eyebrows and sighed heavily. "Well, father...if you're going to start swearing..."

"*Damn* you, Katherine," he bellowed, hitting the table with his hand. "I've had enough of you telling me what to do. If you can't answer my questions I'll tell you...tell you what's been going on. Read this if you must," he snatched open a drawer and scrabbled for the letter which he threw on the table. "That's from Sir Girven Archer," he pointed. "Lydia Acland's cousin. Read it if you must...go on." He began to pace the room then swung suddenly to face her.

"To be blunt, you're continuing to see that groom of Knight's. In fact," he picked up the letter and thrust it towards her. "If we're to believe *half* of this, then you're doing nothing less than having a goddamned, blazing relationship with the man. According to Archer, you're consorting with the locals and generally dragging our name through the mud...and they're laughing, all of them. *And*, what's more," he leant across the table. "I gave you clear orders to have nothing more to do with the man. *I*, your father," he jabbed at his chest. "How *dare* you disobey me?"

The only sound was the duke breathing heavily as he mumbled to himself in an attempt to find the right words. Her mother had taken hold of her brother's arm and they stood side by side looking out of the window with their backs to Katherine and her father. "Well," he snorted. "Answer me, Katherine...*answer* me, I say."

"All right," Katherine had moved to another sash window. She was staring unseeing across the parkland unable to shut out her father's deafening tirade. Now she rounded on him. "All right, I'll tell you. Look at me then Herbert...and you mother. If you've been pulled in to witness this, there's no point in pretending you aren't part of it." She was speaking quietly.

"I *have* been seeing the man you dismiss as a mere groom. I've been seeing him because I love him." She ignored her mother's cry. "He's a wonderful man. I love him dearly and that's the way it's going to be."

"Dammit, Katherine." Her brother's face showed his disgust. "The man's nothing more than a farmhand, a...a...clodhopping great peasant. You can't *possibly* do this...I mean you *can't* go debasing yourself like that."

He could afford to be bold, she thought acidly, hiding behind her father's tails and snapping away like he usually did. "Oh yes I can, I'll..."

"Your brother's right , for God's sake," the duke spluttered. "Herbert's quite right and I'm damned if I'm going to have my family made a laughing stock around half the countryside." His hands were on his hips. "How dare you go mixing and sully-ing yourself with the lower classes like that. How *dare you!*" He was shouting again, his voice shuddering.

"I've given you my reason," Katherine cried, drawing herself up. "It so happens I believe that there're other things in life other than just titles or money…or both. Honestly, father, class, class, class. That's all you ever think about. It makes me sick…d'you hear…sick. What do you think I am for God's sake…some sort of brood mare waiting for you to send me off to stud as soon as you've found the right stallion? She wiped the corner of her mouth. "I mean, just look at some of the woeful creatures you've lined up for me. *Look* at them! Archie Gloucester – so wet and pathetic he can hardly walk the dog. And that ghastly Kenton Knight…don't you ever even *think* about mentioning that creature's name. Godfrey Bolun? The 'Dear little Duke of.' You should know all about him, Herbert. All this whoring and gambling in London. Yes, you."

"What on earth d'you mean…"

"Oh, come on, boy," she sneered, sauntering up to him. "Don't think we don't know what you all get up to. The servants talk, you know…I'm not deaf *and* stupid. The cabbies that drop you off and wait for you talk to the footmen. Even I've heard about your nasty, sordid little forays into Cheapside. What is it? A guinea a time for some poor little virgin? Word get's around, y'know. I'm not the *only* one in the news" She leant forward, her fists clenched. "*But at least mine's honest and genuine.*"

"Damned if it is," the Duke shouted. "I'm *damned* if you're going to go round picking and choosing whoever you fancy. How d'you think the rest of us feel about it? It's got to stop, I tell you. Right here and now."

Katherine watched contemptuously as her mother moved to place her hand on her father's shoulder; she could feel her haughty disdain. The very way she stood with her chin pulled in and looking down her nose like that gave lie to her thoughts. "Father, just let me tell you about this *peasant*, as Herbert calls him. Apart from the fact he saved my life at Simonsbath, d'you realise his father was killed at Waterloo? Charging the French line. *"No wait!"* she held up a hand for silence. "And his father before him, wounded fighting in Bengal. And our peasant's younger brother? D'you know about him? Wilmot? Well, let me tell *you*, Herbert.

"Graduated from Trinity, Cambridge. *Cambridge*, for goodness sake. How about that, brother dear? Harrow was it not for you? And every inch of your way paid for…and what have you done with it all? *Nothing!* Nothing but fiddle around with your bunch of wet fops and dandies. God, you're useless."

"Ohhh, That's *quite* despicable," the duchess shuddered with rage. "That's a *terrible* slur on your brother."

"*Enouuugh!*" Now the duke was purple with rage. "That's enough…enough, I say." He stood glaring at his daughter. "How *dare* you speak to us all like that? How *dare* you?" The four of them stood their ground. It was an impasse and nobody moved, the long, awkward silence broken only by the duchess muttering to herself. In the end it was too much for the duke and he glanced around furiously. "Herbert, take your mother into the morning room," he pointed dismissively. "Go on, *now*. I order you...I want to talk to Katherine on her own." He waited until the door had shut.

"Look." George Northborough walked up to his daughter. As he took a pale silk handkerchief to his face, his shoulders sagged. "I'm not having this, Katherine. I just can't be having it...it's dreadful, awful." His voice had quietened and he took a deep breath. "You simply can't go on like this."

"Like what, father?" She had gone white. The last few minutes had shocked her and her breath came in short gasps as though she had just run up the main stair-case.

"Oh, for Heaven's sake, girl." She waited while he paced up and down the long carpet with his head lowered and his hand on his chin. "You're behaving *dreadfully*, abominably...and you know you are," he groaned. "The reputation of the whole family's at stake. It's quite intolerable. If you go on like this I'll have no choice." He pulled up a chair and sat, shaking his head. "I'll have no other choice at all. If this continues it's either *you* or the family...and there's no alternative. None."

"Why not?" It was Katherine's turn to lean across the table. "Why not, father? What's so terribly wrong with what I've done...and what I want to do? I love him and I want to be with him. Is that some sort of a crime? Is that really so dreadful?" She waited for him to look up at her. "This is nothing sudden, for God's sake, father. I don't go picking and choosing this and that, as you suppose...a man here, a man there. I don't go round behaving like Herbert or that Kenton and the rest of them."

"Katherine, Katherine, Katherine," he held up his hand. "Don't go on, *any* more...*please*. I've made up my mind and that's that." Father and daughter looked at each other. She knew what was coming. "If you don't stop consorting with this man *right now*." He paused, biting his lip. "If you don't stop...then I shall disinherit you. Cut you off." He paused. "The family will formally disown you."

"I knew as much." He looked up startled at the immediacy of her response. "I thought you'd say that, father. So, there we have it. Either I submit meekly and return to this cha*rade* of a lifestyle here, or...or out I go. Is that *really* it? " She pushed herself away from the desk.

Her father looked resigned. Suddenly the anger had gone. The face had greyed. "Katherine, look," he attempted a smile. "I don't want to lose you, I can hardly bear the thought," he cleared his throat. "I'll give you one more chance...please. Give up this man, my dear...you've too much to lose. Give him up and return to the family."

"Father." She spoke slowly, with one finger idly tracing along the edge of the desk. "Listen...I've tried. I've tried so *hard*, believe me I have. But...I *can't*," she whispered. "I could never leave him now...it's been too long." The two looked at one another, each waiting for the silence to be broken. "But I'll not upset you. I won't cause a scene…don't worry . If I have to go, I'll take myself away, quietly, on my own. I'll never give you cause to order me out of your home, Never."

Long after Katherine had left the room, the duke sat on alone. He heard the gong sound for lunch then, after it had sounded a second time, Evans came to find him.

✳

"So that's it, Lizzie." The two sisters sat on her bed. "I've done it now, said my piece and there's no going back."

Her sister took her by the hand. "But don't do anything just yet," she whispered. "Honestly, you can't just walk out of the door. It's a *huge* decision and everyone's up in arms…the place has gone mad. Even the servants…they know there's a terrible row going on. Now's not the time for a decision like this. Papa wanted me to be there too, but I refused…couldn't bear the thought of them all ganging up on you like that."

"Thanks," her voice wavered. "Thanks, Lizzie." Suddenly she fell on her sister's shoulder, her sobs muffled in her hair. Lizzie put her arms around her.

"Listen. Nothing's going to happen, not for the moment anyway. Papa gets like this, doesn't he? Shush, now," she rocked her gently. "No one's going to push you out and lock the door. Anyway, tomorrow he's back to London."

"Mmm, I know." Katherine sat up. "Oh, I'm sorry Lizzie," she sniffed and shook her head. "I'm so sorry." She dabbed at her tears and laughed. "I suppose it all had to come out some time, didn't it. Go on…go for your lunch, I'll get Sarah to bring mine to my rooms.

✳

"Anything more, m'lady" Sarah stood back from the dressing room table.
"No. Thank you, Sarah," Katherine smiled warmly.

For a moment the maid stood undecided then she spoke. "Beg pardon, m'lady."

"Yes…what is it?" Katherine half turned but looked away nervously, afraid of what she might hear.

"Well, m'lady, 'tis a bit difficult. I mean…don't know 'ow to put it but we and the others. Downstairs, I mean. Well, we've 'eard there's been some trouble. Couldn't 'elp it, really. We heard you might be going." The maid hesitated. "And, well, if yer was, m'lady, then…p'raps I could come with yer. Help yer move an' that."

Katherine felt the tears welling again: her mouth was no more than a grim line.

55

"Thank you, Sarah," she choked. "Thank you…it's very sweet of you. Nothing's certain yet but where I want to go, well, there'll be no room for servants. I'll be doing it all myself." She laughed but could see the maid was saddened.

"I'll still come, m'lady. Honest. I can 'elp yer somehow…scrub an' clean an' that. We'll do it together, you an' me."

"We'll see," Katherine replied. "It won't be yet, though. Maybe not for a long time." She rolled her fingers along her pearls then back again. "Oh…I don't know," she shrugged despairingly. "Maybe never, and perhaps it'd be better that way…better if it all came to nothing."

4

Wilmot Tucker heard the sound of voices. Then the front door slammed and he could hear them clearly in the hall below. The three men in the room with him would have to leave so he collected the papers in front of him and shuffled them quickly. "Well, I think that's all isn't it?" He laughed with his short nervous laugh.

The manager's house, built solidly of local stone and with tall windows set high under the slate roof, lay back from the road. It was a comfortable and well-appointed building, a far cry from the miner's cots less than a mile further up the valley of the River Mole. The four had gathered in the sunny, freshly wallpapered office. For weeks now, Heasley Mill, the centre of mining in North Devon, had been buzzing with news of the new equipment ordered to speed work on the deep lodes in the Florence and Prince Regent mines.

"As I said before, I might have come along with all the bright ideas but there's nothing like experience. I'll be needing your help and advice, just as the Davy props and the steam pumps will be helping you in return…making life much easier for you. And there'll be no jobs lost, none I assure you," he added seeing the suspicion on their faces. The three sitting in front of the walnut desk looked back. One nodded understandingly, another smiled to himself but the third leant forward.

"So long as that's so." The speaker was the shortest of the three and a sinewy man, but his weather beaten face, yellowed by cordite, hardened his features. His knuckles rapped on the table. "If we can do it like that, mister, then it's fine. If not, then forget it." A hand cut through the air and his eyes glittered menacingly. The three waited expectantly for the assistant manager's reply.

"And that's quite right." Wilmot rose, ready to greet the approaching footsteps. As he did so, he winced, reaching down to ease the stiffness in his leg. "I've checked with both the company and with Camborne." His voice was raised so he could still be heard as he walked across the room. "As it so happens we're going to have to take men *on*. We're going to need *more*, not less. It's all very exciting so please don't worry. I'll come up this afternoon, Captain Pope. We've got to decide where to put the engine house." He turned stiffly to open the door for those about to leave.

"Aye, sir. We'll be by the pump house." The Welsh mine captain rose and pushed the other two in front of him, all three standing back respectfully for the well dressed stranger who had just arrived and who was standing in the doorway.

"Mr Curtis?" Frederic Knight glanced at the three miners and nodded then took off his glove and began to introduce himself.

"No, sir. Tucker, Wilmot Tucker." The younger man held out his hand. "I'm his assistant and very pleased to make your acquaintance." He saw the look on Knight's face. "Have no fear, sir. I daresay I can read your thoughts." Wilmot smiled warmly, anticipating the next question. "Jack's brother? Yes, indeed I am. And as soon as we received your letter, I knew exactly who *you* were, sir. And you were instrumental in saving my sister, too...my sister, Charlotte, during the Tiverton riots."

Wilmot laughed in delight at the newcomer's surprise then paused, frowning as if a thought had suddenly crossed his mind. "Yes...this is certainly a remarkable coincidence, no less, but then I did apply for the job, seeing it's so close to Molland. My home, you understand."

"Yes indeed, of course." Frederic turned slowly to put his hat and gloves on the sideboard. "But tell me, if I may be so bold...how did you come by all this?" He waved a hand, still in disbelief, then sat in the chair offered to him. "How did you manage...it's very forward of me, I know." He paused while Wilmot sat also, momentarily embarrassed at his own curiosity. "*Most* intrusive, in fact, but pray how did you make it here, to this position, for goodness sake?"

"Started out at Cambridge...well, no...before that Blundell's. They were good enough to give me a scholarship, then up to Trinity where I read mining and engineering. After my degree I got seconded to Merthyr Tydfil to learn the ropes. Whilst there I did *everything*...everything from a full shift at the coalface to manning the pumps, the cages...the lot. Then Camborne in Cornwall." Knight inclined his head, listening intently. It seemed scarcely credible.

"There it was safety mainly. Safety and deep shaft engineering plus, by the way, a chance to look at the mass of new equipment that's coming along. And I'm desperate to get some of it in here by the way...especially steam machinery. The trouble is they're all terrified of losing their jobs. That's what that little deputation was about."

"Can't blame them." The two men paused as Wilmot reached for a file. "It's the same everywhere...town and country."

"Yes," Wilmot sat back. "Anyway, sir, to business and your letter. Look...here we are." He moved the papers and inkwell to one side then opened the map.

It took no more than a few minutes for him to answer the queries in the letter but, even in that short time, Frederic could see that the dark, intense young engineer knew a great deal about his job. The problem, Wilmot explained, was to know where to start. Evidence of ancient or disused shafts was all over the moor and in the surrounding valleys. A detailed survey was required but that would cost a great deal of money.

"It depends on your time scale," Wilmot opined, looking down at his hands. "A survey is indeed possible and I believe we must have a good one. There's a number of good companies. If you asked me I'd go for Schneider and Hannay. They're from Ulverstone in Lancashire, and there're several good names over in Wales. But…as you say, it's going to cost a great deal."

"Well, there's no great hurry," Knight replied. As he did so he paused and crossed his legs. "In all honesty we couldn't take it on just yet. In a year or two maybe, so perhaps really we could do it your way."

"That's grand but I'll have to clear it first," the engineer cautioned. "However, my own times's my own. And if you're serious about a horse and a guide, I can't see a problem. I've done a bit of research already and there are a number of possibili-ties…Simonsbath perhaps, Cornham and Hangley Cleeve as well. I know your father's men have been crawling all over the place but technology has moved on…and moving faster than ever right now." He bent over and tapped the map. "Even here at Brimley, just outside Molland. There's supposed to be copper in there, somewhere. And if there *is*," he paused. "It'll be elsewhere too."

They talked on for several minutes before Knight drew out his watch. It was time to go but he was intrigued at the prospect of Wilmot surveying for him. "Would you be so kind as to tell Mr Curtis I'm very keen to use your expertise. Very keen indeed…but I'll be writing formally, of course. The company'll be well paid…and so will you." Frederic watched as Wilmot Tucker pulled himself to his feet and eased his leg.

They shook hands. "Oh, one thing, sir…Jack. Would you be kind enough to pass on my thoughts…my warmest and best wishes as well?"

"Of course…my pleasure." Frederic glanced at him inquiringly. "You've heard about his last little escapade, I dare say? He's fine now and everything's healed up nicely but I've advised him to steer well clear of that lot…those contraband runners. They're bad and there's nothing but trouble there." The two men looked at one another; one nodded knowingly then both grinned.

Chapter Four

Preparations for Barbrook Fair had been underway for three days. Bill Floyd's field, at least that was what he called it, was situated on the higher side of the bridge over the West Lyn river. It was really no more than a triangular patch of grass and bracken occupied occasionally by gypsies or stray ponies.

Beyond the field steep woods rose in tiers giving the young men and boys in the trees a wonderful view of the day's events. The preliminary rounds of the wrestling were yesterday and, today, Floyd's field was the venue for the finals. They had always been held there and the crowd could watch from the field itself, the bridge or from anywhere else they could find a vantage point. Bill's haywain, to be used as the officials' stand, had been squeezed in between the ring and the river.

"Don't you worry boy...jest keep me cool in between the rounds an' rub my back or shoulders, I'll tell 'e which." Leonard Grant grinned and rolled his arms backwards. They had wrestled together behind the barn at West Lyn but Jack had been no match for Leonard's bulk so Hector had found Jed Stanner, a Lynmouth fisherman. The two grappled and fought every evening for a week with Jack refereeing. Later Nancy had rubbed crushed wintergreen berries mixed with pig fat into his tired muscles. Now they were walking down from the farm.

"Main thing for 'e, Jack, is to watch t'other man. Watch his eyes an' his feet then, in between, tell me what you see. Right? An' keep plenty o' water handy...like a bucket an' damp cloth. An' make sure I gets up an' out there when the whistle blows." Grant chuckled. "Us'll be fine, boy...can only do our best."

"D'you know any of em', Len?" Jack queried. "See any you know hereabouts?" The two had just passed the Methodist chapel from where they could see the rows of tents and stalls lining either side of the road through the village way beyond Bill Floyd's field. The crowd, already several hundred strong and spilling out of the village, was beginning to gather at the ringside.

"Aye, there's one or two," Leonard's eyes were roving. As he walked, he rolled like he always did as if there was a limp or a stiffness somewhere, but his face was a wreath of smiles as he nodded and called back to anyone they recognised. "They say there's a soldier 'yere what's done a bit. Bin fighting for a number o' years or so...not much else though."

＊

"What d'ya reckon, Bill?" Ned Kingdon looked from one militiaman to another. The Redcoats, sent up from Barnstaple to show the flag, had their eyes on the wrestling prize. Their man, Private Billy Daniels, a swarthy, thickset Cornishman, had promised not to drink but his earlier successes had given him a thirst. The Rising Sun at Lynmouth, like all the other taverns, had its own ale and pie stall at the fair. It was lunchtime and the soldiers had decided to gather there. Business was brisk.

"There's naught 'ere." The man from Liskeard put down his tankard but waved away the chance of a refill.

"What about that big lad? The big curly haired boy from the farm up the road?"

"Naaah," Daniels shook his head. He had watched Leonard the day before. "Big enough and strong enough but 'es never no wrestler...hasn't a clue, mun. D'you see his feet? Clumsy as a girt ox, 'e is." The four soldiers looked up as the recruiting sergeant approached.

"Steady on the booze, lads." Sergeant Barber took off his shako and undid the top pair of twin metal buttons on his heavy scarlet jacket. "Now then, Daniels, yer rogue, I've got money on you...no more of that stuff. Right? Don't 'e bleedin' dare."

"No worry there, sarge. I ain't forgot nuthin'." Daniels grinned broadly enough to reveal his bare gums. "Got 'alf a sovereign on meself, I 'ave. Jest like old times, eh?" His body, by no means all fat, shook with laughter. Then he turned like the others, all eyes now on the two well-dressed strangers striding purposefully towards them. Soldiers everywhere tend to keep themselves to themselves; their little world being a private business and they treat with suspicion those who try to intrude, especially if they are smart and well spoken. The group fell silent.

"You wrestled well yesterday, my man." The black, heavily lidded eyes glanced quickly around the group before settling back on Daniels. His short overcoat of dark blue cloth with a black velvet collar was handsomely cut as were his plaid tweeds over the neat, well-polished boots. His companion, a pale, overweight and slack-jowled man, looked grander still but hung back with one hand resting on his hip, the other on his cane.

"Thankee, sur," The soldier rose clumsily.

"A guinea for you if you win today...I've placed five on your head."

"Aw, thankee, sur." Daniels nodded respectfully and scratched behind his left shoulder. "I'll do me best...best as I can, that's fer sure. Thankee, sur."

"Here, listen you." Kenton Knight looked round furtively then back at the wrestler. "See here, now. I don't care how you do it...but beat them an' beat them hard." He paused. "And if you meet Grant, that local man in the final...I want you to *thrash* him. D'you hear? Take the very hide off his back." He nodded to confirm his instructions then turned to his companion. "Come on, Herbert. That's set the pace...that'll sharpen his spurs."

Jason Hawkins and his family managed to squeeze onto one of the few benches by the ring. Next to them Orwell and Kath Govier sat with Abel Tarr and two maids from the manor. Lunch over, the crowd was pressing in around the ring. The surrounding banks and hedgerows were already full and a number of boys were perched high in the trees like rooks. "Good luck, Len." Meg Smales blew a kiss from the bridge and turned to Nelly Combes. "He'll be right enough, love. I used to go with one of they soldiers. Jest a load of talk they are…you wait." She rubbed her hands, but the blonde was not so convinced.

✱

As the final was being announced Leonard rolled his shoulders and stretched before taking off his shirt and climbing into the ring. There already, Daniels seemed deaf to the noise around him. Standing facing his corner he had hold of the ropes and was bending and squatting, listening to his second who was rubbing his man's shoulders. Boots were allowed in the final and, as his own were worn smooth, Leonard had borrowed a pair from Hector. Jack checked them carefully. "Take yer time, Len." He had been studying the soldier and had noticed the heavy flesh around the belt. "The Redcoat's carryin' a bit o' spare, y'know. Go steady to start with…pace yerself. Best of three mind…and look out for they boots. He's a cunning devil…I'll shout if I see ort but you've got the reach on him." He patted Leonard's shoulder and ducked out of the ropes.

Almost before the whistle had blown the soldier was half way across the ring. He was circling warily, crouching low and held his arms ready. Leonard followed him, both scowling in concentration. Daniels, whose broad neck and powerful shoulders were covered with black hair, was shorter but equally thick set. He lunged suddenly, catching Leonard by the thigh and the fight was on.

The groom had been taken by surprise and never managed to regain his balance. For a minute or more they grappled, Leonard doing his best to control his opponent but the soldier knew his game. Eventually he broke free, swung and caught Leonard in a bear hug. They fell together but the soldier half turned and pinned his man, waiting for the whistle to blow.

"*Wake* up, Len…for God's sake get on yer toes man. Use yer *strength*." Jack wiped his face then turned to rub grass and dirt from his shoulders. "*Don't* wait for him to get in his stride, like that. He thinks yer slow an' he'll try it again…*don't* let him." He looked up to check their opponent. There, in the far corner, Kenton Knight had just finished speaking to Daniels. As he stepped away, he called out to the soldiers gathered around their man's corner and whatever he said made them laugh. Even Daniels turned on his stool and grinned, lifting a hand and raising his thumb in salute.

Leonard's speed across the grass took even the Redcoats by surprise. Only one of them near Daniels had time to shout a warning but even he was cut short. The others simply looked on in amazement. Leonard Grant leapt at his opponent, grabbed him with one arm under his crotch then picked him like a sack of corn. Holding him high, he turned and dropped on to one knee then threw Daniels onto his back before crashing on top of him.

"*One...two...threee.*" Fishborn's whistle was drowned by the roar from the crowd. One fall each and all to play for. Jack watched as they sluiced Daniels with water. Kenton Knight was nowhere to be seen but the wrestler was soon on his feet, pulling on the ropes and bending his knees. His pride had been hurt but the fight was still in the man and now he was angry, hell-bent on revenge.

The round began slowly. Both men were manoeuvring warily. First Leonard lunged, then Daniels, then Leonard again and so it went on until, all of a sudden, they were locked in combat. Time and again one twisted free or broke the hold only for them to come together once more. Strength for strength, cunning for cunning, the two were well matched. Twice Daniels caught Leonard's neck in a lock and twice he broke free, both times turning the soldier. Several times they fell, struggling together, rolling and twisting until separated by the referee's whistle.

Sensing the hatred between the two, the crowd pressed in more closely. Friends, supporters and all those who had wagered on the result, were cheering their man on. But the fight was hard and soon both men were staggering, their faces were red with exertion and the sweat ran freely. The whistle blew again and they sat wearily with their eyes closed waiting to be doused with buckets of river water.

No sooner had the next round got under way than Leonard felt the bear hug around his ribs tighten. At once he was struggling. He could feel the militiaman swaying in an attempt to trip him and the two shuffled towards the haywain, locked together and struggling hard. It was a battle for survival and the crowd knew it.

But then came the soldier's boots. Daniels was stamping cleverly but no whistle had blown. "*Boots, Len...his boots.*" Jack was screaming at him. "*Watch his boots.*" It might have been an accident but a second later the soldier's boot drove down onto the top of Leonard's foot and he shouted again.   Then suddenly, with a hoarse shout of pain, Leonard tore himself out of Daniels' grasp. Now blind with rage he spun round and picked the soldier from the ground. It was his turn. With the strength of a giant surging through his body, he half turned and staggered with the helpless man held high before tripping and tumbling through the ropes next to the haywain. The two of them fell together but Daniels, with Leonard on top of him, crashed into the heavy steel-rim of the axle, the full weight of both men behind the fall.

Jack saw what had happened and immediately forced his way through the throng to where the two men had fallen. Some onlookers were trying to hold the crowd back, others tried to stop him, telling him to give the man air but he pushed his way to where Leonard was bending over his opponent. The soldier's skull had been crushed like an eggshell and he lay still.

*

"Bloody killed 'im, you did." Two Redcoats tried to pull Leonard round. "Bloody killed 'im."

"*Rot.*" Jack pushed himself between them. "'Twas an accident as ever there was…everyone could see it was. 'Twas nobody's fault." He had a hand on Leonard's shoulder. "Don't worry, Len…'twas nort but an accident." Leonard looked around helplessly, staring at the crowd of faces. Some were reassuring him while others accused him of foul play. Somebody gave him his clothes.

As the four men pushed their way through, the crowd fell silent. Two of them knelt to check the body. Rob Hannaford, the Special Constable was the first to rise. "Aye, the man's dead, I'm sorry to say. No life there at all." He looked grave. "He's dead and by your hand, Grant…I'll be takin' you in. I 'ave to…'tis my duty."

"No, never," Jack gasped. He knew the constable from Barbrook. "Can't do that. 'Twas an accident, Mr Hannaford…a pure accident, so help me."

"Aye, but 'tis the death of a man, Tucker. A man's died, killed by another an' that's that."

"Plain murder, officer…saw it with my own eyes, we all did." Kenton Knight, standing on tiptoe to see better, called out again. "The man never had a chance. Here." Knight elbowed his way towards the constable. "Take 'em both in, the pair of 'em, that's my advice," he cried. "The fella there commited the deed right enough, we all saw that. But take the second as well…his accomplice. It's your *job*, man, so take them *both*. Here you are, look…well done, you." He took the constable by the hand. "Go on, my good fellow…don't hesitate." Hannaford stood back, reached deep into his coat pocket for his fob watch then, as he took note of the time, nodded thoughtfully.

"For God's sake, man. Are you mad?" Jack stared angrily then caught hold of Hannaford. "Don't listen to him…'twas an accident…we all saw it. It couldn't be helped…no *way.*" More and more onlookers were crowding round. Many were simply curious but there were others in the crowd, none of whom Jack recognised, who were calling for Leonard's arrest. For a moment Hannaford wavered but the highborn stranger had been right, of course. Others also. There had been no doubt about it.

"Honest, Jack. Honest to God." Leonard was desperate. "I never meant no harm. Us slipped, the pair of us." He lowered his head sorrowfully.

"'Twas murder," another voice shouted. " 'E killed 'im deliberate, so 'e did." A chorus of voices replied.

But Hannaford's mind had been made up. He knew he had to act and act quickly. "'Tis my duty to arrest you, Leonard Grant, in the name of the law and to hold you in custody, 'til charges have been considered. Seeing as you's a military man it's my duty also to pass you on to Sergeant Barber here, of The North Devonshire Militia...here, look. You'll be taken to Barnstaple and held there."

"No, sir," Jack caught hold of Hannaford's coat. "Look at him, will yer. He's a broken man....'twas an accident. Honest it was. I swear to God that's what it was."

"Make way, come on now, stand back, please." The soldiers forced their way through the crowd. Two of them stooped to pull Leonard to his feet. A third began to tie his hands.

"Away with you, for God's sake." Jack turned from Hannaford and grabbed at a red tunic. But he was held from behind with his arms pinned.

"No more of that, my son." The sergeant's grey-whiskered face was close. "Like it or not we're taking him in...any more from you and you'll be there as well. Count yerself lucky your own name weren't called."

2

There was little they could do. For three days, before he could be brought before the Barnstaple magistrates, Leonard was held in the Guard Room at Ebberley Lawn barracks. However, the charge, although now the lesser one of 'Unlawful Killing' was beyond their jurisdiction and the prisoner was remanded in custody to await trial at the Taunton Assizes.

✳

"*Grant*, you say...*killed* a man? Dear God, what next?" John Knight had been resting but they had decided he should be told. He was tired and his eyes moved wearily from one to the other.

Frederic had pulled a chair round to the other side of the bed they had placed in the front drawing room. Elizabeth-Jane held on to her husband's hands. The old man had been walking for a week, a little further each day but no more than that, exactly as Collyns had ordered. He had managed to dispense with one of the walking sticks yet his body remained weak, the muscles no longer able to do what he wanted. "What to do about it, then? Eh?" Again his head lolled from wife to son.

"I'm getting after him father. They've taken him to Ebberley Lawn and will be holding him there. But I'll go for Jack Russell first."

"Russell?" John Knight frowned. "You don't want to go bringing him into this? Leave him out of it, my boy. It's none of his business."

"I dare not father. The parson knows them all...and Sir George Gale better than any of them. If they listen to anyone it'll be to him."

Knight remained silent, staring balefully out of the window. "Take care, Freddy," he said eventually. "Don't go tinkering about with the law now...and don't go getting in their way, telling them how to do their job."

"No, father, but they need to hear the truth and we've got witnesses, any number of them."

"All right," he murmured. "See if you can't get Russell to give you a hand...he certainly knows 'em all, that's for sure. Oh, Freddy." A hand was raised. "Look, there's a purse in my desk...a little black leather one in the top left hand drawer. Take it will you. I keep it handy, just in case." He smiled impishly. "Surprising where it's needed."

✳

The two riders clattered down Taunton's Staplegrove, Frederic riding with Sir George Gales's letter in his saddlebag. In it the Chief Magistrate asserted that he could see no case to answer whatsoever. They crossed the Tone at Bridge Street before turning south towards Billetfield Park and making their way through the town. As soon as they breasted the rise and caught sight of the prison walls they could see the crowd. Along a ledge at the top of the prison wall, next to the main entrance, a wooden platform had been erected. "That's them," Russell muttered. "The gallows...and above the gate, for mercy's sake. But maybe there's time yet."

Two carpenters were securing the crossbeam to the uprights on top of the platform. The ropes were yet to be swung in place. Russell's face was grim. "It looks as though they've got Shaddick on today...Devil Shaddick, they call him." He likes them in a line like that.They were riding side by side and the parson saw Frederic's face.

"Shaddick plays to the crowd," he explained looking at the men working on the scaffold. "I've seen to a number of these and it doesn't have to be done the quick way...with a drop. Shaddick, and there're others too, gives the crowd a laugh by pulling their victims up. Literally dragging 'em up and make 'em dance on the tips of their toes for their very life before heaving 'em into eternity. Love it they do...just look at 'em, will you." The early arrivals had taken up their positions near the scaffold already. Many were drunk. "Oh aye, if it's Shaddick, they'll be getting their money's worth."

✳

"Don't rightly know." The jailor, a thin, unshaven man with suspicious eyes, studied Gale's letter, impervious to the urgency of the visit. "Can't say one way or t'other," he shrugged. "Aye…one of them were a big lad for sure…curly hair and all. Saw 'em with the chaplain an hour or so back." He looked through the letter again. "Could be the one, mind. Difficult to say," he chortled. "Too late for all that rubbish, that's what I say."

"Come on man. Time to see the governor, for Heaven's sake. Here." Frederic opened the black leather purse and held up a half sovereign. "One for now…and there's another if we get him out." He bent over the table. "But get on with it, man…press on, press on." The jailor smiled knowingly. They always shouted when they came at the last minute like this. But, so what? If the man was there then he was there. Play for a little time and the rich always paid handsomely.

The Assistant Governor was not to be hurried either. Today, as far as he was concerned, was the same as any other. But he greeted them cheerfully enough, patting his taut, patterned waistcoat before fingering the tightness of his collar. "Well, you'd better go and check," he shrugged. "But as soon as they see there's a chance, they'll *all* be swearing to the Lord God Almighty their name's Grant. Wouldn't you?" he laughed, then giggled loudly before glancing at the wall clock. "Don't be long though…I'm going for my breakfast and then we begin. Stay and watch if you like."

The sour stench of raw sewage hit them long before the warder opened the gate. Once through, they stood uncertainly while waiting for the second gate to be unlocked. They could see that the narrow flight of granite steps below had been worn smooth by countless years of heavy feet. "Right…follow on." The voices and clash of metal echoed together in the narrow passage as the new warder, this one tall and bearded, called up to them. "Stay well away from them mind or they'll have you."

Frederic followed Jack Russell, both clutching at the rope handhold as they descended to the main prison floor. It was a cold, evil-smelling zoo. The animals, clothed in rags, stood on their hind legs baying and howling at the bars as the two newcomers stared grimly ahead, their way lit dimly by smouldering torches. Hands reached out to grab them. Some shouted obscenities. Others, when they saw where the party was heading, rattled their chains and demanded clemency for the condemned. The stink, the noise and the spectacle shocked and numbed the mind.

At the top of the next flight of steps, the jailor turned into a wider, brighter corridor and walked to the far end. As he worked the locks, his keys jangled musically after the harsh din below. "There you are…take a look." He stood back and nodded. "D'ye see yer man?"

The difference startled them. Here the cell was spotlessly clean and the early sunlight shone through the high, barred window. Sitting side by side on a wooden bench and with their legs shackled together, the condemned men were finishing their very last meal. One had been weeping. Another, thin and hollow cheeked, cursed to himself. The third, little more than a boy, started up and stared imploringly, hoping beyond hope. All three were dressed in white linen shirts, their hair cut short.

Frederic felt his stomach turn. He was looking directly into the eyes of men about to be put to death, eyes from which life would soon be snuffed. He could smell sheer terror in the room and sense the feeling of dread. He lowered his gaze, unable to decide whether he felt guilty about his own freedom, or whether he was sickened by the thought of what was to come.

Lying neatly folded on another bench under the window were the hoods which Shaddick would collect when he came to measure them up. Once everything was ready and the prison bell had begun to toll, they would be led to the scaffold by the governor where the chaplain would be waiting. As soon as they had made their final statements, the hangman would place the hoods over their heads and tie them securely, leaving just their chins exposed.

It would be their very last glimpse of daylight and was the final act before the executioner eased them gently forward and fitted the rough, hemp noose around their necks. It would be the moment the crowd had been waiting for and, as the rope tightened, they would roar. Even now, as he stood in front of the three who would soon be meeting their Maker, Frederic could hear distant shouts and whistles.

"He's not here." As they turned to go, two pleaded pitifully. Then the boy began to weep. Knight stared unable to move until the jailor pushed them out and locked the door.

✳

"Well, Exeter it is." The Assistant Governor smiled warmly as they returned to his office then looked at the list that had been brought by his secretary. "And it is, too. Here we are, 'Grant. L.J…unlawful killing. To be transported…seven years. No appeal'" He turned to face them. "Well, he's lucky, if you can call seven years down there lucky. They left here three days ago. Should be there by now. Topsham Quay, just south of the city." He raised his eyebrows and shrugged.

"But look. Get this to the Custom's House…I've endorsed Gale's statement." As he checked his writing so his hands stroked gently at the fat of his cheek. "Here we are. They're being held on the old '*Spartiate*'…she's a prison hulk. A shame really seeing she fought on both sides in the war…an old seventy-four. A chap called Laforey had her at Trafalgar. Anyhow, they'll be loading soon and…let's have a look." He glanced a second file. "The '*Saint Mairie*'," he announced. "Some Saint, she is," he chuckled merrily at the picture in is mind. "An old slaver converted into a convict transport. Lucky to make France, I'd say, let alone Australia."

✳

Long before they were within hailing distance, they could smell the hulk. Standing off nearby with her bow turned into the running tide, a convict ship was loading. As the boatman turned their skiff, Frederic could see the figure of the officer of the watch standing at the companionway.

"Grant, you say?" Dressed in a blue marine jacket with silver epaulettes and cuffs, the officer bent to take the letter which he studied carefully before shouting down the main stairway. "Below there," he called. "Mr *Bates*, please...Mr Bates, do we have a man called *Grant*?" Frederic and Parson Jack watched the officer's face. "*What?*" The officer leant forward to hear better.

A muffled reply came back from somewhere below but both Frederic and the parson had heard what it said. "None on the list...no one here called Grant." The officer looked up and shook his head. "You sure he's supposed to be with us? The *'Josephine Bell'*...is that what they told you?"

"No, no...not the *'Josephine Bell'*, the *'Saint Mairie'*." Frederic look puzzled. "We were told he was going on the *Saint Mairie'* and that she'd be loading just now...this is her isn't it?"

"No, 'fraid not." The officer shook his head once more. "We're the *'Josephine Bell'*. The *'Saint Mairie'* went last night...on the evening tide."

"*Gone*, did you say?"

"Aye...she'll be off France right now an' heading sou'west...well on her way. Sorry my friend."

3

Bert Mathews knew exactly where the barn owls were nesting. He had been watching the ivy-covered stone linhay across the stream from his aunt's cottage and saw how the birds came and went.

Each Spring Bert, barefooted, longhaired and now twelve years old, collected wild birds' eggs. He knew which would sell best and had been doing it since he was nine. He tried to open the linhay door but had to put his shoulder against the broken woodwork until he had forced a gap for himself. Only then was he able to step carefully over the stinging nettles. Inside it was dark and, at first, he thought it was a sack someone had left hanging. However, when he pushed it, it swung heavily and it was then that he saw the clenched hand and, above it, the bloated face, blackened and staring.

Rob Hannaford was in Barnstaple at the time, at least that is where he had told them he was going. News of Leonard Grant's pardon had reached the village two days after his release had been ordered, but the news about his deportation had taken longer. Lynton and Barbrook were divided; there were those who thought their constable had been right and who congratulated him while others shunned him angrily, turning their backs and closing their doors.

Many looked forward to seeing Leonard back home again and why, they demanded to know, was he arrested in the first place? But others were full of admiration for Hannaford, assuring him that he had only been doing his job. Now they were confused. What, they asked, was the law doing changing its mind like this, and a Justice of the Peace at that?

It was Frederic who brought the news of Leonard's deportation. He told Hector that he had gone, that the law had moved too fast and they would never see him again. Shock in the village turned to anger. Some argued that justice had prevailed in the end, but most demanded that Hannaford should be held to account for he should never have touched the man in the first place. By his actions, they cried, an innocent man had been condemned to deportation. Stones were thrown at his house; Ruth Hannaford was knocked down in the market. The mood was ugly and Special Constable Hannaford was warned to watch his back.

He left home in the evening. "I'm off to the inquiry," he told his wife. "It's in Barnstaple...at Ebberley Lawn barracks." When they asked her later she told them she had made his supper, but he had left it and hurried off to borrow Ben Prout's pony. But Ben Prout had never seen him. He had never been asked to lend his pony and, in any case, the little mare was in foal. Nobody seemed to know where the constable had gone.

*

All that was a week ago and it was three days before Bert Mathews hammered on Hector and Nancy's door, burbling hysterically about a body hanging in the barn. Hector and two others went out and cut the poor man down. Now those who had criticised him were ashamed. How the man must have rejoiced to hear the news of Leonard's pardon, they told one another, but how terrible it must have been for the poor man when news of the deportation came through.

The village felt bad. They mourned the passing of an honest man and the manner of his death. At his funeral everyone turned out to see off the Special Constable who had only done his duty as best he could, but who could not face up to his terrible mistake. There had been no need for Rob Hannaford to take his own life like that, no need at all.

Nancy Coward went to help Ruth Hannaford clear his things. It was difficult for the widow to go through her husband's clothes so Nancy took it upon herself. The letter and the four sovereigns were tucked into the inside pocket of his constable's dark blue coat. Had he not taken the bribe, the thin spidery writing said, then Leonard Grant would be with us today. The boy was innocent and, had not the well-dressed stranger pressed him so hard, then he would never have ordered his arrest.

It was all too much, he wrote. He could never look his family or friends in the eye again, neither could he bear the thought of dear old Mrs Grant losing her son like that. The money he took, he said, must go to help the dear lady. He had no choice but to punish himself; begging forgiveness from those dearest to him, and for the Good Lord Himself to have mercy on his soul.

＊

"So what d'you reckon?" Hector watched Jack studying the letter. "Poor old Hannaford...what a mess."

"Hannaford be damned, Hector. Hannaford and the rest of them can rot in hell...'tis our Len. He's the one. No...sorry," Jack could see his friend had let the wrong words come tumbling out. "I know you didn't mean it like that but...Jesus, man, with all that lying and bribing goin' on about who did which or what, then everyone twisting an' turning like they've been doing....'tis our Len's the one who's gone...an' gone forever."

"Who was it then?" Nancy Coward bent to put more sticks on the fire. "Who was this well-dressed stranger who wanted to see Len taken off like that?" Her voice rose incredulously. "Who could have a mind like that and what was it all about, for Heaven's sake?"

"D'you know, Jack?" Hector rose to turn up the lamp hanging from the beam. "Who'd have done a thing like that? And *why*...for God's sake?" Jack stared at the fire now coaxed back into life.

"You *do* know don't you, Jack?" Nancy's voice was hushed. "You *do* know who dunnit."

"Go on, Jack," Hector muttered. "There's summat there. What's on yer mind?"

"Kenton Knight." The name came quietly.

"Never!" *"What?"*

"Kenton Knight paid Rob Hannaford. I as much saw it. I swear to God I did when he took the man's hand but could never prove it. An' the man'll go free...'cos no one can stand and say for certain. Even if they could the swine'd buy his defence. The world will never know, but I do."

"But *why?*" Hector stared at his friend. "Why go and do that to dear old Len...the man who saved his sister from the dogs. Len's never hurt nobody."

"Because of me." Jack saw the look on their faces. "Oh aye, Kenton Knight hates my very body...were I dead in front of him he'd kick my corpse. The man's as full of hate as ever I've seen and if ever there was a way of getting at me, he'd find it. Ever since us were boys together, 'ees detested the very sight of me...and me of 'im for that." He paused, the memories of those rows at Simonsbath flooding back. "What better way of hurting a man than by destroying a good friend in front of him? Someone he loves dearly, eh?"

"D'you *really* think a man could do that?" Nancy's face was in her hands. "Take the freedom of a man like that just to hurt another."

"Oh aye. When you're Kenton Knight you can. Ever since we was young, he's hated my guts. Back in the stables...remember, Hector? All the shoutin' an' kickin' an' screamin' bout this an' that...then when I went to see the Master about him? Oh aye, Kenton Knight'd do fer me all right, just as he did for me and Katherine. He'd get at me anyways he could."

"Can't be true...just can't." Hector sat slumped against the wall.

"I saw him, Hector." Jack's voice was certain. "Saw him hobnobbing it with the Redcoats afore the match...saw 'im with them while the fight was on and saw 'im with Hannaford after, when the soldier fella was dead. Saw him take Hannaford firmly by the hand, an' all." He raised his eyebrows. "What would a dandy fella like Kenton Knight go doing that for...what would he go mixing it with them roughnecks for? Eh? You know 'im, Hector...the damned man wouldn't walk across the road for they lot...never in his life."

Jack paused. "But 'tis summat he won't forget...and nor me neither."

Chapter Five

The thick, black eyebrows and chaos of dark red hair would catch the visitor by surprise and it took a second glance to confirm that the great frame was stooping under the taproom beams. Hardy Cockram was a giant of a man, which was just as well for Sandyway remained a wild and lonely place. It had taken him more than two years since arriving from Lynmouth to beat order back into his public house.

Those who crossed him, and there were some who did without realising it, thanked their good fortune they had chosen a seat near the door. The very worst of the drunks and layabouts had gone, yet the cutlass and fowling piece remained ready behind the bar. But Hardy loved life. His laugh, when it came, exploded like a gun, causing the unwary to spill their beer and the dogs by the fire to glance up and shift uneasily. When the mood took him he would sing, his deep voice silencing all but the most persistent. His songs were the songs of the sea, of Mont Saint Michel and Quiberon Bay.

Sometimes, late at night when most had gone on their way, strangers would come to The Sportsman's Inn. Men, dressed in thick jerseys and heavy boots, would leave their long line of ponies waiting patiently at the hitching rail and knock quietly. The deal would be done swiftly, as if it had been well prepared, but anybody in the taproom at the time would have been careful to avoid the landlord's eye. Hardy would then fill the glasses one at a time, pausing to check the rich tan of Normandy calvados against the lantern.

*

The track up to Sandyway from North Molton was a long, hard pull. The first crest, reached after a steep climb out of the village, led the traveller to believe that the worst was behind him, indeed the road levelled before descending slightly. But it was an illusion and gradually, if it was not shrouded in mist, the great shoulder of high moorland came into view and the real work began. As the land rose higher so the farmland fell away. The track, by now rough and broken, twisted its way through gorse and ling, following the centuries-old route over the moor. Riders and those on foot were free to pick their way across the open countryside but carts drawn by horse and bullock had to keep to the main track in order to avoid the softest ground. Finally, just before Darlick Moors, the ground levelled before falling gently towards the high Sandyway plain.

Oliver Chanter held a hand in front of his battered top hat to shield the evening sun. The builder had waited long enough at the inn and decided to ride back down the track and meet his team. Chanter, a short, swarthy man with big teeth and now in his fifties, had been building on Exmoor for years. As he stood in his stirrups the warm April breeze straight off Barnstaple Bay ruffled his hair and long coat tails. Durno, his evil-eyed gelding with the one white sock, blew hard and pulled at the reins before reaching down to pick at the early grass.

Above him lapwings, angry at this intrusion into their territory, dived and swooped, shrieking in protest before wheeling away at the last moment. Curlews, not so bold, circled warily, their soft, plaintive cries carrying far across the uplands. As he searched for signs of movement, his ears picked up the call of black game and the harsh croak of a passing raven. Way above them all skylarks filled the air with their urgent, bubbling song, climbing ever higher before suddenly falling silent and plunging back down to hide in the grass.

It was almost twenty years since Chanter had first been commissioned to build a moorland farm. Since then he had built two more – Barkham and Ferny Ball – and now he was back again. Further to the north his cousin, Gratton Bawden, had been engaged by John Knight to build several others. There was talk, Cockram had told him over the bar, that the moors were to be settled with permanent farmsteads, where the land would be enclosed by high banks then ploughed and cultivated. "A poor do," the giant had grumbled. "Won't be able to move…peace and quiet o' the place'll be gone for ever."

Cursing to himself, Chanter collected his reins and trotted towards the jumble of ox-carts further down the hill. Even from a distance he could see the leading wagon had shed a wheel and was blocking the track. The second had tried to move round it and was stuck while the remainder waited patiently, one behind the other. "What happened then?" The builder pulled up and dismounted.

"Rose up on a boulder then crashed into the stream bed." The leader of the train jumped down from the beleagured wagon. "Axel's gone…'ere look. Nothing us can be doin' right now." The tall carter rubbed his nose and fiddled with his clay pipe. "Goin' to load t'other wagons then hitch an extra pair o' oxen to each. Us'll come back and fix this in the mornin'."

Chanter looked at his team now moving the stores. Most had been with him for years. They were a good crew, the new men he had picked himself from the long line of hopefuls seeking work at the market. He hated the task, finding it difficult to look into the eyes of those he had passed over. "Right, Jed." He led his horse away from the melee. "We need to get up to where the farm's going in, before 'tis dark. Leave all this to Sutton," he nodded towards the portly carter still working under the wagon. "There's a couple of ponies here. Take one for yerself an' give t'other to Walt Holland."

Three hours later and the meal behind them, Chanter's builders gathered in the low-beamed taproom of The Sportsman's. Some had been here before but most were new to the place and felt Cockram's cold eyes following their every move. The notice pinned to the outside of the door was plain enough.

THE SPORTSMAN'S INN
SANDYWAY
No Miners, no Irish and no tinkers
welcome here. So says the landlord.
God Save the Queen

"We'll be away good and early," Chanter had been holding their attention. "First things first, I want to get the site o' the farm up here pegged out. Sandyway 'tis goin' to be called...Sandyway Farm, only a coupl'a hundred yards up the track." Apart from one man with a cough, the room was quiet: everyone was listening intently. "While we're about it I want to have a look at the next one after that...Sherdon, as 'tis to be known. Barely a mile further on but 'tis a right devil of a place to reach." Chanter looked at the faces around him. "As soon as us 'ave seen to Sandyway, us'll get over. Young Mr Knight wants a place in there...Sherdon Farm. That'll be you, Walt, Reg and meself."

Sherdon, Oliver Chanter knew, was going to be difficult. It would be the hardest one yet by far.

2

As George Northborough stepped through the pile of clothes he had left for his valet, the carriage clock on the mahogany dressing room table chimed the hour. It was four o'clock in the morning. It had been a long evening and, for the last hour at least, he and Amelia had sat talking in her rooms.

However they tried to get round the beastly business it kept returning to haunt them. It had got to the point when they could think of little else and he was becoming used to the all-pervading sense of dread. It was miserable. He went through to his sitting room, shut the door and poured himself a brandy.

The annual spring ball at Broadlands was always fun. Tonight should have been no exception but the duchess, despite his words of caution, had made too much of an effort over Katherine and Marcus Fitzmaurice. Recently appointed to command the second battalion of the Grenadier Guards, Algernon Marcus Fitzmaurice, the Earl of Kinsale and Master of Clonakilty was one of the south's most eligible bachelors. He and Katherine had met before, in London a year earlier when Amelia, much to her husband's consternation, had wasted neither time nor energy in arranging their daughter's introduction.

This evening, looking splendid in his scarlet and gold dress uniform, the tall guardsman cut a dashing figure: a point not lost on the duchess. His attendance upon Katherine had been no less dutiful. Three times they had danced including the waltz and its encore. He had escorted her to the fun fair in the gardens and they had dined together but that had been that. Katherine, to her mother's despair, had discouraged further attention, preferring instead to sit out the remainder of the evening. The journey home had been difficult.

＊

"What *ever* was the matter with you?" Amelia Northborough enquired tartly the moment the state coach began to move. "Marcus is a *most* delightful man. Exquisite manners and...so frightfully brave." The duke grimaced and shut his eyes. He knew what was coming and steeled himself for his daughter's riposte.

"I know, mother." Her sigh was audible. "He's wonderful company and perfectly charming but...oh, really, do we have to go through all this yet again?"

"And he's *very* well spoken for," the duchess ploughed on undeterred. "Magnificent estates in Ireland and all that property in London. I mean, I just wish you would *try* to see it." The duke coughed, then coughed again.

"Come, my dear," he soothed. "I think we know how Katherine feels...and it's all a bit late now." It was indeed. *"Hey, you up there."* He banged the roof angrily with his cane then lowered the window. "There's miles to go yet, dammit," he shouted into the darkness. "Less chatter and more action." Feeling better momentarily, he sat back and closed his eyes once more. The interior of the coach was now silent, each of them quietly brooding over the same vexed subject.

＊

"I don't know where we go from here." George Northborough, blinking in the sudden brightness of the newly installed gas lighting and, smoothing his hair, passed his cloak to the footman before turning and waiting for his daughter. "You really are set on heading off aren't you, m'dear." The very thought was haunting him. "It'll be the death of your mother, you know." The duchess had retired for the night, leaving the two of them together. "She can hardly sleep for thinking about it all...and I'm not much better meself."

"Father, listen," Katherine turned slowly from the drawing room fire, then looked in surprise at how the lines of concern had drawn his face. "I *do* know how you all feel, really I do. You've told me again and again and it fills me with sorrow. Whenever the subject comes up it starts quietly then ends in tears...or shouting...or some kind of a scene. It's *awful*." She flopped onto a sofa, tucking her white satin ball dress under her knees. "The more you all go on the worse I feel...and the more determined I seem to become." His mouth opened but her hand silenced him.

"You keep telling me how everyone's talking about it, how Herbert has walked out of my life and that you're going to disown me. I *know* father...I *know*," she sighed. "But there really is nothing else to say about it. I just so wish it didn't hurt you all so much." Her eyes followed him as he paced up and down the room. He was blowing heavily then stopping suddenly as if he was about to speak yet kept shaking his head as though he was afraid of the outcome.

"But enough! Really, father, look at the time. It's far too late for all this now. We're both tired and I'm going up. We can talk about it tomorrow if you'd like but…this evening's made no difference, honestly." She leant forward to put on her shoes. "Under any other circumstances I'd be delighted and flattered by Colonel Fitzmaurice's attentions. He's a very special man and will be a wonderful catch for some fortunate girl…but he's not for me."

She had reached the door and her hand had closed on the handle but she turned suddenly. Her father, now with his back to her, was standing in front of the fire with his hands clasped beneath his tails and his head bowed as though studying his feet. The heavy, imposing figure had gone. He had shrunk. Instead she saw a little boy, chastened and hurt, alone in the corner. So she ran, losing a shoe on the way and caught his arm.

"Papa," Katherine pulled him round. "Papa…look at me. *Please*…listen. Don't think I'm enjoying all this. I'm not, I hate it…hate every wretched minute." She reached up to stroke his face. "Really, papa, I can't bear it. I'll always love you whatever happens…love you dearly, you know that." He stood staring into the fire. One hand was gently rubbing his cheek where she had kissed him but he dare not turn round as she left the room.

✳

"So, what's the girl got to say for herself, then?" The duchess lay propped against a wall of pillows at the head of her oak four-poster. She had adjusted her nightcap and was rubbing the sore spot on her forehead where she had scraped at her rouge, before leaning forward to pull the side drapes further back. "I'm at my *wit's* end with the girl. *Simply* can't believe it, throwing up the chance of a man like that. It's awful…I despair of the stupid child."

"That's nothing new." George Northborough lifted his feet onto the green and cream striped sofa and stared at the shadows on the ceiling plasterwork. It was late and his wife's incessant carping had drained him."Her mind's made up, m'dear. It's been tested often enough by us all and it's nearly four years now since…"

"She met that terrible man," Amelia cut in. "It's quite dreadful… *awful*. I'm just hoping you're going to stick to your word, George. If she's going to behave like this then she'll have to go without…and I mean just that, not a penny." She ruffled the bedclothes in irritation. "She'll have to leave here as she is…. or it'll look as though we're condoning the whole wretched business." The duchess glanced at her husband then stared hard in grim alarm, sitting upright as she did so. "You aren't about to tell me you've relented? Are you, George? *Well…are you?*"

"No, no, no," he sighed heavily, now quite resigned to being pulled in different directions by his womenfolk. "I've made that plain enough but she can take her things. I've told her that, too. Hang on, dear," he noticed her look and raised both hands in weary protest. "*No*, you listen to me…anything that's hers is hers. We can't go taking it back…her clothes, jewellery, furniture. None of that's anything to do with us."

"Well, I think it's quite outrageous," the duchess fluffed up her bedclothes again, this time slapping them into place around her body. "I mean her rooms'll be emptied as though…as though she's going for good."

"That's exactly what she *is* going to do…leaving us. She's going, m'dear, and there's no stopping her but I'm damned if we're going to be seen persecuting the girl, making her life wretched." He got up, now thoroughly exasperated by his wife's intransigence. "She's not going to leave here like…like some refugee. I'm damned if she is."

"And what's she going to do with it all, for goodness sake? Her things? She can't take everything into some…some pokey little hovel on the top of Exmoor. I suppose she's going to sell it off to keep this man. Oh George, it's *monstrous*…all those lovely things of hers. I simply can't bear it."

The duke rubbed his eyes. The subject had exhausted him. "I'll talk it through with her, m'dear. She's not a fool you know."

"But that's *exactly* what she *is*…a stupid, pig-headed little fool. And we're seen to be com*plete* fools. It's no good, George, you're being very weak…pathetic. Giving in to her like that. I mean it's the family *name* that's at stake. You know how people are talking, for goodness sake. I saw the Dorsets and the Van Beaumans discussing us this evening. It's horrid." Amelia Northborough studied the handkerchief she had just screwed into her ear.

He sat again, hands clasped over his midrift, looking at the pattern of the vine trellis on the carpet. He had heard more than enough from all sides and was sick to death with it all, wearied to the point of exhaustion. His early rages, when he first heard of the affair, had long since abated. He loved the girl now as he had always loved her in spite of their wild shouting matches over her headstrong ways. She was his daughter, the same happy, smiling little girl that used to skip along at his side chatting away merrily. The one who laughed the longest and whose very presence now made powerful men truckle in her company.

He could barely face up to the fact that she would soon be gone from his life and it would be he who had dismissed her. The sneers and pointed fingers he could take and had done just that, but the pain was hard to bear and he was damned if he was going to see her trodden into the ground. Damned if he was.

"George, I've had enough. Will you leave me now." From the corner of his eye he watched her settle, now beating at the pillows and pulling again at the bedclothes as if to vent her frustration. "And get somebody to turn out that gas thing…I don't trust them." He rose wearily but knew he would be unable to sleep.

3

The Great Hall of Simonsbath Manor was very quiet. Save for the flames dancing around the logs crackling in the open fire, nothing moved. Frederic, dressed in white tie like the others, lowered his head to squint through the candlelight and look down the table. At the far end of the hall, beyond his father, the tall, spare figure of Peterkin in his green livery was barely visible in the deep shadows but the house steward caught his eye and nodded.

As he rose, Frederic's chair scraped harshly on the flagstones. There were only seven others, nothing to be nervous about especially as they were the family yet, as he glanced at the faces turned his way, he felt emotionally charged; sadness, love and pride all came tumbling together. "With the exception..." His voice barely managed a whisper and he had to clear his throat.

"With the exception of mother and father, I would ask you to rise." He coughed again and paused, waiting. "Tonight needs no introduction," he announced once the others had stood. "It is a great milestone in our lives, *all* our lives. Mother and father...over the years you have given us everything, everything any of us could wish for...and, today, that has been quite literally so. It's impossible to express how we feel so I will not attempt to try." Both parents were looking down at their hands. "This, now, is just to say we will miss you...miss you desperately, mother dear, and father. All you have created is now in our hands and we will do our level best to carry on your great works...here and elsewhere, but particularly here on your beloved Exmoor. Our thanks and our love go out to you both...and may God speed you, now and always." He picked up his glass. "To you both."

He waited until the others had put their glasses down then walked up to his father. One by one the others left their seats and followed him until the whole family, save for Elizabeth-Jane who sat beaming with pride, had gathered round the old man. Each in turn embraced him.

They knew the retirement had been in the offing, indeed one after the other they had been called into the panelled study at the back of the manor; the small, dark room from where their father had driven his empire. There they had heard the news. But tonight, midsummer's eve, eighteen forty-one, John Knight formally handed over his Exmoor interests to Frederic, his business domain having been broken up already and shared out amongst them all.

Finally, after twenty-five years of struggle and endeavour, the master had had enough. He was seventy-six. He was tired and age had finally taken its toll. Elizabeth-Jane, still only an elegant forty-six, had persuaded him to retire, to pass on the torch to younger hands that were ready and eager. The villa she had found for him in the Tivoli Hills outside Rome was a far cry from the heights of Exmoor but the countryside was gentle, the climate was warm and relatives were waiting to receive them.

✳

Frederic had spent the last week with his father, going first to review the books in Barnstaple with Durnford Morgan. That had not been difficult for he had been there often enough and know most of the figures by heart. The last decision his father made was to transfer funds from two of his foundries to clear what Morgan called the deep shaft of his mining account. The news that he, Frederic, had little interest in further extensive prospecting had been well received. A quiet survey, the banker stressed, was one thing but digging deep into nothing more than speculative evidence was quite something else.

Father and son had then ridden out together to the farms where they listened to Maxwell's account of progress. Finally, beginning just three days ago, they had followed the line of the boundary wall. The moor was dry, where even the high, wet ground beyond the gates on Brendon Common turned to dust under the tread of hooves.

"Castle Heights went this week." John Knight looked at his son. "Or rather Castle Hotel as is their wont to call it now." They had made a rendez-vous with the grooms to change horses at the furthest and most westerly corner of the wall from where they looked northwards to the coast. The old man was standing in his saddle trying to see the rooftops of Lynton but they were hidden by the dips and folds of the moor as it fell away in front of them. "A fella called Baker apparently. Paid a good price, too. But your mother was none too happy with the news." He turned and waved the two grooms on their way. "Claims that part of her soul's down there…I can't see what she means, though."

"But it's just as well, father." Frederic had dismounted and was checking the girth of his fresh horse. He spoke cautiously, picking his words carefully, knowing his father's concern over his ability to manage everything he had taken on. "I haven't told you yet but it looks as though West Worcestershire's going to adopt me as their prospective member. I heard this week and I've got to get back for the formal adoption." John Knight said nothing; he had sensed his son's awkwardness in breaking the news.

"It'll mean I'll be on the road a lot, and just the one residence here'll be more than enough." His mind went back to the first early days…of Jack, Hector and Leonard at Castle Heights. "Sad though, I was fond of the old place, for all that."

"Hmmph, not me," Knight took off his hat. "Couldn't abide the place. Summat odd about it. Used to bring out the pimples on your mother as well in spite of all she says about it. Give me Simonsbath any day." The two prepared to ride on, chatting as father and son do when minds are as one.

"Tell me, Freddy." Knight handed the reins back to his son. "How's life treating you just now? Is there any one there? D'you have a companion…anyone special?"

"The fairer sex, father?" Frederic stood, ready to mount.

"Well…yes. To put it like that. The last I heard was young Jessica Orchard. Your mother and I were wondering…well, how things might be coming along. You'll need company up here ye know…someone to share the problems of life and to keep you sane. I'd have never done it without your mother, never."

"No, father. 'Fraid not. Jessica's away to Hampshire and London…not the sort of girl for Exmoor." He was in the saddle. "I'm on my own right now but there's plenty of time."

"True, true." Knight turned his horse. "You know, of course…know your mother and I always thought that…" He paused. "Oh, phoey…it's all long gone now."

"Go on, father."

"Och, no…it's over and done with."

"No, come on. Who'd you in mind."

Knight glanced at his son. "We-ell, it's all too late, dear boy, but we always thought Katherine Darcy would've been the one for you. She's a lovely girl and loves the moors…and financially they're more than comfortably off…substantially so."

Frederic rode on. He was amazed, not at what his father had said but that it was exactly as he had heard so often before. Charles Acland had told him so, even little Isabella had mentioned it. He had got used to the idea but had never had it put to him like this. "I don't know father. She's lovely, Katherine, but she's always had a mind of her own…and look, now. As you say, the moment's passed. And money's not everything."

"No, but when its there it's like varnish…varnish on a painting. If someone's comfortable enough financially you can tell what they're like, their true colours stand out. They're at peace with themselves. Take the Northboroughs…they've had it all and more for generations and you can tell…wealth sits easily with them. But, *without* it," he wagged a finger. "If it's *not* there or it's new money, you're never quite sure what you're looking at or what it is they're after. Everything's a bit murky. Most likely they're on the make…or trying to impress, to buy their way in." The old man paused, reflecting. "Look at the families we know…those who have and those who haven't. It sounds hard put like that…cruel maybe, but it's true."

They talked as they rode, pausing now and then to see where sheep or deer had scrambled over the wall. At Pinkery they stopped again where they looked down from the high ground behind the lake he had created. "Well," John Knight slapped his thigh. "Here it is…just look at it. Ready and waiting. There's the end of the canal, down there look, just below the dam wall on the left. Open the sluices and away you go…it's all here, Freddy. One lucky strike and you'll be away," he muttered.

"I haven't forgotten it, father." He knew the subject remained dear to him, and the closure of the mines had hurt more than he ever let on. "And that's just what we need…as soon as we get a really good find then we're off…and I need it. I've got to get lime for the land up here somehow…Maxwell's screaming for the stuff and dragging it all the way in by the cartload is never going to be the way. Copper's what I'm after. Ore will do but copper's the one we're looking for…right now in fact but quietly and steadily. Wilmot Tucker certainly knows his stuff." As soon as he mentioned the name, Frederic knew the subject would change.

"Hmmph." Knight gazed into the distance. "Odd that…the boy turning up like he did. Local lad and all that. *But,*" he turned to his son. "A rare old tale though, coming up through life like he has. Remarkable…that's Charles Collyns for you. The man seems to find them and then gives them a chance in life…a chance the lad took with both hands." Frederic knew there was more to come. "Mmm." Knight took off his top hat, rubbed his brow then scratched at the mane of hair, still thick and long but now snow white. "Talking of the Tuckers, what of Jack? What've you got in mind for him, or West Lyn for that matter?"

"I'll take him out of the place." Frederic knew of his father's suspicions and decided to press home his decision. "He's had his ups and downs but he's far too good to be wasting away there. I trust him, you know, and we've discussed him often enough but I'd like to give him a chance to see what he can really do. Reckon I'll hang on to the farm though. Put someone in to help old Slocombe but someone who likes his Bible." Both laughed.

"But as for Jack…I've earmarked Sherdon for him. I'm going to put in a farm on that bit of land we've bought, just south of the wall. Old Joshua reckons Jack's a natural stockman and he's done wonders at West Lyn."

"Mmm. Sounds right enough." Knight's hand was on his chin. "And his other business…what's happening there? D'you know?" He spoke quietly, half turning his head to look back over his shoulder but the question was direct enough.

"They both seem dead set on it." Frederic caught his breath.

"But what on earth are they going to *do*? They can't keep on behaving like this….it's driving them all mad at Blagdon, y'know."

"She's planning to leave home."

"What d'you mean leave? Get away for a spell? A tour or some such thing?"

"No, no, father…nothing like that." Knight looked up at the urgency in his son's voice. "No. Katherine's coming down here. She's going to leave Blagdon for good, or so they say. The family's washed their hands of her and she's planning to leave before she's ordered out."

"Dear God alive," Knight closed his eyes. "Heaven forbid. I'd heard as much but thought it was just old George looking for sympathy. So it's true?"

"Yes, there was one hell of a row...several for that matter." Frederic had to declare his hand. "I'll get Jack out of West Lyn and give them a bit of time together to sort things out. She's dead set on the idea but...well, you know Blagdon, father. Life's been pretty difficult."

"I'll wager," Knight snorted. "Poor old George. Must've damn nearly killed him, poor chap. And as for Amelia..." he shook his head. "Glad I wasn't around when the old girl got going." He chuckled quietly, savouring the thought. "But I just wish to God we'd all found out some other way...I've never really been able to forgive Kenton, you know."

"Nor have any of us." Frederic was surprised at how his words tumbled out. "I'm sorry father but he's so damned full of himself about it all. Even now he plagues us about it. He even saw fit to blame Jack for getting Leonard Grant taken away." His stepbrother's pleasure at Jack's anguish over losing his friend still rankled deeply.

"Mmm." Knight was brooding. It was the first time he had discussed it like this. It sounded simple enough but, to him, it spelt trouble. A girl like that tied up with a man like Tucker could only end in disaster. It was all so wrong, dangerously wrong, of that there was no doubt. But the young had to make their own way and there was nothing he could do. "Not sure I like it, Freddy," he said eventually. "Not sure I like it a bit...you'll have to keep an eye on things. But if that's the way it's going, then keep Kenton well away from them or there'll be trouble...I can see it now. Can't understand it." John Knight shook his head. "Every time he and Tucker set eyes on each other there's all hell to pay. Everyone gets caught up in it...everyone."

4

Throughout that long summer, Katherine existed rather than lived at Blagdon. For much of the time, her father, whose presence she never resented, was away. It was her mother and her two aunts that made life so difficult. The three of them, in particular Mildred, the tall, austere spinster, seemed to take it in turns to watch her every move.

Whether it was from a distance such as from across the park or in the Spanish sunken garden, or else in the house when one or the other would sit with her as she sewed or painted, one of them was always there, shadowing her is if waiting for something to happen. Perhaps, Katherine mused, they thought she might suddenly collapse or be looking for a chance to turn and confess, finally admitting to the error of her ways. Whatever it was, the constant, silent, omnipresence played on her nerves. She yearned for privacy, longed to escape their prying eyes and the senseless vigil, but she knew, and knew they knew, that time was slipping by. They could do what they liked but she would soon be free.

More and more she removed herself to her rooms, avoiding family meals whenever she could. The tense atmosphere in the vast, soulless dining room, presided over by silent footmen whose expressionless faces missed nothing, served only to strengthen rather than weaken her resolve. Sarah brought her her mail, the letters from Jack coming from Holnicote or Simonsbath. The sight of the letters never failed to quicken her heartbeat. When she broke them open, every one folded carefully with her name written lovingly in his quaintly laboured hand, she could feel herself trembling.

Each day she would ride out with Lizzie when they would saunter for hours, chatting and laughing together having made sure that their accompanying grooms were well out of earshot. Twice James Acland came to stay, Frederic once, on his way to London. Her brother, either through oversight or malice, brought Kenton Knight. And how her mother and aunts relished the occasion.

"Come, Katherine, dear." The duchess was at her most effusive. "All that silly nonsense has been forgotten. Kenton Knight is a *very* charming young man. And in any case," she rounded icily on her daughter. "You might have the good grace to behave in a civilised manner towards my house guests...at least whilst you're still here." Katherine ignored her Aunt Mildred's sour looks.

"But of course." Her quiet reply was never meant to sound disarming. "You know I'll always behave with propriety, mother, just as you taught us...that is, to those who are civilised whoever they might be. It makes no odds and you know that. But as far as Kenton Knight is concerned, he's nothing but an odious, little braggart. He's a *liar*, a *cheat* and one who takes our family name into the whorehouses of Cheapside and Whitechapel."

"*Katherine!*"

"Don't worry, mother. I shall give neither you nor him cause for any embarrassment." With that she rose and picked up her skirts. "The man is simply not worth it. *If* he wishes to pay his respects he knows where to find me...but he won't. And my advice to my brother is that he, *dear* Herbert, would do well to find better playmates...those of a little more substance."

＊

The first idea the staff had of Katherine's imminent departure was the arrival of two four-horse pantechnicons to remove her furniture. A day later, Frederic and Edward Knight called. The duke, home from London, entertained them but Katherine met them later in Lizzie's apartments.

"And what was Jack's reaction to my suggestion?" Frederic had not seen her since her last visit to Exmoor. By now worried at the idea of them living right out at Sherdon he had suggested they look for a farm on lower ground. "It would be simple enough, Katherine, and you could easily raise the money. Far, far more comfortable than right out there."

The more his father's words had come back to him the more he had thought of her. Sherdon was going to be a bleak and desolate place, hidden away at the top of a high lonely valley more than a mile from the nearest track. He was angry with himself for having offered it to Jack in the first place but Jack had seized on the idea. He would relish the challenge and survive no doubt, but for Katherine, Lady Katherine Darcy from Blagdon Park, life would be way beyond her cruellest nightmare.

"He wouldn't consider it, Freddy." She sat back and put her arms behind her head. "Wouldn't even entertain the idea and, to be honest I was glad."

"Why so?"

"Well, *his* reasoning was that he is determined to work for you. He knows you've had all sorts of problems finding tenants elsewhere and he wants to see you well." She moved herself closer, now gaining in confidence, and sat perched on the edge of her sister's camel back sofa. "He'll never forget all you've done for him and...well...I know he feels indebted to you. But, also," she hesitated, looking from one to the other. "He says his heart's out there. He loves it in the wilds and can't see himself anywhere else."

Frederic looked away. She obviously had no idea. Her love for the man had blinded her to the realities of what was coming. This lovely, sophisticated woman was about to give up everything she knew and held dear. She would be giving him everything she had and he could think of nobody else who would be prepared to relinquish half as much. What man could ask for more? Who would not be grateful for such loyalty and who could not but love such a woman in return for the sacrifices.

Jack was a lucky man indeed and he envied him. It was there and then, quite suddenly, and as he sat watching and listening, that he began to understand his own emotions and why he had been feeling like he had. He saw it immediately. It was for her: Katherine, the woman now sitting so close to him. His father had been right but she had pledged herself to another: Jack Tucker.

"And you?" Edward Knight, leaning forward from the window seat, cut across their thoughts. "What do *you* want, Katherine? You know it's going to be merciless up there. No creature comforts, nothing like that...it's going to be devilish hard." Edward, shorter and broader than his brother and now a banker with Sir Crispin Barclay, had no ambitions towards such a life.

"I know." Katherine dropped her hands and sat thinking before looking up again. "But my heart's out there, too. It's mad, I know it is...and I can't help it."

She laughed shyly, momentarily taken aback at this sudden intrusion which had forced such words from her. "There's a magic about the wild loneliness of the place and some great force is drawing me on irresistibly. It's for me, I know it is." Her face had flushed in sudden embarrassment at having spoken with such emotion and she paused. "I know exactly what you're all thinking," she said quietly. "You think that things might change, don't you? You think that one day I'll wake up and want to gallop away from it all? But I won't you know. I'll never turn back. No matter what happens, I'll never leave him," she said looking from Frederic to Edward.

"Then, if that's the case, you won't be needing a great deal of money," Edward threw an arm over the back of his chair. "It sounds awful, I know," he laughed. "But it's true. However you *will* need a decent sum to get going and then a modest income after that…just to help things along.

Katherine nodded thoughtfully, as did the others. "But how does she actually get *hold* of money?" It was Lizzie who had been sitting quietly and listening. "When she actually wants to *buy* something in a shop…food for instance? It's all very well for you men but we never touch the stuff. *No* respectable woman does, no matter who they are…you won't let us," she laughed drily and sat back looking at her sister again. "But you're going to *need* money, dearest, and in your hand. Jack's got nothing at all…*nothing*, for heaven's sake."

"Right." Edward leaned forward again. "It's easy and I'll tell you how…so permit me to introduce you to your new banker," he joked. "We'll set up the trust in London and arrange for the income to be paid into your account down there, Freddy. Katherine can let you know what she wants, then you make the necessary withdrawals. In that way her trust's safe and the income's on call. So there we are." He reached across and squeezed her arm. "We'll look after you, my dear…it's as simple as that."

5

She announced the plans for her departure the day before she left, surprising and confusing her self-appointed chaperones by attending dinner that evening. Her presence at the table and her news took them unawares. None of them knew what to make of it let alone what to say to her. It was her turn to take the initiative, exactly as she had intended. Surprised at her own gaiety and confidence, her conversation prevailed for a while, making it ever more difficult for her dinner companions. However, in the end, after her high spirits had finally ebbed away, she gave up and listened wearily as the dreary small talk droned on before dissolving eventually into the usual, awkward silence.

The farewells came in the drawing room. She would be leaving early, she announced. Her departure from their company would relieve them of further discomfort, and the picture in her mind of the scene once she had left amused her, but she no longer cared. By now she had had enough of the whole charade.

"Mother." Katherine rose, noticing how quickly her mother scrambled to her feet, as if she had been expecting the move. "I'll take your leave if I may." The words sounded wonderful. It was as though she was at last throwing back the curtains in a dark room, or ordering the prison gates to be opened before setting out into the bright sunlight. "It's time to bid you all farewell."

"*Katherine*," her mother whispered, looking first at her sisters before shaking her head in disbelief. From the corner of her eye Katherine watched her two aunts as they stood nervously together, Mildred's arm linked through her sister's. "Oh, Katherine." Her mother shrugged in resignation then let her hands fall against her side. "Well, it's your decision, my dear. I don't know, really I don't. I'm so upset about it all and yet..."

"Don't worry," Katherine said quietly, taking both her hands. "It's not necessary to say anything..." She paused, wondering if there was anything else to say but there was nothing, nothing at all. "Good bye, mother." She felt no warmth, no life in the brief embrace and there was no emotion in her voice. Mildred's hand was cold, her face frozen. Eunice, the aunt she barely knew, simply grizzled and snuffled into her handkerchief.

✳

She saw that Sarah had left an oil lamp by her bed exactly as she had asked. Her clothes for the morning were laid out on the chaise longue. She had decided on the rough, thick clothes of countryfolk. They would leave at dawn for Stockbridge in order to catch the Mail at The Grosvenor and the drive along the river promised to be chilly. She hated the cramped, malodorous conditions inside public coaches and winced at the prospect of being trapped against total strangers, rocking from side to side for hour after hour, confined and subjected to the sights, sounds and smell of others. Fine clothes, from what she had heard, only attracted unwanted attention, most of it crude leers or heavily pressed thighs and wandering hands of men old enough to be her father.

Before she climbed into bed, she put on her housecoat, took the lamp and wandered through her rooms. Most of her clothes had been boxed. The five cases to go with her were labelled and strapped, ready to be loaded onto the wagonettes. The furniture, or what was left of it, had been dismantled and wrapped in preparation for the move to London. Whatever was to remain had been covered by drapes.

It was strange. She knew she ought to have been saddened, tearful even, at leaving the home that had shaped her life. As she moved between the shadowy covered shapes and piles of boxes, she realised that there was nothing left to do. Everything that needed to be done in order to assist her departure had been done. Even if she had wanted to there could be no going back. She was committed and thrilled at the very thought.

Later, as she pulled the sheets up to her chin and stared up into the inky black-ness, she saw the long locks of golden-brown hair ruffled by the breeze. Gradually the face appeared, strong and sun tanned, then the eyes. It was him. She could see he was watching her and she smiled back before a finger went to his lips, warning her not to cry out.

Then the face changed. Now it was grim, resolute and mud flecked. Whenever she moved, she could feel the bog shaking around her. A hand, his, came reach-ing out for her, the fingers stretched wide in desperation. His voice was urging her to hold on. He called out her name and their fingers touched. She felt his grip tighten then her hand slipped from his grasp and she lost him. Yet he was still there somewhere…she knew he was.

Then she heard him again. This time he was whispering her name quietly. The sunlight shining directly into her eyes made her want to turn her head away but his hands still had hold of her face until he began to fade from sight. She watched helplessly, crying out after him, urging him to stay but he had gone leaving her cries to be hushed by the wind.

*

"'Tis half four, m'lady." A hand was on her shoulder. "Come on, m'lady. Come on, wake up." Having just drawn back the heavy curtains, Sarah was bending over her. "'Tis half four an' near light already. Brought you yer tea and 'ot water."

Chapter Six

Head and shoulders were buried in the thicket leaving just the tattered, knee-length blue trousers and bare feet protruding. Suddenly, when the voice called again, the figure began to move, wriggling backwards until it could stand. "He…he…he's way down." Davey Tucker, for that was his name, pointed at the large rabbit hole. His freckled and, by now, very muddy face was red with excitement.

Jack walked up and pushed back the brambles before treading them flat and crouching beside him. "Don't 'e worry, lad, he'll be fine. Leave him be…he'll soon tire." Minutes later Scamp appeared. He shook himself vigorously then raced off down the hill towards the cottage. Jack had been at Badgercombe since mid-morning but it was now almost a month since Fred Loosemore had come over to Grace's cottage at Luckworthy to tell him that he had found somewhere for them to live. The place would do; it would have to.

✳

The family had just about grown used to the idea that Lady Katherine Darcy would be coming to live with them in Molland. But it had taken time. Initially Grace had been dumbfounded, quite literally terrified at the thought. Her friends and those close to her had been unable to comprehend the news and it was Charlotte who had been the first to offer a practical solution. Embarrassed at her own situation with Davey, she offered up her cot, assuring Jack that she and the boy would be able to find lodgings elsewhere. "'Tis no problem, Jack. We'll be all right. Her won't know anyone, poor lass." That only made it worse.

"What*ever's* she going to make of us all here…an' me on my own like this?" Grace wiped her hands on her apron. Her face was lined and drawn but her eyes, although he could see she was dreading the idea, were the same bright eyes he remembered. "There's no room nor nothing, Jack…an'…an' she's a real high-born lady. Her'll know nort about cottage life…cookin' an' washin' and that." She waved a hand nervously at the back of the door where two rabbits were hanging. "Skinnin' an' cleaning rabbits…doing the pots an' all that. Whatever's us goin' to do? Bain't right."

Jack had long since realised that he would have to ride out the storm of protest and ignore the gossip and speculation in the village. Fred Loosemore, as he had done so often in the past, calmed the situation. If needs be, he and Tilly would take in Charlotte and her son while Jack looked for somewhere to live. "'Twill be just for a day or two, if that," he advised, drawing on his pipe, as if he knew the matter would be solved. "Don'e go worrying, Gracie. We'll find summat…there's any number of places about. Anyhows," he coughed, waved aside the smoke and sat upright. "If the maid's bin stoppin' at Lynton, her'll know what 'tis like in the country. An' if her don't, her's goin' to find out soon enough." His laugh turned from a wheeze into a shout of a cough. "Aye," he croaked, wiping his eyes. "Aye…that's for sure."

Grace was far from sure. The thought of sharing her few rooms with a total stranger, one from a different world, was horrifying. Even being in the same building was going to be difficult. But Fred was as good as his word. "Us have found somewhere and 'tis proper," he announced, beaming with pride, the little round face ruddier than ever. "Edgar Rumbelow out to Twitchen's got a place…just the job so 'tis. Old mind, an' needs a touch 'ere and there but 'tis a proper job."

*

All that had been a month ago. Jack took the boy's hand and stood back. Edgar Rumbelow had already kept his part of the deal; the old woodman's cottage, hidden away behind the trees above the bridge had been put right as he said it would. Two days work a week from Jack in lieu of rent was fair enough but the rest was now up to him. Badgercombe cottage needed more then just Edgar's new tiles and doors.

The creeper, now turning blood red, had been allowed to run, covering the porch and reaching up under the eaves, almost hiding the faded lime wash on the cracked walls and the powder-blue window frames. Somebody had once planted flowers in the beds under the windows but they had long since gone, nettles and docks hiding all but the boldest of the surviving blooms. The woodman and his family had left more than two years ago and it showed. Nature had crept back. The place was overrun, now little more than a haven for jackdaws and rabbits.

Even the track down to the road was covered by a thick archway of brambles that tore at their clothes and tripped them as they forced their way through. The tall grass in the field where he had put his few sheep had run to seed and needed to be scythed. Davey had shown him that the gate in the garden hedge, where the path ran to the edge of the stream, had been broken and would also have to be fixed.

Earlier they had opened the windows, pushing gently against the frames that were stuck, before lighting a fire to dry the cottage. Three times Jack had asked Davey to fetch more kindling but the fire had caught in the end when smoke filled the rooms while waiting for the chimney to dry. But now the blue haze curled away lazily towards the trees before being snatched by the breeze. Once a sudden down draught had caught them, forcing them to turn and run outside. Davey, the quicker of the two, spun round and laughed helplessly as Jack coughed and fanned the smoke from his eyes.

Farmer Rumbelow returned, beetling together his black eyebrows as he studied the roof. "That's it, lad…bain't much mind, but 'twill keep 'e warm and dry…an' 'tis somewhere for 'e to call home fer awhile." Jack followed the heavy, rolling tread of the farmer as he toured his property. "Come winter 'tis sheltered, mind…right out the wind. Better so than some of they places up top." His great shaking laugh echoed through the woods. "Oh aye…'tis better down 'ere than up over…b'lieve me, it is."

One step behind him, Jack brooded. Grateful though he was for the deal that had been done, he remained disturbed. Katherine had talked about life at Blagdon Park often enough for him to imagine the size and elegance of the place where the dog kennels, the ice house and even the potting sheds were bigger than the cottage. Yet she was coming here to *live* in tiny Badgercombe. It was run down and overgrown and he could see her looking at the place in disgust like she had looked at Kenton Knight. He had seen something of her haughtiness and knew how dismissive she could be. She would laugh cruelly, he surmised, toss her head and pick up her skirts.

He had never had a home before and had no idea where to start. The dark, low-beamed kitchen together with the cobwebbed scullery still full of rubbish and the back larder where ivy came through the broken window were all places he had taken for granted. Now he had to clean and prepare them then furnish them. He had never thought of curtains or rugs, beds and tables but now he had to. He sensed Edgar Rumbelow's eyes as the older man read his mind.

"Don 'e worry, boy," the heavy hand shook his shoulder. "'Er might be comin' from some fancy, girt place upcountry but there's nort wrong with Badgercombe. Coupl'a weeks work 'ere an' 'twill soon be straight. Now then," he turned and contemplated the garden. "My advice is to get the garden y'ere goin'. There's time enough yet for't gets too cold."

"But it's much too late *now*, isn't it?" Jack asked uncertainly.

"No…late for some but not for t'others." Rumbelow bent clumsily for a handful of soil.

Later Jack worked as the farmer showed him, clearing the weeds then breaking and tilling the soil before sowing his lines of winter greens. He cut and laid the low fence, protecting the garden against rabbits and tied strips of white cloth to the fruit trees to scare away the deer that came down through the woods from the moors above. As he replaced the gate and secured the outhouse roof and doors the valley echoed to the sound of his hammer and saw.

Word spread. Ralph Rudd, his cousin Lorna's eldest son, brought a cartload of old furniture from Winsford, apologising quietly that some pieces were broken while others were scratched. Ann Cox, Nan Ball's pretty, flaxen-haired daughter brought tools and implements, while Stan Thorne, his mother's long-faced elder brother, rode over from Dulverton to see what goods his nephew might need from his iron-monger's shop.

Each evening he would harness up Fred's little grey cob and set out with the shorter of the two haycarts to collect what had been promised to him. Gradually, piece-by-piece, he began to assemble what they needed most. Fred Thorne, another uncle and still making cabinets in Withypool, offered his services. For nigh on a fortnight the two worked together, repairing broken and worn tools and damaged furniture. Those for which Jack had no use he took into South Molton and bartered for differ-ent or better ones together with wire and nails, for stakes and for goods he knew he would need on a farm. His time at Simonsbath and West Lyn had served him well.

※

He grew close to his sister. Charlotte never spoke about her time with Naylor but he sensed the wounds ran deep, while in Davey they were there for all to see. The boy was frightened of life. Withdrawn and sullen, his eyes flitted nervously whenever he spoke, never settling or able to hold his gaze. He hated school and twice ran away. Then came the pilfering. "Just dunno." Charlotte slumped back in the kitchen chair. Her puffed, sallow face was a mask of despair. "'Twas terrible…I could've died. First candles then a tinderbox…now a knife. Jessie's father, old Sid Daniels saw him. I dunno, Jack…just dunno. First school an' now this." Jack went to see the shopkeeper offering to settle the matter. Then he asked Davey to help him.

At first he said little, simply waited for the boy to be there. And he always came, indifferent at first, shrugging or scowling whenever they spoke with his mind still locked away in its own silent world. Even when they sat resting together, side by side with their backs against a tree, he would turn away, choosing to throw pieces of twig rather than talk. But if the boy preferred it like that then Jack was happy enough.

In time he thawed, slowly like a block of fish-ice in the cold room. Then it was he that was first out of the door, whistling to himself while he waited, calling to the dog and whittling his stick. One word became two. A quick glance slowed to a straight look. Where the frown had once glowered a smile now flickered and where the tongue had stammered a voice began to emerge. The boy learnt fast and it was the stream in particular that held his fascination. For hours he would wander watching the dippers and wagtails or searching for signs of otters on the mud banks before running back and blurting out what he had seen. He learned to mimic the songs of wild birds and the call of animals then stand silently with his head cocked listening for the reply. Time and again Jack would raise his head to the sharp cry of a vixen or the whistle of a dog otter only to find Davey lying hidden nearby.

He perfected the rumbling call of a young stag and the warning bark of a hind, then sat calling by their tracks in the woods, crouching low behind cover as they edged closer until they caught his scent and shied away. He listened carefully as Jack taught him how to spot rabbit runs and the points in the hedgerows where pheasants would creep through. Then he would stare, watching intently with his black scowl, as Jack taught him how to set the snare and net. Jack promised that, come the move to the moors, he would show him how to tickle for trout under the overhanging banks and gaff salmon as they lay in the deep pools before beginning their run upstream.

2

Katherine waited patiently. James Acland, the tall mischievous one she liked, now married and living at Holnicote, helped collect and store her belongings then he and Eleanor, his young wife, took her into their home. The apartment they lent her in the older part of the house was but a fraction the size of her own rooms at Blagdon but it served well. The last few hours at Blagdon had not been easy and, although several weeks had gone by, she could not forget her final moments. It was strange that parting from those who worked there had hurt the most.

✳

She smiled at the memory of how the footmen and burly watermen, fearful of waking the household, crept down the servants' stairs with her cases and trunks. She had waited with Sarah until the rooms had been emptied then tiptoed across the main landing to see if her mother was awake. The duchess knew of her plans for Katherine had told her twice but the wing was silent and there was no light showing from under her doors. Although her father was away she paused outside his rooms, tempted suddenly to throw open his door in the hope that he might still be there. It would have been wonderful. He had said farewell two weeks earlier before driving to London and she remembered with a heavy heart the look in his eyes as he left, leaving her standing wondering when she might see him again.

Lizzie was awake and dressed. She had been waiting as planned and they clung to one another with their cheeks pressed and their arms around each other. Neither spoke, they just held on tightly whispering between the tears until Katherine hurried from the room.

On her way down, she stopped briefly and tidied her face before taking one last look at her rooms. As she walked slowly from one to the other, the sound of her calf-skin boots echoed off the walls. The apartment was cold, no particular spot holding memories for her. She might have been anywhere. Outside a thin morning mist had chilled the gardens, blanketing whatever colour had been creeping into the day. She had asked the coachmen to meet her at the rear of the house and walked briskly to the window to check before making her way down until she could see the light under the kitchen door.

The brightness of the room made her blink but she stopped, one hand still on the door the other shielding her eyes. Seven, eight, ten, a dozen even of the staff were waiting in line, their solemn faces turned her way. Moments before, she had heard them talking but now the room was strangely silent.

"Beg pardon, m'lady, but I couldn't stop 'em." Ranger, the tall, softly-spoken second butler broke the spell, stepping hurriedly from behind the table, pulling his shirt cuffs out from under his tailcoat sleeves. "I'm sorry, ma'am. Hope you don't mind but they…all of us, rather, we just wanted to be here…to say farewell."

"Oh, you shouldn't have." Katherine, the hand at her mouth now tightly clenched, looked swiftly from one face to the next. "Really you shouldn't," she whispered, shaking her head. "I just wanted to slip away…quietly, on my own."

"Come, m'lady. Mustn't stop too long or you'll be late for the stage." Ranger took her arm. "We all know 'tis not right like this. Shouldn't be done but…well…we couldn't just let you go without seeing you away." He looked down at her and smiled, squeezing her arm encouragingly. She was never able to remember what they said as she took their hands. Their faces were a blur in front of her. One by one they told her how they would miss her, three of the maids were weeping, several wanted to go with her and they all wished her God speed.

"Morning, Middy," Benson, bald and gaunt and with his body stiff with rheumatism, stood at the end next to the door, his best black leggings gleaming with polish. Now long since retired, she knew he must have walked the five miles from Romsey. 'Middy,' the old gardener's pet name for Katherine since he had heard the little three year-old call out, was never used unless they were alone together. It was their little secret and now the creased face was smiling kindly. His eyes were twinkling but she could see the tears as he leant forward.

"Here y'are, m'dear...here look." The hand that took the cloth from the basket was gnarled and swollen, the skin leather hard. He tried to steady himself as he passed the basket to her but she could see it was shaking. "Daresay you'll be needing these," he whispered, stepping forward to catch his balance. "Might come in handy, someplace. Here, look." Each little box or bottle of seeds set around the nest of moss had been labelled, the trowel and fork, polished and oiled. He told her that his daughter had written the message on the label tied to the roses but she dare not look.

Katherine put the basket down and took his hand in both of hers. "Thank you, Benny," she whispered. "Dear Benny, thank you and thank you again for coming...*all* this way...and for everything." She threw her arms around the old man and hugged him before moving on quickly, unable to say more.

Outside, the forgathering of grooms, coachmen and gardeners fell silent as Ranger guided her from one to the other. The farewells, cheerless and sad, were often little more than gruff mumblings as the right words were sought in the dawn half-light. A soft glow showed from the first floor window where Lizzie's curtains had been drawn back.

Sarah was at the step by the brougham's open door. Katherine had been dreading the moment and the two stood looking at one another. The maid started to speak, faltered then fell into Katherine's arms sobbing unashamedly. She remembered the girl's fingers clinging to her clothes as she cradled the head against her until Ranger eased her gently away. Even now she could hear the deep clunk as the carriage door shut and feel the sudden jolt as it jerked into life before it was brought to a halt once more.

The shout was breathless. "Whoa...hold on." It was Ranger and the butler had been running. "Here, m'lady," he gasped, forcing his head inside the carriage. "Almost forgot and t'would never have done." She took the letter from his hand. "Papers from the church, m'lady. The ones confirming your banns've been read...the curate's man brought 'em last night. Said to tell you they were read at evensong, all three times...just as you asked. Said there were no problems, nobody said nothing…said also to wish you luck, m'lady. That's all he said." Then the brougham jerked forward again.

3

"When d'you reckon you'll be able to make a start?" Frederic Knight leant against the beam over the open fire then prodded at a log with his boot. "I'd like to get an idea of what might be there as soon as possible, then get the analysts in to have a look."

He glanced up as he spoke even now amazed at Wilmot's self-assurance. Initially he had considered him to be somewhat shy and withdrawn, diffident almost but he had been wrong. Underneath that nervous abruptness and tucked away behind the sharp mind was a warmth and a kindness he had not detected before. The man intrigued him. The more he saw the more he liked and he could think of several he knew who would delight in his company.

"Oh, I've been at it for sometime now," Wilmot laughed, his eyes darting away as usual. "Chipping away whenever I get the chance. The trouble is that Heasley's a little out on a limb and it takes a bit of time to get out on the ground. But here…" He unrolled a map. "Have a look at this." They moved to the table, catching the best of the light from the window. First they stood, then sat engrossed in discussion, stopping only when a hand came to move the lamp. Next they ate quickly, talking as they did so, with their plates on the map and the food mere sustenance swiftly devoured.

"Nelly? Nelly Coombes?" Frederic turned surprised at the serving girl. "Goodness, I'm sorry…only just seen it's you. What brings you out here, to Sandyway?" Wilmot saw the look of surprise on his face as he rose. "Here, allow me." Frederic laughed and helped with the plates. "Wrong side of the moor for you surely? *No?* But, what a surprise." She had been watching from the kitchen, waiting for the two men to finish.

"Hardy, sir. That's Mr Cockram…he's dad's cousin, 'e is." Nelly Coombes brushed back the curls and crossed her plump white arms. "Didn't fancy working on with they new folks at Castle 'ights so dad spoke with Hardy…and 'e got me out here. Proper job an' all. Busy though." She glanced at Wilmot and caught his eye before bending forward to peer more closely at him.

"'Ere, 'ow's, Jack?" They both saw him start. "'Tis no bother, sir," she laughed, her body shaking with delight under the thin cotton dress. "Hardy told me that you've bin in an' out of here from time to time. I hear he'll be out afore long. Out to Sherdon, isn't it, sir?" she glanced at Knight.

"That's right," Frederic looked at Wilmot then back at the girl. The man he could see was easy, happy to be known as Jack's brother. "He'll be married by then," Knight glanced at her. "A married man, I guess…if it all works out," he added as an afterthought.

94

"Oh aye..." The laugh had gone and the sparkle and bounce with it. *"Married?* Oh, aye...'tis true what they say then." Nelly inclined her head but Wilmot had seen the line of her mouth as she turned to go

"That's your brother for you." Frederic laughed, getting up and reaching for his black, high-buttoned coat. "All the girls loved him so they did, but now he's gone and left them. Incidentally," he turned to let Nelly Coombes help with his collar. "We'll be passing the turning down to Sherdon but it'll be a year or so before they can move up." As they made their way to the door, the taproom fell silent.

"He'll do you well, sir...you know that. If anyone'll do the job out here, it'll be him. Jack lives for his farming."

"And her? Katherine?" Frederic spoke quickly. "Have you met her yet?" Wilmot didn't look up but the question had come in a rush.

"No, but Jack an' I've talked often enough. It's been hard for them both but they'll be together soon...free to get on with their lives at last." They reached the stables together, both deep in thought.

✳

The road took them to Landacre where they turned up the Barle valley. "There's evidence of old mine workings up here, you know." Wilmot pointed towards Simonsbath. "A fella called Billingsley wrote about it years ago, around the turn of the century. I've had a look...it's difficult to tell but there're definitely all the right signs."

The two rode on until they came to a patch of wet ground where the river swept wide in a smooth black arc. Frederic reined in and watched as his companion stood and searched. "There you are." Wilmot eased forward pointing at the water lying between clumps of rushes. "See the colouring here...it's like rust. Almost *is*, in fact, and look at the film on the surface. That's one of the best indications of iron trace elements. See, here...and again over here." Knight followed the younger man, studying the ground until he pulled up again.

"Now then...we're not the first to be digging about round here, you know." Wilmot's horse swung as he pointed to the hillside. "Ah yes...there we are...over there. You can see the scree under those grassy mounds."

"How old, d'you reckon?"

"Phew, difficult to say." He screwed up his face. "Could be medieval, Roman perhaps...even earlier. That's just the sort of open cast work they liked doing. But it looks as though they attempted an adit," he saw the frown. "Oh yes...they would have had them then...perhaps a drift or two running off inside as well." He thought for a moment. "To be honest we'd do best to take a lot of samples first then go for a main shaft."

"That'd be a fair task in itself, would it not?"

"Oh, for sure, and out here in particular. We'd have to be absolutely certain before bringing in all the equipment. And that *would* be some undertaking...machine houses, pump house, blacksmith's shop, plus enough room for two horse-whims...everything. Plus the living accommodation, of course...and all to be paid for. Sorry, sir," he laughed at Knight's face. "Bad news, I know, but now's the time to hear it, not when you're a hundred feet down."

"Well, I'm prepared to have a go. If we can be just a bit more certain...then I'm game."

The two men had reached Simonsbath and Wilmot was about to turn for home. "Why don't I see if I can get the Prince Regent mine captain up here with a couple of his team from Heasley Mill." The two studied one another. "It'll take time and a bit of money but it's far better to have a really good look first. We'll get some samples out then send them off to Camborne or across to Dowlais...somewhere where they know what they're talking about, then we can consider the next move." It made sense and they planned to meet again.

Frederic watched until Wilmot had turned the corner. The man was doing just what had been asked of him and, for that, he was grateful. But the curse of it all was money. Once again he was tempted to throw caution aside and go for a quick strike. Two of his father's last team had urged him to do just that but he had resisted and was glad he had. Now Wilmot Tucker, as straight and direct as his brother, was urging caution. So who was right and where should he go from here? As he dropped the reins to let the horse take him over the bridge, the young master of Exmoor turned up his collar and rubbed his chin. He was sorely tempted but it needed a little more thought.

4

"*Sah!*" The chair hit the wall but not before Sergeant Fanshawe was on his feet. "Very good to see you again, sir." The eyes were glinting as brightly as ever and the ends of the smoothly waxed moustache twitched urgently as he thrust out his hand. "An' looking very well, too, sah." Fanshawe checked him up and down. "In the pink...the very pink of nick, so I see. Time for a cup o' tea p'raps?"

"Thank you, Sarn't Fanshawe." Frederic took off his top hat and reached for the black wicker chair under the window.

Fanshawe sat and listened to his officer's request. "*Him* sir...*Tucker*? One of them 'eathens you brought out o' the mountains with yer, wasn't 'e?" Fanshawe filled his cheeks and blew, working furiously on the ends of his moustache. "In to all that wrestlin' business, wasn't 'e? I dunno...should 'ave shipped 'im orf to Orstrailia with the other fella...Grant wasn't it? That or strung the pair of 'em up in Taunton.

Too kind you was, sir…too soft on the men. The big stick…that's what they need. Now then…let's 'ave a look."

He consulted the nominal roll, reading aloud and stopping only to curse roundly at the names of those he considered had crossed his path. "Well, sir, seein' it's the break o' the week and seein' you can bring them four savages in with yer, should be no problem. We can use the Master Chef's cart, sir…nice little one it is. You leave 'im to me…'e knows what's good for 'im. Owes me a favour or two, so 'e does." Fanshawe scowled. "By the way, sir, who's 'e marryin'…that Tucker? Who's having *'im* for Gawd's sake?"

Frederic watched the sergeant's face as he explained the circumstances. The eyebrows crashed together then shot up, pulling the eyes with them. "Bleedin' heck, sir. What's an 'igh born lady like that doin' grubbing around with the natives? Gor bless my soul. I bet 'er old man had summat to say about that, an' all. I dunno…*cuh*." Fanshawe shook his head. "Cuh." He was silent again. "I'd 'ave told him soon enough, sah. Put 'im straight, so I would. *Tucker*…Gor, bleedin' 'eck."

5

"No, Jack. You can't go behaving like that." Charlotte rounded on him. "Just bain't proper to go living together like that. You know very well you'm not married yet. And I don't *care*," she stamped on the protest he was about to make. "I made a right proper mess of my life and mother's had enough on 'er mind without 'aving no tittle-tattle goin' on. Bain't right."

Jack glanced through the door of the small annexe, now used as a wood store. "But I can't live in there, Lottie," he remonstrated, snatching at cobwebs from his clothes and speaking rather too loudly. "Look at it the state of it…and why should I? We'll be married in a week or so…and what does it matter anyway."

"Oh don't go giving us none of that, Jack Tucker." By now Charlotte was at the stone sink across the room cutting vegetables with her back to him. "You know full well what mother says and, anyhow, the vicar'll be along just as soon as 'er arrives and you know what 'e'll be thinking…an' be lookin' for. What d'you think people'll say when they know you've been…well…down here together?" She turned and pointed the knife at her brother. "An' think of *'er*, Jack. 'Er's come all this way on 'er own and 'er's got 'er position to think of. 'Er won't want none of that talk goin' on. Don't be so mazed."

He tried to reason but Charlotte would have none of it, not even the idea of him sleeping inside, but downstairs by the fire. "Don'e be so daft, Jack. That's just as bad and yer know it. You just clean up that little place and put your head in there. 'Tis only for a few days and…bless my soul, it's not cold nor nuthin. Honest, man, there's no other way an' that's the end of the matter. Katherine'll be in the end room and I'll be next to 'er with Davey…an' you'll be outside…you an' Scamp." Jack knew he was beaten.

It was just before dark when he found the letter left by the messenger. His heart leapt: Katherine would be here tomorrow. Then he paused, still concerned about how she might react. He had worked hard but the cottage was all so basic, it was half empty and quite dead to the senses. When he showed his sister the letter, she laughed, ruffling his hair. "There we are," she nudged. "Told yer she'd be comin', didn't I. All this nonsense of yours about 'er turnin' back an' that. Nuthin' but a big silly, so you are."

Charlotte and Davey helped Jack clean the path leading to the stone porch then left for Molland, leaving him to greet her on his own.

✳

It was the dog that heard the horses. By the time Jack had brushed the sawdust from his clothes and wiped his face, the wagonette had unloaded and was on its way back down the track. He stopped at the side of the cottage and watched her with his body half hidden by the rain butt and creepers. It had been nearly three months.

He watched as she knocked on the door then held her dress and stepped back to look for signs of life. Adjusting her fur collar, she picked her way forward again, this time leaning forward and peering through the windows, getting ever closer to where he was waiting. He could see her eyes searching the rooms and he smiled at the little flick of her head as she brushed back her hair each time she bent down. "Good evening, m'lady."

Her hands, gloved in smoke-green kid, flew to her mouth. "*Jack,*" her voice was barely audible. "Oh, my God, Jack." Suddenly they were in each other's arms, her hair and long, velvet cloak billowing behind as he swung her round. "Put me down, put me down," she laughed, leaning back to look at him with her eyes dancing merrily. "Let me see you," she whispered, her arms now round his neck. "Mmm… my dear man…my dear, dear man. Oh…it's been so long." They kissed tenderly, holding on to each other as if afraid to let go.

"So this is Badgercombe?" Her hand was squeezing his arm. "Oh, Jack, it's beautiful…quite beautiful." Her voice trailed off as she tried to take it all in. "Come on," she turned and held out her hand. "Show me, I want to see everything…everything." Minutes later, her peals of laughter rang out.

Jack stared, puzzled. "You mean, you don't mind? Lottie said it wasn't right but I told her it didn't matter."

"And Lottie was right," Katherine's finger pushed at the end of his nose. "*Every*one'll be wanting to know what we're up to down here and I'll wager that parson…parson…"

"Froude," Jack interjected.

"Yes, him. I'll wager he'll be down making sure we're not getting into mischief. *No…*" she burst out laughing once more. "No, you're outside in the shed, just as you said, and your little sister's with Davey upstairs between me and the devil himself. *Listen*," she took his hands in hers. "It's only a few days and then…we'll…we'll…be man and wife." She gabbled the last few words and pulled him towards her. "Just think," she stood on tiptoe and kissed him again. "Mr and Mrs Tucker…d'you realise that?" It was then that he knew she was going to stay.

"Aye," he took her face in his hands. "Aye, I know. Been thinking of nuthin' else these last few weeks. But you won't be just plain Mrs Tucker, will you?" He pulled away from her. "Someone, can't remember who, said you'd still be a lady or summat…Lady Katherine Tucker, isn't it? That's what they'll be calling you…summat like that?" His eyes searched her face.

"Oh, phooey, we'll keep all that for the snobs…to out-snob the snobbies when we've got to. But, to everyone else, and I mean *everyone*, I'm just plain Mrs Tucker…Mrs Jack Tucker, so there."

She remembered a great deal about the following week but not in the order that things happened: there was too much of it. Parson Froude called and she could see he was uneasy. The look of relief on his face when she gave him the letter containing her banns only confirmed his anxiety. "Don't worry," she assured him. "Everything, but everything's in order."

"Will the family, or…er…members of the family be present? I mean, can we help with the…"

"Just my sister." She saw his look. "You must treat it as though I have nobody else. It's been their decision to…disassociate themselves. Sad…sad for them that is, but I've learned to live with it. As for me, I'm at peace with myself and what I've chosen to do. My sister will be by my side and Mr Frederic Knight…Freddy, will bring me to the altar. He, one of his brothers and just a few others will hold my hand, as it were. And…that's that."

"I see." Froude nodded slowly. "Yes, I see. *Well*," now beaming with relief, he rubbed his hands vigorously. "It really does seem, Lady Darcy, as though…"

"Stop." Katherine put a hand on his arm. "I've stopped all that. To you, Grace, Lottie, little Davey even, I'm Katherine, simply Katherine. I know, I know," she sensed his disappointment. "But it's far easier like this, then everybody knows who I am, not *what* I am."

✳

Charlotte ordered Jack out two days before the wedding. "Go and calm mother," she advised. "Wilmot's staying up there as well…just leave Katherine with me. Honest, Jack, stop fussin' around so. 'Er's lovely and Lizzie's coming tomorrow. Oh yes. 'Er and Mr Knight came when you were in Barnstaple. We're goin' to look after Katherine, all of us are. You just gid on and sort yerself out.

"And Emma's coming in as well, so there'll be more'n enough of us here." She moved him to one side and examined the pot simmering on the ashes. "See if you can 'elp Fred Loosemore an' Wilmot. Troy'll be up there, too. They're goin' to do the weddin' feast just like they did for Emms…up in the big barn."

Katherine watched Charlotte as she ran her hand down the length of the satin wedding dress. Her fingers looked hard and rough, ingrained with grease and blackened with dirt against the soft, pure white material. Her hair, chopped short to the neck, was beginning to grey at the roots. How long, she wondered, before she, too, was like that. "Aw, Katherine, 'tis bootiful. Real, real bootiful. You'll look real lovely."

The two had become close. At first Charlotte spoke quietly and Katherine had barely been able to understand the soft westcountry burr. Jack had told her about his sister and she had been as nervous as Charlotte when they first met. But it had been Charlotte who had laughed first. "Y'ere," she had cried, taking Katherine's arm. "Us'll make a right 'ansome pair, us will." Katherine caught her twinkle. "Can'e 'magine?" by now she was giggling with one hand to her mouth, making her even more difficult to understand. "Can'e 'magine when some fine gennelman or lady calls for you and 'er gets me at the door? Or someone comes for me, Arthur Vellacott, say, or Bill Scriven, summat like that, and sees'e at the door? Can'e see the look on they vaces?"

Little by little Charlotte showed Katherine about life in a country cottage, where and how to draw the cleanest water from the stream, how the handymaid, the crocks and trivets worked around the hearth and how the spits and water-boiler kept working for hour after hour. Katherine watched, grimacing in horror, as Charlotte cut up raw meat and gutted fish, explaining what could be eaten and what was boiled up for the dogs. "Don'e worry, m'dear," she chuckled, her short dumpy frame shaking with mirth as she watched Katherine's first feeble efforts. "'Tis easy really. 'Ard at first but then comes nat'ral like." She soon learned that most of the clothes she had brought with her were useless in and around the house and garden where the voluminous skirts and petticoats got in the way and tore themselves on the brambles and wild rose thickets.

Only once did her confidence falter, just for a moment soon after Jack moved out. Charlotte had gone into Twitchen and the cottage was silent, even the birds were quiet. She was alone, alone and suddenly afraid. It was all so new. She knew of no one from her station in life who had ever done this before, there was no one to guide her or tell her how she should behave. She walked slowly, almost fearfully, to the broken wicker chair by the door where she pulled it round and sat, contemplating what she had done and wondering nervously about the future.

Scamp, his legs now not so strong, scrambled clumsily into her lap then sat testing the air. She studied her hands, felt the rough skin then looked at her nails that were already chipped and broken. How long, she wondered, before they became like Charlotte's? She had seen how country life hardened and coarsened the women, ageing them early and bending them. The hem of her dress was torn and her tiny shoes looked muddy and scuffed. The face that peered back at her from her gilt travelling mirror that morning was rosy cheeked and sunburned rather than pale and powdered. The hair had been combed roughly and tied back, no longer groomed for hours and set by Sarah. And all in little over a week. She sighed heavily and the little dog craned its neck backwards. Before she could move, he had licked the end of her nose. She flinched and laughed, her contemplative moment now passed.

But it was Jack's life and already she felt part of it. Here, unlike her own strictly regulated world, everyone knew everyone. Shy and wary, they had stared blankly at first and kept their peace as country folk do with strangers. When Charlotte had taken her to the mill and the bakery, they had smiled politely and passed the time of day but no more than that. In the shops they had glanced briefly and nodded before turning away and chatting to Charlotte. The children had simply backed away and stared. But now, even in this short time, the curiosity was over. There was a warmth in the smiles that greeted her and a cheeriness in the voices that called out her name.

"You'm one of us, now," Charlotte had joked. "But don't 'spect for things to happen too quick, mind. Takes time in the country. But don'e worry, m'dear, they knows you're Jack's and they love'e for that. They know you belong 'ere with us."

Katherine smiled to herself at the memory then closed her eyes before settling back in the chair with Scamp in her lap.

*

The six soldiers making up their escort for the short drive over Cussacombe Common to the church, were gathered around the gaily decorated military wagon with its canvas cover raised over the side hoops. As soon as she saw them she clapped her hands in delight.

Frederic, in full dress uniform, took her mind back to the balls at Blagdon and Broadlands, the glittering chandeliers, the long dresses and the periwigged footmen and the strict, orderly way of things. Where were the others, she thought, searching in vain for a moment while her ears strained for the sound of music. But only Lizzie was there; dear Lizzie, sitting surrounded by flowers and waiting for them to join her. Nobody had told her about this, they had kept the surprise to themselves.

The heavy cart from Ebberley Lawn was never a bride's carriage. It was a kitchen on wheels or had been until somebody had removed the boiler and stove and the racking for pans before installing the two narrow bench seats. It might just have passed as a landau from Blagdon or possibly a dog cart from Simonsbath but it was impossible to tell with the cushions and rugs piled high and the sides decked with ribbons and bunting. Frederic sat facing Lizzie and Katherine, their legs entangled in the narrow space between them, their laps covered by the hoops of the dresses and the long bridal train piled carefully like whorls of cream.

She was chatting to her sister, the two of them holding hands and laughing gaily as they gossiped, stopping only to draw breath when the wagon bounced or rolled. She was going to her man with a song in her heart and a light in her eyes. She was radiant, a woman in her prime, serene and confident about all that was coming to pass. Whether or not she noticed the glances of the troopers riding beside her Frederic could not tell. What man, he wondered, would not have given his own life in return for hers, the life she was giving so freely having forsaken all else.

He had been dreading the ride to the church for he knew he could do nothing but sit helplessly and look on as Katherine Darcy was transported from one world to another. She could not begin to understand what lay ahead and yet it was he who was taking her to her destiny. It would be his hand giving hers at the altar. In his own quiet way he had tried to warn her but it had not been enough and when she brushed aside his concern he had stopped. He should have done more, tried to reason with her, enlisted the help of the others to make her see sense. But he had failed. He had not been able to summon the courage for it was not her safe deliverance that was on his mind but Katherine herself. For months he had struggled with his conscience yet, however hard he tried to cast aside such ignoble thoughts, they had never quite left him, rather they kept breaking in on his mind and stirring his heart. If only she could draw back, not for her own salvation but for him, Frederic Knight, because he coveted her for himself. He had known it in his heart but now he knew for certain and there was no point in battling against the truth. He desired her, loved her maybe, yet her heart lay elsewhere.

✳

As soon as they reached the porch Jack turned, as did Wilmot. A dash of coloured light splashed across the two brothers as the sun burst through the stained glass south window, suddenly lighting up the dark grey of their tailed coats. From where she stood, she could see that his cravat, under his high winged collar, had been secured with the gold pin she had given him. His hair, sun-bleached and trimmed but still long, was tied back with a black velvet ribbon.

When their eyes met, she smiled then half raised the spray of wild flowers in her hand but the sudden scrape of scabbards and spurs on the flagstones as they moved forward made the villagers turn and stare. Many had never seen a soldier in uniform and here were several, dressed in dark blue jackets with silver lace, their white belts and gold sashes creating a blaze of colour in the deep shadows.

She had dressed as she had always wanted to for this occasion and had to move slowly so as not to displace her great aunt's bridal tiara that kept her veil in place. The long train of her white and cream satin wedding gown had been laid out behind her by one of the troopers before Lizzie took his place. Moving now in time with the music, she glanced shyly through the fine Bruges lace at those who had become part of her life, many of them whispering and pointing or beaming excitedly when they caught her eye. But her finery was too much: she should not have dressed like this in front of these warm, gentle people who had little more than their workday clothes. They would, she was sure, think she was reminding them of who she was and felt a sudden pang of remorse.

*

She recalled little of the evening at Luckworthy; just a sea of rugged, weather-beaten faces and twinkling eyes, and the loud squeals of laughter as the children scampered between the tables. Several men from the village danced with her, their hard hands and powerful arms holding her gently as she swirled and turned, each one carrying her further and further into her new world. Jack danced with her twice, Frederic danced with Lizzie and Emma before he asked for her hand. He seemed quiet, she thought later. He asked her again, twice, but she never had time. Everyone seemed to be there…Charlotte and Hector, Bill Scriven, Stan Thorne and Ruth, the carters and millers, the shopkeepers and tanners and farmworkers she had met, all of them dancing and laughing and dancing again.

Two troopers saw them back to Badgercombe then turned and left, the sound of their voices and the hooves on the track gradually fading. They were on their own at last. The noise, the music and the shouts were no more. It was late.

The night was still and very quiet. What little of the harvest moon that was left shone through the open window to play on the wall behind them. "You all right," he whispered. "Not upset nor nothing?" She felt his hand reach out and gave him hers, twining her fingers through his.

"No," she murmured. "I'm fine…anyway it's too late for all that, isn't it? Far too late." There was a long silence before she wriggled closer allowing her naked body to press up against his. Her hand began to stroke his chest.

"What are you thinking about?" he asked softly.

"Oh, all the usual things…home, the family. Mother and father. What they're doing…and what they must be thinking about. But it's all so far away, isn't it…and so different." She paused, wiping her cheek. "What about you?"

"Same really," Jack sensed her moment of anguish and turned towards her. Brushing the hair from her face he moved gently over her. "We'll be all right," he whispered. "Don't worry, my love. Things might be a bit strange for a while but…we'll manage. You'll see."

As their lips touched she relaxed and her mouth opened in response.

Chapter Seven

It was to be nearly two years before the move to Sherdon finally took place.

Long before, Frederic had been asked by Chanter to go up and discuss progress and Jack accompanied him. At the farm they met up with the builder and two others. One, Tom Webber, Jack remembered from the time he accompanied Frederic's father to watch them building the Exmoor wall. Webber, now over seventy, lived in Brayford, a quarrying village tucked snugly into the woods to the west of the moor. The second, another Irishman, had been brought over from County Kerry.

"It's been the devil's own job." Oliver Chanter picked his way through the building material ahead of Frederic. Jack could see by the sweat marks on the back of his shirt and by the way he walked that the man had been toiling hard. Twice the start had been delayed and Frederic, now irritated by the constant excuses, had them working against the clock. During their ride over in the morning he had been testy, something Jack had rarely seen before, and there had been long silences when Jack wondered if he might somehow be the cause.

"The wars've sent the price of oak sky high." Chanter kicked out at the stack of roughly hewn beams. "The navy took everything and the young trees aren't ready…won't be for years. You can see how much we need." They followed his hand across the plain stone walls of the house where the empty windows stared blindly and the doorway gaped wide. "We need so much of it…there look, near on a hundred for the roof alone. Pine's fair enough in places but it's oak that bears the loads." Frederic nodded.

"Then there's the slate. That's gone up too. Everyone's after the stuff, especially in the midlands and north…factories, docks, mines, whole new towns going up. It's there all right but the beggar's are asking fer gold."

"And for everything else as well, I suppose," Frederic muttered. They had reached a pile of stones just where the pegs began for the line of the new barn. Each found a seat, Jack on one from where he could see clearly what was soon to be his home. Chanter was depressing. His news was all about problems and he detected the hard edge to Frederic's voice. He too sounded dejected.

"Pretty much, I'm afraid, sir…aye, pretty much. And if that's not enough, I'm losing good men, too. The money's better in the towns what with all the development. Look at they two…the lads over there. Boys, barely out of school but that's all there is." Chanter paused. "Aye, it's not easy. But never mind," he slapped his thigh. "We'll manage…one way or t'other we'll get the job done. It's a fine place you've found out here."

"What about Lower Sherdon, the shepherds' cot over the hill?" Frederic tugged at a long grass. "Once that's up I'll put the hedgers in. Webber tells me there'll be more than twenty of 'em…*twenty*, for God's sake." He laughed cynically then pulled a face.

"We're there, sir, very nearly there." Chanter rubbed his bare arms and looked round for sight of the two wallers. "Another month, two perhaps and they can move in."

"But why so many? They'll be tripping over one another. A dozen maybe, but *twenty*…" Jack watched his master's head shake angrily. "Costing a fortune. Plus all the working horses." He could see the father in the man. It was all there, as plain as could be: the drive, the burning impatience and the same boiling frustration.

Chanter studied the ground. "I know," he nodded despairingly. "That's what I feel but it's what Tom Webber reckons and the man knows his job well enough."

"Did he go through those figures of his with you?" Frederic stood on the stones and stared impatiently down the valley.

"He did indeed, sir…twice."

"Well, where is he for Heaven's sake? Said he'd meet us." His hands were shielding his eyes. "No doubt looking for more expensive work to do." Chanter glanced at Jack. "Well, go on…tell me the worst." Frederic turned back and sat again. "Let's hear it, then. May as well get it all over at once." There was little humour in his smile.

Chanter checked himself, collecting his thoughts, then reached for a short oak plank. It wasn't his job but he could see an explanation would have to be given, and a good one at that. "'Tis like this…an' he reckons he'll need every one of 'em. Here we are now…here at the top we have the wall." He rested one end of the wood against his knee, the other on the ground. "He'll have the wallers up here…three or four of them. They're good, mind…got them from up north, Westmorland, I think. Then next there're the ditchers…two or three at least ditching and packing the earth between the stones. Here, say." He tapped the middle of the wood. Right? Right so far?" he waited for the nods.

"Now, here's the problem…the stones and where the devil to find 'em." Chanter shrugged. "We've looked for signs everywhere but there's very little about, hardly any so it's the river beds, down here." He prodded at the bottom of the plank with his foot. "He's planning on a dozen or so to work in the rivers and streams…remember they're going to have to lift the rock first, then split and size enough to keep the party on the wall busy…and they work fast. Less than a dozen hard at it down here and you'll be paying for good men up top to be doin' nothing." Jack and Frederic leant forward, both listening intently.

"Then…and here's the point, then we've got to get it all up to them and it's a hell of a climb. Bullock carts're no good…far too steep." The builder shrugged. "So they'll be using ponies but the wee fellas can't carry more than two-fifty, maybe three hundred pounds at a time…'specially if we keep 'em at it all day. An remember it's more than a ton of stone for every yard of wall so we'll need a dozen or so ponies…and a man can handle no more than three at a time on the steep ground. So," he frowned and looked up, then back at his piece of wood. "That's it then…eight, ten, eighteen…twenty, twenty-four all told."

"Hell fire and damnation." Frederic's head dropped, the two with him waiting patiently. Jack could sense the man's disappointment. It was hard. He was trying desperately to get ahead yet everywhere he turned, something or someone caught hold of him and dragged him back. Wilmot had told him about the mines months ago and he had heard also how Maxwell was struggling. That was bad enough and now the builders and wallers were running into one thing after another.

"Not too good, Jack." Frederic looked up, weary at the weight of it all and caught his eye. "You won't be up for a while, I'm afraid. What d'ya reckon Chanter? A year…it has to be doesn't it?" He clambered to his feet and dusted his cream breeches. "A year at least."

Chanter drew in his breath and scratched the soil with his boot. "Has to be, sir. Has to be that…all of it."

✳

They were two fine looking men, even Chanter could see that as the two stood talking together. Young Knight, as he was known, was bound to be angry but he had taken it well. Both had been hoping for better news but it was nobody's fault.

The youngster was going to have to pay more; prices were rising and he had accepted it with good grace. He was a big man, a shade taller than Tom Webber, and broad at the shoulders, around thirty or so he reckoned. Handsome as well in a fine sort of way with his thick, dark, well cut hair and neatly trimmed side-burns…and the money was still there. The high-buttoned coat with its black velvet collar and the well-cut breeches with the brown-topped boots gave it away. Same with the horse, a beautiful thoroughbred stallion. Yet there he was…still a bachelor funnily enough.

Frederic Knight was big but Tucker was taller still, almost half a head as they stood together. Quite a lad in his day they said. A bit of a ladies man too and he could see why. Mrs Chanter would for sure and he smiled at the thought. And they were still talking about the wife he had found for himself, a titled lady from up country or somewhere like that. There'd been a right old rumpus about it all, so Cockram had told him but here they were, man an' wife and Sherdon it was going to be. Good luck to him. Chanter rose stiffly and rubbed his arms.

"Not too much is it, sir?" Jack knew what was on the other's mind. The day had been difficult from the start but Chanter's news must have hurt. His master had been more than kind already and he would be happy to work anywhere for him. "I mean…couldn't help hearing those figures an' that. P'raps you'd rather us go someplace else."

Frederic paused. It was Jack through and through, typical of the man. Having had his own hopes of an early move dashed already, here he was offering to forgo what had been promised him. Nobody would farm the place better. It would be hard and he needed a hard man, but then there was Katherine. Would it be too much for her? Perhaps he should find them somewhere else further down; might even see a bit more of them. But no, that would be wrong, possibly even dangerous. "Thanks, Jack, but I'm keeping Sherdon…don't worry yourself. But what d'*you* reckon? Come on, honestly…what would *you* really like to do?"

The two men stood looking at one another, both reading so much. Frederic saw a man he admired more than any other and had done so since they were boys and had first played together. He had offered Jack a chance and he wanted him to accept yet he could not deny there was now something else. He prayed she would not come between them but it worried him: worse still it excited him.

Jack knew his master had given him everything, had saved him time and again and now he was offering to help once more. "Heavens, sir, what have I done to deserve a question like that? 'Tis a wonderful thing for any man to be asked, an' with all else that's on your mind." Frederic smiled diffidently, for a moment uncertain. "'Tis here, sir. Sherdon. If you'll have us here then here's where we'll be. And I'll see you right…we'll build a home where you'll always be welcome, more than welcome…as long as ever we're here."

"Fine, that's it." Frederic clapped his shoulder. "We'll have to wait a while, but Sherdon it is…that'll be your home.

*

A little more than a week after he had broken the news, Katherine announced she was expecting a child. The baby, Dr Collyns told her, would be born in June. "So we'll still be here." Katherine came up behind Jack's chair and put her arms round his neck. "Our first child'll be born here and baptised at St Mary's."

"Strange, you know." Jack took her hand and looked up at her. "Never thought I'd feel like this. But it's wonderful," he gasped, scrambling to his feet. Suddenly he was serious. "But you'll have to take care, be careful what you do." His arms went around her. "No more of the heavy work, all this gardening and.…"

"Oh, for Heaven's sake…listen, you," she kissed his cheek then pushed him back into his chair before settling on his knees. "Listen, I'm not an invalid or a weakling, you know. Charles Collyns told me to do whatever I wanted, until he tells me otherwise."

＊

Winter came early, the first snows falling before Christmas. Farmer Rumbelow had seen it coming, noting how the deer had come down from the moors to shelter in the woods before raiding the fields for roots and the low lying pastures for food. Flocks of fieldfares gathered earlier than usual, woodcock and snipe collected on the marshy ground around the springs. The storm, when it came, raged high above Badgercombe, where the gale roared through the tree tops but the little cottage was spared the worst of the wind, and the snow fell gently. When Katherine looked out of the window just before dusk the ground had been covered, small drifts appearing, blown by eddying gusts. It should have been dark but the day hung on to the grey evening light.

Next morning the world had a silent whiteness about it. The clouds were higher and broken with patches of blue in between and the breeze was ruffling the branches, spilling flurries of snow to the ground. "Here." Jack called her to the window. "It's deep already and maybe more to come."

"What's that moving in the wood over there? Over there, look." As she spoke, she pulled the rug tightly over her shawl and picked her way across the bare boards.

"Where?" He wiped the window with his sleeve.

"Over there...under the trees. There look, it moved and there's another...and more behind."

"Stags." Jack rubbed the wet glass again, this time with the corner of her shawl. "They've left the hinds now and are living together. And there's the leader...cuh, a great big fellow." She caught his arm and, for a moment, they stood motionless. "See the antlers on him. There're three a' top either side...twelve points in all. That's a royal...what they call a royal stag. Magnificent beast...and just look at the ice on his mane. Must've been cold way back up there."

Badgercombe, like everywhere else, was cut off for a time by the heavy snowfall when the narrow, steep-sided lanes had been filled to the hedgetops. Three weeks took their toll and almost all the food. Only a few vegetables were left and most of them rotten, bitten deep by the hard frosts. The hens had stopped laying, three of them and the cockerel were taken by a fox that chewed and scratched its way through the gap at the bottom of the henhouse door. The house cows stood empty of milk with their ribs and hips sharp against their hides. Charlotte and Davey queued for hours at the bakery. Jack killed a lamb, then an older ewe.

But they were warm and lived better than most, moving their mattresses into the kitchen, all five sleeping huddled together around the fire. Others were not so lucky. Several had perished so Parson Froude told them when they got to the church. Only two in Molland had succumbed but several in Hawkridge and Withypool, further up the hill. Out on the top it had been terrible.

2

Easter that year was late and it was on the way back from church that Katherine felt the first pains. "Jack," she tried to sound unconcerned. "I'm not feeling too well. Stop the cart for a minute can you...let me walk a little." Twenty yards further on, just where the track twisted through the high banks of gorse, she stumbled then fell and lay on her side, this time doubled up in pain." Charlotte ran and crouched beside her. It took just seconds to see.

"Can you feel movement?" she cradled Katherine's head in her arms.

"No, but I should, shouldn't I," she whimpered, fighting back tears. "I haven't felt anything for days now...a week maybe and it should be moving and kicking and things." She gripped Charlotte's sleeve. "There's something wrong, isn't there Lottie? Something's happened?"

"*Jaaack*," Charlotte beckoned furiously but he had already left the cart. "Give me a hand, quick. 'Tis the baby. Get 'er to the cart quick. Gentle now. Soon as us're home, go for mother. I'll take care o' the maid."

That evening she lost the baby but there was nothing that Grace and Charlotte could have done. Harriet Maud never opened her eyes. She was beautiful, a perfect child but far too small and delicate.

When at last Katherine had fallen asleep, Jack went outside. It was a warm spring evening and the first of the nightingales and warblers had arrived. He settled himself on a large moss-covered boulder by the bridge, listening to their singing and the sounds of the evening, unable to understand why it had to be them. He remembered the fear on his wife's sweat-streaked face as she gripped his hands and her pleading look before she contorted with pain, then her loud cry of anguish just as his mother closed the door. She had tried so hard. It seemed so cruel and unfair.

He knew instantly, the moment Charlotte's face appeared as she ducked under the beam over the stairs. Even before she shook her head he knew their hopes had been dashed. Katherine, who had been living for the moment when they would hold their child together, had been distraught. Her cries and deep sobs of grief still rang in his ears as he sat by the water. Charlotte came to join him just as the light was fading and the two of them remained together until the day had gone.

The child was buried at St Mary's in the corner plot under the tall trees beyond the south door. Wilmot and Emma joined them for the service with Fred and

109

Tilly Loosemore. Katherine, haggard and red-eyed, wrapped in her long, dark green velvet cloak, clung to Jack as she listened to the sombre words spoken by Parson Froude. He spoke gently and Jack could see she was comforted by what he said, both then and later when he called to see her.

Slowly, as the weeks went by, she learned to live again. Her strength and colour returned, as did her smile then her laughter and brightness. Only his own harsh bitterness remained, smouldering and smoking inside him like fire deep inside a rick. It was as if there remained a dark corner of life he could not understand and, because he could not understand it, he did not trust it. Katherine sensed his moods, doing what she could to cheer him through the spring and summer months. Charlotte noticed how she fussed around him. She would take his arm and show him her efforts in the garden.

"Look, dear. Old Benny's seeds...the gardener from Blagdon. See how the carrots are the first ones to show." Jack watched as she crouched to examine the line of tiny seedlings, her fingers picking twigs and pebbles out of their way. He saw that she had cut her hair shorter, showing off the white nape of her neck as she bent forward. "Oh, it's easier like this," she laughed when he asked her why, standing again and pushing it back with both hands to tie what little she could find.

No man could fail to be moved by her love, by the way she always put him before herself. He saw how her blouse still stretched against her body, showing that the fullness of her figure had returned at last. "Charlotte did it for me," she mumbled, taking the two pins from her mouth and smiling shyly. "You're not cross, are you? I'd lost without her, Jack. She's a wonderful person, you know that don't you?"

Suddenly, after the months of cold, he wanted her again. In that moment of desire his own love returned. She was as vulnerable as a child, and she needed him. "Here," he whispered hoarsely, pulling her gently to her feet and drawing her towards him. "It's *you* that's wonderful. You've given every-thing...everything you've ever had, haven't you. You carried our child, nurtured her inside you. It was your loss not ours...yet still you can smile and look kindly at life." His hands reached down past the small of her back. "All those little things you do for me. I *do* care...really I do, y'know." The fragrance of her warm, soft body sent a surge of life through him. Once more he was alive and it was Katherine who had done it, as though she had banished the demons lurking at the back of his mind.

Jack reflected also on how Charlotte had scolded him. 'You're a lucky devil an' all. Don't deserve her sometimes, you don't,' she had chided. 'All day long, the maid's been thinkin' of yer, doin' this an' that. Won't let me do the supper now. Says she must learn 'ow but I can see she's doin' it for you, bless 'er.' He knew she was right. 'Took the little dog cart and called in to see mother on 'er way back from Dulverton. 'Er's a real good maid, 'er is Jack. You look after 'er.'

They marvelled at her courage and faith and when, in the autumn, she told them she was pregnant again, the whole family rejoiced.

*

A second bad winter delayed work at Sherdon further. It was Hardy Cockram who told him that two men had been lost hedging. "Anyway's that an' the weather's put 'em right be'ind again. Mind you," Cockram shook his head. "'Tis none too good right now. Chanter'll tell you when you see him."

Jack rode on. By now he knew the route well. Less than a mile past Sandyway, he took the left hand fork to Landacre before turning off down the steep Sherdon track and dropping down to the bridge over Sherdon Water. He noticed the small cottage by the bridge was occupied but, beyond it, his farm remained far from complete. "Sorry, Jack," Chanter came up to the pony as Jack dismounted. "Nothing us could do 'bout the weather. We were the only ones working out here for sometime...they stopped everywhere else, up at Emmett's and Wintershead out over...over at Honeymead as well." The two men walked around the yard and buildings, Chanter explaining the layout.

"End of August, Jack. That's what I said to Mr Knight. Us'll have most of it up by then, enough for you to move in, like. Then finish off outside afore the weather comes in." Jack returned to hear that Dr Collyns had pronounced Katherine and the baby, now due in a few weeks, to be fit and well. And so they were.

Two days before the birth, Grace moved into Badgercombe, the family once again relegating Jack to his earthy, cobwebbed store, this time with Davey as a companion.

"Gid on up to Sherdon then," Charlotte urged. "You keep tellin' us there's so much to be done...the garden an' that. 'Tis no use hanging round 'ere moaning, Jack, waitin' for things to happen. You'm best out the way. Anyway's 'tis not due for a week yet." Katherine had asked him a number of questions about the house and he left after breakfast, taking Davey with him and Scamp in his saddlebag. The little dog with the patch over his tattered right ear was fourteen. He was also half blind and his master took him everywhere.

On the way home, they stopped at The Sportsman's, knowing there was no need to hurry. "Someone up here asking for yer, today." Hardy glanced at him as the two men stooped under the black beams to see each other more clearly before Jack settled into the corner seat by the fire.

"Oh, aye. Go on, then." Jack wiped the froth from his mouth before turning to study Davey. The boy had taken to the horses and he watched through the cobwebbed window as he picked up their feet to check for stones then ran his hands lovingly over their flanks.

"Good little lad there," Cockram followed Jack's gaze then paused. "Luke Harper, it was."

Jack looked up sharply. "Working from here now, is he?" He saw the big shoulders shrug. "Heard word 'e was looking for a new route. Played Moles Chamber too often, 'e did. Too many times…too many people."

"And too many villains," Cockram's laugh erupted. "Aye, lad, you're not far off it. Wanted to know if you're interested. He'll be along now an' then…want to see yer, no doubt."

✳

The first they knew of the birth was when they caught sight of Charlotte with her skirts held high, flouncing towards them. Jack stopped dead, searching her face. He knew at once. "Both fine, Jack. Real fine," she gasped before stopping in front of them. "Honest to God, Jack, they'm fine…reely." He sprang from his horse but she caught him, throwing her arms around his neck. "He's a bootiful baby, a lovely little boy. Charles, that's 'im isn't it?" Jack heard no more. He pushed past her and ran for the door behind which Charles Lionel Tucker, tiny, wrinkled and noisy lay with his mother.

✳

Less than a month after the christening, Jack's cousin, Mary Westcott, came to see them. Dan, her husband, had been taken ill and had had to give up his farrier's business in Hawkridge. Times were difficult, very difficult she explained, and she had come to ask if they would take on Billy, their son. "E's not the sort for school," Mary announced. Katherine had never encountered such helplessness before where a mother had begged others to take her children. But then she remembered how Grace had had to part with Jack and Emma and the diminutive, mouse-haired woman in front of her now was desperate. "Never bin in trouble nor nuthin'. Just can't do his sums, nor read nor things."

"They'll *all* be off to school." Katherine was adamant. She had been sitting quietly, listening to the woman's dilemma but now she understood and her mind was made up. Jack, she knew, was going to be short of help. "No…I'm sorry," she noticed the look on their faces. "But that's the way it's going to be. They'll need it later on and I'm not going to let it all pass by. School and church…those are the two rules in my house." Then she paused. "Oh, Mary," without thinking Katherine reached out for her hand. "I'm sorry. We'll take him, of course we will. He'll be no problem…and you can come up and see him whenever you wish."

Billy Westcott, short, wiry and a mass of brown curls arrived a week later. He and Davey took one look at each other and began to fight. They fought for three days, rolling around the floors, locked in grunting, gasping combat, struggling

112

to get the better of one another. Chairs fell backwards, crockery crashed to the ground and twice they knocked the wooden cradle sending the baby into fits of screaming. Outside they threw water and hurled stones at each other, chased one another with sticks and tumbled, arms and legs entwined, into the mud by the water trough. At first Jack laughed. "'Tis only normal," he cried. "It's good for them. One or other'll come out tops and that'll be that."

"Sort 'em out, Jack," Charlotte shouted back. "Sort 'em out or I will. Proper little monsters, the pair of them." Katherine's gentle pleadings had no effect; still they fought, goading and taunting one another into violent reaction. She began to regret her decision, wondering how they might return the child to his parents.

"*Jaaack.*" He knew the scream. "*Stop 'em*...stop 'em this instant, I say. *Stop 'em, Jack!*" Charlotte had one by his hair.

The following day he woke them early. The big bow wagon, pulled by six oxen, had to be loaded with logs for Sherdon. He worked them, one against the other till lunch, then on to tea then on again until it was dark. "That'll put a stop to 'em," he whispered as they looked at the boys now asleep on the mattress in the old wood store. One lay curled on his side, his thumb near his mouth, the other on his back, with an arm across his companion. Neither had eaten, neither had washed and neither moved as Charlotte drew the horse blankets over them. Jack was right: Davey Tucker and Billy Westcott became inseparable.

In August, when Charles was four months, Frederic came and told them that the farm was ready. "Take it steady," he warned, looking from one to the other. "Get the important things in first then bring everything else on as soon as you can, before the weather breaks. The builders'll be away in a week or so, then it'll be yours. Oh, and one more thing," he added. "There's a young Irish fella up there looking for work. Declan somebody or other...Declan O'Hara, I think. Webber speaks highly of him...says he's a wonder with horses. Comes from Kilgarvan in Kerry, not far from mother's place."

3

Wilmot touched his mouth with the linen napkin and glanced across the table. George Elworthy was ugly and a coarse brute of a man. His face was sweaty and red because he was too fat; he spoke and drank with his mouth full and his eyes bulged.

"Mining you said...that it?" A few moments earlier the garishly dressed merchant, most of whose buttons were too tight, had broken in on his conversation with the shy young woman on his right. Before dinner Wilmot had watched him easing his way among the other guests, gobbling the canapés and talking too loudly. He looked rich and was, he suspected, used to having his say.

"Indeed I did, sir." Wilmot nodded dismissively and turned back to Rebecca Deveraux. By now he was certain that the engraved invitation which had been delivered to his home two weeks previously had been on account of The Honourable Mrs Piers Deveraux's elder daughter. Why, for instance, had he been placed on her left? The only other single man, and one more than a generation older, was sitting next to their hostess. Horace Carpenter, bald apart from a frizz of grey hair behind his ears, was a modestly dressed little man. He had not, so Wilmot decided, been invited to contest the issue.

It was Frederic Knight who had first mentioned the Deveraux family to him when Piers, the Bristol ship owner, had bought Court Hall in North Molton a year earlier, and he could now understand why their arrival had caused such a stir in the mining village. The house, he noted, had been enlarged then refurbished with taste and furnished well, comfortably rather than opulently. The well-attired groom who had taken his horse, and the liveried butler had been both courteous and respectful.

Court Hall was, according to Frederic, the Deveraux's third home and but one indication of the Western Steamship Company's continued success. The invitation had surprised and intrigued him and he wondered what Frederic must have said about him for his existence to have been acknowledged thus.

"Just here at Heasley Mill, you mean?" Rebecca smiled, half inclining her head. "My *goodness*, how exciting, Mr Tucker. I *never* knew that, most certainly not." Turning towards him, she put down her knife and fork then dabbed her mouth delicately. "But please, do tell me more. We hear it's dangerous and so hard for them all. It must be dreadful down there." Her small eyes screwed up in abhorrence. "*Do* tell me about it."

Wilmot could see she was no beauty. He had studied her earlier, before dinner, as she moved between the dozen or so guests and decided that she was too small and too thin, her hair looked a wiry mess and her features a mite too sharp. But appearances could deceive, sometimes woefully so, and he was more than encouraged to find she laughed easily and talked intelligently, far more so than the horsey, gaudily dressed creature on his left. In fact he was more than encouraged.

"Well, sadly that's so," he turned to decline the offer of more wine. "But we're making good progress all the time. Even when I was at Camborne, that's the school of mining where they study these things, we managed to cut back on the number of accidents." He saw her quizzical look and went on to explain how the arrival of steam power had eased the burden on those working underground. It was when he was telling her about how young children and women were sent into the narrowest of shafts that he noticed her tender nature. Later, and after he had changed the subject, she chatted freely about their new home in North Molton and how she had fallen in love with the wild, open countryside.

"So different to Bristol, even out at Clifton where we live." She laughed lightly. "I *love* it here, but Susannah," she nodded towards her younger sister. "She and mama are bored. They prefer London…our other home," she explained. Wilmot was surprised to find himself disappointed when they rose to allow the ladies to withdraw, vowing to seek her out when they met later.

✳

"Now then, Mr Tucker." Piers Deveraux, his wavy silver hair elegantly cut and smoothed neatly back, gathered the six men around his seat at the head of the table. The smile was warm enough but Wilmot felt the eyes, though a mite glazed with drink, were studying him closely. "Freddy Knight tells me you're doing wonders for him. Anything up there? Found anything yet…or can't you say?"

"Well, sir." Wilmot knew the question was innocent enough but he dare not reveal his hand. The room had gone quiet, the others he knew were waiting on his reply. He paused once more and wrinkled his nose. "It's a bit early just yet. There're signs here and there…quite positive in fact and there's still some way to go but…"

"Oh, go on, man. Don't be so damned cagey." Elworthy leant forward. His lower lip, Wilmot could see, was hanging loose. Onions and tobacco tainted his breath. "You miners are all the same…terrified we're all going to rush up there with our picks and shovels…*ha. Ha!*" he crowed again turning to those he supposed would enjoy his humour. Wilmot looked down and Elworthy missed his quick glance.

"Come, come, George." Deveraux waved a finger admonishingly. "That's not fair…don't push the boy." He smiled benignly. "You're quite right, Tucker. Quite right…shouldn't have asked you that. Too many ears about the place." He stretched for the port.

"Thank you, sir, perhaps it's better that way for the moment. I'm so sorry," he glanced at Elworthy and shrugged. " But there again *'Satis est equitem mihi plaudere.'* No?"

"What's all that rubbish about?" Elworthy lowered his head further to glower suspiciously.

"Horace, sir, the Satires." Wilmot smiled politely. "It's Arbuscula shouting above the crowd as they attempt to mock her. Roughly speaking, "Tis enough for me if the knights applaud.'" He turned to Deveraux, raising his voice a touch. " But then she goes on *'Ut audax contemptis aliis explosa…*but I don't give a fig for the rest of the house.'"

"*Haaa,*" Deveraux shouted with laughter then banged the table in delight. "*Haaa*…oh, dear. That's marvellous. There you are George…there's a riposte for you. Where's yer answer to that, my man? Admirable," he muttered wiping his eye. "What a line. Right, come on everyone." Still laughing to himself, he clapped Elworthy on the shoulder and led the way through the hall.

*

The moment he re-entered the drawing room, he could feel Rebecca's eyes on him. She made no secret of her delight at seeing him again and he smiled back encouragingly, boldness paying homage to boldness. The footman with the tray of snuff and sweet ginger caught him before he reached those around the fire and he hung back, easing the pain in his leg and leaving open the way for her to reach him. "Freddy tells us that you ride a lot...always out and that you're *very* good." She smiled encouragingly.

"Oh, but no...nothing like him or his brothers," he replied hastily. "I enjoy it though, that I will freely admit. And you, Miss Deveraux? What about you, might I ask?"

"Well, yes. Me too." She shrugged and smiled coyly as if too timid to say more and he waited sympathetically. "We, that's Susannah and I, ride out whenever we can. But father forbids us to go far unless one of the grooms accompanies us. He says there're so many tales of...well... *highwaymen* and people like that. Can it really be so?" She studied his face, frowning as though it could not possibly be true.

"It has been said, but that was some time ago," Wilmot replied. "However you should never go unaccompanied and I mean that." He wondered if she knew what was on his mind and continued hesitantly. "But Miss Deveraux...perhaps your father would permit me to accompany you one day? It would indeed be an honour and the moor is a beautiful place...quite wild and very mysterious. Maybe I could accompany both you and your sister? Or perhaps...you would prefer that we should ride out alone with your groom?"

Her eyes dropped. "Thank you, Mr Tucker," she spoke quietly almost in a whisper. "I am much flattered by your kind offer and, yes, I would like that. Why, *yes*." She looked up, her eyes now sparkling. "Yes, thank you, it *would* be very nice." He noticed Susannah approaching and the three of them talked on until it was time to go.

Wilmot took his leave as he saw the others preparing to depart. "*Mister* Tucker." Mary Deveraux sailed between her daughters, offering him her hand. "*Thank you for your company...and,*" acknowledging his bow, "Thank you again. My husband tells me you are something of a classicist...as *well* as an engineer."

"Hardly, madam," Wilmot's eyes widened in surprise. "No, no...a mere amateur if that and certainly nothing more. But whilst at Cambridge it became one of my hobbies."

"And the others?"

"Er," Wilmot looked cornered. "Poetry, I suppose," he said shyly. "Poetry and literature. I was up at Trinity with two who're making their way just now. We were in residence together...William Thackeray and Alfred Tennyson; their names'll mean nothing just now, of course. I contributed one or two scientific articles for Will's journal and the three of us used to read together. They wrote but I only read and it was marvellous," he laughed shyly. "It was a wonderful new world for me...a refuge from the laboratory and I loved it."

4

"Hold it there!" Jason Hawkins ran round the cart and took the rope. "Well done, lads. I've got 'er now." They had been loading since before dawn.

Jack had taken much up to Sherdon throughout the week yet every cart and wagon had been filled already and still more was waiting to be loaded. Davey and Billy, both barefoot, ran off to collect the pony then let out the sheep and cattle. Jack wanted them on ahead. As soon as they were ready, the boys set off, Davey walking in front of the Tuckers' own sheep and cattle. Billy, bareback, rode behind with the dogs.

"Too warm, right now." The heavy face, creased and running with sweat, grinned up at Katherine. Jason's hair had all but gone but his belly was there, lower and heavier perhaps, causing his legs to stick out further as balance and support. "Mark my words, there's a storm about somewhere." The shepherd wiped the worst from his red face. "Best stay close to they covers, m'dear." She had been sitting in the front of the large bow wagon for sometime, watching him moving from cart to cart checking the ropes and stays before talking to Jack.

Above her head the canvas cover was pulled taught over the metal bale hoops while behind and nestled securely in between two sacks lay Charles, asleep in his cradle, his face half hidden in Tilly Loosemore's lace bonnet. He was frowning, concentrating hard on something or other, his tiny fists balled tightly, and there he remained even as she started to rock him, humming quietly. But it came as an effort for she was puzzled, perhaps disconcerted, at why she felt so helpless. She should have been filled with the same sense of adventure as the others who seemed to have so much to do; yet, for her, there was nothing. Jack, Jason Hawkins and Ralph Rudd, Lorna's son, had refused to let her get involved. She believed them at first when they said it was because of the baby, but she noticed Jason's deference towards her and Ralph's shyness. She was in the way, of that she was certain, and had been put in the cart where she would come to no harm.

Charlotte was in her element. She had watched her chatting easily and laughing with the others as they swung boxes and pieces of furniture onto the carts. Even Grace climbed nimbly up and down the front of the tall wagon, while she, herself, had staggered and almost fallen before pulling herself aboard breathlessly and catching her clothes. They had told her to sit there with the baby but that was the excuse and she wondered why they felt she was so inadequate.

She had grown to love Badgercombe. She loved the warmth and peace of the cottage and the thought of leaving it all and the village life saddened her. Jack had taken her out to Sherdon and she had seen, at, once, how things were going to be different. There would be no village, no windows or doorways from behind which to peep, no chattering children or dusty streets. No longer would she be able to sit in the sun and listen to the distant church bells, or hear the screams of the swifts as they twisted and raced overhead. Although it had been June with the moors at their best, the wild, bare expanse of the country surrounding the half-built farm had been daunting. There was an emptiness up there she had not detected before.

They had stopped at Sandyway where she met Hardy and was introduced to Luke Harper. Jack had not seen him for two years or more and she smiled at the memory of how they had greeted each other. The landlord and smuggler fascinated her but there was no common bond. Their craggy faces and hard, lean bodies seemed so much more in keeping with the elements of the high moors while she hated the very idea of the wet and the cold, even at Badgercombe.

Wilmot had come to see them soon after the birth. She had forgotten he was so much shorter than Jack but broader and his features were darker but, for all that, no one could have mistaken the fact that they were brothers. She had seen the delight on his face as he held his young nephew and how he had chatted excitedly with his brother and sister about their future. But when they had been alone she noticed his concern especially when he asked her outright if she thought she would be happy at the farm. His intensity and earnestness unsettled her and she wondered if he knew something they had kept from her. Later, when he relaxed, they had talked about literature and just two weeks ago he had brought a green leather-bound box of books, promising to come out to Sherdon and change them.

✳

"All ready, my love?" She started as Jack's hand pressed her thigh. "That's it…off soon." His hand remained and their eyes met. "Hey, now. What's up?" he jumped onto the footboard and crouched beside her. "Not afeared, are you?" he asked softly. "Not worried nor nothing?" She shook her head and tried to smile.

"No…" her voice wavered. "I just feel so…so utterly useless. Look at me…you've sent me to sit up here, to keep out of the way. Honestly, Jack." Katherine leant against him wearily. "Everyone else is dashing about, even your mother…look at her." She glanced up as he stroked her hair. "I'm meant to be one of the family, you know, not some sort of…of, oh, I dunno." Her head shook sadly. "No, it's nothing…I'll be fine." Jack remained where he was, one hand behind her neck, his fingers kneading her gently.

"'Twon't be long, dear." He bent and kissed her forehead. "As soon as we're in, we'll get settled. It's going to be your house at Sherdon. Up to you to say what goes where…you know that." He turned at Jason's shout.

"What's *that*?" he cried suddenly and turned. "*What*? Right, hang on a minute." He kissed her again and jumped to the ground.

*

Less than an hour later they were on their way. Jack set the pace in the covered bow wagon pulled by the six brown oxen. There was no talk, just the crunch of gravel and stones under the iron rims of the heavy wide wheels.

Behind them Ralph Rudd drove the first farm cart. Charlotte rode with him while Jason Hawkins followed, driving the two horses pulling Farmer Rumbelow's cart. As the covered wagon turned to cross the bridge at the end of the lane Katherine stood to see better, holding on to one of the hoops for support. She craned her neck, standing on tiptoe to catch the last sight of the home that had meant so much.

She stared at their bedroom window, as usual half hidden by the virginia creeper, already turning red just as it had been when she first saw the cottage. It was there, behind the little half-covered window, that their first tiny child had been born. The little one had not lived but they had been blessed with a second, born in the same room and now he, like the rest of them, was leaving the home that had done them so well. Grace stood beside her and she felt the older woman's arm around her waist, knowing that she had read her thoughts.

"It's funny really," Katherine gazed back into the warm, brown eyes. "I never felt like this when leaving Blagdon but here…Badgercombe's been so friendly. It's just as a home should be, just what it should feel like…and so much has happened."

"I know, dear, I know…it's difficult just now. But try to look ahead, to see what's coming." She steadied herself and caught Katherine's elbow. "Come, now. Best take Charles inside, into the shade. 'Tis too hot already."

The great clouds, white at first, built up behind them as they climbed the track out of Twitchen. By midday what little breeze there was had dropped. The clouds, now black and menacing, had swollen into towering columns piled high, one on top of each other, blotting out the sun whose rays reached out helplessly from behind. "Goin' to catch it soon," Jack called over his shoulder. "Leave the front open 'til the last moment…it's going to be heavy and there'll be a wind, too, most likely." Jason had been right. Moments later she heard the first heavy drops tapping against the covers as the hot wind blew eddies of dust and dried leaves into the air.

The gold and purple flash came first but only just. It was the tearing, splitting crack followed by the deep boom of thunder that woke the baby as the patter of drops increased to a hiss on the canvas before rising to a roar. She heard herself shout with fright as the wind suddenly hit the side of the cart, buffeting it violently and sending sprays of icy water through gaps in the canvas.

"Here, take this." Grace was on her feet, her hair already plastered to her face and her clothes wet through. She saw her slip as she threw the empty sack. "Put it over your shoulders...your *shoulders,*" the old lady shouted before stumbling backwards again as the wagon rocked wildly.

"Mother...*mother*. Here, take the reins will you." Jack forced back the front cover. Water was streaming down his face and he was gasping at the sudden cold. Katherine could see he was worried. Behind him lightning rippled and flashed across the black sky. "We're turning down the steep," he was shouting above the noise. "An' I'm going to walk in front of the bullocks or they'll run away with themselves."

Suddenly she was on her own, clutching the baby and struggling to sit in the dim light of the swaying, rolling wagon. Every time it lurched, water poured through the joins in the canvas, soaking her and their belongings. Twice she tumbled, once heavily when she grazed her arm. For what seemed an eternity she was slithering and falling, clutching wildly to support herself and protect her child.

Not until they had crossed the river and begun the long climb up past the cottage did the thunder rumble away, grumbling to itself, and the wind, now fresh and cool, begin to ease. When Grace at last tore back the cover, Katherine was standing half-crouched and blinking with the baby in her arms. The sun had returned and the world appeared as though it had been washed clean again. And there, with its stonework glistening wet, was the farm behind a curtain of steam rising from the sedge below the house.

She sat back against the high, wooden side of the cart and for a moment closed her eyes. She had lost her shoe and her arm hurt where she had knocked it but they were there. The carts had finally stopped. She took the baby's raised hand playfully between her teeth and smiled down on him, quite happy to remain as she was. But there was work to be done and they would be waiting for her, Jack had told them that.

"*Daaavey.*" Katherine jumped. Charlotte had left her cart and was standing just the other side of the canvas with her hair and clothes layered against her body and her fists clenched on her hips. "Where's Jack, mother? Did yer see that fella over there with the boys?" She swung round anxiously, looking up at them. "Mother, did yer see him? Katherine, no?" She started forward purposefully with both arms swinging. "Don't want they boys 'aving nothing to do with strangers up 'ere. There's too many tales of this an' that."

Then they saw him in the distance. He was dark like Wilmot and had much the same build. She could see that her husband had been expecting him and watched as they walked slowly together talking, before he pointed in their direction.

✳

120

"O'Hara, ma'am. Declan O'Hara's t'e name." He held out his arms to Grace. "'Twas a terrible tempest, to be sure. Here, now, take my hand, t'em both if you wish." Katherine glanced suspiciously. Even allowing for the thick stubble and the weather beaten face, the features were dark and gypsy-like, the eyebrows and long eyelashes as black as night. But it was the eyes that caught her attention. They were blue, a startling blue: as he spoke so he smiled and the eyes danced.

"Here, ma'am," he held out his arms. "I'll take the wee bairn." Katherine blinked in surprise at the wink then shrank back from his hands, clutching her child defensively. "Come now, you're looking as though you're starin' at t'e very divil hiself." He lowered his arms then raised them again. "I'm the oldest of ten, ma'am, and know more about the ways of little people than any man should. Here now." He cradled the baby then let her down lightly. Only later, when Grace reminded them, did she remember what she had seen.

"There's something about the boy," the old woman said quietly, glancing furtively through the empty kitchen window. "Did you notice the dogs…'specially Glen? See how he behaved?" Grace looked at the others. "You know what he's like usually with strangers. Goes for them, just like that…real savage sometimes. But he wouldn't leave that Irish boy alone, just like a puppy he was. And the pony, Cherry. Did you see her? Followed him as though he had a head collar on her."

"I dunno," Charlotte stood back from the freshly lit fire. "If 'alf the things they say about that lot are true, even 'alf, then there's trouble out there somewhere. 'Ee's best where 'e is, outside in the barn…an' even that's a mite too close."

Chapter Eight

"But I couldn't." The room was silent and the two sat looking at one another. It seemed as though there could be no alternative and Frederic shook his head. "It'd be nothing less than blatant robbery." Without waiting for her reply, he took a draught of the watery beer, taking care to hide the taste.

"Oh, don't be silly, Freddy. We've simply got to face facts." Katherine got up and walked across to the window. "We've talked round and round the subject for weeks now, and it's got us absolutely nowhere."

Frederic settled back into the threadbare sofa and glanced at her silhouetted against the afternoon sun. Even now she looked magnificent but rural life had begun to take its toll. She was thirty-four, only a year older than himself but the little creases had started to appear when she smiled. And why not? She had no potions or creams to feed her skin, no protection from the frequent wind or the sun whenever it shone. When they met he had been amazed at the strength of her grasp and the roughness of her hands. Her leather bootees were worn through and the hem of her skirt, even where it had been taken up, was stained and frayed.

She had greeted him with her usual warmth and friendly smile, but he had sensed a wistfulness about her. Wilmot had told him how much she enjoyed their visits and they both recalled her melancholy when it was time for them to go. It was not easy and he was never quite sure how to react. Wilmot felt the same.

"We've all been doing our sums and it just does *not* add up," she insisted. "We're simply running out of money." He could detect the worry in her voice. "It simply can*not* be done all at once…it's impossible. Come on, Freddy, think about it," she rounded on him aggressively. "Jack's been ploughing solidly for three weeks now…he hasn't had a break…and there's still a mass of other work to do besides. It's been piling up. Burning off all that sedge and heather took much longer than any of us expected.

"And once he's finished the ploughing, he's got to harrow it all…*then* lime it. And that's going to be a killer, almost two cart loads for every acre dragged all the way up from the coast. And *then*," her voice rose, "Then, if all *that's* not enough, once he's done that, he's got to put in the roots. Honestly, it's a massive undertaking. We won't be putting any stock on the fields for at *least* two years…three probably, maybe more. Even I can see that."

She turned at a noise in the yard and watched the two boys on the pony, lifting her head and stretching to see them disappear round the corner. "If the sheep are going to arrive next week they'll have to go out on the high pasture. Then what?"

She turned back to Frederic. "What happens when winter really sets in? What are they going to live off?" She shrugged and let her arms fall back to her side. "Thin air? They can't survive out there on nothing…nor the horses…or the cattle. They need fodder, and lots of it. And so do *we* for God's sake…there'll be nothing in the garden until May at the earliest."

"But can't I lend you the money, instead?" he leaned forward. "I mean, these are heirlooms. Look." He opened the felt bag, spilling just her ruby and pearl necklace and the matching gold bracelet and earrings into his hand. "Van Damens'll pay hundreds of guineas for them, hundreds. How old are they? Two hundred years? For goodness sake, Katherine. It'd be mad to part with them…*mad.*"

"No it's not…not at all. For a start, a loan's right out of the question…it only puts off the evil day. We've gone through all that already. In any case you can't afford it…can you?" Katherine stared at him. "Well, can you? Come on, you've told us how things are with you…and the whole estate for that matter. If the mines were up and running it would be different but they're not. Honestly, Freddy." She sat next to him and took his hand. "You've got huge financial worries yourself…so where's this wonderful loan coming from?" She bent forward, toying absently with the jewels. "Your brothers? The banks?" She knew he had to agree.

"I'm afraid the facts are staring us in the face," she continued. "It's no good even thinking of making money out of a farm up here while it's still being created…*hacked* out of the wilderness. It's going to take years…*years,* and I don't care what Maxwell or anybody else says. And even then, even when the income starts to drip in, there's heaps more to do…and the markets are miles away." She threw her hands in the air, slapped the sofa and stood.

"But what about Jack…?"

"He'll never know, and don't you dare tell him. Not *one* word." He was surprised at the sharpness of her tone. "The poor love's got more than enough to worry about. And, in any case…he doesn't know I brought my jewellery down with me."

"*What?*" Frederic gasped. "You mean you…"

"Yes, I'm afraid so," she caught his look. "It was my idea…nobody else knew. They're here, tucked away where no one'll ever find them, for just this sort of thing. Anyway," she sighed heavily. "It doesn't really matter, honestly…it couldn't matter less. There won't be too many grand occasions up here, will there? It'd be nice if there were but…" her voice trailed off forlornly and she pulled a brave face. "It's wonderful here, really it is… but sometimes I just long for…oh…well, company. Yes…I suppose that's it. A few friends to laugh and chat with."

Suddenly Frederic was on his feet and standing over her. She looked at him in surprise, searching his face to see why he had moved like he had. "You *are* managing, aren't you?" he reached for her hand. "I know I've asked you several times before but I hate to see you like this. I...we all worry about you, Katherine...all of us...Lizzie, Charles...even Wilmot, and I've got to know him very well."

Katherine lowered her head. "I *do* love it here," she murmured. "And that's the truth. I adore Lottie. She's great fun and's always saving me from something or other. And Grace and Ralph and the boys...and Jack, of course, bless him. He's been marvellous...quite wonderful." She smiled suddenly at Frederic's look of concern. "Believe me," she urged. "I'm fine, really, but I do so look forward to seeing you and the others. You'll come out from time to time, won't you, Freddy? Please say you will." She glanced down at the hand holding hers, patted it softly and smiled before releasing it gently.

"Yes." He had to clear his throat. "Yes of course I will." He had wanted desperately to keep hold of her hand but dare not. It would be his privilege and a pleasure to ride out to see her but it was going to hurt. Each time he saw her it hurt a little more.

✳

Before leaving the farm, Frederic rode out to where Jack was working. The big plough was biting deep into the soil and he could see that he was struggling to hold the line behind the two oxen. Katherine had said it all...creating the fields was going to be a slow and tortuous process. It would be years of hard work before the grass they had to sow would be able to support stock the year round, and time enough after that before the farm became viable.

"The sheep are due next week, Jack," Frederic dismounted and undid his coat. "The *'Glendower's'* coming in to Ilfracombe towards the end of the week. We'll put the shepherds into Lower Sherdon. There'll be two of them...Little and Gourlay, both from Scotland." He waited until Jack had secured the rope lines.

It was then that the thought came to him. How it came into his head he had no idea but it sounded as though he had planned it well. "And, listen, I've arranged for the winter feed to be brought in...all of it...for the sheep, cattle and the horses, the whole lot. There's room enough about the place. If we can do that, d'you reckon you can see the hard months through?" Jack slapped the rump of the nearest beast before turning and leaning against it.

"Aye, sir," he kicked out at a piece of loose earth then unrolled his sleeve to wipe his face. "As long as the fodder's here we'll be fine. If we're talking about lambing in April, the rams'll be going in soon." Jack thought quickly, working backwards. "Next two, three weeks as it so happens and if it's cheviots and blackface that're coming down, they'll be wintering up top. They'll have to," he laughed. "There's room in the shippens for the cattle and horses but that's about all."

He thrust his hands into his pockets and looked at Frederic who he could see was studying him. "It's been a devil of a race against time, you know," he muttered. "Too fast, really. The days are beginning to draw in now an' the weather won't hold for much longer." It sounded as though he was complaining but he wasn't. Frederic nodded, snatching at his hair in the wind. "We'll manage 'cos I've got a good team, even so it's difficult to know what's got to be done first. Ralph's up on the high ground right now, burning off the next group of fields and Declan's away for more lime...a good young lad by the way. Even the two littl'uns have gone down to Badgercombe for more wood. There's none up here for miles..."

"Listen, Jack." It was Frederic who broke the awkward pause. All he had seen today bit deeply into his conscience. It was as though he had sent in his friends only for them to become his slaves; the sheer graft and toil of it all appalled him. "D'you think it's really going to work out? Can it be done?" he put a hand on his shoulder. "I mean *you*...not just the work, but Katherine and the family?" Jack looked past him, wondering if he had asked her the same thing. He wagered he had and was just as sure she would have shrugged it off.

"How's she coping?" Frederic felt his friend tense, perhaps he thought he was intruding.

"We're all finding it hard just now, sir. All of us. But I know what you mean...and thanks for that. She's grand." Their eyes met and he smiled. He could see he was concerned as he always was. "No, Lottie and mother're seeing to her. She'll be all right. But what about *you*...yourself, sir," he nodded. "How're things with you?"

"Hell's own," Frederic laughed bitterly. "They're all after me...the banks, not Durnford Morgan thank the Lord, but the rest of the pack. And I can't even find tenants that'll stay on the farms. Another lot have gone, that old couple couldn't take a second winter. They're *all* agin me...family, banks, everyone. I told you about the family, didn't I?" Jack cocked his head.

"They're all wanting their share of the estate and by yesterday at that...all of 'em, shouting and screaming for their income from the farms. I've *got* to strike it lucky with the mines...simply got to. Wilmot's doing what he can but the damned stuff's elusive and I've had to call a halt to all father's old plans. The railway and the canal, that sort of thing...all those grand ideas of his."

It was hard for them all; both could see it yet the difficulties seemed to bind them together. The worse the situation, the closer they became, yet somewhere there had to be a break.

2

Jack's chestnut gelding, Larkspur, lifted his head. For a second he stopped chewing and listened with his ears cocked, then made his way slowly through the heather towards the farm. A few moments earlier the three ponies had done the same while, behind them, Farmer Rumbelow's two draught horses followed more slowly. It was as if they had all been called in, or drawn by the swish of oats in a bucket.

Billy Westcott looked at Davey. His eyes were wide with astonishment. *"There,"* he whispered. "Told you, didn't I? *There...listen."* Davey squeezed past him and looked through the dung window at the far end of the shippon.

"Yeess," he breathed, standing on tiptoe. "Listen, he's playing that sad one. You know...the slow one they all like."

"Come on, then." Billy pulled at his sleeve. "Let's go and ask him. Jack said we should." At first Declan did not see them, it was the horses who gave them away and he stopped playing. The boys had crouched in the ditch under the hedge to watch the animals, now gathered round the Irishman. Two threw their heads in the air and squealed with their ears back, but the rest were looking at him, as if they were waiting for the whistle. One of the draught horses pushed her way through and stood just feet from him, head lowered and breathing heavily; curious but unafraid.

"Chk, chk, chk, chhk." Declan rose from the bank and walked amongst them talking quietly, stroking one and feeling the mouth of another. "Tck, tck, tck, tck." Ralph Rudd's pony, always nervous to catch, stood patiently then lifted his head when O'Hara leant forward to rub his face against its muzzle.

"Wow." Davey gasped as the Irishman swung himself lightly onto the pony's back. "Look at that, Billy. No one's done that. Never...not even Jack." Still talking quietly Declan nudged the animal forward, the others following, stopping only when they saw the two boys.

"Ah, 'tis gone...away on the wind." Declan tossed his hands in the air, slid from the pony then ran across to settle beside them under the newly made hedge. "They're happy enuff, op here" he grinned. "Least that's what they've been telling me." He looked at Billy, now staring open mouthed, and ruffled his hair. "'Tis an old oirish secret...but true. True as I'm here today, so cross me heart." He slipped the whistle into the lining behind his waistcoat pocket. "Me granfer was taught boy a tinker from Tralee. Passed it down to me, so'e did. Said I had the charm."

"What was that you were saying to them?" Davey nodded slowly and blushed. "Something funny, wasn't it, Declan?" He glanced at Billy for support. "You were talking all strange, different like."

"A little bit o' Gaelic, so it was," Declan winked. "'Tis t'e language o' the bogs. The little people speak it, and the ponies at home talk back to 'em."

"Will you say some more...*now*? Go on, Declan." Billy tugged his sleeve. "Say something...*please*."

"Yes, go on, Declan. Let's see if they can hear you. Talk to them."

"Away with yer, now," O'Hara got to his feet. "Some other time, maybe...when there's something to be said."

Only Charlotte remained dubious about the Irishman. The boys begged Jack to let him have a room in the house. Grace asked also and even Katherine relented. "It's getting colder now," she urged. "Couldn't we find him a space somewhere, even in the loft perhaps?"

"Well, it's him or me." Charlotte leant back against the sink with her arms folded defiantly. "Once we let one in, there'll all be here. They're all over the place, living here and there, fighting an' carrying on...sleepin' rough an' that. And we've heard what they get up to." She crossed to the kitchen table and lifted the cooking pot. "Just listen to Hardy Cockram...hear what he's got to say. *No*...Mr Declan O'Hara's fine where he is. Takes his meals with us, then's got his own place above the cows. 'E's got his bed and his blankets...and a washbasin. That's enough."

It was Declan, not Jack, who taught the boys about life on the moors, warning them to note how the herds of native ponies, the little ones with the mealy mouths and cream-coloured bellies, moved before the weather changed, and to watch for signs of deer in the combes. October, he told them, when the swallows had flown and the curlews had gone back to the estuary, was the time of the rut, when the stags fought for the hinds.

"Steer well clear, now," he advised, wagging a finger. "They're worse than the fighting oirish, that's for sure. One minute he'll run, the stag that is, then suddenly he'll turn...change his mind, just like that." He clicked his fingers. "Quick as a blink, he'll be turned about an' facing yer. Then look out...he'll paw t'e ground like a bull, toss his head in the air and scchheeew." O'Hara clapped his hands. "He'll be on to you like a mad thing, he will. And they're still looking for the fella that can run faster than a stag. No man can do that...and you won't be the first."

✳

The route to Withypool school followed the Barle past Landacre Bridge then onto the high ground before dropping down once more into the woods along the river bank. By now the first autumn winds had begun to strip the leaves from the trees and the bracken was turning. Colour had faded from the heather. Jack and Ralph had given themselves the two months before Christmas to sow the roots.

Billy was cupping his hands and blowing as Davey had shown him how. The two ponies, reins loose over their necks, were walking side by side as their riders chatted and laughed together. The wind had dropped so the bracken by the corner of the wood should never have moved.

But it did. "Billy," Davey called his name quietly. "Billy, look…a stag, no two." The first animal, a young male, trotted onto the track less than a hundred yards away and stood looking at the boys. "Stop, Billy," he warned. "He's not frightened like he should be." Davey had pulled up. He remembered Declan and could see his finger warning them. *"Billy, stop!"*

"Rubbish. It's only a young'un, no more'n a pricket. Come on." Billy looked over his shoulder, beckoning. "Come on, cowardy. Let's get on…oh, come *on*."

"Stop!" The shout was too late even as the young stag barked a warning and disappeared. The beast that stepped onto the track in its place and whose flanks were covered in mud, lifted its head and blew loudly, scenting the air. There was foam around his mouth and the nostrils flared wide. The stag, as tall as the pony, with his pointed antlers spread wide and high, blew heavily a second time then pawed the ground and turned towards Billy. As it broke into a trot, Billy's pony turned and reared up before putting his head down and bolting

Even as Billy was tumbling, Davey's heels drove into his pony's flanks and he was waving the sack he had snatched from around his shoulders. "Roll into the ditch, Billy," he yelled. "Roll. Go on…I'm coming…" The stag stopped and turned to face him then snorted but Davey raced at the animal still screaming and whirling the sack around his head. For a moment the creature stood uncertain. Then it sprang from the track. "Get up, Billy. Quick…jump up, there's more, I heard them in the bracken." Davey reached down to help.

"Got, me?"   "Yes."   "Quick, kick hard."   "I can't."   "Hang on." "I'm trying to."

"Come on, pull… pull hard. That's it, hang on."

The tears came later. "Don't say nuthin' to anyone, will yer?" Billy pleaded. "Not to the others. Don't tell nor anything."

"C'mon, Billy. 'Tis…'tis…'tis nort, nort at all. Did yer think I would leave yer lying…lying there like that. You didn't, did yer? I could never have done that…*you* wouldn't 've."

3

Three weeks after the sheep arrived Jack decided to kill two of his own, one for the farm, the other to barter with his neighbours. Hardy Cockram had told him how things were done on the moor and it was the same as back in Twitchen.

Harry Fisher from Ferny Ball, a mile down stream, had been to the farm already. He and his daughter Gaile, a slim, doe-eyed girl two years older than Davey, had come with him, riding bareback and dressed in boy's breeches. The boys shunned her at first but she knew the moor well and even Jack was impressed with her riding. "Don't go round joking about 'er just 'cos she's a girl," he laughed. "I watched her go down over the steep the other day, cracking on she was too. I'd be proud to ride like that meself and her could teach you boys a thing or two. You want to watch 'er and learn…not go messin' around."

"Us 'ave got the mill at the farm." Fisher, stocky and bow legged with bushy, black eyebrows had been born in Withypool where his elder brother had taken the mill after his father. He had met Jack earlier but this was the first visit to Sherdon and Katherine had left them sitting round the kitchen table.

"'T'ain't worth going all the way down there for that, so us grinds the corn up yer abouts. Easier that way. Now then," he tipped back his dirty felt hat, the one with jays' feathers stuffed in the band, and set about relighting his clay pipe. "If you can let us 'ave two stones of fresh lamb…then we'll see about they crushed oats and the flour…and the winter greens." Fisher lifted his wrinkled face and exhaled, then coughed. "That's so long as they last, that is." It was a fair deal.

✳

A week later Cockram took Jack to Sandyway Farm. At first old Jeremiah Gillard had not wanted to see them until he learned they went to Withypool church each Sunday. "Ah, yessir," he wheezed, struggling for breath. "Never mind whom they pray with, so long as they fear the Lord and respect His day." Jack stood restlessly. He had not come for this and he looked away from the old man's one good eye. "Sometimes the minister comes to preach an' sometimes it's me. Yessir." He stopped to suck in more air. Anna, his wife, and Arthur, his son who farmed the land joined them, agreeing that Jeremiah would do their shoes and boots. "Us can settle up later on," he beamed cheerfully. "Anna here'll keep the book an' us'll see how it goes, but a stone of good lean meat, well…'tis the usual start." Jack went next to The Sportsman where Hardy wanted some lamb. He would be paid well, the landlord promised. It might take a week or two, a month maybe but when it came it'd be worth the wait.

Luke was there and Jack knew he wanted to talk. "Be on yer guard, man," he said eventually. Only Hardy Cockram was left in the room with them. "There's word about that Braddon's riding again…working the Exford road, down Landacre Bridge way." He paused but his eyes remained fixed and steady. "Word is that 'e knows you're the man what cut 'im up rough that day."

"'Tis true, Jack…true an' all," the landlord nodded. "Someone's let on to 'im an' that's fer sure. He and another, they're after anything that's going…dogcarts, traps, folks on their feet and the like." Jack saw Cockram was serious; Luke, too, but the smuggler had said enough. "'Tis getting bad up here what with the sheep

129

gangs, an' all. More'n fifty were taken on Molland Moor. Seems as though the more folk're about, the more trouble there is. Us needs to keep an eye open. Don't forget where you are at Sherdon, mind," the landlord warned. "Way out on yer own there…just you and yer wimin. Young Rudd's no more'n a boy. And the Irish lad? Ha," the great man shrugged dismissively. "Think on it, Jack…think carefully now."

Jack took no chances: he couldn't afford to. Braddon and others would go for him if they could. He showed Ralph Rudd and Declan how to use his swords, sending them in with whoever went to the markets at Withypool or Exford. Luke pressed a musket and two pistols on him. They were old but well oiled. Jack sniffed the wooden stock, then examined the metalwork. "French, yes?" he looked up and grinned. "That's French oil fer sure."

"Aye, well…just say the fella didn't want to let go of 'em…best leave it like that. Nor these, neither." The bag swung heavily, almost falling through his hands. "Two hundred, Jack…the best lead balls there are. And two horns of powder, American grain. Teach 'em well, boy. Like you was taught yerself. Only one man wins, remember…the second man's dead." He left his stool to close a chink in the curtains. "Same for you, lad…keep yer own hand in, too. Never think you're too busy for that."

He knew the smuggler was right.

4

The three horsemen pulled up at the crest of the track to Sherdon. One turned his collar against the strong westerly breeze as another snatched at his horse when it reached down to pick at grass. The farm, less than half a mile away, was half hidden by the mist. Only the faint outline of buildings was visible. "They're in, that's for sure." The leading rider stood in his stirrups and turned to his companions. "Smoke from the chimney and more at the back of the yard…there look…the varmits."

"Let's try the house first." The second rider, a well dressed, dark haired man, grinned at the idea. "Wait t'you see the look on their faces…but it's their own fault, damn 'em." The man at the back laughed and the three rode on.

✳

It was Charlotte who saw them first. "'Ere, Katherine. Not 'specting no one, are we?" She stared from the bedroom window. "Three riders look." Katherine bent to see but the group had dropped into a dip. They reappeared much closer, riding fast, three abreast. She stiffened and grabbed Charlotte's arm.

"Oh, my God…*no*." She stared at Charlotte. "Lottie," she gulped, then grabbed at her. "Lottie," her voice was an urgent whisper. "Get Charles and get into the kitchen…quick."

"Whatever's..."

"Just *do* it," she cried. "Do as I say, *now*. I'll tell you...when I'm down. *Listen*," her eyes were wide, both hands clutching Charlotte's shoulders. "That's my brother, Herbert, and Kenton Knight and it can only mean trouble. Lock the doors quick, *quick*...and don't move. Don't answer their knocks. Go on, Lottie. *Run*."

＊

"Nothing doing." Preston leant down once more and hammered on the door with the bone handle of his crop. The hollow sound echoed throughout the still of the house. "If they're here then they've run scared." He turned his horse and followed the others.

Jack had killed and skinned the sheep two days previously, leaving buckets under the carcasses to collect the blood. One had been cut up and was lying under a muslin cloth on the trestle table. The two fleeces had been stretched and salted then hung from a beam. The air was thick with the warm, creamy smell of offal and the sharp tang of tobacco. Those waiting had been talking quietly but fell silent as the riders approached. Somebody coughed.

"*So*...and what's all this? Just what have we got here?" Kenton Knight led the way, peering from face to face until he saw Jack. "Aha...*Tucker*." He savoured the word. "I thought as much. Tucker the groom, then Tucker the farmhand...now Tucker the butcher, eh? And who's sheep are these, might I ask?" He stood in the saddle, flicked out the tails of his coat, then rode closer. "And what the hell's going on here...on one of our farms?"

"Just cutting up the sheep, Master Kenton. My own sheep, no more'n that." He stepped forward, wiping his hands.

"*Mister Knight*, to you, Tucker. *Mister* Knight and let there be no mistake."

"Damned right." Edgar Mason, the third rider, dismounted. "There's a stench of villainy about the place, Knight...an' sheep stealing at that. I've seen it before, my friend." His horse backed towards the group by the table forcing a dog to slink away. "Straighten them out, my friend. Go on...sort 'em out."

"No, no," Jack turned at Cockram's angry growl. "'Tis all right, Hardy," he nodded. "Steady now, friend...steady." He smiled briefly. "No, sir," he squared up to Mason. "They're me own sheep. Born and bred here at Sherdon."

"Show me, Tucker. Where's the proof?" Kenton Knight nodded towards the carefully rolled fleeces. "Here, I s'pose," he scowled contemptuously. "Open them up. Let's see your mark on them. *You*," he pointed at Arthur Gillard. "Open'em up and show me...if they're there to see."

131

"Won't find nothing there, sir. 'Twas on their heads, a coloured mark but now the heads are burned, along with th' offal out there. Be'ind the barn, sir."

"So...*no* evidence to say they're yours. Eh?" Kenton Knight came up to Jack who held his stare. The face was fuller, more flesh around the collar than before but the eyes were the same cold, humourless eyes of old. "Yours, eh? What rot...what putrid, foul-mouthed *rot!*"

"Yer pardon, sir," Harry Fisher stepped forward. "Yer pardon, like, but 'tis the way things're done, here. Ye see, sir, they..."

"Hold hard, damn you." Knight spun round and pointed with his crop. As he did so, his heavy, dark green redingcote swung open. "This farm's no public charity. It belongs to my family and is part mine. *Mine*," he tapped his chest. "So just hold your tongue."

Jack caught Luke's arm, then turned to bar his way. "Steady, man. Steady now," he hissed as the smuggler tried to push his way towards the new arrivals. "'Tis best left to me. Stay calm."

"*So*, Tucker," Knight's hands were on his hips. "It's theft, is it not? And you can't prove otherwise, can you now? Plain theft and you're the one. What say you to that?"

"'Tis not true, sir. All of us here know that and..."

"*To hell it is...damn* you." The shout was high-pitched, just as he remembered at Simonsbath. "We've caught you at it. Look at your hands, covered in blood. Don't lie to me. Hey, Herbert," he shouted to Preston. "Ever seen a thief caught red handed like this? Ha, Tucker, I've got you at last...at *last*. Haven't I just!" Knight cocked his head. "Know what they do to sheep thieves, Tucker? Eh?" He sneered at those by the table. "They hang 'em, Tucker...hang 'em high, so they do. Make 'em swing."

"Just a minute, Kenton," Preston rode up behind Knight. "Look...not so fast, old thing...."

"*Pah!*" Knight grimaced. "What's to fear here...with this lot? I've waited a long time for this. By the Almighty, so I have...a very long time indeed."

"'Tis no use, sir," Jack cleared his throat. "They're me own sheep and that's all there's to it." He waved his arm. "All the witnesses a man could want. You're wrong, sir, and badly wrong at that."

"Tucker," Kenton Knight had lowered his voice. "You're a *thief*, and you're a liar. D'you hear? A thief and a liar...and damn you for that."

"Knight." Lord Preston's voice was raised anxiously. "That's enough, old thing. Quite enough. There're other…"

"Hold hard, Preston. Hold hard" Mason interrupted. He was a lean man, with a thin head and narrow, lidded eyes. "Let Knight speak for goodness sake. Let him have his say for there's truth enough in it all." Jack caught his bridle and pushed the horse to one side.

"Is that a charge, Mister Knight? Or is it a challenge against my honour?" He half turned and held out an arm to steady the angry voices behind him.

"All *right,"* Kenton Knight straightened himself. "If that's the way you want it to be." He took off his glove and threw it at Jack's feet. *"Yes,* and so be it, Tucker. I challenge your word…or whatever honour you've got. Pick me up, man…*if* you've the courage. Pick me up…or remain the coward you are. Huh."

The barn was very quiet. Jack felt all eyes on him. He paused, then took a deep breath. "Look, sir," he appealed. "Enough's been said, 'tis madness. There's no need for more. Surely us can…"

"See there," Knight crowed and pointed. "No courage…a coward as well if ever I saw one."

"Right," Jack snapped. "I'll take no more…not from you nor any man alive." He stooped, snatched up the gauntlet and glared at Knight. "Now, I've taken you up. We'll both of us appeal to the judgement of God…and it's to be all the way, Mister Knight. All the way, d'you hear me, man?"

As he strode up to Knight and held out the gauntlet, now shaking in his hand, someone behind him shouted, then another. His jaw was set. "And we'll fight with swords," he declared, looking his man up and down. "Rapiers…or cutlasses? 'Tis no matter to me. Your choice and your answer now, sir."

"Only peasants fight with cutlasses…rapiers it shall be. And where do you wish to take your chance, might I ask?"

"I'll think on it." Jack took a deep breath and blew slowly. "My man will inform you…be advised of that."

5

Hardy's knock woke him. For a moment he lay still, arms behind his head, surprised at how relaxed he felt. The last two weeks had been miserable. Perhaps he felt like he did because the aftermath of the challenge was now way behind him.

Charlotte had hurried into the barn as soon as Knight and the others had left, Davey having run to the house with the news. Harry Fisher and Arthur Gillard had tried to calm the distraught woman. "Needed to be done, m'dear," Fisher had taken hold of her. "Don'e worry about it, our Jack can handle 'eself. Luke'll see to that...eh Luke?"

"I'll be at the inn, Jack." Luke clapped him on the shoulder. "I'll be waiting for yer...send word for me there."

"We'll see you, Jack," Hardy Cockram, took both of his hands. "Good on yer, my boy. Good on yer, lad."

Grace had been weeping by the fire and Katherine was in their bedroom. "For God's sake, Jack." He felt her whole body shaking as she threw her arms around his neck. "D'you really have to go this far? Ralph, no Davey, said that it's...it's..." she looked up, choking with tears. "Said it's to be...the whole way...that's...to the end...the death. Oh, God, no. Please, Jack, no." His shirt muffled her loud sobs.

That first evening had been hard and he smiled wryly at the memory. Time and again, he explained, that it was he who had been insulted and Knight who had thrown down the gauntlet. There was nothing he could do, he told them, save withdraw, leaving Knight victorious and himself liable. The charges, when they followed as they surely would, would mean death by the rope or life in Tasmania.

"*Never, never, never.*" He had banged the table savagely, those around him sitting back stunned. "I'll never submit to such accusations, nor such a slur on our family name...my father's name. *Never.* D'you understand what's at stake here? No? Well *think*, damn you, *think.* 'Tis the *truth* that's at stake...the honest truth and our honour." They had never seen him like it before, not even his mother.

"Knight made the running and Knight has to withdraw...and he won't. He's nort but a vain, arrogant fool. Nothing will make the man see sense. He showed us all what he was and now he's stuck with it." His chest was heaving. "'Twas he who made the charges and 'tis he who has to live or die by what he said. *Nobody* but *nobody* says all that and makes a challenge, *then* expects a man to back down. No...never." The fist crashed down again.

✳

Frederic and Edward Knight called the next day, then James Acland. Dr Collyns rode in from Dulverton, Fred Loosemore and Jason from Twitchen. Wilmot came twice, Hector and Abel Tarr from Simonsbath and Parson Froude from Molland. All wanted him to stand aside but when he asked them how no one could answer him. Word was out that he had been publicly insulted and humiliated, then threatened and provoked. Word was that he had held back, kept calm even when the gauntlet was down. Even then he had held his peace. But word was also that when he had taken Knight up, there was a rage in his eyes and that he would never back down.

He fought only twice with Luke, first for more than two hours, then for less than half. "'Tis enough, Jack," the smuggler had saluted then taken his hand. "Can go on for ever like this and get no better. Your head'll get too full of worry, 'Tis there, Jack, all there…just need to stay calm." They had talked for a while then left it at that. "Fight extended, lad. Use yer reach to keep 'im at bay. Either he'll collapse in a funk or else try to rush you. Keep 'im at bay and watch his eyes, d'yer hear? Just like us 'ave always said."

Two days beforehand, Jack sent Ralph to Simonsbath. The rendezvous, the letter said, was to be at the two gates on Brendon Common, the time half before eight, dawn. Mr Tucker's seconds were to be Mr Luke Harper and Mr Hardy Cockram. The doctor, appointed by mutual consent, was to be Dr Baillie, assistant to Dr Collyns, and the Director of Combat, a Mr Jethro Swain, Master-at-Arms of The Royal North Devon Hussars. Mr Jack Tucker, the letter concluded, would be much pleased to see Mr Kenton Knight on the ground as appointed and as agreed.

*

"Can't see a way out of it." Sir George Gale sat back. "Witnesses by the handful." He waved at the letter in front of him. "Duelling's not yet illegal…frowned on by the Royal Court fer sure, but when a man's insulted and provoked like this then it has to be. All swear blind the boy was accused wrongly in front of family and friends…then had the challenge thrown at his feet…that's it." He raised his hands helplessly and let them fall again. Parson Russell pursed his lips. Frederic stared at the painting on the opposite wall and nodded. The two had met the magistrate in a final attempt to have the duel declared illegal. "Even that fellow Preston admits Kenton went too far. I'm sorry Freddy…very sorry, my boy. It must be hard for you, just now…hard indeed."

"Thank you, sir." Frederic pulled himself stiffly from the leather chair. As he extended his hand he smiled thinly. "It's my kinsman through and through, you know," he shook his head. "The man never knows when enough's been said. T'would have come some day, somewhere but…wish to God, 'twas not here and now."

"Come, Freddy." Jack Russell, speaking softly, took him by the arm. "Thank you, George. We know you did your best and were there a way you would have found it…but, no. Our thanks, my friend."

*

The last night had been spent at The Sportsman's and the two men left long before dawn. Ralph Rudd, who was to carry the news back to Sherdon, rode with them. The mist, thick in places, was damp; the ground, Jack knew, would be wet and slippery under foot. Several dogs barked as they clattered past Simonsbath Manor and turned up the hill. Jack peered at the lamplight already glowing through the windows of the house and the stable cottages beyond. He wondered how Knight had spent the evening before and what Mrs Strong had prepared them for breakfast. What, he wondered, would she be thinking; she and all the others.

On the last long climb up to the moorland, nobody spoke. Both gates had been opened wide and the line of coaches, some with lanterns still burning, were little more than boxes in the grey first light. Jethro Swain, dressed in the Hussar's black and green patrol uniform called for Jack.

"Twenty minutes, sir. Time's tight and there's much to do. Show yourself to the doctor and check the ground if you like. Your man's here...over there by the horses." He pointed to the figure Jack knew to be Luke. "He's been marking your piste. 'Tis but fifteen paces each way an' no more'n that...should do the job nicely for us this morning." His smile was warm enough. "Organise yourself how you will, sir, then be here in fifteen minutes...the other's are by the coaches." Jack peered into the gloom and saw them. One of the shadows would be him. He could hear them talking. One called out, others laughed.

Dr Baillie was sterilizing his instruments and the weapons to be used. He paused, wiped his hands then took Jack by the shoulders. It did not take long. "No problems?" he queried, bending the wrist and elbow of the fencing arm.

"No, sir," Jack had been watching the doctor's soft pink hands but now he saw the line of instruments already laid out on the white cloth. Beyond the table the plain, pine coffin lay by the doctor's cab, its top open and ready. It would, he knew, be used within the hour for they were going all the way. He had insisted on it and felt his pulse quicken as he glanced at the two slim, steel blue rapier blades of tempered steel, their points honed needle sharp. 'Unbreakable,' Luke had warned him. 'Slip in through the flesh, ever so easy. Little or no pain, not like the slash an' cut o' the sabre.' Which one, he wondered, would he be holding and which of the two tips would be poised, dancing menacingly in front of his naked chest?

"Strip, gentlemen, please." Swain's voice sounded muffled in the mist yet the order was simple enough. "As we're goin' all the way it's strip right to the waist please, then street gloves and the silk wrists. Thank you, gentlemen. Five minutes called...just five minutes."

"Why all this?" Jack asked Baillie as the surgeon tightened the silk bandage around his wrist.

"The main arteries, lad. Aye, I know," he glanced at his frown. "All the way it might be but we can't have you dying from the loss of blood," he grinned encouragingly. "'Twouldn't be right, now, would it?" Jack stared at him, then glanced up.

Kenton Knight had approached and been watching. Now he nodded in recognition. His body looked heavy and Jack noticed the bulge above the waistband where the line of hair from his chest dwindled on the white belly. *'Never mind the body,'* Luke's voice again. *"Tis the eyes, Jack, the eyes that matter. See into them an' you'll see yer man."* The man was evil and Jack glared until he looked away.

"Gentlemen, please," Swain called them together. The final instructions were brief. "And now, gentlemen," he looked from one to the other. There was an air of *'irrevocabilite'* in his voice. "'Tis my bounden duty to ask you both if either would seek to withdraw…one final chance…after this 'tis too late…*no?"* Nobody spoke. "Right, gentlemen, 'tis left to the judgement of Almighty God."

"Take Post!"   "Salute!"   "Gentlemen…On Guard!"   "Fence!"

*

Knight had a plan, Jack saw that at once…and he could fence, too. His eyes were sharp and alert…his body finely balanced and his feet were moving well. The man was not going to fall apart, he was going to fight and fight hard. Jack parried, the tips of their blades scraping harshly. He parried again and feinted. Knight slipped his guard…Jack withdrew…then again. Suddenly Knight lunged and Jack jumped, but not quickly enough.

"Stop fighting!" Swain's rapier split the points of their swords. "Time out and see to the wound." Jack saw rather than felt the blood trickling down his forearm, wincing only when Baillie pressed home the iodine.

"Salute…On Guard…Fence!" Knight was confident. It was there in his eyes. They were hard, now glittering determinedly as he sought his final opening. He advanced swiftly, feinting and ducking as he came on, their blades clashing and ringing against each other's handguards. Jack parried, feinted and lunged, forcing Knight back. He could see the sweat running down the man's face. His eyebrows were scowling in concentration but the eyes still flashed brightly.

'Use yer reach,' Luke had warned on their way back from the doctor. *'Play him at length and he'll tire.'* But still he came on, this time ducking low and reaching up. Jack parried then slipped.

"Stop fighting. Time out and see to the wound."

It was the laughter coming from the group by the coaches that fired him. Even as Baillie was bandaging his forearm, Jack was impatient to return. The fops were lounging against the vehicles, watching him casually and mocking, joking amongst themselves with not a care in the world between them. He could sense their feelings; expectant and ready for the kill yet wrapped warm and safe against the morning chill. Bets on the outcome, he suspected, would have been wagered. Typical of that sort, typical of Kenton Knight's friends. Much longer out here and they would be bored. Not for them the stinging sweat or the flash of rasping blades. For them it was a morning of fun, the placing of bets, then a casual glance at the still warm body on the ground. Next round, perhaps, or the one after that?

"Salute...On Guard...Fence!" Knight rushed his swordplay. Jack had seen it coming. He drove forward then withdrew and backed away. "*Aaah,*" the man lunged to a cheer from his friends. Jack backed further, jumped back again then dropped, almost to one knee.

*

Even as he went down, he knew he had found his mark. His blade was waiting, poised and steady as the soft, white belly impaled itself further and further, sliding on so smoothly...just where the hairs came down from the chest. Jack had done all that he needed to do, used his reach and held his ground. The man was dead, even as he withdrew his blade.

"*Stop.* Stop fighting," The urgency in Swain's voice brought them running. "*Seconds...doctor...*quickly now." It did not take long. One deep cough and blood came from the mouth. The body twitched, then the legs then the feet last of all. The head turned and flopped to one side. The eyes stared but saw nothing. Everything was still.

Jack never felt the cloak Cockram put around his shoulders, nor heard Luke's words in his ear. He was leaning forward, hands on his knees, trembling and gasping for air, the sweat running freely. He saw Baillie look up and glance round, searching for Swain. Then the doctor shook his head. As the white sheet was pulled across the body, so Jack sank to his knees. He was spent, exhausted and tumbled forward retching violently.

Nobody looked round as Ralph Rudd spurred his horse down the road.

PART TWO

A Shadow in the Dusk
August 1850

Chapter Nine

"Ooops...mind away." Katherine lifted the tray higher in order to see the child.

"Ici, ma petite...Marie-Christine. *Attends, doucement!*" Lizzie leapt from the rug and ran to pull the toddler from under her sister's feet. It had taken the little girl almost a week to get over her shyness and run half naked with her cousins. Henry Tucker, now four, and Francis, almost three, had long since shed most of their clothes in the August heatwave, so turning their bodies nut-brown and their hair the colour of straw. Their feet were grey with dust and their mouths hidden behind circles of grime. Earlier there had been a rumble of distant thunder and now the sun bore down heavily.

The front porch of Sherdon opened directly onto the main yard so it had been Katherine's idea to clear the area behind the house. It was her escape from the world, her own haven of peace and quiet she told Declan and Ralph when they grumbled about having to lay flagstones and cobble around the well. The area of sheltered grass now grazed tight by the house goat had become something of a lawn, while the descendants of old Benny's seeds from Blagdon filled the beds under the wall.

There was little breeze, enough only to touch the tips of the tall foxgloves that stretched high above the clumps of blue cranesbill and bracken on the grassy knoll. From the tangle of dog rose that Jack had tied to the corner of the house a chaffinch called while, further away, a yellowhammer trilled plaintively in the afternoon heat.

"What's he saying, mama?" Henry pointed, frowning in concentration. "*Listen*, mama," he insisted. "That one over there. Papa says he's saying something when he sings like that. There."

"A little bit of bread and no...cheeeese." The two older children squealed with delight as their mother shook her head and bared her teeth.

"Chi-i-z," Marie-Christine copied her aunt then stopped abruptly with one finger in her mouth, overawed by the sudden attention she had aroused.

"Can we have some honey comb, mama? *Please?*" Henry begged, his eyes rolling from mother to aunt. "Or a piece of sugar cane? Can we?"

"No, that's for the others but you can share one of Lottie's cakes. Here look...but only if you're good." Katherine leant forward to wipe the worst from his mouth. "Charles'll be back from school soon and he's bringing his friends from Ferny Ball." The others pushed their way forward to where the spiced bun was being sliced. "Why don't you take the little ones and see if you can see them coming up the lane. And look after Francis. Go on," she waved her hand. *"Oh Henry...go on, dear. And keep your hats on."*

Lizzie, twice widowed and now La Comtesse de la Sainte du Massac-Seran, watched the three children picking their way over the cobbled yard. On her way, Marie-Christine squatted suddenly to discuss something with the little black cat that had come to greet her. "Five years...no *six*, isn't it?" She turned to her sister. "Six, since you've been living up here? What with Charles coming up seven now it must be nearly that. Goodness." She settled back onto the horse rug, placed Jack's straw hat over her face to shield her eyes from the sun then lifted her skirts to her thighs. "Where *does* the time go, for Heaven's sake?"

The two sisters rested side by side with only the yellowhammer to break their silence. A little over a year after Henry King's death in the South China Sea, Lizzie had announced her engagement to Count Henri-Marcel and the family had been delighted.

"It helped everyone to forget," her mother, the duchess, announced loftily, unable to disguise her delight at the string of titles, few of which meant anything to her. "Life's absolutely fine, marvellous...quite back to normal so it is. He's *such* a nice young man," she convinced her friends. "And those Huguenots are just like us, aren't they? Even more so...don't you think?"

It had not been quite so much fun when Lizzie had been removed from their London home to south west France in order for her husband to claim ownership of his uncle's Chateau Jonquieres outside Toulouse. Henri-Marcel, heir to one of the great cocagne dynasties, had introduced his young wife to the Toulousain society with a flourish causing her letters home to become ever shorter and less frequent.

But that adventure, too, had ended in tragedy. Just a year ago, Henri-Marcel, for many years a leading Pyreneean climber, had been killed. He, two friends and their guide, had been climbing high in the Circle de Gavarnie behind Lourdes when they had fallen, roped together, and tumbled for hundreds of feet down the ice and rock face. There had been no survivors and a week later he had been buried near their home in Lavaur's Cathedrale Saint Alain. Grief stricken and alone with her children, Lizzie returned home to England.

She had arrived at Sherdon almost two weeks ago, bringing three year-old Marie-Christine with her. Arnod, her son, now one and already ennobled, was at Blagdon with his nurse and her maids. The two sisters had been chatting endlessly for days bringing together the last six years of their lives. Lizzie looked well, Katherine noticed at once. The hips that had borne her children had broadened a touch but the couturiers of Paris had done their best with the silks and cotton patterns; only those who remembered her of old would be able to tell. Her skin, still the same pale peach under the tumbling hair, had remained unattected by her tragedies while her hands and feet remained as neat as ever they were. She was the just same, as the laughter in her eyes bore witness.

At first Charlotte had been wary of the visit, afraid that Lizzie, so elegant and now titled, and with so much to tell, would come between Katherine and herself, unsettling life's pattern. When the coach pulled into Exford the farm boys had been curious and silent. It had been Ralph who chatted away on the wagonette, winning the heart of little Marie-Christine when she sat in his lap as he drove with her mother beside them. Davey and Billy, riding as guards, glanced shyly at the finely dressed newcomer in her silk-gauged bonnet with her bone-handled parasol.

Lizzie remembered how they had all been standing in the cool of the kitchen when Jack's boots rang out on the stone floor. He had said nothing, just wiped his hands on his breeches before moving the two sisters together and standing back to look from one to the other. "Well…I don't know," he muttered. "'Tis difficult to tell, that's for sure. S'pose there're those about who might be able to tell one from t'other but 'tis mighty hard."

Then suddenly he had thrown his head back and shouted with laughter like he sometimes did, sweeping them up in his arms together. Grace had joined them then Charlotte in her own stumbling way. But, to Lizzie, La Comtesse, it mattered not. The family were Katherine's and, if Katherine loved them and they her, then so would she. Her bonnet had seemed ridiculous so she had taken it off and shaken her hair free.

✳

Banter and chatter at the table fascinated her and she was happy enough to sit listening quietly in particular to Jack as he held court. "So what did they say?" The man of the house held out his tankard for more beer. "Two years yet, I'll be bound. Two or three."

"No, just over a year," Davey and Billy answered together. "Us'll 'ave to wait 'til Davey's eighteen before us can join," Billy went on. "The officer said we could go back next spring tho' and join 'em for camp an' that. Just got to bring the 'orses like you had to, Jack. Remember?"

Jack nodded. "Didn't see Sergeant Major Fanshawe then?" His face creased at the thought of how the men of the Royal North Devons would have reacted to the man's promotion. For months, since after lambing when a detachment of the hussars had called at the farm, the two boys had been pestering Jack to let them sign on. A week ago he had relented, and yesterday, after a tearful farewell from

Charlotte, they had paid their first visit to the barracks at Ebberley Lawn.

"No, thank Heavens," Davey grinned. His eyes opened wide at the idea. "But they told us about 'im, didn't they, Bill. That fella in the stables, the one with the beard. He an' that other one, they told us. Sounds real bad, 'e does...scary too."

"Did you ask about Declan?" Lizzie half stood, stretching across for the salt. "You said he asked you to find out the other day." She had become intrigued by the closeness of life at Sherdon and now felt part of it. Everyone seemed to know what everybody else was doing and wanted to do. Problems were discussed freely with hopes and worries shared.

It was the same with their neighbours and already she felt involved with the community. In spite of the distances between the homesteads, hardly a day passed without someone calling about something or an offer of help, or news about this and that. It was, as Katherine said in her letters, so different to life at home. It was open and honest, more natural than life at Blagdon where the different strata of society were segregated into their strict, stupid tiers, where contact was so formal and where insincere politeness so often hid the truth.

Yet Sherdon was never for her. For all the freedom and homeliness, she could not have survived in the wilds like this. She had seen how hard Katherine and the others worked; just to watch them frightened her. For the first time in her life she had seen what it was to be in the kitchen or the scullery and washroom. She felt sick and had hung on to the door when Katherine pulled the chicken she had killed earlier and shuddered at the memory of the bitter stench of the flyblown privy.

She had seen Katherine's hands, witnessed the strength in Charlotte's body and the broken frailty of Grace. How many years, she wondered, before her sister, too, became stooped, bow legged and toothless. Twice when they had been alone together, she had spoken of her concern but Katherine had sworn she was happy enough. She loved the life, she replied, but the answer had come a little too quickly and Lizzie had not been convinced. She had seen how her sister had glanced at her clothes and how, like a child, she had helped select what jewellery should be worn and how she had tried to help her with her hair. The questions about home, the staff and her father, slow at first but then more searching, worried her.

It was unsettling. Katherine was trapped, committed to this strange, savage world by her deep love for Jack and her loyalty to his family. At night, Lizzie lay for hours in Charlotte's wooden cot, bent and cramped and unable to straighten her legs, wondering what had happened to the wild, free spirit she remembered.

*

"Mmm, mmm," Jack waved his knife at the mention of Declan then put his hand up to his full mouth. "Not 'ny more," he said swallowing hard. "Told me t'other day, he's happy enough back here. Now we've done up that place in the barn for 'im, 'es happy to stay on…an' a good job too. Anyhows," Jack took another mouthful. "Can't 'ave everyone off to the army," he mumbled. "Plenty of work to be done 'ere."

"That's Bess Cockram, that is," Billy glanced up but his remark had been heard.

"Oh, so that's where 'es bin spendin' his time? Up at The Sportsman's, eh?" Jack tore off a chunk of bread to chase the gravy round his plate. He had heard from Hardy that Declan was now a regular visitor and that Bess, his daughter, seemed to know when he was next due. But the Irishman was not alone, Hardy warned, others had taken a fancy to the girl with the long, dark hair. Jack hunched his shoulders.

"Saw Bamber today." Now it was Ralph. As he passed behind Charlotte with a fresh jug of ale, he glanced down at her. "Said to see yer at market, Saturday. Yeah?" Katherine saw the startled look on her face before she blushed and studied her hands. So it was true. She had thought as much and smiled to herself. Almost a year ago Jack had told her that Bamber Heard, a widower with two grown sons from Withypool, had been inquiring about Charlotte.

"Can't offer much, mind," the stocky hill farmer had muttered to Jack as they stood by the pens at the sheep fair. "Been by meself now nigh on three year. The farm pays well and the two boys are still there, like. Them's company enough, good company an' all." Jack listened as the older man struggled with his words. "But 'tis summat a bit more'n that, Jack. Now Jessie's gone, 'tis the heart that's lonely…that's what I'm missing just now."

Later Charlotte admitted to Katherine and her mother that she found the man pleasant enough. Twice he had waited for her after church then walked with her, his cap clutched in his hand, back to the cart. There he had paused awkwardly before offering his hand to help her step aboard. Later still he had begun to call at the farm after checking his flock on Withypool hill.

"You'll be coming to market then, Lottie?" Katherine tried to sound casual but Charlotte's flustered look said more than her reply.

"Don't rightly know." Charlotte's chair scraped on the flagstones. "Don't know what I'll be doin', Saturday," she shrugged and it was her mother, Grace, who reached out and pressed her hand reassuringly.

2

Hugh Pemberton, the new manager at Heasley, and Captain Pope heard the stick on the stairs. Without doubt it was him.

When they met for lunch Wilmot Tucker had promised to deal with the matter swiftly that very same day but he had other business to attend and they had been waiting for more than half an hour. The brief was prepared and they were holding the man in the locker room. Two others had been detailed to stand watch over him.

*

"Sorry about the cane," Wilmot grimaced and sat heavily before pulling himself forward in the hard-backed leather chair. "Not usually this bad but it plays up when I've been in the saddle too long." Earlier he had ridden over from the offices of the Brendon Hill Company to which he had been appointed manager and his leg, the one he had broken in the mine at Camborne, ached in the cold. "Now…let's hear about this fellow. Burgess, isn't it? These stories're pretty grim, you know…so what's he really like?" He grunted and stretched his leg but was in good spirits nonetheless. The Deverauxs had asked him to stay and had told him that Rebecca would soon be home. Furthermore Alfred Tennyson, whom he had first introduced to the family two years ago, would be staying at Court Hall on his way to Bideford. The poet loved Devon and had asked to be shown the moors.

"Well, sir," Pemberton glanced at Captain Pope, still captain of the Poltimore mine. "To be honest he's *bad*…a nasty piece of work. Manages to alienate every-one." Wilmot shrugged dismissively and caught Pope's eye.

"Mr Pemberton's right, sir." Now it was the mine captain and Wilmot nodded at the sing-song voice he remembered so well. "A right detestable blaggard, if you'll pardon my words. Nobody's got a good word for him, sir. The men 'ave threatened him twice, y'know."

"Well, I can't sack him just because he's not nice or popular, for mercy's sake." Wilmot eased himself back and pulled a face. "Come on…what about his work? What's that like?"

"Worse." Pemberton crossed his legs. "Won't work underground…refuses. Says it's his health so we've found him a surface job. Made him a shift leader…that's a polite name for head dogsbody but he's often the worse for drink when he comes on…an' what's *more*," he laughed incredulously, "He's set himself up as some sort of God fearing Methodist. The youngsters detest him…terrified of him they are an' we've warned him time and again about sending them down to cut the new faces." Pope nodded. "Nobody less'n twelve years old so we said but 'e takes no notice."

Wilmot sat back allowing the tips of his fingers to play together. Then he scowled, pulling his two black eyebrows in towards one another. The very idea sickened him. He had seen it further north where he watched horrified as chimney sweeps held down six and seven year-old boys who screamed as they had brine rubbed into their red-raw knees and elbows. And he had seen it down the mines where children as small as his nephew pulled trolleys on their hands and knees. "And you're expecting me to dismiss him just to keep in line with these new union rules? Code of Practice or whatever? Uh?" The men nodded. "God's truth, what's become of us all." He glowered at the papers in front of him and shifted his seat. "All right," he sighed. "Let's get on with it."

They had been right. As soon as the man opened his mouth, Wilmot sensed the venom. The eyes were shifty and the malice was there, written all over him. "'Tis their own damned fault, the beggars. Won't get on with it down there. A touch o' the cane's all they understand…never harmed no one." Wilmot forced himself to hear the man out. Pemberton spoke, then Pope but the man denied everything.

"*Right*," Wilmot raised his hand. "That's it, I've heard enough. You'll leave tonight. Give him his pay, Mr Pope." Burgess lurched forward.

"Get him away," Wilmot glared at those who had caught hold of him. "Get him out of here and keep him out." As soon as the door shut the three remaining relaxed. One blew hard while the second shifted uneasily.

"Be surprised if that's the last we see of 'im." Pope took Wilmot's hand at the door. "He'll be around, sir. One way or the other. Mark my words. Convinced the whole world hates him."

"Not near any of *our* mines, that's for sure." Wilmot took his hat from the manager. "And I'll be warning Mr Knight…he's got problems enough as it is."

"Wheal Eliza, sir?" Pope had heard word that the ore lode had thinned.

"Not too good sadly…and that's against the predictions." Frederic had asked Wilmot to monitor progress at his works, in particular the ore shafts at Simonsbath. "Started with a bang, a year ago in September but then slowed and they've had to close the initial shaft…little sign of deposits and there's always the flooding up there. Mr Knight wants me to have a look at the new ones. Anyway," he sighed heavily. "Let's hope things here settle a bit…and thank you for lunch." He nodded then turned and reached for the handrail before descending carefully.

Outside a raw November wind blew down the Mole valley from the moors to the north. Wilmot lifted his high collar and bent forward, urging his horse into a trot. The ride to North Molton took little more than half an hour, yet he was grateful for the shelter afforded by the steep banks of the narrow lanes. It would be good to see the Deveraux again, even better if there was news from Rome.

✳

"And you, too, sir," Harvey, the Court Hall butler and as bland as ever, turned and adjusted his cuffs. "Madam expects to be back within the hour. Sends her apologies, sir, but asked me to ensure that we see to your every need. Oh, by the way, sir, this arrived for you yesterday." The old butler's bespectacled face was expressionless. "Rome sir...so the mark says."

"Aha." Wilmot took the letter from the proffered salver. It was Rebecca. Her hand and the green ink gave her away and the envelope felt heavy; several pages again.

"Will that be all, sir?" Wilmot's eyes were skimming the first few lines. He had seen enough already – Rebecca was as pleased as ever she could imagine to be, sitting under the palms in the water gardens at Villa d'Este while writing this letter.

"Er...sorry Harvey. Oh, I do apologise." He pushed the letter into his inside pocket. "Tell me...Mr Tennyson, has he arrived?"

"The library, sir. Told madam he would be quite happy to be left alone, but asked to be informed as soon as we knew of your arrival." Wilmot saw Harvey's look. The butler had guessed what was on his mind. "Not awfully well, I'm afraid, sir. In a dreadful hurry as usual and his eyes are getting no better. Shall I...?"

"Thank you, Harvey, but no...I'll find my way."

Tennyson was exactly as he expected. The tall, spare figure was sitting hunched over a book in the window seat with his shortsighted eyes frowning in concentration just inches from the page. The brown hair, already receding, was tied back as badly as ever, as was the apple green cravat. Even as he stood in the doorway, Wilmot could feel the nervous energy in the man as he flicked hurriedly from page to page muttering to himself. He watched sadly as the poet tore off his glasses, replaced them with a monocle then bent forward once more and stroked at the ends of his beard. His eyes most certainly had deteriorated. "Alfred, my dear good man."

"Aaah...*aha*." As Tennyson jumped so papers swirled to the floor. "Tucker, 'tis you as ever it was." Then, as he leapt to his feet, the book in his lap crashed also. "How are you, my man...how are you...let me see, let me see...make way for the blind." He turned Wilmot to the window and clapped his shoulders. "There, 'tis good to see you, and looking well, too, by jove. *Now then,* hear this: 'His broad clear brow in sunlight glow'd; On burnished hooves his war-horse trode'. There you are...take it from there," he giggled, holding out both arms. "Come on, come on...on you go."

"Heavens, man." Wilmot's hand flew to his forehead. "I knew such a test would come soon enough. Wait...wait," he shut his eyes. "Er...er...yes, 'From underneath his helmet flow'd his coal-black hair as on he rode'. Yes?"

"Not bad, not bad. Coal-black *curls* it was, not hair...'his coal-black *curls* as on he rode'." Tennyson dug him in the ribs. "Sir Lancelot had curly hair, didn't he just?"

146

"Come, Tennyson, enough of that." Wilmot pulled up a deep wicker chair behind him. "Let's hear your news. Tell me about Emily and about the wedding. I want to hear it all…and explain how you could possibly leave your new bride like this after just a few months? And I want to know what you're doing down here," he slapped the poet's thigh. "All that *and* what news from Westminster? Eh? Tell me. Have they made the decision yet?"

He could see the poet was exhausted, far more so than two years ago when they were at Somersby together. But the man had always been like that. Even at Trinity he had dashed everywhere like a mad thing when others walked, then worked prodigiously far into the night while others slept. He had to escape, he explained. Journalists and literary critics were hammering at his door. Ever since Wordsworth's death he had been hounded for his views on the succession. Only last month the Prime Minister had offered the post to Samuel Rogers who had declined. Alfred's name, together with two others, had gone forward and the announcement would be made before the end of the month.

"*Desperate*," Tennyson muttered. "*Desperate*. The Laureate's mantle's hardly worth it all…honestly. Emily fled back north. Drew the blighters away from me and I made a run for it down here." Emily apart, Tennyson's family was in disarray and Wilmot listened quietly as his friend unburdened himself, his tears falling freely as he spoke about his brother's addiction. "The boy's in a dream world, Tucker." He shook his head sadly. "The damn stuff ravages the mind, it's terrible…*terrible*. The drug has such power. Worse than the drink that did for father," he whispered, wiping his eyes.

The long silence that followed was just as Wilmot remembered. High emotional drama followed by a deep, silent abyss. Tennyson sat hunched with his eyes closed, just the mercurial mind a blur of constant activity. Slowly the right hand was raised and a finger wagged knowingly, then stopped and pointed at him before wagging again.

"Tonight, after dinner," he sat up and blinked. "Mary and Piers have asked me for 'In Memoriam' to dear old Arthur Hallam. Hey now…remember how we used to read together, we Apostles, then you and Arthur would scribble down my thoughts? When the eyes first began to go? Ha, what a dear, dear friend…I still miss him so. But now," his face lit up. "I said it'd be an honour. 'Tis the poem I've chosen to go forward for my selection so 'twill be timely."

✳

It took over half an hour. Neither Mary nor Piers expected him to begin at the table and Wilmot caught their surprise when Tennyson motioned for silence and began to recite, as ever hunched and bent half sideways in his chair with his knees tucked high and his eyes closed. He spoke slowly with a deep, mellow huskiness in his voice that rose and fell with the emotions of the work. Just one arm was raised occasionally as if to amplify his words.

147

The poet had been distraught when Hallam died so soon after becoming engaged to his sister and the oration reflected the deep sorrow. What they were hearing now was the culmination of almost twenty years' work; Tennyson forever polishing or amending single lines, stanzas or whole sections year after year until, at last, he was satisfied. It was not until the very end that he turned towards them with one finger raised. His head was bowed and his voice was low. *"Behold, I dream a dream of good...and mingle all the world with thee."*

The hand dropped and the poet sat motionless with his head now high on the back of his chair. His beard was pointing ceilingwards and his eyes were closed. The room was very still. Wilmot could see by the light of the candles and fire that the others had been moved. By the door, Harvey's white glove reached up to his face. He had heard it himself many times but, even now, the beautiful, haunting lyrics spoken from the author's heart stirred him deeply.

"Dear God," Piers muttered eventually, shifting carefully in his chair. "You made the whole world stand still, me boy. It was marvellous...marvellous, Tennyson. Quite marvellous."

✳

Only after lunch the following day did Wilmot see the different side to his friend's character. "Keep 'im at it, sir." Cornish, the young groom, had advised Tennyson at Court Hall before they set out. "He'll do you fine, 'e will, sir, s'long as yer keep pushing 'im on." The ride up North Molton hill had gone well and they paused at the summit.

"Look at that." The poet stood and turned his face towards the wintry sun. "Can't see so much now, sadly, but I can feel the space. Can you not, Tucker? It's infinite, *timeless*. And what light...and the *air*. So fresh." He filled his lungs, then filled them again. "The very stuff of England, my friend. Nowhere else, nowhere else at all is it quite like this." He breathed again.

"D'you know?" Tennyson remained standing. "Look east from here, from this very point and there's nothing 'tween you and a thousand miles on from Moscow." He raised his head then turned his horse. "And here to the west...this way, nothing 'twixt here and Shenandoah in the land of Virginia. What a thought that is...*what* a thought. Eh? How's that? Up here, high on your beloved Exmoor there's nothing but nothing for so many thousands of God's miles either way. Come on, man. Let's go...before the Lord casts his spell any further."

✳

Sherdon intrigued him and he made Jack and Ralph lead him stumbling from shippon to barn, from linhay to shed where he peered closely at the livestock and machinery as his questions came tumbling out, the next before the last had been answered.

148

Wilmot noticed at lunch how the young were fascinated. Davey and Billy sat open mouthed with food still on their forks, as Tennyson told of his travels, sometimes breaking into his own poetry or the languages of the Levant. "What's that?" Billy asked once, screwing up his face but Davey waved him back to silence.

"Listen to these young minds," Tennyson turned to Charlotte and Katherine. "These're the important ones, these ones here…uncluttered and unspoiled as yet, pure and thirsting for knowledge. Ours're made up. They're fixed and entrenched, set already but with nowhere to go 'cept down their preordained path. *Too late!*" he chuckled and shrugged, causing the children to burst out laughing with him before stopping suddenly and glancing around uncertainly.

Jack forced himself from the table. Wilmot left with him, then the women faded, leaving Ralph and the boys with their visitor. They talked until the light began to wane, their voices muffled behind the door save for the occasional shout of laughter. But, suddenly, it was time. "What have you done to them, Alfred?" Katherine queried, standing with her arms around Billy's shoulders as he leant back against her. "I've never known them so quiet. Look at them," she bent down and brushed the boy's cheek with her own. "You've defeated them."

"T'other way round, m'dear." Tennyson's body jerked clumsily as he struggled into his tweed sack coat. "'Twas they who kept me on the edge of my seat…all their hopes, their plans and ambitions. What faith they have in what lies ahead. What dreams…and such optimism. 'Tis like an opiate…such thoughts would do us all well.

"But look out, all of you," he rounded on the shadows in the parlour doorway. "I'll be back…just as I vowed and then we'll see what's what."

3

Jack watched Jasper Harper's eyes following Bess from the room. Hardy had closed at midday and the four men settled into the old cattle byre now serving as the back parlour of The Sportsman's Inn. Snow, frozen hard by the sharp frost, clung to the bottom corners of the windowpanes but the bright glow from the peat fire between the two mangers gave out barely enough warmth. "You're sure it were him, are you?" Hardy turned to look at the young highwayman as soon as the door closed. "He's a hard 'un, yer know, that Braddon." The landlord cocked a questing eye at the others.

"Aye, sure as sure can be." Jasper Harper, hollow eyed and staring, sat slouched in his black three-quarter coat. His head was hunched low between his shoulders and half hidden by the high collar turned up around his ears. Steam rose from his coat where ice had once frozen the wet serge. The burly, compact frame was slumped deep into the chair as though someone had dropped him there like a part filled sack. He nodded and sniffed, then glowered at his own thoughts.

"I'ad the dog fair an' square, I tell yer. They picked 'im outa the water 'alf a mile below Landacre Bridge."

"Dead right enough, was 'e?"

"Come on, man." The young highwayman's look was one of contempt. "In the Barle for three days...what d'ya think?"

Like a cock in the pit Hardy thought but he could see what his daughter saw in the man. Four years on the clipper ships between Shanghai and Rotherhithe had hardened and sharpened him. Silk and spices were the listed cargoes but the excise men had got wind of the opium. Harper and three others had slipped the dockside cordon but the others had been taken. "Nort but self-defence, it weren't. True as I'm here, oh aye." He laughed at the memory then threw himself forward to sit upright. As he did so his black tri-corn hat fell from his knee.

"Oh aye, my friends, Mr Josiah Braddon jumped a bit too quick that night, so 'e did. Just beyond the bridge where the road turns up the hill. I had it in mind they might be there." He loosened the tie and shook the half-thawed ice from the ends of his hair. "Had myself ready and caught him before he could get off a shot. 'Ere look." Jasper half turned to reach deep inside his coat. As the coins, rings, and an amber necklace followed by a gold fob watch clattered on to the table, the others leant forward to see. "'Ere we are, see." When he opened the case to read slowly, the heavy chain dangled and swung.

"'*To Arthur from Mary. With love. 12 May 1817*'. Ha," he chuckled. "Hangin' in his weskit so it was...an' this in his coat, too." He held the fine court dagger by its blade. "Been at the game a bit too long had our Mr Braddon...a bit too long an' a mite too slow. Aye...'twas 'is turn t'other night."

Jack had heard about Jasper's swordsmanship from his uncle, Luke. "So fast," his friend had complained. "Once I might have stood a chance but now...'tis over like that." The fingers had clicked. "He's got the balance and the killer streak." He studied the newcomer and could imagine the scene at Landacre: a shout to halt and a glint of steel, perhaps a wild, loose shot or two followed by galloping hooves. Grunts of exertion as the body was picked up, then a heavy splash beneath the parapet on the lower side of the bridge where the water ran deep.

"Just take it steady, my son." Luke had somehow materialised from the shadows and was standing next to Jasper. Jack saw the momentary flicker of wariness on the younger man's face. "None of yer 'Jack o' Lantern' games up here, my little lad. Us'll need to use the taproom here and use it quietly mind."

"That's fer sure," Hardy Cockram leant forward. "I run a proper 'ouse 'ere, you mind. Fair enough...maybe a run from Luke and the ponies from time to time, but that's it. Any robbin' or sheddin' blood an' the law'll be here."

"What law?" Jasper tugged at his collar impatiently. "Bain't none of they up around 'ere abouts. Anyways they'd be right strangers out 'ere…wouldn't know one from t'other, nor the moor nor nort like that." The caution of those in the room had irked him but his bravado had failed to impress.

"No matter." Jack could see the landlord was irritated. "Once they know anyone like you's operating out this way they'll be on to us. Redcoats an' Yeomanry an' all. Us can do without they lot. Right, Jack?" Jasper's glance came with the toss of his head.

Arrogance or confidence, Jack could not tell but he watched carefully as the young freebooter rose then followed him as he made his way to the door. Bess was there. He could see the outline of her pale dress as she took their tankards, then watched again as her white hand came up to the back of his neck when he bent forward. Her father had seen it too and they moved their legs to make room as Jasper picked his way back to his chair. Somewhere there was perfume in the air, heady and rich from the Languedoc. Bess Hardy had made herself ready.

For two hours they talked. Luke, now past fifty, had had enough. The money had been good but the way of life had got harder by the year. "More'n thirty coast-guards now…'twixt Bude and Porlock," he grumbled. "'Tis difficult enough jest getting' off the beach. Then there's the takings. Duty's reduced on baccy 'n spirits, now. Bain't like it was. No ways." He stared wide-eyed at the peat before pushing at the turf with his boot. As the cloud of sparks were sucked into the chimney, up high to where the wind rattled and boomed, the others watched silently. "An' the ships're changing an' all. Bring less now and want more for their trouble…bain't like it was."

"Still a market up y'ere, then? Eh, Hardy?" Jack's voice broke in.

"Oh enough…aye, enough. Must be a dozen drinking 'ouses and more if yer takes in the Moltons an' Dulverton." The landlord lifted his chin and scratched thoughtfully. "Even more'n that if yer looks so far as Tiverton. Plenty o' trade, 'specially now that Moles Chamber's gone."

"What about the family, Jack?" It was Luke. Hardy glanced up with eyebrows raised for the smuggler had spoken his own thoughts. Jack was half way into his topcoat and swung round. A week earlier Luke and Hardy had come out to the farm. Jack had taken them into the shippon and showed them the space between the hatch in the hayloft and the roof above the cattle. It had taken time for them to see where the knife went between the boards.

"Right old roastin' they gave you last time, didn't they just…after that Moles Chamber run." Hardy's frame shook with laughter.

"They won't know nothing," Jack shrugged. His coat was now on and the collar raised. He paused at the door. "Young Irish lad's the only one that saw us last week. A squeak from him an' he'll be back with his road gang. 'E knows that, an' all…'tis more'n his life's worth. Let me know when you're coming."

As soon as he stepped from the warmth of the room, the chill wind hit him. The money was still good and the odds at being caught were long, but it was the thrill of it all that drove him on. The risk of losing everything, the meetings like this in the black of night, the gruff whispers and rough handshakes, the ripple of unshod hooves on the track and the solid feel of the weapons. It was a drug that sent the pulse racing, but he needed the gold as well. By the devil himself so he did…that poet would have understood.

Pulling his tail of hair from the back of his collar, he grinned to himself. Katherine would go mad if ever she guessed, the more so now the baby was due. It should have been May but Dr Collyns had said it would be early, just a few weeks away. He had missed the warmth of her love in the night, the feel of her body against his and her soft cries of pleasure. Patience, she had whispered soothing him gently. *Pah!* Patience, always more patience. Well, patience be damned – look at young Harper and the landlord's girl. He rammed his hat down and leant into the wind.

4

The harsh north-easter took three long days to swing back, the change bringing with it enough rain to tease those working in the fields. But today it had cleared and the high, pink evening clouds promised a settled spell to come with the dawn.

Jack had just crossed the bridge by Sherdon cottage when the shoe came loose. He saw it at once and dismounted to check before beginning the half-mile walk back to the farm. The little stone cottage, set back from the river, had changed hands before Christmas and he had been meaning to stop by. But now it was late and already the clear, cool dusk was falling.

He remembered seeing the new tenant, as the man made his way to and fro along the riverbank. Wally Sexton at Barkham had spoken of his new hand and he knew that Declan and Ralph had met him. As he led the mare, he could see the lamp in the back window down on the left behind the beech hedge, and he moved across the track to see better. It was the sound from the shed behind him that made him jump. "Whoa, steady," he soothed the animal then turned. It was barely a laugh, more a chuckle as though she had been watching him and was waiting for him to pass.

"Oh my and what a to do." She was not beautiful, rather a little too short and a bit plump for that, but pretty and lively in a comely sort of way. And she was close enough for him to see that her eyes were twinkling mischievously as though she knew she had surprised him. "Sorry about that…you'm from up the road? Yes?" The hand that pulled the sack tighter around her shoulders then snatched at the locks of auburn hair and held them against the evening breeze. "I've seen yer now an' then, but 'tis nice to meet at last. E'en like this, so to speak." She laughed, a light bubbly laugh and held out the basket of eggs "There see, an' not so many at that...but they'm all in to roost now."

"Yes, for sure...'tis good to meet. I've seen your husband...seen him often, on his way to work."

"Oh, ah." The green eyes danced as she studied the man in front of her. "I'm Kitty...Kitty Rawle." She moved the basket from one hand to the other and took his. "'Tis Jack, isn't it?" she confirmed. "Jack Tucker, from up the farm?"

"Aye, that's right...indeed it is." Her hand, when he took it, was warm and soft and held on to his own until he eased it away. "And very good to see you at last." Why he stammered, he never knew. "We'll call by directly...my wife and I that is, but the mare's lost a shoe an' I best be getting on. Another time...soon p'raps."

"Oh, ah. Best to be gettin' on then, I s'pose." The eyes never left him. "'Tis getting' late...cold an' all." Her shoulders hunched as though she needed a shawl to be wrapped tightly around her.

Jack nodded and started up the hill. He never really knew why but twenty yards further on he stopped and turned. She was still standing on the track looking at him with her legs part astride and her head on one side, both hands holding the basket in front of her. He knew she had seen him so he raised a hand. It should have been bold and cheerful but it wasn't; just a sign that said something or other. He thought he saw her smile as her hand rose in reply but it was getting dark.

Fifty yards on he turned again and there was a shadow, a shadow in the dusk. It might have been her, perhaps not...but he hoped that it was.

Chapter Ten

Declan drove the peat cutter into the ground, stood for a moment then pulled himself out of the trench. For the next half hour he was bent double, stacking the turf sods into neat piles knowing full well that he would be back every two months to turn them until they were dry. They were nothing like as good as the turf around Kilgarvan or Killarney, but there was less rain here so they dried more easily.

It was now almost three months since Bess Cockram of The Sportsman's had thanked him for his company and wished him well. He had tried his luck once more but her smile was no longer there and when he had gone to leave, folk round the fire had nudged each other knowingly. For a while it had hurt until Jack had taken him aside. Later they laughed about it but his master had been right and he had doffed his cap to her. Good luck to the fellow whoever he was and, in any case, life had to move on.

For once his feet were not too wet, at least no water squelched from the eyelets of his boots as he made his way over to the wizened blackthorn tree where he had placed his coat and lunch. He knew she would be coming and the old tree was their marker. Whenever it was fine she rode and today was one of those when God smiled on the world. Even for May it was warm and he watched idly as a honeybee searched the pink wortleberry flowers next to the bare patch where the wild ponies stood to rub.

It was when a curlew called out in alarm that he sat up and craned his neck. It had to be her.

✳

Declan took her face in both hands. "'Tis grand to see you. The very thought of it's kept me at the peat all morning." As she stretched up to snatch a kiss, her hands clutched at his sleeves.

"Can't be long today." Gaile Fisher saw his look of disappointment. "Sorry." she reached out and squeezed his hand. "Father wants me to go into Withypool with him. Wants to get something for those late lambs, the little ones in the field next to the house." She sat on the grassy bank and waited until he joined her before settling close to him. "What're you *doing*?" she laughed, screwing her face in disgust.

"Emptying me buckets o' water," he grunted bending forward to unlace his boots. "'Tis me feet. They're only half drowned today...but mighty cold at that. Away with yer." He removed his coat, wiped his feet on the sleeve and wiggled his toes. "Och, they're not that bad...an' they've had a fair good bath, for that. *Hey, you!*" The Irishman fell on his side as she gave him a push.

"That's *horrible*," she chided. "*Dreadful* and just before lunch, too."

Ever since she had seen him netting rabbits above Lower Sherdon she had been fascinated, tossing her head angrily when her mother warned her about the ways of the Irish on the moor. Her father had tried to tell her as well and she knew he had spoken to Jack. Davey told her that he had heard them talking in the hay barn. "The girl's eighteen," Jack had said. "Many're married by now, you know...mothers even and she's got to face the world sooner or later." Arthur Fisher had told him how he and his wife had heard about the likes of Declan and their wild ways. "The lad's nay a bad 'un, Arthur. He's gentle with the little ones an' they love him, really they do. Mind you it could all be hidden away in his blood, like the rest o' them but I'd give him a chance."

It was the dancing blue eyes that captured her, that and his soft lilting brogue. She knew he was different but, oh mercy, he was *so* desperately shy. Twice now she had reached for the buttons on his shirt and he had backed away. "Just the touch of a kiss, my love," he warned as his hands closed over hers. "No more...*no, no, no*. 'Twould break the spell. You're a lovely wee colleen, honest to God you are, but 'twould never be t'e same again. T'e magic would be gone so it would...*crash*, just like that and gone for ever."

It infuriated her and made her more determined than ever to make this madly attractive man her own. "Dear Mother of God," he had complained holding her wrists. "You'll have me down there with old Hades, shovellin' away for me sins. 'Tis enough, Gaile, enough...me little mischief maker." She had laughed as he tried to look severe but he was a man of his word. Today, though, it was different and she wanted to know how serious he was.

"You remember the other day?" Her knees were tucked under her chin. "Up here, when you talked about leaving. Moving on, you said. Did you mean it...?"

"'Twas just a thought. But a thought none the less...there in me mind all the same." Declan sensed that she had come to find out. "But it would be just me by meself. I'd go on my own, over the hills and away in the night."

"But you even talked about *America*. That's miles, I mean, it's forever...across the sea and you'd never be back." Gaile knew he could tell she was worried. "And you said that half your family's gone already. Sailed away, just like that."

"Well now, listen here, will you." Declan scratched at the mop of black curls in frustration. "Nothing's for sure...and that's for certain, too," he chuckled and winked. "But there's nothing at home across the water in Killarney...nothin' at all after the famine there. Me cousins, that's Mathew an' Frank, they're speaking of goin' and asked if I'd come. I showed you the letter." She nodded. "They'll be going from Liverpool, that's op in the north. On a packet boat or one of them new-fangled steamboats...made out of iron they are, no sails or nuthin'. Magic. Just a big engine thing inside and two big wheels to push it along...something like that."

"But you'd sink. If it's iron you'd go down like a stone."

"They canna do that, even." Declan shook his head vigorously. "A fella in the shippin' office explained it to Frank. A thinking man, he was…spoke right fancy, he did. Too strong for that, he said. Too big, so they are an' they canna sink." He bent down and looked into her eyes. "And hey, why all the fuss about *me* just the now? You should hear the talk at the farm, about Billy and Davey…and the army. That's what all the gossip's about just now. It's driving the wimin there crazy with worry." Declan shook his head. "Lottie's in a right old lather o' sweat. Killing this and shooting that, she cries. Gallopin' here an' there. 'Tis a sight more dangerous than sailing o'er the sea, that's fer sure."

Gaile was silent. He was right. They had all heard the stories about sailing to America – the New World as they called it. But if he went he would be gone for good and then somebody else would find him. "Don't go," she whispered. "Please…not yet anyway. Not until you're sure about things." She paused briefly before the words came tumbling out. "But if you *do* go…just *if*, that is…take me with you, Declan," she pleaded. "I'll come, you know." She leant her head on his shoulder. "You'll be needing me there. Oh, please Declan." She took his hand and wriggled close as his arm went round her. "Take me with you," she begged.

"Sweet Jasus," Declan looked aghast. "There'd be half the men of Exmoor out there puttin' salt on me tail. Can ye imagine it, now? Yer father an' Jack, young Ralph an' the ruffians up at the pob. Dear God, they'd catch us before Landacre bridge and skin me alive, so they would."

"No they wouldn't." Gaile pushed against him. "Don't be silly. You're just making it up, aren't you. I don't mean *now* but if you do go…if *we* go…it'll be different then."

"For sure." Declan wiped the tear from her cheek before he kissed her.

2

Victoria Alice was two months old. She had arrived on St George's day, as expected, and proceeded to spend as much time as possible asleep. Or else she lay with her tiny eyes screwed up against the light and her lower lip protruding as though she did not much care for those peering at her. And why should she?

Most of them looked horrible. Some of them smelt of unpleasant things and they all bent down to within inches of her face to leer goggle-eyed before turning and bellowing to others across the room. Somehow she knew already that if she opened her eyes, took a deep breath and screamed, the face would go away and not come back again. It was but one of her first lessons about life and it served her well.

＊

"I really need to see the boy but if he's away out on the farm, it can wait awhile." Dr Collyns crept quietly past the wooden cradle and tiptoed to the window seat. Without thinking he moved the dirty plates then brushed at the dust and crumbs before sitting beside Katherine. "His mother's none too well and I'd like to tell him what I think." A week earlier, Grace had collapsed and although now stronger she passed much of each afternoon in her cot. Collyns had called to see Katherine and the baby but spent most of his time upstairs. "She's not far off seventy now and her life's not always been too easy.

"My surmise is that she's had a mild attack of apoplexy. She's tired, very tired and should stay where she is." The doctor frowned and pursed his lips. "I don't much like that lack of movement down her right side. There," he bent to demonstrate. "And she's finding it difficult to talk. Now then, I've given her some laudanum and you should see she has a drop or two each evening." He passed her the small, brown bottle. "It's opium really, so go carefully. I would have liked to have seen Jack and told him myself...next week perhaps, when I'm back. But you can pass it all on." He sat back and scratched his forehead. "Phew, what a day." His body sagged and he paused, wondering how to continue. "And...how are things with the lady of the house?" Charles Collyns took her hand.

Katherine shrugged and forced a smile. "Oh...so-so," she sighed and shrugged, momentarily lost for a reply. Then her shoulders slumped and she looked down.

The doctor, now over sixty himself and wise to the ways of his fellow beings, had seen how life was treating her. "All these changes can't have been that easy for you," he muttered, almost to himself.

There had never been anything quite like John Knight's picnics and rides from Simonsbath and he could well remember the two Northborough girls; beautiful, elegant and graceful, escorted across the moor by the young men of society with their servants and grooms following discretely. He had seen them at Filleigh, at Holnicote and Dunster, dressed and attired exquisitly, laughing and joking as they danced the night away. "There must be a number of things you miss. Your family...friends? Home, for instance? It can't have been easy, my dear." He spoke quietly, watching closely as Katherine fiddled with the end of her cloth belt.

"Oh, this and that," she shrugged. "Just the little things, sometimes." He sensed her voice quavering and watched as she bit on her lip. But it was easy to read her mind. Here was another one who had seen the changes, she was saying to herself. First it was Freddy, then Wilmot and Lizzie and now him. I must look a sight but I don't need anybody to tell me. I can see it all for myself.

But she could not hide from the truth and shook her head. "Look..." she whispered taking her hand from his. "Just look at this." Now her voice was louder. "The nails...they're all broken and cracked, aren't they? And the rough skin..." She rubbed her thumb across the side of her forefinger. "And my clothes and my shoes." Her voice choked shrilly as she fought back the tears. "My hair, my face, my figure…it's gone, all of it." Her clenched hand was at her mouth.

He could feel her body shaking before she sobbed noisily and shook her head. "Oh…I don't know, Charles…I just don't know." She caught her breath then sobbed again. "But it's not important, is it? It doesn't matter really…it's nothing." She took the handkerchief he offered and blew. "Oh, I'm sorry…I didn't mean to speak out like that, honestly I didn't." She laughed then sniffed and dabbed at her eyes.

"I know, m'dear. I know." Collyns patted her hand. He had thought it might be like that but the die was now cast and the world was moving on without her. The society she knew had left her behind, forgotten her and she knew it. "Jack's a fine man, they all are…you've a wonderful family. But sometimes these great changes are not as easy to make as they look. Everyone's as happy as larks and the whole world seems to be smiling *but*, well, sometimes deep down it's not quite like that…and then it's good to talk." His eyes creased kindly. "That's what your old family doctor's for." It was only later, when she gave him tea that she learned about Wilmot.

"A cracking lad…and done well, by jove." Collyns put the cup and saucer down. "And Rebbeca Deveraux's charming. Did they not tell you? *No?*" he looked surprised. "A family secret I daresay. It's nothing serious mind you," he added hastily. "Nothing like that, at all. It's just good…how should I say? Just good to see them together and enjoying each other's company so." He went on to tell her about his evening at Simonsbath.

"Freddy Knight's found himself a young lady and a lovely young girl so she is…barely eighteen, would you believe. Florence somebody or other, I never got round to anything more than presenting myself. I missed her on the dance floor…too old for that sort of thing and I would have frightened the child to death. But Freddy swears blind he fell for her the very first time he set eyes on her…in London two years ago. We're all wondering if anything'll come of it especially as he claims he stole her away before anyone else got the idea. And he's still smitten so it seems…but we'll see, there's time enough yet." There had been twenty or so to dinner and it sounded as though the clock had been put back.

"James and Eleanor, the young Aclands were there, both asking after you. Two of the Luttrell boys, also, and a crowd up from Filleigh. And the Chichesters…Giles and Caroline from Arlington, all hoping to see you soon and wishing you well."

She was staring out of the window, her face half hidden from him. "The house was full," he continued. "So they put Wilmot and one of the others in the cottage with dear old Jenny Squires. And *what* a fuss she made of the lad," his eyes shone merrily. "Quizzed him non stop about Jack. He really should get up to Simonsbath and call in on them sometime. The old folks're none too strong now and they both adore the boy." It was another hour before he left.

She had loved seeing him. His comforting words and quiet, fatherly manner had helped but once he had gone she felt empty and depressed, lonely and rejected by those whose friendship she had cherished so dearly. Simonsbath must have been fun; she could imagine the noise and laughter. It would have been wonderful to have seen them all again and to have met Freddy's young companion. What, she tried to imagine, was she like? Men were hopeless at descriptions and the dear old doctor would have had no idea of what she would have wanted to know…her clothes and her jewellery, and the little things like that.

So…Freddy was settling at last, was he? Oh well, the girl was lucky, very lucky. Suddenly she was hurt and envious, jealous of this child who had arrived on the scene so dramatically only to sweep away one of her dearest and closest friends. A friend she had known since…since before *Florence* or whatever her name, was born even. And, if she *had* captured him then he would no longer be around, no longer be free to ride over and see her. No longer able to do so many things. Would he be there at all, she wondered. No, he would have gone and her sudden pang of jealousy turned to one of fear, fear of losing the one who had always been around; the one who might in some sort of way have been the rock on to which she could have clambered were her world ever to fall apart.

They had all missed her, so the doctor claimed, but she had known nothing about the house party. It had been kept hidden from them. She and Jack had not been invited yet they were only four miles away, far closer than any of the others. Wilmot had been invited. Why *him* and not them? Was it because of Jack, perhaps? Because they felt he would have been out of his depth, sitting there miserably uncomfortable while trying to make polite conversation about business and politics. Were they saving him from that or was it because the rough farmer would not have fitted in, or might have said the wrong things, or been awkward and an embarrassment to those on either side of him?

Or was it that terrible duel perhaps? Yes, perhaps. It would be easy to think of that as the reason. Yes, indeed that might have been it, although Jack had returned from seeing Frederic convinced that all was well. And in any case they had met here many times since and it was simplest and easiest to believe that nothing was amiss. But was it though? It would have been a miracle if that were really the case. If only she had been there at Simonsbath when the two of them met soon after the duel, she would have seen for herself, sensed the atmosphere beneath the bonhomie and detected any simmering animosity or mistrust.

On the other hand perhaps it was *her*? Perhaps *she* was the one who would have been in the way at Simonsbath. Yes, her, Katherine of Northborough, Lady Katherine Darcy…the one who ran off with the groom. The one all the talk had been about. The one with the crude, short cropped hair, the ruddy cheeks and spreading hips. The one who fell from grace and out of favour, the one the family had cut off and spurned. Perhaps that was it. Perhaps she would have been too much for them all; she and Jack together, between them spoiling the party. Easier therefore to omit them.

She began to feel angry, a deep smouldering anger that she was going to have to hide from them all, resentful that he, her man, or both of them for that matter, should be considered like that. How dare they? Jack was a better man than any of them. She knew it and they knew it. Only he did not.

✻

The moment he came in she could see he was exhausted. Since late morning, as soon as the grass was dry enough he and the boys had been out. Arthur Fisher and his son, Rex, had come to help as had Wally Sexton from Barkham bringing his new man from the cottage down the lane. But even with the seven scythes, the large field above the house had remained less than half cut. She and Lottie had taken lunch out to them and they all sat quietly in the sun watching three young stags working their way through the bracken on the far side of Sherdon Water.

The men had laboured until tea when Jack stopped them, but he and Ralph had pressed on with the pitchforks, turning and shaking out the rows of cut grass. They would turn it again tomorrow, then start to build the hay into stooks. After that, as long as the dry spell continued, the three fields on the lower side of the lane would be ready.

"Tired, my love?" Katherine stood behind his chair. She was leaning forward over him with her arms around his neck. "Why don't you rest awhile? Mmm? There's only the milking and Lottie's seeing to that with Billy…and he can feed the dogs for once." She bent down and kissed the top of his head. "Ooh look," she brushed her hand through his thinning hair. "Who's going bald then? Just on the top. *There*," she kissed him again. "Just there. Perhaps we can have an early night. Mmm?"

"Be nice." Jack looked up. His head was cushioned between her soft breasts. "Just got to get round the lambs. The ones across the way…down the lane. I'll take the pony…won't be long, then we'll go on up."

Two hundred and thirty it should be and forty of them his own. Whenever he looked at the mark on his own sheep he remembered the duel. The very sight of the red cross on the head triggered a stream of memories beginning with the confrontation in the barn when Kenton had asked him for proof of ownership. He had never really worried about the outcome of that fateful morning. God had been with him. He knew in his heart that he had been right all the way through, but he knew also that Frederic had been devastated.

It had not been easy to summon the courage to go and face him and it had taken him more than a week. Once they were certain that no charges would be pressed, Dr Collyns had urged him to do so, telling him that Frederic wanted to see him.

160

He remembered how Abel Tarr, now head butler, had greeted him warily as if he, Jack, was a man to be watched; that he was now something of a danger rather than the Jack of old. As he walked across the stable yard, he could feel their eyes on him and, when he reached the kitchen, one of the maids ran from the scullery.

Frederic had welcomed him cordially enough but it had been hard. How does a man look at a friend whose brother he's fought and killed? But then how can a man stand the very sight of another who's taken the life of his own brother? The atmosphere had been strained, broken only when it was time to leave. "Honestly, Jack," Frederic's hand was on his shoulder. "It could never have been any different, you could have done nothing else...nothing at all, my friend. Had you stood aside from all that, he would have despised you. It had to be done." Then he paused. "And had it been *you*, my friend...you who mean so much to me. What then?"

It was his sad, brave smile that did it. Suddenly Jack was back in time, back at Lynton all those years ago, outside the forge with the smell of hot metal in the air. The bully, Ben Holder, had gone, sent packing by his fists. Hector and poor old Leonard were there somewhere, he could see their faces while Frederic's hand was in his. The little boy's eyes were shining with pride. '*What a fight that was,*' the hand tugged as he skipped with delight. '*It was great, Jack, and he deserved it.*''

'*That's right, Master Frederic.*' He remembered how he had felt so pleased with himself. '*When 'tis a matter of honour, you've got to stand your ground.*' Those had been his words and that was what he had done to that little boy's brother.

The study at Simonsbath had become hazy, the figure in front of him a shadow. He knew he could not hold back and neither could the other. The two of them had wept, holding on to each other. The tension and awfulness of it all had been impossible to live with, like storm clouds building but that one hour alone together saved them. Something terrible had passed and, once again, they had been able to sit together, then laugh, then ride out as of old.

✳

He counted the flock twice but three of his lambs were missing. Eventually the dogs found them in a patch of brambles across the bridge and brought them back to where he was holding the gate. The cottage by the bridge, barely a hundred yards away, looked empty although the hens were still out and the washing still on the line. Jack was on edge. He was always like that when he remembered the duel; the heart was beating a mite faster and his senses were sharper, more aware. The clothes on the line made the pony start.

He stopped. They were her clothes. Those shapeless pieces of drab, white cloth, flapping emptily in the breeze, would soon be pulled tight around the body he had seen the other evening. Her soft warm flesh would fill them snugly, her earthy fragrance perfume them. Some were slim and intimate, shaped to hold and caress her dark secrets. Even as he was thinking so, his eyes flitted from one to the other.

How, he wondered, would her body look dressed like that? And suppose she was standing in front of him now, what would those green eyes be telling him? Her mouth would be smiling, her lips parted and ready like they were before. And what would she be saying, he wondered. But then he started suddenly and looked round, kicking the pony on and now angry with himself. Yet he felt the heat in his body. He had become alive and excited. His body was on fire.

*

"Hey, you." Katherine nuzzled against him. "What's the matter?" Her fingers played lightly on his chest. He blinked but said nothing, continuing to stare at the ceiling with both hands behind his head. She moved further across the bed, hooked one leg over his naked body and lay half on top of him. "Not going to sleep, are you?"

She brushed back his hair and put her lips to his ear. He could feel the warmth of her breath and the moistness of her tongue. "Well don't…not yet, my love," she whispered, nibbling gently. "Not for a while, anyway," she pleaded. His chest rose and fell under her body but still he did not move.

"Come, Jack." She rolled away and tried to pull him on top of her. "Come here. I'm all right now." She was breathing hard. "'Tis safe again now…and I want you," she whispered huskily. "Come to me, my love." Her lips found his once more and she opened her mouth but he did not respond; he just lay there for a moment longer before slowly turning away.

3

A little white head peeped out of the saddlebag that had been placed on the ground. Two ears, one black, pricked at the sound of the base drum. "'Ere, steady you." The hand, hardened by years of toil, lifted and held the small body. Strong fingers curled around the fat, pink belly. His snarl, as savage as his eight weeks could make it, was serious. But he thought better of it and licked frantically at the hand now settling him back into his nest of hay.

"Don't go doin' that." Her hand pushed his arm away. "Not here, Bamber. There's too many folks about and's not right." Bamber Heard grinned impishly, quite indifferent to whoever saw them. He pushed back his felt hat festooned with autumn flowers, and surveyed the scene. Minutes before he and Charlotte had been standing quietly together in St Andrew's churchyard.

Three years ago, he, his brothers and his two sons had buried Jessie. His wife, and her family before her, had been born and brought up in Withypool and it was only right that she should be laid to rest alongside her parents. Each Easter since and on the first day of the autumn sheep fair, Bamber made the short pilgrimage to lay flowers on her grave.

"That's better." Charlotte stood back to survey her handiwork with her head on one side. "Can't 'ave weeds all over the place, poor dear. Us'll tidy 'er Mum an' Dad's in a minute." She bent down again to adjust the spray of wild flowers and heather under the headstone. Bamber watched her lovingly; it was all he could do not to crouch down beside her as she worked. She was no longer a sprightly lass, he could see that, and her own boy would soon be away to join the army, but he knew she was the one he had been looking for. He was certain of it and his heart sang with joy.

His parents' grave took a little longer. "That'll do, dear. That's real nice. Mother'd be pleased with that." As she rose, he slipped his hand under her arm and the two stood in silence. "'Er was a wonderful soul, 'er was," he muttered.

"Don't doubt it, dear," Charlotte patted his hand. For a moment the farmer was lost for words. "Come on," she whispered. "Let's step away an' leave 'em in peace. Bless 'em."

*

"'Ark, to they dancers." Charlotte swung the saddlebag across her shoulder and the two of them walked towards the church gate. The bag moved then wriggled impatiently. "Oh, come on then." She reached inside and put the terrier puppy on the ground. It had been over a year since Scamp had died and Wally Heard, Bamber's brother from Winsford, had pressed the little dog on them. Patch, as he was known already, trotted across the path to examine a dandelion but it was of little interest so he turned to see what else was about. "Come on, you," Bamber bent to pick him up.

"There 'e be." Their hands touched briefly and for a moment they stood as any couple might who have found each other. Bamber regarded her fondly. Slowly his round red face, edged with greying whiskers, broke into the warmest of smiles. His whole face creased, half hiding his eyes until only the smallest of twinkles could be seen. Charlotte looked away and her eyes dropped: she had never felt like this. Could it be that, here at last, was a man who actually cared for her and respected her. She longed for his visits to the farm and their walks along the Barle after church when he would tell her about life in the village. She loved his stories; they reminded her of her own childhood, those happy, carefree days at Molland.

Whenever they came to Withypool they passed close to Brightworthy, his farm above the river, but she had yet to be invited inside. "No, bain't proper," Bamber had shaken his head when she asked him if she could have a look. "There's time enough, dear, plenty o' time for that, but 'twould be wrong to hurry it all along." That was eighteen months ago.

"Look at yer smock, man." Charlotte licked her finger and rubbed at the stain on the white cloth. "Real messy, you are. Bad as the little ones." She took his smock in her hands and rubbed vigorously, just where the two lambs she had embroidered skipped across his chest. "There'e be, look." She brushed the material flat then flicked at some dust on his shoulders. "That's better…there we are."

Bamber's grin grew wider still. He was enjoying the attention, loving it, and glanced round furtively. Nobody was looking so he took her hand and bent forward. She felt his warm breath and the tickle of his whiskers on the back of her knuckles and smiled happily, allowing him to hold on to her fingers a few seconds longer than he should. "C'mon, Bamber. Us'd better find Jack and the others," she urged. "Said to meet us by the sheep pens."

As they approached the bridge, the beat of the drum grew louder. The drummer, withered and bent and with his hair tied in a knot, stood over his drum beating out the time with his leather thongs. A second man, his hair a mad frizz, leapt up and down with a tambourine while the two fiddlers, one standing and one sitting, nodded and bowed as they played. Around them all a gaggle of children jostled and fought. Beyond, and surrounded by the crowd, the morris dancers in their yellow and red costumes hopped, skipped and turned to the music as the bells on their batons and clothes jingled rhythmically.

"There look. T'other side, the Hawkridge crowd. Daresay Molland's there too." Bamber rubbed his hands together. "An' there's Exford…*there*, see. By th'girt big tent." Young men and women from the surrounding villages had walked to the fair in procession, dressed in their Sunday best, their hats decorated with flowers and corn dollies. Each village had its own emblem decorated with bright ribbons and raised high on a pole by a young man especially chosen for the task. Hawkridge had a lamb's fleece, Molland a cow's skull. Exford a pair of antlers and Winsford a fox.

The young villagers, shy and nervous at first, paraded around in their groups, both men and girls together, waving and shouting back to their friends in the crowd. Many of the ones promenading for the first time knew nobody and peeped shyly at the world from the protection of those around them, knowing that they themselves were being watched. Later at the dance, and if they could summon the courage, their chance would come.

"Cuh…how's about that then. Never seen so many as 'ere's today. An' all them fair young maids jumpin' about…Oh…my," he gasped. "Cuh, dearie me, there'll be fun out there tonight when the dancin' starts." Bamber hitched up his smock and suggested a little skip.

4

Grace died a few days before Christmas after her second attack that came towards the end of November. Dr Collyns had prepared the family for the worst and Charlotte nursed her until the end.

Katherine marvelled at her patience, sometimes sitting with her as she spoon fed the old lady, cradling her head like a baby as she mopped away the dribble from the side of her face. Somehow, between them, they lifted her from her cot to change the soiled linen and found time to keep her washed and dressed.

They both knew it could not last and her final attack came when they were with her. "Steady, mother…steady. There now…steady." The two women glanced at each other. "Can't be long," Charlotte whispered, lowering the grey-white head back on to the pillow and wiping her brow. "Could feel the struggle inside 'er as 'er eyes rolled up." She shook her head. "Did yer hear 'er, Katherine? Voice all rattlin' as 'er tried to say summat? T'ain't fair, though. Fought so 'ard, she did…but 'tis no use."

Katherine pulled the exhausted woman over to her. She had seen the sorrow in her eyes. "You've done everything, Lottie," she whispered. "Everything you can and we've all seen that. Everybody says you've been more than a mother to her. Perhaps…well, perhaps it *is* her time."

Jack finished early that evening, coming in to spend an hour with his mother as soon as he had done the milking. Billy and Davey sat with Declan in his room, one carving a flute, the other making nets. "She's very frail, Jack," his sister warned quietly as they stood by her cot. "Hears what you're saying but can't say nort back. Moves 'er 'ead from time to time, that's all." Jack said nothing in reply, just nodded then held his fresh lamp higher to see more clearly. His mother was lying still, a wisp of lifeless grey hair had fallen across the smooth, marble-white skin of her forehead. The black hole of her open mouth, wrinkled tightly around the toothless gums, gaped at the ceiling. Her eyes, he had to bend forward to see them, had shrunk into the deep hollows of their sockets. Only her frail, empty chest moved. One glance was enough.

He turned quickly and beckoned to the two women. "Get Ralph and Billy to fetch Wilmot…then go on for Emma," he whispered urgently. "But give 'em a bite to eat first." He paused, thinking quickly. "Tell Ralph to come an' see me before they leave. We'll keep Davey here…just in case. Lottie's right but they'll need to be quick."

He crept back into the room, to the stool by her cot and pushed the Bible across the table to make room for the lamp. Then he took her hand. It was tiny, frail and felt so light. And it was cold so he covered it with both of his own before lifting it and rubbing his lips gently along her nails. They were neat, shiny and now smooth from the lack of work. "Mother," his breath ruffled the hair by her ear. "Mother, 'tis Jack." He sat back slowly watching her face before leaning forward again. "Mother." His voice was a little louder. "Can you hear? 'Tis Jack." His eyes searched for movement.

"Jack." As her eyes opened slowly, the whisper came from one corner of her mouth. Her hand moved as if to close round his and he could see she was trying to smile yet only one side of her face moved. But it was still her: the smile belonged to nobody else. He saw the smile as he remembered it   and, in that brief moment, felt all her warmth and strength.

"'Tis me, dear. I'm here." He squeezed her hand then bent forward to brush his lips across her forehead. "I'll stay awhile," he murmured. "I'll not be leaving yer. Everything's done outside. Animals all fed and bedded down so I'll stay…sit with yer an' we can talk…when you've 'ad a little rest." She smiled again and closed her eyes, happy at what she had heard. "Another baby, mother. End of June." He watched her eyes open wide at the news then felt her other hand pat his before she relaxed once more.

"'Twill be another little girl, my love," she whispered, opening her eyes. "Tell Katherine, dear. 'Twill be another loverley little maid. Little sister for…for…"

"Victoria, mother. A sister for Victoria. Katherine'll be in directly." Jack spoke out loud for the first time. "When she's in, you tell 'er, dear. 'Er likes to hear from you." Wilmot and Billy arrived soon after midnight, Emma and Ralph just after dawn. Her two children and Davey joined Charlotte and the four sat quietly by the cot until Wilmot sent them running, one outside for Jack and the other for Katherine. The end came peacefully at noon.

✵

"'Er's stopped, Jack." Charlotte looked around searching anxiously for her brother. "Mother's stopped." She nodded as though confirming it. "Look. The breathin…'er's still." For a moment the heads around the cot searched anxiously for signs of life.

"Aye, she's gone." Wilmot held Katherine's arm while Emma, with both hands to her mouth, stood alone. Davey saw his mother's face and knelt beside her, pulling her close to cradle her head on his shoulder. Only Jack stood apart.

His face was empty and grey. "Aye," he whispered then coughed to clear his throat. The others glanced up uncertainly, surprised at the sudden frailty in his voice. " 'Er's at peace at last, bless her." He inched his way past Charlotte and Davey and bent down to kiss her again before easing the sheet over her head.

Chapter Eleven

Christmas at Sherdon had been difficult: it was as though Grace was still there. Despite the funeral at Molland, her spirit had seemed unwilling to leave them. And this was in spite of the fact that Jack had told Katherine and Charlotte to leave the house while he cleared out her clothes and moved the furniture around.

Declan had helped. "'Tis the young house, Mr Jack, that's the problem. It's the first time, you know, and the place won't let go of her. The spirit seeps into the woodwork like t'e smoke gets into yer clothes. She's here with us now 'cos she's happy. Smilin' and carin' like she did in her life." He grinned back at Jack's startled look. "Oh aye, 'tis fer sure. Me mother was fey an' could talk wi' the departed. I canna do that but, y'know, there's a difinit feel for her around the place. D'yer not think?" The Irishman rolled his shoulders and shrugged. "'Tis normal enough. She was the first to leave us but she won't be the last...an' ye can be sure of that."

Wilmot paid for the funeral. The others had wanted to help but he insisted. "I couldn't just stand by," he remonstrated. He, Jack and Charlotte had gone into the parlour. It was cold. The mist outside pressed up against the windows while, in the hearth, the newly laid peat fire smouldered miserably unable to compete. "Listen, Jack." Wilmot flicked back his hair. "The two of you did everything for mother...*every*thing. Fair enough and I know I couldn't because of all my travelling about the place, but now I can. And I want to." They could see his old, intense stare. "I want to play my part or I'd feel...well, as though I'd simply been standing aside."

"We'll share the cost, 'tis only right," Jack sounded adamant.

"It's nothing to do with rights...honestly, Jack. We don't share out something like this, like children sharing a gingerbread man." Wilmot waved his hand at the thick smoke and opened the door to let the fire draw better. "You've got more than enough on your hands keeping this place going. And anyway, it so happens that things are going well for me just now and it's...it's just common sense. Put another way, it'd be niggardly not to and I'd never forgive myself." He turned to face them and the others knew he would not give way; he never did when his mind was made up. "Come, Lottie," he appealed to his sister. "*You* see it...surely." The lowered head and slight lift of the shoulders told them she had heard what had been said but had nothing better to suggest.

"All right, all right," Jack sighed and looked wearily at his brother. "Thanks, Will...you're right. If things were a bit different here then maybe we could all have done something."

"Then I shall see to it all," Wilmot assured them as he left after lunch. "Please now, all of you, leave it with me." He checked his girth and nodded to the two men from Court Hall he had brought with him before mounting the grey. "My thanks again, Katherine dear." He put on his top hat and leant down. "Thanks," he whispered taking first her hand, then Charlotte's.

✳

The glass-sided hearse, adorned with black ostrich plumes and drawn by two Belgian blacks, brought her from Dulverton to St Mary's where Parson Froude met them. The box pews were packed even before Bert Loosemore, Fred's nephew, began to toll the bell. More and more villagers squeezed their way into the tiny church, leaving many to stand between the font and bellringers until the sidesmen turned people back and closed the door. Those shut out remained where they were, huddled against the wind while waiting to pay their respects.

The internment, near the cemetery wall did not take long. Jack barely noticed the faces that turned and watched as he and Katherine left their pew to follow the pallbearers down the aisle. Some smiled kindly in support as they waited their turn while others stared balefully, craning their necks to see how the mourners were faring. Froude led the way to the far corner of the churchyard.

Jack could hear him reading but had little idea of what he was saying, remembering only Katherine's arm through his and how tightly she was holding him. His foot slipped at the edge of the cobbled path and again on a tussock of damp grass near the grave. "*For as much as it hath pleased Almighty God of his great mercy to take unto himself….*" Froude knew the words by heart and barely glanced at his prayer book, his eyes instead checking those gathering behind the family. When he nodded, Jack, followed by Wilmot, bent to pick a handful of loose earth from the mound by the grave. "*Ashes to ashes, dust to dust; in the sure and certain hope of the Resurrection to eternal life…*"

He was the first to step forward and felt all eyes on him. Parson Froude's voice seemed to get louder and he remembered watching as the vicar's cassock and surplice billowed out in a sudden gust. He knew he had to be strong but in the sudden silence that followed the oration, he felt lonely and reached out for Katherine's arm. People nearest saw him pause uncertainly as he stepped onto the boards left by the sexton. For a moment he stared into the grave, his face now grey and lined with strain.

It was deeper than he expected but the coffin, lying at the bottom of the cold, winter tomb, did not look out of place. It seemed to be at peace, strangely comfortable as though it was how things should be. His mother had finally come home to rest and somewhere down there, behind the polished oak and the tightly bound shroud, was the voice and smile he remembered. He inclined his head as if to listen and peered more closely but there was nothing. She had gone. Even when the earth he let fall rattled on the wooden lid, he showed no emotion but just stood with his hand half outstretched. Froude saw Katherine whisper.

"Come, dear." He did not want to leave but Katherine led him firmly. As he turned he heard Wilmot's earth falling onto the coffin, then Charlotte's and Emma's, Davey's and Ralph's. The mourners parted to let them through and it was over. "Come on." His wife wrapped both arms around his. "Let's get something warm inside you."

*

Cold though it was, winter waited awhile as though toying with the idea. But when it came it struck with a fearsome icy blast. Jack stood in the porch and searched the evening sky. "What you looking at, papa?" Henry lifted his feet and swung on his father's arm. "What is it...what's up there?" His father frowned. It looked as though Bamber may have been right for today the sky was different. There was a feel of snow in the air but something else as well. Last night the wind had veered round to the north and now it was still...too still.

A week ago, just after the year had changed, Arthur had walked over to warn them. His father reckoned the snows would come and with them a terrible cold. Jack had seen it already; each night the frost had been sharper than the last when a thick rime coated everything from the grass and trees to the metal on the implements in the yard. Even at noon the sun was no more than a faint red glow in the freezing fog. Thrushes and fieldfares had gathered in the rickyard squabbling with the finches and sparrows.

Old Fisher had watched the deer and ponies come down to the low ground, the snipe and woodcock having left already for the shelter in the deep coombes beneath the moor. Wild geese, divers, even eider duck collected on the Barle, something Noah had not seen since the blizzards of thirty-nine. Here at Sherdon rats and mice started to come into the house from the outbuildings.

Nature was on the move, all the signs were there. Jack crouched by the boy who put an arm around his father's neck and leaned against him. "See the clouds up there. There look." The child followed his hand. "They're grey, Harry. Grey as grandma's hair used to be. Remember?" The five year old nodded, thumb in mouth. "It means there's lots of snow up there, much more than last year and old Mr Fisher says so." Jack nodded slowly to himself as though confirming his own thoughts. The last six weeks had indeed been difficult but each New Year brought hope and promise although, right now, the omens were not good. He watched his son as the boy took his thumb noisily from his mouth.

"Is it going to fall, papa? Come down? D'you remember last time...when the chicken house got full, and the hay shed?"

"I do, I do." He rose slowly. Most of the lambing flock were in the water meadows below the house but the younger stock and cattle were out on the high ground, some right out on the rough sixty acres. They would have to be moved down tonight. Even those below the house, where the snow tended to drift against the hedges, needed to be brought closer to the farm.

2

He decided to work through the night so they ate early. "Wind's veered round further." Declan and the others had gathered by the stables and saw Jack glance up at the sky.

"Aye, out to the north east...the last place we want it." He put his other boot against the mounting block and adjusted the canvas legging before stamping hard to shake his trousers into place. "Now then...." He swung round looking at what had to be done. For a moment he was undecided.

"D'you want me to come with you?" Billy was fastening his coat.

"Not yet, my boy, not yet." Jack patted his shoulder. "No...I'll get out there myself and bring the cattle down. Give Davey a hand, then the two of you can open the swede clamp...we'll give the lambing ewes a good feed. Then open one of the ricks...the smaller one next to the yard. Get the thatch off this end." Even as he left the shelter of the lane beyond the farm and started to climb, he knew the temperature had fallen again and it was when he reached the rough pasture that the first tiny flakes of snow danced around him. They were taunting him, making him guess at what might follow.

It should have been dark by the time he arrived back with the cattle but the snow had increased, settling on roofs and around the yard, bringing with it that strange silence and soft light. The flakes were larger now, falling gently yet covering everything they touched.

"Move 'em right up, Davey," Jack shouted. "Go on...right up...get they cows and young calves up to the far end." Billy had hung a storm lantern from one of the beams and Jack could see there would barely be enough room. He slapped the rump of the nearest bullock and whistled. The beast lifted its head and pushed urgently against those in front, blowing loudly. Tails swished and heads lifted in agitaion. And it was the same for him. Now frustrated, he raised his arms. He shouted and he moved from one side to the other behind the scrum of cattle while the dogs darted in to snap at their heels.

Later, water for those at the far end would be a problem but, right now, they were settling and feeding on the hay the boys had forked into the racks. Cows and calves called out to each other; somewhere a bullock lowed hoarsely. The air was thick with the rich smell of dung and the steam rose from the sodden beasts. Every now and then two or three struggled for more space but they were safe.

❊

As soon as Jack saw the yard his heart sank. Old Fisher had been right. It had taken much longer to sort the cattle than he wanted but, even in that time, the wind had risen, bringing with it smaller, ice-cold flakes that blew across the yard in sheets before sticking to whatever they touched. One moment they floated and danced in the still air while the wind drew its breath, next they raced madly into the night, driven on by the icy blast. High above the sky was black. Somewhere up there the clouds that brought the first snows had been swept on by this terrible wind that old Fisher had said could blow for days.

"The lambing flock." Jack bent forward and held his hat. "Get down to the lea and start bringing them up…two hundred and thirty. Take the dogs but don't rush 'em, mind. The pens should be ready." It was calmer behind the shippon where the land dipped sharply towards the stream. In the half-light below, they could see Ralph and Declan knocking hurdles into the iron ground. Where they faced into the wind, their two bodies were covered. Even as he came up to them it was beginning to freeze.

"Ready for 'em now, Jack," Ralph tested the hurdle. "Should keep 'em fast, they should."

"I'm going up top." Jack tightened the sack round his shoulders and turned to go. "See them in here, lads, then give 'em hay. We'll clear a way to put the roots down in the morning." But it was not to be.

"Hold it, Jack." Ralph struggled alongside him. "I'm with you…better off with two up there tonight." Jack saw the snow in the man's hair and watched as he tried to wipe his face dry. Even then some ice remained frozen to his eyebrows. Rudd, now twenty-six, and a few inches shorter than him, was hard and lean. Jack had often seen him at work and was glad of his company but the lane leading up to the high ground was blocked where the drifting snow had crept over the high bank. They took to the open fields yet the further they climbed the harder they had to battle into the storm. "We're going round in a circle," Ralph clutched at Jack's arm. He had to shout to be heard.

Jack's storm lantern was swinging wildly. A sudden gust caught his hat. He snatched for it but too late and it was gone, blown like a leaf into the night. "I know," he cried. "I'm trying to find the gate onto sixty acres…looks as though it's drifted over."

The younger man bent forward, his coat billowing behind him. "Over there, look…further up." The drift had curled like a giant wave into the gateway, hiding everything under a great sheet.

"We'll check here first." It was Jack's turn to shout. "I said we'll check *here*. My guess is they've been driven down the hill and are up against the bank over there…buried most likely."

"D'yer reckon this'll ease, Jack, or are we in for one of they ones we've 'eard about?" Ralph's boot slipped. "Wha' d'yer reckon?"

"Could get worse still…far worse." They had reached the lee of the hedge and crouched down out of the wind. Behind them the tempest was blasting at the far side of the bank, whipping long spumes of snow from the crests of the drifts, some higher than the bank itself. No sooner had they stopped than the iced powder began to cover them, some filtering down the back of their necks before melting and trickling further down.

It took them more than half an hour of tripping and stumbling through sedge and ice covered pools to search the rough ground. The land had been swept bare with not an animal in sight. "We must find 'em tonight…not so much the cold but the lack of air once they'm covered." It was the high drifts against the banks that worried him yet there was nowhere else for the flock to be and the banks would have to be searched. The two inched forward, feeling their way carefully as they prodded at the drifting, powdery snow with their crooks.

It was slow work, exhausting and freezing but they found them in the end, just where Jack feared they would be. The flock was buried, huddled together and entombed against the high bank. The warmth of their bodies and hot breath had hollowed a cavern under the snow. Several were down in the slush already and Jack could see they were too late for others. Too weak through the lack of air, the rest stood exhausted.

"They won't move." Jack had watched Ralph working ever more slowly. His head had dropped and now he sounded despondent. "Can't get 'em to leave the drift…won't even try." Minutes later he stopped and slumped against the bank. The snow was above his waist yet he seemed not to care if the freezing blizzard covered him or not. Jack struggled through the drift. He took the man's face in his hands but the lips had blued. The eyes were rolling unfocussed and his teeth were clattering. Even as Jack held him, the younger man was weakening and he had to be got off the hill now, right away. Jack bent low and waited until the body had fallen across his back. Then he rose slowly. Having stood, he juggled the weight to let it settle more easily before beginning the long journey down to the farm.

❋

Later that night, Declan watched Jack leave the yard. After ten minutes he returned. The young sheep was slung across his shoulders, held safely by its feet, while its head hung loose. The man's back was hunched against the weight yet his stride was steady and firm. Two of them tried to stop him, the others offered to go with him but he would have none of it. "Make them safe here. Tend them well…feed them and water them…see they want for nort." As he rested against the barn door, the ice on his hair and eyebrows gleamed in the lamplight. "I'll take my time…they'll not be moving tonight and I know where they be."

Frederic Knight never heard the full story of how his flock was saved. Rumours reached Simonsbath about what one man had done throughout that wild, winter night and for most of the next day. Twice, so he heard, they brought him soup and once, in the bitter hour before dawn, they took his shepherd's coat, by then solid with ice, and changed it.

Nobody saw him pause to huddle under in the lee of the high bank by sixty acres, where he gasped for air, where every muscle and sinew in his body ached and his sodden feet were frozen numb. Nobody knew why he drove himself on, forcing his body, time and again, to face the brutal climb into the teeth of the blizzard, only to stoop and pick up a frozen ewe before turning to come back down with the animal safe on his back.

Dawn did not break that morning, the night simply faded, making way for daylight to filter gradually through the gloom. He stopped to eat then turned once more to face the steep climb. This time they came with him but were unable to collect one for themselves, struggling instead to pull and push a few back down the hill. It took longer that way and it was harder so he stopped them. It disturbed the flock, he said, so he toiled on alone.

Just before noon, his strength began to give. He sensed it was going when he could no longer swing the animal up onto his shoulders, rather he struggled and fought with the weight before stumbling to keep his feet. But he dare not stop. Later he ate again then changed his coat once more. Several times he fell, not with a sheep on his back, but on the flat ground when he thought he was safe. When he came down with the last ewe, leaving the dead where they lay, the light had started to fade. By now the storm had eased but the snow was hardening and, as he came into the yard, his boots crunched noisily on the frozen ground.

✳

"*Why?*" Katherine turned and looked at Declan appealingly. "Why did he do it?" The Irishman placed the books back in the box. Each time Wilmot brought her a pile to read she let him pick and choose. He would sit reading in his room for hours, wrapped in blankets against the winter cold. When he finished them all he would start again, delighted at finding things he had missed on the first occasion and impatient for Wilmot to return with more. Burke and Boswell, she knew, were his favourites but she had let him keep hold of 'Smith's Sermons' as well.

He sighed, inclined his head then cocked an eyebrow. "'Tis difficult to say," he muttered. "I have me own ideas…but they're mine and only mine, you understand."

"Well, come on." Katherine put down her darning. For weeks, since the end of the long, cruel winter, she and the others had wondered at Jack's labours that night. Frederic had been aghast, furious that anyone should put himself at such risk but he, like so many others, marvelled at the tale he heard.

"'Tis difficult to explain." Declan smiled bashfully. Ever since he first borrowed her books, the two had enjoyed talking together. He knew she confided in him and he had told her much about his own younger days, about how he had fallen in with the wallers and what he hoped to do with his life. Even so it was not going to be easy for him to explain. "You see, the man's burdened himself. Neither he nor the others canna see it...but 'tis plain to me."

"But *why*? And what do you mean?" Katherine sat back. "What's this *burden* all about? Worry...or what?"

"Och, a number of things. He's a very proud man, is Mr Jack, yet he sees himself as a vassal to the place. Drives himself on. Like a man demented sometimes, so he is. Ever more determined to get t'e best out of every last drop. And he never stops, for mercy's sake."

"But everyone's the same, Declan. Breaking a new farm out of the moors was never going to be easy. Honestly, everybody works all the hours God gives...we have to."

"Aye, I know, I know." Declan leant forward, elbows on knees, and scratched at his mop of curly black hair. "But...well, 'tis more than that. He's Mr Knight's man, you must see that. He adores him, worships the man...'tis mutual."

"Go on." Katherine stared at him.

"Well, for me 'twas the duel that did it...and the manner it ended. It broke t'e both of them. Cut them to the bone it did and between soch a wonnerful friendship at that."

"But what's that got to do with rescuing *sheep*?" Katherine laughed and stood. She felt the baby move and smoothed her belly, then stretched and pressed her hands into the small of her back. "Not some sort of debt repaid? Is that what you mean?"

Declan bent forward again. "There's a saying at home that when a man wants to get something behind him...out of the way, call it what you will. We say he has to scrub his soul clean till it bleeds." Declan stood beside her. "That's what 'twas that night," he whispered. "No more'n less than that...to be sure it was. The master was cleansing his soul out there in the wild o' the night, purging himself and the flock was his soul...Knight's sheep at that. It was something he had to do...or perish the while. But he's fine, the now."

Without thinking he had taken her hand. "Really he is, you know... as fine as can be. *Now* then, ma'am." He had seen the sudden look of sadness in her eyes when she smiled. They seemed to be pleading with him, searching for confirmation, begging him to be right. He could see he had said something that had given her hope. But hope about what? He picked up the books, checking them carefully yet remaining disturbed by her reaction. "I'll be off wi' me readin.'"

Katherine picked Victoria from the cradle and held her over her shoulder. The baby gurgled as she patted her back and she swayed herself gently to and fro. Walking over to the window, she watched the Irishman cross the yard to his room, on the way shouting something to Davey and waving cheerily as he went. She had always marvelled at his perception. Perhaps it *was* that ghastly morning that had been praying on Jack's mind all this time, haunting him night after night as he lay silent, still and cold in bed beside her. Perhaps, as Declan suggested, his soul had been purged of guilt. Perhaps things might now be different and she prayed it would be so, for she wanted her man back.

3

"So...tell me, dear boy. Come on, tell me, quietly now while there's some peace." The gardens were at their best and the two men were strolling together having returned from church. "What the devil's happening in your life? Eh? All this about the job, a house...and Rebecca? Mind you, Tucker, she's a lovely creature...and such fun. Why...you old dog." Wilmot stumbled at the slap on his shoulder then laughed at the familiar high-pitched giggle that followed the cascade of words. Life, as ever, was rushing Tennyson along and the weekend was to be but a brief affair.

Earlier in the year, the poet and his wife had seen Farringford House for sale and were about to secure a deal when Emily announced she was pregnant. Matters had become complicated, he explained, and last night they had laughed fit to bust as the Poet Laureate tried to excuse his procrastination and constant changes of mind. The house and land were now his but he had decided to delay the move to the island. Impossible, he had decreed, until mother and child were fit enough to face the winds that swept in from Freshwater Bay. 'It's about as far away from the damned critics and their wretched quills as we can get,' he had huffed. It was his last point that decided matters and they had moved barely two months ago.

"*Well*," Wilmot took a deep breath. "It all began with Rebecca, of course."

"I'm so glad she accepted you," Tennyson cut in. "It couldn't have been easy for her, mind." He lifted his coat tails and joined his friend on the wooden seat. "I mean, just look at the very state of you, dear fellow. You're not exactly everyone's first choice, are you? Even for those of us who knew you at Trinity. Huh...*away there!*" The cat leapt from the sun bed it had scraped among the roses. "Can't stand the beastly things. They're always after the little birds...all that wonderful bird song. *Go on!*" he yelled, the gravel he had thrown falling well short. "I'm sorry, Wilmot. My dear good man, do continue...it was most rude of me."

"It was after the engagement party the Deveraux gave for us in Bristol, when the old man approached me. He whisked me off to his study then asked two other fellows to join us. Board members I think they were, and he came straight out with it. They wanted to purchase my release from Dowlais Iron and set me up in Bristol…offered me a very good post in their head office."

"So why all the fuss and dithering?" Tennyson scraped at his beard.

"Oh, come on Alfred." Wilmot flicked back his hair. "First of all it'd be quite some move. Dowlais are one of the biggest iron and steel companies in the country. Then, well…what do I know about ships, for God's sake? Or commodities and markets. Any of that? Docks, cargoes, all that sort of stuff? They'd eat me alive up there, and once they'd done that I could never return to my old job."

"*Rubbish!*" Tennyson exploded. *Non*sense…absolute stuff and nonsense." The poet half turned away from him and threw one leg over the other. "Listen, dear boy. All that's far too easy. Any fool can mug it up and trot it all out. A man like you'll have it mastered in a week. They're after what's in there." He turned and stared at Wilmot then tapped his friend's head. "In there, huh?" His body shook with laughter. "There's supposed to be something tucked away up there…isn't there? What did he say? Percy Shelley?" Tennyson held up an arm, appealing to the sky. " *'Teach me half the gladness that thy brain must know, such harmonious madness from my lips would flow'*."

"Birdsong, Alfred. Those were his skylarks, not people."

"Mmm…but only in one sense." Tennyson wagged a finger admonishingly. "Old Deveraux's been watching you and not only while you were prowling around his dear little precious. Why d'you think he's had you over so often, meeting all his business associates, his bankers and so on? All that lot, eh? He's been weighing you up, my man. You're a stubborn brute, Tucker, but you're quick…quick to pick up all the points flying around the room and then put 'em together." He leaned back with a finger raised. "Remember how you and Will Thackery used to argue? Oh, dear God, how it went on and on…exhausting stuff, but good to follow. That's what he's after, my boy, your grey matter…not what you know about his ships, for God's sake. And what's all this about Court Hall?"

Wilmot was silent, embarrassed. He had mentioned it to Emily last night. Rebecca had alluded to it earlier but he had been the one to let it slip. "It came as a wedding present, no less. The rest of the family can't stand the country and they've bought a bigger place in Bristol…a veritable palace up on Clifton Heights."

"You'll be near Jack," Tennyson mused. "That Sherdon's a wonderful spot. Such peace out there…I *must* get down again. And Katherine, of course, and Lottie…and those boys. What're they up to…hearts still set on battling away for queen and empire?" He lurched round to face him and slapped a thigh. "Any more confrontations with stags, eh? What a tale that was."

The two friends talked on. Wilmot told him about Katherine's difficult birth the previous month. Collyns and Bailey had saved the child but Anna Grace was to be the last. He saw Tennyson's worried look, then remembered that Emily's child was due in a few weeks. "Fear not, Alfred," Wilmot put a hand on his arm. "Fear not, old thing. I would not have mentioned it but that Katherine's...well, she'll not see forty again, forty-one to be exact, and they were warned about the risk."

"Forty-*one*," Tennyson gasped. "And still *such* an elegant woman...beautiful, and so sweet natured. But it hurts to see her working so." He left his words unfinished and the two sat quietly. Wilmot sensed his concern.

"We all worry, Alfred. They've done miracles up there and Jack's good to her but it's a hard, hard life. Even Lottie says so and she was born to it. The beauty of Court Hall and North Molton is that I'll be close and...well," he shrugged. "One never knows." He went on to tell him how he took up books for her to read and stole a few hours with her whenever he could.

Tennyson looked dejected, frowning deeply and with his head bowed low, almost between his legs. "They have to go on," he muttered. "'Tis very paradise itself up there. Virgil said it, didn't he...'*Non equidem invideo...*'"

"'*Miror magis*,'" Wilmot whispered. "His Eclogue, yes?"

"Just so...and to the shepherd, believe it or not." Tennyson tossed a handful of stones onto the path. "'*As for me I grudge thee not – rather I marvel.*' Eh?"

Suddenly there were footsteps on the gravel and the moment had gone. Wilmot watched his host trying to identify the intruder. "Beg pardon, sir...gentlemen."

"Ah, Hoskyns, yes," Tennyson smiled at the voice and held out his hand. "But why this now? What are you about?"

"Compliments of Mrs Tennyson, sir. Madam would welcome your presence without delay. Mr and Mrs Browning and Mr Lear are to catch the four o'clock ferry. From Yarmouth, sir, and she wishes luncheon to be as soon as possible. Their carriage will be here soon after three."

"Goodness." Tennyson scrambled awkwardly to his feet, pulling a fob watch from his waistcoat before holding it close to his face. "Heavens above. Now let me see." Wilmot watched as the poet turned the timepiece to the sun and lifted his glasses. "Shortly before one, no less. Right...yes...Hoskyns. Tell her we'll be with her directly. Come, Tucker," he crooked his elbow. "Your hand, dear fellow...around these plants and things if you please. Poor Browning will have caught it from his wife, I'll be bound. The good lady's a terrible one for the clock...a right stickler and she rides her poor man with such sharp spurs, so she does. As though he's a lazy nag...such a bore so she is." The two men linked arms.

4

Jack tried to move quietly. One of the floorboards by the door creaked and he grimaced. "Don't worry, dear. Nothing wakes her." Katherine smiled warmly from the bed. "Honestly, she's the best of them all." Anna was asleep in the cradle, Victoria next door in Charlotte's room. The boys had taken Francis down to the river and the two eldest would not be home from school for at least an hour.

Katherine was getting stronger but Charlotte insisted she did as Dr Collyns had bidden her and take an hour after lunch each day, and today it was hot and sultry. Charlotte and Declan had gone to Withypool and the house was quiet, slumbering in the August heat. Even the dogs, lying in the shade, were listless. Jack sat on their bed and took her hand, the signal for Patch to creep from under the covers and press up against him. The moment his master looked down, the little dog rolled onto his back and looked up enquiringly.

"Saw that girl from the cottage again this morning." Katherine shifted her position on the pillows behind her. "Gillan Rawle's wife. Er…Kitty, I think her name is. Isn't that it? A pleasant little thing."

"Oh, aye." He was sure she felt him flinch. "What's 'er about then?" He swallowed awkwardly but managed to catch his breath.

"Selling eggs and things. Clothes pegs…and what looked like a lot of old rabbit skins. She was away to Exford with her baskets just as I was seeing the boys down the lane."

"Oh, yes." He was thinking quickly. "Can't say I've seen much of her. See Gillan from time to time on his way to Barkham an' back." Jack took his hand from hers and scratched his shoulder. "Wally Sexton keeps him hard at it, I dare say."

"Never see any children there…boys haven't either. D'you think…"

"Don't 'spect so," he blurted. Too late he realised for he had no idea of her question.

"What d'you mean?" Katherine laughed and pulled his hand away from the loose button on his shirt. "Don't keep on doing that, dear. You'll make it worse. No…what I was wondering *was*, that if Lottie *does* go…then I'll be needing some help. I mean, there're five little ones now and I don't think I can manage it all. D'you think if I asked her she might consider coming in to help from time to time? Daresay they could do with a bit more money."

Jack stared down at the bed. Kitty *here*? In the house? That slow smile and those green eyes? He could imagine it. No, he couldn't. It would be impossible, dangerous beyond words…a keg of powder too close to the fire and getting warmer all the time. It could never last. But then…why not?

Katherine laughed mischievously and put a finger to her lips. "What on earth are you looking like that for? As though you've seen a ghost. Oh well...it was only a thought." She shrugged and pulled a face. "Don't worry dear...we'll find someone, there're plenty of others. Anyway, let's see what Lottie wants to do with Bamber...and what's to do about Davey." They both knew Charlotte was getting worried about her son joining the hussars. They had talked about it before when the three of them were together and again on Sunday when Gaile Fisher had been to lunch.

"Can't blame him. Neither of them for that matter...they're both in it together." For a moment he had been angry with himself but now he relaxed. The very mention of Kitty had excited him, the more so with Katherine's suggestion which, as if by some cruel twist, made it sound as though she was actually encouraging their union. But she, of course, had no idea of his reaction to what she had just said. She had no idea of his thoughts and could never entertain such thoughts herself. Her mind was pure. Seeing her lying there chatting away so trustingly, he yearned to close her in his arms and tell her how much he loved her but he held back. It would have been too much and she would have thought it strange just now. This was going to have to be his own private battle. Somehow he had to wrest this other woman from his mind. He had to or it would be the end, and if ever Katherine got to know.... Yet Kitty was there at the cottage, day in day out, and so close. Barely half a mile away, and on her own for most of the time.

"Saw Hector at Simonsbath the other day," he announced. He and Dan Webber were there at the sheep fair together. Said the lads did well at camp and the Royal North Devons are after them." Jack warmed to his theme, relieved he had been able to move talk on. "No choice, is there really? What sort of life 'are they goin' to have up here? I mean to say any youngster like them that sees a soldier's life...an' hears all the tales. They're bound to be keen."

"But they're not going for ever, are they?" Katherine sat up shocked. "Not taking the shilling...and signing their life away?" Jack nodded. "Oh, dear God. Lottie'll go crazy. She's terrified at the thought of them even joining the Yeomanry...thinks they'll get caught up in these riots and things. But the *regulars*...oh dear. Poor Lottie. And what about you? What on earth are you going to do if they both go off? *Jack*...you'll be stuck without them."

"Oooh, there's plenty of lads about. George Snell's boy out to Bishop's Nympton. Young Herbie. Comin' up for twelve now. Farmer Rumbelow reckons 'e's ready to go out to work. An' Stan Bawden, Ed's lad. He's another...we'll manage."

"Well, make sure our two let you know in plenty of time." She reached out and touched his nose. "And don't go forgetting about it...or not wanting to ask anyone, then make it worse for yourself." Jack looked down at her. As always she was thinking of others, worrying about their hopes and fears, their problems and their families yet she had so much to worry about herself. Slowly and gently he lifted her chin before bending down and kissing her softly.

"Jack," she whispered when he drew back. As she reached up and stretched out to run both hands through his hair, her eyes narrowed with affection. "Oh Jack...dear, dear Jack. Come here. If only you knew..." For a moment she was lost. "If only you really knew how much I loved you. *Here*," she murmured, holding his face in her hands. They were now very close. "You darling, darling man. I love you so much...come to me." As their lips met once more her eyes closed.

"There you are. See?" She was breathing more quickly and looking up at him, watching his eyes search her face. "That's all, I'm afraid. Go on. Away," she chuckled and pushed him gently. "You know the rules...the doctor spelt them out." He wanted her there and then but knew it was not possible for the doctor had warned him. He felt proud and strong. He loved his wife and wanted to show her how much he cared but that, he knew, would come later.

✳

Nobody could remember what time it was when the dogs started to bark. Then, as soon as they heard the first horses, the geese began to call. By the time whoever it was had reached the yard, the place had gone mad.

"Stay here." Jack threw back the bedclothes. His gun was in the kitchen but he lost a few moments finding his trousers and boots. Years before, Luke had warned him never to get caught in bare feet. *'Never mind clothes,'* the smuggler warned. *'Ye can move an' run just as fast with or without. But yer boots...can't do nort without summat proper on yer feet.'* The loud, echoing knocks began before he was half way down the stairs. Ralph was in front of him.

"Get up behind the front door, lad. Get the lamp goin'. Talk to 'em...but through the door. Don't open, whatever they say. I'm goin' out the back." The yellow moon was three parts full but still high in the clear sky. There were two riders in the yard while a third, the one who knocked, stood dismounted by the door. Further back down the lane he could see more silhouettes. Somewhere a horse blew. Across the yard, Declan opened his window causing the riders to turn quickly.

"Stand or I shoot...and I've got the two barrels on yer." Jack was behind the hedge and knew he was hidden. "One move and I shoot...who are you and what's yer business?" The riders hesitated. "Answer me or I'll take the first man right now, just as you are...answer me, I say."

"Jack...Jack don't shoot." The rider at the door turned this way and that trying to get sight of him. "'Tis me, Jasper. Jasper Harper...we need yer help, Jack."

180

"Stay where you are! Move and I'll shoot!" Jack's voice echoed round the yard. *"Declan…down here man, and quick about it."* He kept to the cover and waited for the Irishman. "Their guns and swords…take 'em one by one. I've got yer covered," he advised. "Let the dogs out first, they know who's a friend or not."

"Jack, thank God it's you we…"

"Hold yer tongue, blast yer eyes." Jack could feel the rage inside bursting. "Damn you, Jasper Harper. Damn you to hell and damn you again." By now he was close and could smell the drink. Savagely and without pausing, he picked up the younger man and threw him against the porch wall. What in the devil's name're you doing out here…at this time of night…and up to no good I'll be bound?"

"Jack, let me down. For mercy's sake man." The younger man's eyes were bulging. Strong and fast though he was, the strength of the great farmer made light of his efforts. He could feel the hand around his throat tightening. *"Jeeaack,"* his voice croaked. *"Pleeeese."* He fell to all fours, coughed and rubbed his throat. The figure was towering over him. "Ye God's man…where did all that come from?"

"What's yer business, Harper? Tell me now an' tell me all." Jasper climbed to his feet and leant against the wall still rubbing his throat. The smugglers had been tipped off, so he explained. A party of shepherds at Kinsford Gate had warned them of Customs men at Sandyway and more out at Moles Chamber. They could not go on, but neither could they turn back for there was no place to hide at Simonsbath. It was a large run, one organised by Luke.

"Can yer help us, Jack? Above the cows…there's room enough. Seventy casks and two bales of baccy." For half an hour they argued and pleaded. Once they almost came to blows but Jack stood his ground. Enough had been enough out at the Acland Arms. They had talked at the Sportsmans but he wanted no more of it…nothing…never and no matter even if Luke was his old friend.

"Damn yer, Jack. Have you no honour? Where's yer shame? Think on the man you're turning away…maybe turning in, for that." Jasper now stood with his feet astride. His hands were on his hips throwing open his coat of claret velvet. "'Tis not for me, man, nor any here, but for *Luke*. D'ye not owe him, Jack? Owe 'im for all yer know, all what 'e's taught yer down the years? If yer send us away now, how'll yer face the world? Eh? Answer me that before yer have to answer to others."

He tugged at his stock then bent down to pick up his French cocked-hat. "Come on, man…'tis only this once an' I'll pay yer well. Half the takings, d'ye hear? *Half*…that's more'n a hundred guineas. Jack…come now."

It took more than an hour to hide the contraband and the following day he was up before dawn checking and doublechecking. Before the smugglers left he took Jasper to one side. They walked to the far end of the empty shippon where, once again, he cornered him. "Listen, lad an' listen well to me." Jack's finger was close to his face. "Just two things. Right? Two things an' remember 'em good. *Never again*, d'ye hear? None of this…*never*, ever again. And now listen. If what they shepherds said were true then they're after yer, my lad…the law's on yer tail. An' if it is, then you're a marked man." Jasper turned his head away and shrugged.

"No…come here. You listen to me good, boy." Jack moved closer. "You mark my words. Take care, Jasper. Don't go getting them all vexed. Lie low for a while. Keep away from the Sportsman's or they'll have yer…Redcoats an' all. No…no," he saw Jasper's face. "Just heed my word, boy…don't go pressing yer luck. A man's got only so much of it and most of yours is gone."

5

Declan decided to move on. He had been thinking about it for some time and the affair with the smugglers made up his mind. It would be hard leaving but another letter had arrived from home. They told him there was nothing left in Ireland and they were going to try their luck in America. The family needed him, they said. They wanted him with them and they were pleading. For a week he agonised, turning the matter over in his mind as he worked alone. Gaile would be difficult: it would be best to slip away in the night as he had once threatened, then write later. Jack, he felt sure, would understand. He would warn him in time and there were plenty of lads looking for work. He had heard them talking at the table and Bamber Heard had mentioned two others in Withypool.

But it was Katherine. That was going to be difficult, very difficult. He loved her as he loved his own sisters, sometimes even as much as his mother. They could talk and laugh together, tell each other little secrets, discuss the books, tell tales about their homes. Leaving her would be hard, and the thought of it all disturbed him.

He knew he treated him differently to the others. They all knew that but nobody cared. It was just the way things were and they used to laugh about it. But she would miss him keenly, of that he was sure. She needed his company, lived off it, but who else was there? Who else could take her mind off the drudgery? Who else could brighten her day and make her smile? She needed to talk about the books and she loved it when they sat discussing the meaning of something, or about what somebody had thought or done. He saw it all, especially the gulf between her and her man. He noticed, too, how when the gentry called, even his master's brother, her spirits soared. But now they came less frequently and he could tell how much she missed their company.

That delicate, gentle, sensitive woman would be left all on her own. He, the bridge between herself and the others, would be gone. She would be deserted, trapped and he could imagine her there, caged like a beautiful songbird but silent and lonely as she gazed through the bars at the world beyond.

✳

"Stay," Declan whistled quietly and watched as his collie crouched before lying flat. It paused, watching him, panting eagerly and with its ears pricked, then lowered its head but with his eyes still on him "Stay." He whistled again then turned to pick up the rabbits and nets.

The river had been running high, probably too high for the trout but he decided to take a closer look. The dog would be happy where it was so he clambered over the bank and made his way down to the bridge over Sherdon Water. The wood smoke he could smell would be coming directly from the cottage for the breeze was in that quarter. He pushed back the branch, ducked underneath then stopped.

Larkspur, Jack's horse, was tied up by the gate. The two sheepdogs leapt to their feet but Declan had seen them already. He crouched low, raised his arms and whistled a long, soft note. Both animals slowed to a walk then slunk towards him, wagging their tails submissively. One came to his feet and rolled onto its back. He bent down, took hold of both by their heads and spoke quietly. They settled at once and watched him yet neither moved for he had told them to stay quiet. The horse half turned and saw him. Again he called quietly, took the animal by his head and blew gently into his nostrils, taking in the animal's breath.

He could hear voices so he crept forward, now suspicious and alert. Jack's coat was on the bench by the cottage door but they were inside. Declan heard him laugh…then her voice once more. A door shut and the voices became muffled. A moment later she laughed again. Then somewhere, upstairs so it seemed, a window was closed.

Chapter Twelve

The spring after Declan left, indeed the summer that followed, brought fresh hope to those on the moor. Easter Sunday was one of the mildest anyone could remember when Jack and the boys worked in their shirtsleeves before getting ready for church. The next few days were warmer still and it was Charlotte who remarked that she had never before seen swallows while picking daffodils. A little snow had fallen in February but it was nothing, or that was how old Fisher put it. March was wet and on several occasions the Barle burst its banks. April was not much better but after that glorious weather broke out over the English countryside with May confirming all the earlier promise.

Memories of the great storm faded but a terrible toll had been exacted where stock had been decimated, as though struck down by a plague. For weeks after the snow, skeletons of sheep, picked clean by scavengers, lay in the fields surrounded by shreds of wool. Several farmers chose not to sell what lambs and calves arrived that year, deciding instead to build up their breeding stock.

Those who had prepared themselves wisely fared better and at Sherdon, what Grace had taught them served well. Although full of weevils, the extra flour she always kept lasted throughout. Potatoes and roots, stored carefully in clamps, escaped the very worst of the frosts while the meat, salted and prepared as she had shown how, remained edible and nourishing. But fear about running short of fuel, a legacy from Molland, weighed heavily. Time and again the boys were sent down to the woods at Badgercombe or out to where Declan had stacked the peat.

*

Last year had been one of recovery and replacement as nature balanced her books, but this year promised to be better. Everyone missed Declan, in particular Gaile and Katherine. He vowed he would write and each week they waited for the mail at The Royal Oak but nothing came. For weeks Gaile walked the three miles there and back again until her father put a stop to it. "Can't think of nort else," he complained to Jack. "Won't stop dashin' 'er eyes an' bawlin' about the fella...never stops. Won't eat, won't sleep...won't do nuthin' but lie in 'er cot an' stare at the rafters."

"Aye well. 'Tis always the one that hurts...that first one. The poor young heart's never known ort like it before. All soft an' innocent it is, beatin' away an' mindin' it's own business then *bang!*" Jack's hand slapped against his chest. "All of a sudden, along it comes...just like that." Her father was forced to agree. It was Ralph who brought her heart back to Exmoor: quiet, hard working Ralph, the one who kept his peace and who the others teased but who Jack trusted. It had been he who had noticed her sorrow and he who had got her to smile again.

Katherine saw the change when she came up to the farm and envied the girl her newfound happiness. Only after Declan had been gone for some months did she really understand how much she, herself, missed the Irishman's company. She missed his quick mind that used to feed her own, his knowledge about so many things and his understanding about what he had read. She yearned for his happy, carefree spirit about the place as much as their arguments over the books. Visits from Frederic and Wilmot, or from Dr Collyns and Parson Jack when they passed, meant more and more. She looked forward to them all but they were busy men and never stayed long.

She searched the markets at Withypool and Exford for a friendly intelligent face, one with whom she could talk and in whom she might confide, but she was viewed as a stranger and would always be so. Whenever she tried to make conversation she knew they were studying her, watching her mannerisms and the way she expressed herself rather than listening to what she said. Whenever she walked by the men they would fall silent. Sometimes they would nod or return her smile but, more likely, they would stare ahead silently as though lost in thought, or search busily for something in the distance. Yet hardly had her shadow passed than the pipes would come out again and the heads nod together. From time to time she would hear a titter or a laugh and the shuffling of feet behind her.

With the women it was worse. It was almost as though they resented her intrusion into their world. All smiles while the deal at the stall was being done, they would mutter politely and nod then stand back and search for the next customer. Try as she might she could never get them to talk. As far as they were concerned that was the end of it and they wanted nothing more to do with her. Even in her market clothes, they knew she was different and were uneasy about her presence. It was her fine features and the way she spoke; even how she held herself. Some bobbed respectfully but then glanced away shy and confused, looking anywhere but at her. Her loneliness bore heavily.

2

"Heey...*up*." Jack raised his shears and looked up, watching Billy as he jumped down from the holding pen gate and ran to take the freshly shorn ewe. The sheep, surprised at her near nakedness and sudden freedom, bucked and skipped in defiance as he pulled her across the barn floor. Holding her by one horn, he dipped Frederic Knight's branding iron into the raddle then rolled the 'FK' across her back, keeping it steady while the red pitch soaked into the short, white coat.

"'Tis one of ours, 'er is...so a cross on the head between horns as well, don't forget." Jack stood and stretched.

"'*Eeay*...there." This time it was Ralph who stood. Shears high above his head in one hand, he held the ewe until Davey collected her, then pushed at the fleece with his foot while waiting for Gaile. She had been sitting in the sunlight by the main door with her mother and Jade Sexton waiting for a shearer to call. Now she ran.

The young shearer watched the girl gather the fleece into her arms then toss it onto the floor before stooping to collect in the loose pieces. As she moved from point to point around the floor she crouched low, her fingers working nimbly until she had gathered it all in. Unaware he was watching her she ran her hands through the soft, creamy texture then leant forward to place her cheek against the wool.

"Bootiful, that," Ralph gasped, leaning over to put down his tankard of cider. "Never find clothes so pure's that." Lifting his shirt tail, he bent forward to wipe his face.

"What be you checkin' me for, Ralph Rudd?" She smiled shyly and blushed, happy to be working with him. His shirt was streaked with sweat and his long wiry hair flecked with dust and pieces of wool. Little did he know it but his whole body reeked of sheep where the oily muskiness had worked its way into his clothes and skin. He lacked Declan's impish wit and ready smile; sometimes she thought he was almost too quiet, but he had been gentle with her, understanding her moments of sadness.

"Good for yer skin, that is. 'Ere, try a bit." He squatted beside her, caught hold of her wrist and turned it gently while lifting back her sleeve. Picking a handful of freshly cut wool, he rubbed the soft fibre up and down the underside of her arm before trailing his fingers lightly over her skin. At first she tried to draw back then relaxed, warming to his touch. "There 'e be. Feel that," he murmured, keeping hold of her hand. "Soft, ain't it...soft as cotton grass."

His hand tightened and he pulled her gently towards him before dropping his gaze to her half open blouse. "'Ere, come on. What you lookin' at now?" She pulled back her arm and moved to close the collar of her dress but her smile gave her away. "You keep yer eyes t' yerself...an' away from down there."

"Better for to look where a man's s'posed to look...ain't it, maid?" He held the fleece while she tied it with a short rope she had made by twisting the wool then stood with her, still close. Reaching out, he picked a sliver of loose wool from her hair. "Well...ain't it?" he asked softly. It was his turn to smile.

"'Ere, come on you two lovebirds." Bamber Heard, shearing master for the week, glanced round making sure no one else could hear him. His hip, long since his tormentor, caused him to roll rather than walk as he made his way towards them. "Nuff o' that, buiy." He grinned cheerfully for Lottie would be delighted with this snippet of tattle. "'Tis more than hot enough in y'ere without none o' that goin' on. Now then...ready? Right...*Davey*," he lurched round. "'Nother one, y'ere. *What's that? 'Ow Many?*"

The old farmer waited with one hand to his ear. "Right, lads." It had been a long day and he turned clumsily, uncertain to whom the new information should be imparted. "A dozen it is. Twelve more then that's it," he announced to nobody in particular. "Hour an'a half, p'raps...then finished...all done."

Bamber took off his felt hat and followed the girl across the floor. Old enough to be her father and more yet he could not be blamed for noticing the swing of her hips. No man could for her thin cotton skirt was never meant to hide that sort of thing. Was she, he wondered, taunting her man while he waited for his next sheep or was she letting those watching see how a young maid should really be walking? As he rolled along in her wake, Bamber scratched at the back of his head. It didn't matter he decided, either way young Miss Fisher knew how to carry her fleece.

He passed her father and Wally Sexton, both still shearing. Arthur Fisher was bent over his ewe. The animal, now lifted and turned to sit on her backside, leaning up against his thighs, sat rudely with her legs stuck out like a fat woman. Same as old Mrs Rottenbury up against the rick at harvest time, he mused. 'Cept the sheep are better looking. Wally chose to kneel on one knee by his ewe. The head of the animal lolled close to the shearer's own, her eyes rolling anxiously as she tried to take in the scene around her. Every now and then she would gurgle a bleat. Both men worked steadily, turning their sheep slowly as soon as one part of the fleece fell free. Sometimes they would call out to each other, sometimes laugh out loud at what had been said but their eyes never left their gleaming blades. They were masters of the art yet it was the end of a long day; the sweat on the back of their red necks and the dark patches on their shirts showed how they had toiled.

The evening sun, still high enough over the shippon, made every effort to brighten the deep gloom inside the barn. But it had to struggle for the day had been busy and the thick clouds of dust that had been kicked and scuffed into the air hazed the bright shafts of sunlight on their way to the shearing floor. The two great doors, large enough to allow fully laden haywains inside the barn, had been thrown wide and held open to catch whatever breeze there might be. Bamber could see that the wooden floor had been polished clean by the grease of the wool and took pains to step carefully down into the deep wagon ruts by the main stone archway. Here he paused with one arm across his face to shield the light. "You'm be feedin' 'alf Exmoor tonight then, m'dear? *Eh?*" he shouted, cocking an ear."

"Nigh on sixty, all told." It was Emma that called back. Now housekeeper at Filleigh, Jack's elder sister had long since given up getting her hands dirty yet she was never happier than when spending the whole of shearing week at Sherdon. Some years ago Jack had asked her to help and it had become a tradition.

"Here girls...over here a minute." The two teenagers left setting the table and followed their mother to where Bamber was surveying the proceedings. Hands on hips, his smock was spread comfortably about his girth. Emma, like every-body, rejoiced in his company. The smiling, weather-beaten face with its two dancing eyes drew the best out of people and she had been delighted when Jack told her about the farmer and Lottie.

"'Allo, me dear," he said softly. "'Ow be'e getting' on?" Emma smiled affection-ately as he raised her hand to his lips. The girls stepped forward to take his hand one after the other, laughing shyly at the great show he made of it all. "Loverley maids," he chortled, looking from one to the other. "Summat o' their mother there, I see. And their gran' too...bain't there now?" he added, bending forward to look more closely. Sarah, the younger of the two, ducked coyly as he reached forward to pinch her cheek.

"Now then, dear." It was an important matter that had been playing on his mind and his eyebrows shot up at the sudden thought. "*Now*...what sort o' time are yer reckonin' on?" The watch came from somewhere deep in his trousers beneath the endless rolls of his smock. "Wally 'n Edgar'll be here 'bout seven...they'm comin' early but t'others won't be far be'ind."

"Us reckoned that Jack would have a good crowd here tonight." It was Gwen Fisher and Bamber caught her eye. "'Bout sixty or nearabouts."

"Aye, so her said." He shook his head, contemplating the crowd. "*Sixty*...cuh, bless my soul."

＊

Charlotte watched the last one to be shorn. It was Davey who took the animal and Gaile, her hips still swinging, who collected the fleece. The work was done at last and the boys took the pen of ewes to join the rest in the meadows beyond rick yard. The faces of those in the barn, every one of them, were drawn and their bodies tired to the bone. Some sat, leaning back against the wall, others stood talking quietly among themselves. The barn was empty, even the last shaft of sunlight had gone slowly on its way. There was no noise or bustle, no banter or laughter, nothing but quiet talk and the chirping of sparrows. Shearing was over.

"Right, then." It was Jack, nodding to his sister, who clapped his hands. "Bring in the ale, m'dear. 'Tis time at last...time for the toast." Standing up on his toes in the middle of the shearing floor, he turned slowly. "*Gather up everyone,*" he called. "*Bring in the ale*...cider as well. *Everyone* take hold of summat."

"*Come then.*" Now it was Bamber who took off is hat. "Come, m'dears...y'ere's health to the flock." As he turned to Katherine and Jack, the tankard was high above his head. "To Maister...to Missus an' all they've got. May God bless 'em all...and God bless the flock." One by one the glasses came down. Some gasped at the effect of the cold ale, some laughed, others clapped.

＊

The Chuggs came early as they always did, followed closely by the Buckinghams. The Hibberds and Bawdens came together, then the Heywoods with the Rudds, the Cockrams and the Sextons and all the others, drifting into the yard one after the other, one family at a time, old and young packed into the wagons and carts. It was as though they knew that the day at Sherdon was done.

Katherine watched from her place at the table, just beneath the steps leading up to the front door. She would have been there to greet them but Anna Grace required her attention, so she sat quietly with her child. The young lady herself, with her cheeks aflame and a wet fist pushed determinedly against an even wetter mouth, stood happily and bright eyed on her mother's thigh, her little legs bending and stretching excitedly and missing nothing of the events before her.

Jugs of ale and cider were placed on the long trestle tables that had been arranged around the spit where the pig was turning. Long before, lanterns had been lit and set out between the loaves of bread and the plates of pickles and chutney and the tall jars of foxgloves and buttercups put there by the girls. Lamps had been hung from beams in the barn and the younger children watched as the older boys swept the floor clean.

Katherine hummed as she rocked the baby. Jack was pleased at how it had gone and, for that, she was glad. Everybody had worked well and preparing the food with Emma and Lottie had been fun. Haymaking was yet to come and that might be difficult but, at last, at long, long last, the farm was beginning to pay. No more than a small, miserly return for their efforts but it was a start. They would never be rich but somehow they would manage even with the children growing so fast.

She could see Jack with Hardy from The Sportsman's and waited until he looked her way, still talking as he did so. She could not move but glanced round shyly then lifted her head and pouted her lips. Without thinking or pausing for breath he glanced away then swung back suddenly, realising what he had seen. His smile was slow but she caught the kiss he returned. Hardy saw it too and waved.

Emma and Charlotte moved among the guests pushing the youngest children in front of them with trays of homemade sweet scones and cheeses. Slowly, as the shadows grew longer, the gathering drew themselves in until suddenly, as if someone had clapped their hands and told them to begin, it was all laughter and noise. The men, legs astride and heads nodding sagely, talked farming talk, of the Knights and other tenants, of farms new and old and about their stock. Women, with their heads together, spoke of life in the village. About who was ill and which families had been blessed with a new arrival, about who had bought this or sold that, about who was courting who, and who had said what.

Anna Grace looked on at it all until she was bored when, without saying anything, she rested her head gently against the warmth of her mother's neck and closed her eyes. She had seen enough. She was ready for bed and Katherine rose carefully.

*

"Are you going to sing, Mr 'eard?" Bamber looked down at George Buckingham. The child, with long fair hair and no front teeth, the one who had fallen into the pond earlier and was now dressed in Henry Tucker's Sunday suit, had been sent to ask. The others stood back watching anxiously. "Father thayth you are..." his voice trailed off.

"*What?*" Bamber asked. "*Me an' Jim?*" He picked the child up and watched affectionately as the youngster looked round shyly before pressing his face down and hiding his eyes. "P'raps after supper, m'dear," he said quietly, ruffling the child's hair. "P'raps us'll get Mr Carter and his boy to play on the fiddles and we'll give'e all a song about the staghounds. Eh? Now then." The old farmer lowered the boy gently.

He kept his word but it was not until Jack rose to cheers and shouts and called the two men forward. Then, on his feet before Jim Blackmoor, Bamber went through the chorus with those at the table. Once he waved their efforts away and sat heavily, making as if he wanted nothing more to do with them. But he rose again to more cheers, even then demanding something better, bending forward and shouting above the noise with one hand to his ear. Only at their third attempt, was he satisfied.

Jim Blackmoor was as stocky and black-haired as his name suggested, even to the hairs on the back of his short, stubby fingers. No razor had ever touched his beard, which stood proud from his face that was already half hidden under his old, high-pointed hat. The two men, now the centre of attention, moved to the head of the table beside Katherine where a lantern had been placed that shone up into their faces. The lady of the house lifted her chair back to make room, whispering something that made them both laugh. Old Bamber wiped at a tear. Everybody watched expectantly as Will Carter adjusted the strings of his fiddle, frowning to himself and muttering as he scraped and plucked until he was satisfied. At last he looked up and nodded.

Bamber raised his hand but there was silence already. Softly at first, as they had done so many times before, the two men began to sing, one low and rich the other higher and more easily heard.
>   "The forest above and the coombe below
>   On a bright September mo-orn
>   'Tis the son of a sod that thanks not God
>   That ever his body was bo-orn.

So-o-o," the cry from the table rose. "Hurry along the stag's afoot." Tankards and hands crashed in time.
>   "The master's up an' awa-ay.
>   Aloo, aloo, we'll follow him through
>   From Bratton to Porlock Ba-ay."

By now the dogs in the sheds were barking. Someone blew a hunting horn, somebody else hollered loudly and the younger children stared around in wonder. As far as they could see, their parents had gone maze, carousing and banging the tables without caution or shame, all pride and dignity gone to the wind. The two singers, eyes still fixed on each other, waited for the fiddlers' cue. Bamber wiped his mouth and Jim pulled on his ear.

> "He's all his rights and seven a top,
> His eye is the eye of a ki-ing.
> He'll beggar the pride of them that ride
> Before he leaves the li-ing.

So-o-o-o," again the fists thumped down. Three more verses and justice was done as the two men were cheered into the night.

Dancing began soon after when the younger ones left their elders to sit and talk, but gradually the tables emptied and the barn filled to the sound of shouts and the scuffle of feet on the shearing floor. Will Carter and his son, 'Thin' Reg, sat on the table near the collecting pen. A slow dance was followed by a jig, then a bright and jaunty barn dance with all the clapping and stamping. After that came a square dance, then back to a slow glide.

Jack danced, Katherine danced, everybody danced. Kitty Rawle, her hair swept back and decorated with wild flowers danced, but not with Jack. She knew he would not ask her but she was not concerned. Several times she caught him looking her way and once, when he passed, his arm brushed against the softness under her blouse. He paused for a moment and pardoned himself with one hand on her shoulder, and she smiled at the touch of his fingers. But he did no more than that. Only once, just after the last dance, she saw him nod and smile slowly before turning away.

3

"And tell 'im it's two shillings and sixpence a week... *and that's for both of 'em,"* she yelled. "Each one of 'em, that is. Same as everyone else." John Marley waved in acknowledgement to his wife's shouts then turned and beat his fist on the tenants' door once again. Three times he hammered before putting his shoulder to the woodwork. Eventually the lock gave, causing him to stumble into the front room.

The little girl with blue eyes and flaxen hair had been crying. "Where's yer father, maid?" He tried not to frighten her but he was furious, not only with Burgess but with himself for not heeding the warnings about the man. He followed the child into the dark, communal living room, wrinkling his nose at the rancid smell. Clothes, most of them dirty and damp, lay in tangled heaps. A mouse scuttled from the mouldy bread while another, or perhaps it was a rat, knocked over the beaker by the logs in the corner. The place was cold and dank.

"Burgess...get up, I wanna talk." Marley nudged at the chair with his foot. "Come on, get up, yer lazy brute...*get up, damn you!"* He bent down and shook the prostrate figure, stopping only when the girl scrambled hurriedly onto her father's lap.

191

"No," she begged. "Please don't." Anna Burgess turned to ward off his raised hand. "*Don't!*" This time she cried out loudly and cowered down to shield her father. "Papa's not well." The vagrant stirred aggressively. Unwashed and unshaven, he brushed his daughter to one side.

"'Tis *I*, Burgess, John *Marley* an' I've come to speak about yer rent." He could see the man was still sodden with drink and watched in disgust as the face yawned widely. "Hey, wake up, man…gid on yer feet." It was his boot that brought attention. "D'yer hear me, Burgess?" Marley bent down. The man stank and he shook him violently. "*Come on*, blast yer eyes…*come on.*"

"Le'me be, for Chris'sake." Burgess coughed. He hawked then hawked again before scowling blackly as he focussed on the figure in front of him. "I 'eard yer, Marley." He struggled to sit and rubbed his face, the week-old black stubble rasping against his hand. "I 'eard yer, man." He coughed again. "An' I ain't *got* no money. Right? I can't pay, yer." He glared back at the face above him. "Can't pay and that's all there's to it." He fell back and closed his eyes.

"Two days, man. Just two days an' you're out. *Right?* Out on yer ear an' that's the end of it." Marley stood back but then bent forward again. "An' don't forget it, man. You're a savage, Burgess…an' a wastrel at that."

∗

It was dark before Burgess pulled himself out of his soiled chair. Twice Anna had come to him begging for something to eat and twice he had dismissed her. Now she came again, more timidly this time and fearful of his reaction. "Gid over to Gallon 'ouse…round to the kitchens." He yawned and scratched then turned back to the tinder and matchwood by the fire. "They'll give 'e summat." But Anna hesitated. She had tried already and had been chased away. "*Gid on!*" Burgess pulled her to the door and pushed her into the night. "Do as I bloody say…an' don't come back without summat."

Howard and Barrow, the two lodgers in the next room were away for the night. Burgess had been due to go with them, for the sheep at Honeymead had broken out again. The Irish in the nearby miners' cottages paid well for fresh meat and asked no questions. The money was good but tonight he felt bad and he scratched himself again. Marley was pressing him; the man never let go. Two shopkeepers in Exford were chasing him as well, and those in the bar over at Gallon House had helped throw him out. Young Tucker, the dandy whelp with the limp, had sacked him from the mine and the new vicar at Simonsbath wanted to see him. Burgess rubbed his wrists. The scars itched where the miners at Heasley Mill had tied him before their beating. It was the children's fault, and he cursed them: they had done nothing but sneak and complain until the men had come for him.

Before she went to bed, Anna brought him a discarded piecrust but it wasn't enough so he hit her, then again but harder. His hunger remained and her whimpering

192

annoyed him. Everyone was against him. First it was that lot from Heasley. Then the police had come for him: the ones from Dulverton in their new uniforms. Always on about money so they were, but there was never enough. Whatever little there was had gone, spent on the child…oh and and the drink, of course, where even the slops from the inn had cost him. Now there was nothing, nothing at all yet still he had to keep her. The other two had gone back to their mother but the girl remained. She was a hold on him and a drain on his money. Burgess frowned. She would have to go. Like it or not there was no other way and he shrugged to himself. It wouldn't take long but he would wait until she was asleep and do it then.

*

The door creaked. Anna, lying in their single cot was on her side, holding her small piece of cloth up to her mouth. She heard the noise and turned suddenly. He could see by the light of his tallow candle that she had been crying and he scowled at her welcoming smile. He wanted to do it there and then but he stopped, realising he had come upon her too soon.

An hour later he tried again. This time she was asleep with her small, thin body curled up against the cold and her fair hair half hiding her face. He picked her frock from the bed and began to twist it into a rope but something disturbed her and she turned, muttering quietly to herself. He stopped and backed away. "Sleep, damn you," he cursed under his breath. "Sleep an' lie still. Make's it easier." He waited next door, all the while his frustration and anger mounting. But suddenly he remembered the others, Howard and Barrow. Of course, of course…they would be returning soon and he could wait no longer.

Just as he lifted the blanket, the little girl's eyes opened. They widened in a flash of recognition and she gasped in surprise. Burgess, his jacket off, rose high above her and snarled, then slammed the blanket down.

He could hear her muffled cries. She wriggled and thrashed so he threw himself on top of her body. Even then her legs kicked out in desperation so he knelt full on her, forcing the blanket down even harder and pinning her with his knees. He changed position and half sat so he could trap her head. As he held her down, waiting for her body to lie still he looked round. The canvas bag where she kept her clothes and two rag dolls would do: it was all he needed. The strength of her struggling had surprised him and he was breathing heavily, but the rest would be easy enough.

He removed the blanket slowly and looked down, brushing aside her wavey flaxen hair to see more clearly. Her mouth and cheeks were mottled and flushed but she lay still while her eyes, still blue, stared past him. She was dead but he shook her and slapped her to make sure before nodding satisfied and wiping the spittle from his mouth.

It took him until after midnight but he got rid of the body, burying it close to the mine workings where he and the others hid the sheep they killed. He knew the ground well and was back in the cottage by dawn.

✻

"Bin an' taken her over to Porlock...to her gran's." He went to lean against the doorpost but slipped and almost fell. Sarah Marley stepped back. All the time he had been speaking to her, Burgess had been watching her closely as if he was trying to gauge her reaction to what he was saying. She had asked him where his daughter was and for a moment she thought he looked pleased with himself, smug even. But the man was evil and that might have been just the way he was. "Got her clothes an' that 'ere," he shook the bag. "I'll be back tonight...or in the mornin' maybe." He pushed himself away from the door and she watched him go, now using the doorpost herself.

But he never went to Porlock. Hardly had he returned to the cottage and fallen onto his cot than he was woken. "*Will'am*. Y'ere, *Will'am*." The voice was urgent but his sleep was already deep and it took time for his mind to clear. "Summat's up...out there by the sheep we buried." Lester Howard bent over him and shook him again. "There's a fresh 'un there. Will'am...*Will'am*, d'ya hear? Summats up, man. Must be somebody else out there working the flock. D'ya *hear?*"

Suddenly he was awake, wideawake and listening. Howard and Barrow must have come across the girl's grave. It had to be that and he would have to get out there. It was three days now and the body would have stiffened and started to rot so he would have to cover it well. He was thinking fast like the devil he was. Spoil was difficult to hide so he would have to put the body elsewhere, somewhere deep where there would be no trace. Burgess had worked most of the mines on the moor. He knew them well, both the few still running and the ones they had given up. Wheal Eliza was one of the worst. Deep, dangerous and waterlogged, the main shaft was detested by all who had ever worked there and they had rejoiced when it closed. That would be it; as soon as it was dark.

Lifting the body was not difficult but the corpse was set hard and he had to force the thin limbs together then bind the bag tightly so they would not spring back. She was heavier than he thought and the two miles to the old mineshaft punished him. But he knew where to find the gap in the fence. Even so he was careful, using a stick to feel the ground in front of him. The second fence was lower: they had put it there to keep out the sheep and it was easier to cross. He tried to throw the body so that it dropped cleanly but as it fell so it bounced off the walls. He never heard the splash but he knew she was down and out of the way at last.

✻

His journey home did not take long for he pushed himself across the moor determined to put distance between himself and the mine. Tomorrow he would burn her clothes then make good his escape. The going was difficult and he was gasping for air so he neither saw nor heard the figure crouched in the bracken by the side of the track. Albert Barrow waited until he was well past before he dragged the next sheep's carcass towards the pit he had dug.

It was only later that Sarah Marley recognised the shards of burnt cloth. She could see at once that they were from little Anna's frock. They could belong to no one else for she had embroidered the two white daisies onto her collar at Easter and there they were, the collar and part of one sleeve untouched by the flames. Yet he said he had taken the clothes to her grandmother's. Something was wrong, badly wrong and she sensed it at once. Parson Thornton from Simonsbath should be told.

4

Varney Grayson, Frederic Knight's new agent, tied his horse to a ring on the garden wall. Lammerton, his assistant, did the same.

Grayson was a shortish, thin man with a thin mouth and ferrety eyes. His dark receding hair was slicked back, drawing tight the face underneath. The red waistcoat with brass hunt buttons under his roll-collared frock coat made him out to be a man of quality, as did the well cut boots for that was why he dressed like he did. The narrow beard, trimmed neatly to a point, gave him an air of menace, exactly as was intended. Mr Varney Grayson, he had long since decided, was not a man with whom the yokels would wish to argue or who's shadow they would choose to cross. Before going to the door the two men chatted briefly and laughed.

Tucker, as well they both knew, was Mr Knight's favourite. A review of the books had revealed that; this was quite apart from what they had heard about the place. Mogridge, the agent before him, might have been easy on the man but Varney Grayson was having none of it. The Sherdon books would be straightened and straightened soon, balanced by Tucker's own pocket if needs be. What riled him this morning was that he had been told to deal with a woman, and a farmer's wife at that.

"Please come this way." Charlotte led the two men across the hall and opened the plain, unpainted parlour door.

"Mr Grayson, I take it?" Katherine left the fireplace and waited, expecting him to offer his hand.

"No need for that, Mrs Tucker. No need for none of that." Without further ado, Grayson, shorter than Katherine by several inches and immediately conscious of the fact, dropped his saddlebag onto the table.

"Thank you, Charlotte," Katherine nodded as they had decided she should. "We'll have the tea please, then that will be all." Grayson glanced over his shoulder, angered still further that his presence and authority appeared not to have been respected. It should have been, but if it had not then he would see to it.

"Gentlemen, pray be seated," Katherine gesticulated towards the chairs behind the table next to the far wall. The two men would be looking into the light for she had placed them there while she would be facing them and in shadow. "My husband sends his apologies but he's been called away on urgent business." Katherine's hands were in her lap and she smiled politely, looking from one to the other. "However, as this meeting is simply to consider in outline a draft agreement, we have no need to worry. *Yes?*" She raised one eyebrow. "Good. Now…er, Mr Grayson…pray proceed, if you would be so kind."

She had no idea what effect such a formal demeanour would have but Wilmot had warned them that Knight's new man was a bully. Jack had been determined to be present but she had persuaded him otherwise; Parson Thornton's plea for assistance over the Burgess affair had been something they could not ignore. The man had to be found and, in any case, she would be more than happy to see for herself how the new agent would behave. That was her story.

Deep down she was terrified at what he might have to say. They knew that Frederic was desperate for money and a review of the Sherdon rent was long overdue. To submit to a tyrant would be worse than useless, so she would stand her ground the only way she knew how. Even so she could feel her hands shaking. As they talked on Charlotte served them tea.

*

"So, that's agreed then." Grayson sat back, glanced confidently at Lamerton then turned back to Katherine. "Quite satisfied, I take it, Mrs Tucker? Yes?" He began to collect his papers together noisily, making a show of his importance. "It all seems straightforward enough."

"You well know my opinion, Mr Grayson." Katherine could see he disliked her and everything about her but it made no difference. A bully would try to get his way whatever the odds so there was little sense in making it easy for the man. And she had seen the sly looks between them so it was always going to be the two of them against her.

The agent had gone over the review a number of times, reminding her that he could, should he so wish, increase the new figures by half as much again; the arithmetic was plain enough. They had argued doggedly, Katherine countering him with complaints about the poor quality of the land, of the lack of allowances for breaking the soil and demanding that the building maintenance should be taken into account. She was desperate but dare not show her feelings. Any increase at all would surely break them for they had nothing else to offer. Her stubbornness and attitude riled him. The woman was above her station as her airs and graces and the way she spoke showed. But she should know her place and, if not, she would have to be taught. Well, he would show her; two hundred and fifty pounds per annum was cheap. His hand had hit the table but still she held her ground.

"I will inform my husband accordingly and he will, no doubt, seek a meeting with Mr Knight should he feel such a course of action necessary." She forced herself to remain calm but could feel her fear turning to anger, an anger fuelled by a detestation of this man in her house.

"But *I* am the agent."

"And Mr Knight is a friend."

"Business should not be done that way."

"Allow Mr Knight to decide." Grayson inclined his head. His jaw was set, his own ire plain and undisguised as he took a bottle of ink and quills from his bag. It was time to go but there was one more thing and he clenched his teeth, determined to be drawn no further.

"And now Mrs Tucker." Grayson opened out the draft document. "Just this…one small matter before we conclude." Dealing with her, even speaking to her irritated him. His mouth was a hard, thin line. Who, he asked himself, did she think she was and where did this conceit come from? "We need to know your family details. Should rent fall in arrears, Mr Knight's solicitors would wish to know to whom they may have to turn." He glared at her as though she would do well to understand.

"But I am not of his issue. Who ordained such measures?"

"Never you mind, Mrs Tucker. That is no business of yours, but we need your details as well as your husband's. Now then…your family name, please. Full name…that is if you have more than one." Again the smirk.

"Darcy." She sat back. "Darcy of Northborough. Lady Katherine Mary Elizabeth Harriet Darcy…now Tucker." She watched Grayson closely, well aware that he was studying the legal document by which the tenancy was bound. His quill remained poised. Only his head moved. Then he turned and glanced at her. His eyes were narrowed more than ever yet she lifted her chin and held his gaze. "I assume there is no problem, Mr Grayson? If that is the case then pray continue."

"Are you…is this some jest, Mrs Tucker."

"*Lady* Tucker…Lady Katherine Tucker…and now that you know, let there never be any misunderstanding, no matter what the circumstances. I trust I make myself clear."

"Yes." Grayson's eyes fell. "Yes, of course." He looked up again as though to add something then returned hurriedly to the document in his hand.

"That is my name, Mr Grayson." Katherine stabbed her finger at the document in front of him. She felt quite faint, the pit of her stomach was tumbling and churning. Even breathing the same air as this dreadful little man made her feel ill. "It is my very own and I would not wish to hear comment on the matter. Pray continue but be sure to write it clearly so that it is easy to read. Should your solicitors wish to take the matter up with my family then you had better be quite clear as to who they are…and where they reside. You will need both addresses…Northborough of Grosvenor Square, Mayfair and of Blagdon Park in Hampshire."

＊

Charlotte could barely contain herself and threw open the parlour door. They had gone. At first she thought Katherine was smiling, but she was not. Her hands were at her mouth, her eyes screwed tightly shut and her whole body was shaking. "Oh, my God, Lottie." Charlotte's hands went to hold her face. "What a nightmare…what a ghastly, ghastly nightmare. And to think he came here to brow beat us into submission, like that." For what seemed a long time she was silent, her body shivering before she gasped for breath and sobbed again. "And to think that awful man's going to try to ruin Jack…I can't bear it."

The next morning she rose before dawn. The birds were still greeting the day as she made her way to the well and there was a chill freshness in the air. Although some of the stones were now covered with lichen and half hidden by ferns, they had remained in place. There were eight to move before she could pull the box out and she had but half an hour before Ralph and the boys would wake. By then the box had to be back, the stones replaced and covered. Less than half her jewels remained but they were her favourites, the ones she was dreading to part with, hoping beyond hope to pass them on to her own, to Alice and Anna and to the wives of her sons.

For ten minutes she agonised. One by one she replaced those she could not bear to lose, all of which had belonged to her father's mother. Whatever would he do, she wondered, were he to see her now. Slowly her hand closed around the bracelet. Even in the dawn light the enamelled gold and the clusters of sapphires gleamed while the pearls hung delicately from their clasps. It had come from France. Her grandfather, the third Duke, had bought it for Matilda, second daughter of the Marquis of Hexton, who was soon to bear him a son – her father, her very own father.

Frederic thought he knew how she must feel when she gave him such heirlooms to sell, but he did not. He could not. Nobody could possibly understand her sense of sadness, of the dreadful betrayal, of treachery to the whole family. She was robbing her children of their heritage, abusing the trust her family had placed in her. She felt the guilt of a thief and what she was doing wounded her deeply. Mercifully, though, Jack would never know.

Chapter Thirteen

The kingfisher flew to his usual spot on the broken root where he paused. His prey, a young stickleback, was still waving feebly in his beak. Then he blinked and blinked a second time before darting to his burrow beneath the old willow. A few seconds later he reappeared. Settling back onto his perch, he ruffled his plumage and began to preen his wing but stopped. The magpie's chuckle had alerted him and suddenly he was off, away downstream.

The boy heard it too and lifted the arm that had been shielding the sun from his eyes. He sat up briefly to listen then lay back once more. The steep hollow in which he was lying was set well back from the river. Sometimes, during the winter rains when Sherdon Water broke its banks, the hollow flooded into a shallow, crescent-shaped pool but now, in the heat of August, it was dry. Dead grass caught on rushes and low bushes showed how far the water had once reached.

The tall ferns around the rim of the dell hid him from all but anyone who stumbled across their hiding place. Even the river itself was shielded by the high ground on the far side that pushed the current in a wide sweep towards him. Across the water, under a flat rock, a low bank of shingle and rough sand shimmered in the afternoon sun.

Davey had been waiting for over an hour before he heard the swish of her skirts as she pushed her way through the bracken. Instinctively he reached for his shirt, still hesitant about what might come to pass. But then she stopped: Jade Sexton paused and stood at the edge of the hollow, looking down on him. She had been walking quickly and was breathless but now her heart began to beat even faster. Her cheeks were flushed and she, too, was uncertain about what to do next. Even from where she was standing she could see how pale and slim he was.

Knowing that he would soon be leaving home, she had agreed to meet him. Ever since that moment after the shearing supper she had been thinking of little else. At first she had been nervous, alarmed at the boldness of his approach and by what he had suggested, but they had left early that night and there had been no time to find out. "You awake?" She had approached him quietly and nudged his foot with her shoe. He sat up again, this time twisting himself so her body hid the sun and he could see her face.

"Heard yer way back," he boasted, screwing his eyes against the light. "'Eard they maggies, too...they knew you was there." Davey Tucker moved himself to make room. "Anyhows, I knew you'd come. 'Ere you are, look." He patted the horse blanket. "You were goin' to come, all along...weren't yer?"

"Dunno really." As she took her place on the rug beside him, she laughed shyly, tucking her feet modestly beneath her long skirt. Davey looked at her. The bar of freckles under her eyes showed where her high cheekbones had caught the sun. Her nose was peeling, hence her father's felt hat although she had turned it up at the front. Her hair, bleached almost white, was pushed back behind her shoulder so she could see him better.

"'Twas you that did all the talkin', all the askin'…weren't it?" Jade caught his eye fleetingly but then looked down to study her hands. "Said yer wanted to see me an' that. Didn't yer?" She shrugged demonstratively as if it was of no consequence then glanced at him out of the corner of her eyes. "Anyways, what's it all about?"

Davey turned and pulled at a long grass. He knew perfectly well why she had agreed, and knew that she knew. Now she was just being silly. Ever since she had known he was going to join the army she had been following him around, always wanting to talk but then getting tongue-tied at the last minute. They had grown up together, more like brother and sister than neighbours and he had never noticed her until the other night at the dance. Jack had noticed her as well and had danced twice with her before leaving them together.

Davey remembered everything about her that evening; how her eyes had sparkled when she looked at him. It had made him smile and that had made her giggle. He, too, had laughed out loud, watching her as she put a hand over her mouth. Her eyes had been wide as her bubbling, girlish laughter tumbled out unrestrained. Even now he could feel the lightness of her touch when she turned under his arm on the dance-floor, and the firmness of her body as she pressed against him when the music slowed. Jade Sexton from Barkham was sixteen, no longer the little girl who bounced around on the back of a pony on her way to school, or who chanted away as she skipped under the rope in the playground.

Just before her father had ordered her onto the cart, he had kissed her gently. Her lips had hesitated against his, but her hand had strayed to the back of his neck and he had felt her body rising and falling as she breathed. 'Yes' she had replied nodding against his chest. 'I s'pose so…I'll meet you there, opposite the big rock, down by the deep pool.'

✳

"Why yer sittin' like that?" They had been talking until the shadow of the tall willow covered them. She didn't reply but simply lifted her shoulders. Davey reached out and stroked her arm but still she sat unmoving, yet when his fingers curled around the point of her shoulder, she longed to respond. "You afraid or summat?" She shrugged again. He moved closer and stretched up to stroke the hair from her face. "I'll miss yer, Jade," he whispered. "Miss yer lots, yer know that?" Her startled look surprised him.

"You'll take care, won't yer, Davey…I mean th'army's dangerous." Yet again the thought of him going alarmed her and she turned to look at him. "Dad said so…people getting killed an' that." It was his turn to shrug. His mother was always saying the same sort of thing. Sometimes she appeared to be angry about his decision, sometimes she pleaded. Perhaps it was dangerous; after all, his grandfather had been killed. He looked away, neither proud nor afraid but his pulse was racing.

"I'll miss yer, too, Davey." This time her hand reached for his. "Hurts me to think about it. Does yer know…'onest." As they lay back together, she rolled towards him to press her lips against his cheek. "I'll miss yer, Davey," she whispered. Then, as her hand slipped inside his open shirt, her mouth was on his.

"Us'll be safe, though, Billy an' me." His fingers were following the soft, firm swell of her breasts. "Some say there's talk of war, others that…."

"Don't say that." She wriggled further on top of him and looked down. "Don't never say that…'tis *dread*ful," she murmured. Her hand pulled out the last of his shirt then moved back to his chest. "Never go sayin' things like that." She kissed him again, then came the soft warmth of her tongue.

After they made love, they bathed, then stood together thigh deep in the dark pool under the rock with their arms entwined as the cool water washed their nakedness. Unashamed and uncaring they made love again, this time gently and smoothly as their young bodies moved together. Afterwards they dragged the rug to the top of the dell where the evening sun still warmed the high bank. As they lay together he told her he would not be able to see her for sometime and she cried in his arms. Just before they parted, when he held her face in his hands and kissed her, they both wept quietly like the children they still were. Things would never be the same again; they knew that of course but it was too late to change.

2

"There, there, dear. He'll be fine…they buiys'll be safe enough…army'll know 'ow to look after them." Bamber looked anxiously at his son then back to Charlotte who was sitting with the letter in her hand. Edgar, the elder of the two Heard boys and taller than his father but with the same round face, had just ridden back to Brightworthy Farm from Withypool. There had only been the one letter. Davey had written from Higher Barracks at Northernhay, just outside Exeter. He and Billy, so the spidery scrawl told them, were more than pleased to have been accepted into The Fourth Light Dragoons and would be departing shortly for the Cavalry School in Aldershot in the county of Hampshire, near London town.

"But 'ee's only a lad," Charlotte wailed. "Just a buiy reelly…not gone his teens. Still three months to go isn't it…no, four?" The two men glanced at one another. Not used to such an outpouring of grief, Edgar frowned. Minutes earlier they had watched as Charlotte tore open the buff envelope and began to read. At first her face had been bright with expectation but had grown longer and gloomier as she made her way along the line of her son's handwriting. Now the young farmer wished he had not brought the thing for they would have been better off without such news.

"And they'm goin aways in one of they new railway things...like they'm did to Plymouth two weeks back....goes faster than a gallopin' 'orse...straight through they tunnels an' things like that. 'Ere look." Bamber took it from her.

"Oh, come back 'ere, love." Lottie had seen him turning the paper around and then back again. "Can't read very well, can you. Katherine taught they lads readin' an' writin' real well 'er did. Now then." She turned to the daylight and began to read once more, her eyes keeping pace with her finger. "*...the engine did begin with a great roar which made the horses start madly. Captain Bellew's charger broke free and galloped off so that was all up for him. There was much smoke and a bright fire underneath the barrel on the engine. Two men with black faces took coals from a box and fed the fire such as farriers do. Others filled the barrel up with more water.*" She looked up and laughed through her tears. Bamber and Edgar stared.

"*We led our horses into a cart on the long rails and fastened them by their head collars. Then we climbed into the same cart and sat with our mounts until the sides had been made fast. At that point, the engine commenced to pull us all with much blowing of steam. There were ten carts in all, each one hooked on behind the one in front. So we gathered speed until we were going pell-mell such as only hunters can manage in a fine chase. Billy lost his cap when we sped into a tunnel through the hillside. Mister Evans told us we can do forty miles in just one hour. The wind was rushing past. It was black and there was much coal dust'*...ooooh," her voice tailed off. Walter, younger and shorter than Edgar, appeared and stood in the yard doorway. For a moment all three of her menfolk stood undecided.

"Come, dear," Bamber slid onto the bench beside her and pulled her towards him. "Our Davey'll be fine, you'll see. Soon as they know 'e comes from a farm, they'll give'e summat to do with animals or working 'orses. Haulin' things or pullin' summat...like as he knows best."

"Bet they look smart, eh Ed? Remember Davey with they breeches an' that? Tight they were, tight as that, look" Walter pulled his trousers around his thighs. "Does 'e say anythin' 'bout that, Lottie? Anythin' there in that letter?"

Charlotte looked down. "Oh aye...'ere look." She turned the page and began to read again, louder this time. "'Ere...'*We have blue jackets and pantaloons. The jackets are splendid and have six loops of gold gimp on each side of the breast with their caps and drops.*" She read on slowly and methodically. '*Our trousers have two stripes of yellow lace and the butcher boots a gold boss on front at top. Now, our shoulder belt is handsome. It is of gold lace with a scarlet stripe and a pouch of black leather behind.*'" She checked herself and blew heavily, her head shaking in wonder. "'*We look real swells as we march into town wearing our busby headdress of sable fur and ostrich feathers waving on top. We in the shiny fourth have a red and white plume also. We step out boldly with our capes as cavalrymen should step and even the fine ladies of Exeter town do fancy us which angers the Redcoats'*...there," she whispered, looking proudly at the others. "My little Davey...a man 'e is...a real soldier."

It was six weeks before the two boys left Aldershot. The training had been severe, many falling by the wayside but, no sooner had one course begun its passage through the Cavalry School at Southern Command than another formed up behind and followed the same path. There was a rush and a sense of urgency about their lives. But Davey and Billy were not alone. Concentrating on such matters as quitting and crossing their stirrups or applying oil to their chargers' hooves, they remained blissfully unaware that in London, less than thirty miles away, those responsible for manning the army had become seriously worried. When the Commandant called them together on the last day of the course, he read out a statement. Most stared back vacantly, disinterested and uncomprehending. The fact that Russia had declared war on Turkey meant nothing to them, neither were they the slightest bit interested to hear that the Russian fleet had put to sea from a town called Sevastopol in a place called Crimea.

Of more immediate concern right now was the fact that the passing out parade was less than three hours away, by which time both men and their mounts had to be spotless. The inspecting officer, a man whose name they had never heard before, was the Commanding Officer of the nearby Eleventh Hussars. Lieutenant Colonel The Earl of Cardigan, so they had been warned, was one from whom the very highest of standards were to be expected.

✳

"Stand still…and listen in!" Regimental Corporal-Major Raven of The Royal Horse Guards made himself clear. Today, due to the rain, prize giving was held inside the new cavalry riding school. Lord Cardigan had inspected the stables already and was now taking lunch with the officers in their Mess while the parade schedule was being reorganised. Recruits from the next course had raked the sanded floor before the hundred and twenty men due to pass out were marched in. Now they raked it again while others manhandled a table onto the rostrum. Upstairs, in the gallery behind the main entrance, bandsmen blew into their brass instruments and shook spittle from the tubes.

"When the inspecting party arrives," he shouted, "I shall call the parade up to attention." The ranks in front of Raven stood motionless. "Look *up*, look to your *front* and *no* bobbing about…*Bandmaster?*" he searched the visitors' gallery above him. *"Ready?"* Mr Raven stiffened, swung towards the door and saluted. The visitors had arrived.

"Parade…paraaaaade…shun!" The Regimental Corporal-Major's white glove flashed up in salute while, above him, the lead trumpeter nodded. The whole assembly stood frozen until the last notes of the National Anthem had faded away. Only one horse moved, throwing her head up and down, and pawing at the ground.

The inspection over, all eyes were on the visitors as they made their way to the dais. It was the final moment. "And now…the prize for the champion recruit." Captain The Marquis of Brearley addressed his notes. "The silver spur," he paused. "Awarded by the commandant to the trooper adjudged to be the best all round cavalryman on the course…goes to," he paused again. "Number 470096 Trooper Tucker of The Fourth Light Dragoons…"

"Step forward that man." The Regimental Corporal-Major Raven rose on his toes.

The face that peered down at Davey looked old, the eyes bloodshot and the long whiskers that had been groomed immaculately were curling and grey. Lord Cardigan cut an impressive figure, that was his wont. The young trooper standing in front of him was not only impressed, he was terrified. "Well done, lad, well done indeed." Davey smelled drink on the breath but stared ahead unblinking. James Thomas Brudenell, the seventh Earl of Cardigan, not only expected excellence, he cherished it. "Damn fine show."

Davey reached out for the spur, mounted on a small oak plinth, then took the hand offered to him. The grip was hard, almost painfully so. "You did well…keep it like that and you'll go far." Cardigan nodded at the salute, lifted his hand casually in reply and turned his back.

3

"They've got him." The Reverend William Thornton stood in the hall while Jack took his coat. "Got him yesterday."

"Really…where?"

"Swansea, would you believe? Got across by boat from Lynmouth, all thirty miles of it…currents, tides, the lot." The Parson gave one of his little laughs and shook his head. "Incredible. One of the harbour boatmen, an old boy called Groves, took him over. The man said he wanted to look for work in the docks and there he was…simple as that. Local police checked the work list, interviewed several new faces and the fella gave himself up. Marvellous."

It was while the police were questioning him that Burgess asked if his daughter had been found. It was a mistake, they all knew it, but the man clammed up nonetheless. In spite of the remorseless interrogation, day after day, he said nothing. He was charged with wilful murder but it was no more than an academic exercise, there being insufficient evidence. The Dulverton magistrates were forced to consider his release: that is, until Albert Barrow made his move.

✳

"That's not up to me." Superintendent Cresant Fox turned back from the office window. He, too, was getting desperate with the lack of progress. "Anyway Barrow, you're rotten." The thickset policeman leant over the table, his eyes only inches from Barrow's. He was angry and it showed. "How do I know you're not swinging the lead? Eh? How do I know you aren't in on this an' are trying to nobble Burgess?" He grimaced in disgust at the rabbit eyes that stared back at him from behind the whiskers. "And 'ow do we know *you* weren't in on the very act itself…that you ain't got the poor little mite's blood on yer hand's? Eh...Barrow? Ain't that it?" Fox glowered. "What were you up to with that little girl? Eh?"

"Nuthin'...no...honest to God...nuthin'" Both hands clutched his cap. "Honest, Mister...I swear by Almighty God I ain't touched the child. Never...not me nor Lester 'oward neither." Not liking the face that was glaring back, the rabbit eyes grew wider still. "Honest to God, Mister."

Fox's nose wrinkled. He had touched the raw nerve all right, no doubt about it. The man was panicking, scared witless and probably telling the truth for the first time in his life. "All...right, Barrow." The words came slowly. "I'll see what can be done. I'll talk to the Bench. But you listen to me." As Fox reached out for the man, the chair legs scraped harshly on the floor.

"An' you listen well." Albert Barrow was on the tips of his toes. "If there's no body down that mine...if we get the place drained and find nuthin'...you'll swing, Barrow. You mark my word. You and your friend Lester 'oward'll dangle outside Taunton gaol 'til you're stiff. I've got you now for stealin' sheep and cattle rustlin'. Where was it...Comer's Gate an' White Post, *and* for poachin' deer. Your words, Barrow...yours, not mine, an' for that you'll go the whole way...twice over, easy. So you'd better start prayin' the child's where you're telling us." Barrow slid to the floor.

✳

It took weeks to clear the mine. A diver went first but nothing was found. After that the magistrates ordered the shaft to be drained. The steam pump and windlass, both damaged on the long move out to the site, broke down and work stopped once more. Nobody was getting anywhere and it was Jack who suggested fetching Wilmot. It took them a week to reach him in Huddersfield but he told them to be ready and gave a list of what he would need. Whilst they waited, the police collected storm lanterns, better pumps and hoses, a new windlass and two cartloads of rope from Bideford Quay. Word went out for all those who knew the mine to assemble.

✳

The front parlour at Sherdon, crowded with police and mining engineers, smelt heavily of tobacco and sweat. It was late but they had decided to work on. Wilmot's arrival had put an end to the bickering about who should take charge and who should do what. They knew it was he who had organised the sinking of the original shaft and that he knew the layout and dangers better than anyone. His urgent, decisive authority quelled any further discussion.

"We'll need someone to go down on the end of a rope." Wilmot moved the lantern across the table so he could see better then bent over the plan of the mineshaft. "Those old wooden ladders attached to the walls are slippery as hell and loose...as well as being half rotten." Earlier that day he had arrived from Bristol and had gone straight out to the mine, not even stopping in Simonsbath to see Frederic.

205

The weather was bad. The farmers said it would stay that way and it was the flooding of the main shaft that worried him. The pumps had done their best but had to be kept working to cope with the water pouring back in, not only from the bottom, fifty fathoms down, but from a stream at the thirty-six fathom level where the northern lode had been breached. The underground water, straight off the waterlogged moors, had broken through and was cascading like a waterfall into the depths more than fifty feet further down.

"More than that, I'll need someone, two probably to wait at each level, that's the twelve, twenty-four and thirty-six fathom adits, here...here...and here." He looked up at the circle of faces around the lamp. "We can't just let the one poor devil down by himself. They'll have to have good lamps and we'll need a pulley signal system from the bottom to the top. We need to know what's going on down there or we'll lose someone...just like that." Jack and the others sat back.

"It's going to be hard down there." His face, gaunt in the lamplight, shone ghostlike as he looked at the anxious and expectant eyes staring back at him. "Save for what light we can muster, it'll be pitch black. *And* it'll be cold, cold as a tomb. Those at the bottom'll be working under a waterfall. Here look..." he returned to the plan on the table. "Water's falling all the way from here...down to here." He had everybody's attention but the silence that followed was broken by a sudden commotion.

"I'll go, Wilmot. I'll go...let me be yer man." He knew the voice at once and caught his breath. Glancing up and holding a hand to shield his eyes, he peered over the lamp and tried to see into the darkness. A volunteer it had to be, but could his brother's man do the job? All eyes were on Ralph Rudd as he pushed his way forward, the ones nearest the table making way for him. "I can do it...I can find me way well enough."

"It'll be hard going, Ralph, damned hard." Wilmot studied the man closely, wincing as he eased himself back in the chair. "And it's a very different world down there...something you know nothing about. I mean...d'you think you could manage?" Everyone waited.

"Aye," Ralph nodded. "As well as any man...I bain't afeared."

✳

Two days later the search for the body began at dawn.

Wilmot placed men at each level with lamps and safety ropes then followed Ralph and his two assistants down to the waterfall at the thirty-six fathom level. Here they could see that the water was running from the entrance of the adit before cascading over the edge and into the blackness below with a deep rumble. A chill, wet draught swept up from the depths, turning the air around them into a damp mist. Clothes became sodden and hair frizzed. The ladder, glistening with slime where it had been exposed to the water, and the canvas pump-hose followed the water into the abyss, but that was all.

As they stood at the edge of the shaft looking down, the four men sucked in lungfuls of stale air. It was cold and they struggled to breathe yet there was still further to go. They had to shout to make themselves heard above the noise of the water for their voices, echoing off the towering walls of the shaft above, were muffled.

"*Ready?*" Wilmot looked at Ralph. The man was shivering but he nodded eagerly and seemed confident enough. The three around him watched apprehensively as he picked a large stone from the tunnel floor and tossed it over the edge, his eyes following it expectantly as it disappeared from sight. Nobody moved except the man himself who turned and shrugged before craning his neck to look up towards the pinprick of light more than a hundred feet above. One by one they followed his gaze.

"Right, now listen." Wilmot checked the knots on the rope around his waist. "Any problems, *anything* at all just pull on the windlass rope…here look, and we'll get you up with the safety rope…this one here, around your waist. We'll lower the storm lamps with you, luckily most of the water's running down the far side so we might get away with it."

Ralph nodded. He glanced at Wilmot and shuddered suddenly. "Right then, I'm ready…ready as ever I'll be."

"Well said, my friend…whenever you so wish." Wilmot put an arm around the figure in front of him before clapping his back. "God speed, lad."

At first the descent was easier than he expected and the lamp held good, the metal cover keeping off all but the worst of the spray from the falling water. But it was the cold. Soon his hands were numb, kept that way by the icy slime on the ladders. The chill damp air soaked his hair and soon seeped through his clothes to chill his body. Unable to trust his fingers any longer, he hugged the sides of the ladder using the crooks of his arms to hold on. It slowed him down and, as he slowed, so his breathing became more laboured. His lamp dangled alongside him but it showed him little and nothing at all of what lay below.

It was the icy water at the bottom he felt first then the mud, the deep oozing mud that gripped and sucked at his boots as they filled, before sliding further up his legs as he sank deeper. He stopped, for a moment terrified to go on lest he would be trapped in the freezing mire, alone and entombed with the corpse he had come to find. But he had to move. He reached out apprehensively, one moment feeling along the wall of the shaft like a blind man feels his way, then raising his lamp to see what he could. Around him water was falling like a storm in the night. He stumbled and lurched, half stuck in the mud but straightened himself and tried to move on before stumbling again. He struggled to pull himself free and almost fell when he lifted his leg. As he did so, one foot slid free from his boot.

He tried to move cautiously, leaving the lamp on a narrow ledge but the icy, clogging mire seemed set on keeping hold of him. He knew he should not be breathing so hard, they had told him to stay calm but he was working himself hard and had no option. But he made it at last. Half covered in fungus and with water running off it as it had done for months, lay the canvas holdall he had come to find. It was just across the shaft, hard against the wall where it had come to rest when the mine was drained. It was resting on a mound of shale.

Steadying himself, he reached out but at first he was unable to move it at all. It, too, had become stuck. Time and again he stretched out and scraped at it with his finger-tips yet time and again it refused to move. He forced himself to get closer and tried again, this time managing to draw it towards him, inch by inch across the mud, until it rested against his knees. Then, for what seemed an age his fingers, frozen and slippery, grappled with the windlass ropes and the cords they had lowered. He flexed his joints and beat his hands against his sodden jacket in an attempt to get his circulation back. Then he washed his fingers clean of mud and put them in his mouth to suck warmth back into the flesh. Still he fumbled and it took time, all the while his body getting colder. Slowly and painfully, however, he managed to secure the ropes.

When the windlass started to lift the bag, he followed it to the first adit, clambering desperately up the ladder to keep pace with those pulling from above so he could hold it away from the wall. His hands and feet, one bare and frozen, kept slipping on the wood as he grappled and clawed his way upwards using elbows and knees as well. His breath was rasping, his teeth chattering and his whole body shivering but he made it at last cheered by the sight of helping hands reaching down. At the adit above he paused to wash what he could from his hands and clothes in the clear stream water before beginning the long, agonizing climb to the surface.

"Look at that." "Fetch a coat." "He's done it." "Steady. Here, give him a hand." "You all right?" "Bring a swig of grog for the lad."

The hand on his shoulder was shaking him ever more urgently. "Ralph, Ralph, 'tis me. Come on, lad…'tis me." Someone had wiped him clean where he had retched up the effects of the foul air. Some other kind soul had pressed a blanket round his shoulders. He was still gulping down the fresh morning air when he heard the voice again.

"'Twas the little girl all right, lad." He was sitting against the wheel of a cart and Jack crouched beside him. "'Twas her for certain." So numb and bemused was he that he frowned at the face in front of him. "You did well, boy, as good as any man. Doctors have opened the bag over in the old engine shed. Word is that 'tis the maid herself, poor little soul. Now that devil will meet his Maker."

✳

Burgess was hanged six weeks later. The two men stayed at the Cross Keys the night before then left early for Taunton Gaol where a large crowd had begun to gather outside. "Stay here, lad. I'm going in, the governor wants me there." Parson Thornton took out his watch. "Nine they said. Almost another hour yet but I'll get inside and stay with him 'til it's done."

"Know 'im, d'yer?" The old crone squinted up at Ralph. "Did fer 'is kids, so they say.

208

Did fer 'is bleedin' kids, I ask yer." The mouth was toothless. The woman, like most, was drunk. He spurred his horse on, pushing through the crowd, now revolted by everything he saw. Billetfield Park was filling with those who had risen early to come and watch men die. As one section of the mob called noisily for action so others joined them, the cheers and baying rolling back and forth across the hillside. There was a tension in the air, an ugly blood lust, and even now at this early hour the onlookers were becoming restless.

The toll of the prison bell, as if to announce the commencement of proceedings, sent a wave of excitement across the park and a large section of the crowd pressed forward, jostling and struggling for places nearer the platform. What had caught their attention was the emergence of two men who had come out to fix ropes over the scaffold beam. But it was the ringing of the hand bell by a third that caused the sudden silence. Apart from the odd shout or laugh here and there the crowd had stopped moving. An expectant hush had fallen. As Ralph watched, two more men followed the bellringer and then a third. These three were dressed formally in black frock coats and tri-corn hats. The last of the trio began to read an announcement but from where he was it was impossible to hear.

Burgess appeared next, walking clumsily behind the prison chaplain with his legs shackled and his hands tied in front of him. At this the crowd, now aroused and noisy once more, pressed forward again, this time to the very base of the scaffold. A second prisoner, well dressed in a silk shirt and doeskin breeches followed Burgess. Then came Thornton, and Ralph watched as the parson moved ahead to join the other chaplain and the condemned men. Four warders with pikestaffs brought up the rear and took up their positions.

The second man out was the first to die. Shuffling out from behind Burgess to address the gathering, he spoke briefly until Shaddick, the hangman, collared him roughly and dragged him under the beam where he stumbled and fell to his knees. The executioner and a guard wrestled him back to his feet where he was held while the white cap was placed on his head followed by the larger black hood that covered both head and face. Shaddick fastened this securely before toying with his victim, tugging the cords ever tighter and jerking the helpless man's head this way and that, causing him to stumble about as he tried to keep his balance.

The crowd loved it: it was the moment they had been waiting for and, all around him, people were urging the executioner on. Shaddick obliged and it was only when his audience grew impatient that he placed the noose around the prisoner's neck. As the rope was tightened, so the condemned man rose onto the very tips of his toes where, to further taunting, he skipped and hopped in an attempt to keep breathing. The cheers and laughter grew louder, even more so when finally his feet swung free momentarily. Twice more the hangman lowered his victim, making him dance for his life as his feet sought something firm, before at last heaving him well clear to wriggle and jerk as he died.

Then it was Burgess, and Ralph stared grimly as two of the guards half carried and half dragged him to his place beneath his rope. All hope had gone and when someone spoke to him he merely shook his lowered head. Once more Shaddick played to the crowd, ordering the warders to hold him up and hold him still while he fastened the cap and hood. However, suddenly and now that death was close, Burgess panicked. Even from where he was Ralph could see him twisting his head to and fro in some desperate effort to shake off the noose. But the hangman had firm hold of him and quickly tightened the rope until Burgess, too, began to dance on his toes. The front of the mask over his face was being sucked in and blown out as the lungs gasped for air. Once his legs buckled and Shaddick lowered him gently to allow him to find his feet before hauling him up again. Thornton spoke briefly, gave the sign of the cross and the rope was pulled tight.

Ralph had no idea how long it took. The figure had ceased to twist and jerk but was still swinging freely as the party on the platform withdrew, leaving the crowd to stone the bodies. One hour later they would be cut down and stripped by the hangman who would sell the clothes to the crowd while the warders removed the corpses. But Thornton spared him. His last duty with Burgess now honoured, the parson rejoined his companion, and the two pushed their way back through the crowd.

4

Frederic studied his fingernails. His father might have set about it another way with Sir James and Sir Crispin Barclay but things were different now. Back in those days there was capital in abundance, the virgin Exmoor landscape lay waiting, and above all else the thrill of expectation over copper and ore was in the air. He took a deep breath and pulled out his watch. Time had run on. They had given themselves three hours but without success. It was the end of the matter and time for some lunch.

Sir Durnford Morgan closed the file. Frederic thought Esdaile's successor looked a lot older than his years but, whether he walked or sat, he had always stooped a little and his face usually bore lines of worry. The hair was shorter and grey-flecked where it covered the tops of his ears but it had been cut as well as ever. And the Lombard Street banker had done his homework, of that there was no doubt. He, like they, had tried to see a way ahead but it had come to nothing.

"So...that's your final word?" Frederic glanced across to his brother, Edward, then at the figure behind the desk.

Morgan lifted his chin then rubbed it to and fro before burying his face in his hands. The two younger men waited. "I think it has to be...just *has* to be. I can't see any way out." He looked up, from one to the other sorrowfully then inclined his head. "The Exmoor estate is fine, there's no problem there and your team have come up with the same figure as ours...or very nearly. It's these damned mines...the same as ever it was." He tapped the files angrily and pushed back his chair. Then he rose and walked to the bookcases built into the far wall where he turned and leant back with his arms outstretched and resting along one of the shelves.

"Look," he appealed. "Apart from one or two small strikes we've had *nothing* back in return, absolutely nothing and we've now lent you more than the value of every brick and piece of lead piping out there. In fact if the project collapses then *we* stand to lose more than the sum value of the farms…and that's as it stands now." Frederic nodded ruefully. "And you're asking us to underwrite you *again* to the tune of…what was it…a further eight to ten thousand pounds."

"But surely you can see the potential, sir." Edward Knight lifted his hands. Morgan had taken the rare decision to allow his new subordinate to argue the family's case against him. Sometimes the opposition's advocate made for good listening, the more so when the two were kinsmen. Perhaps, between them all, they and the bank might have been able to see a way. He had felt obliged to make such a gesture for his association with the Knights had been close, and for so many years. To do otherwise would have been unthinkable. And it would have been confrontational. "Dowlais have come in, so have Schneider and Hannay," Frederic's young brother continued. "What more do we need than that?"

Morgan pursed his lips then gave a little laugh as he shrugged but it was a humourless gesture. "Come on, Edward, it doesn't need me to spell that out to one of my fellow bankers." Frederic's eyes moved from one to the other. "The documents they've produced are so full of clauses that we'd be binding ourselves to the very devil himself. We've been through them all 'ad nauseam'…both with the board, and you and I together."

"But it's the *potential*," Edward persisted. "All these reports speak of high quality ore…it's all there, for Heaven's sake. These aren't half-baked companies, sir…they're well known, all of them, and they've done their studies thoroughly. They know exactly what's at stake."

"Then just where *are* all these wonderful deposits? Mmm?" The reply was brisk. "We've had less than two thousand pounds back on our investment thus far…and that's over all these past years." Morgan pushed himself away from the books and strode to his desk. "Look…let me remind you, if that's necessary." He flicked through the papers in his tray. "Those were the early, optimistic reports, but it's no longer the case as you know. *Here* look…Dowlais's most recent prognosis…from Merthyr Tydfil. We've been through it and it's really very bleak. See this here…remind yourselves." He pushed the letter across the table but neither brother moved. "If we're going to underwrite the mining enterprise *any* further…and there's nothing more we'd like to do, then you, Frederic, must match our figures by liquidating assets or increasing revenue from the agricultural estate. I'm sorry…it's really nothing more than simple mathematics. Our decision stands…it has to."

The brothers had no choice. Others in the family, Charles, Margaret and Isabella, had instituted court proceedings against the estate. The full potential of the mines remained impossible to determine and if they were to investigate further, extra resources would have to be found. The banks had turned down their request, even Edward had been unable to raise the capital. Funding would have to come from within and Varney Grayson did as he was instructed.

211

✳

Charlotte and Katherine listened as Jack pleaded with the agent when he rode out to see them. The winter roots had failed, he explained, but not through poor husbandry. Sheep prices were down and wages had risen: it would not be possible to make ends meet. Other tenants had left. The situation was appalling, he declared, surely that was plain. Grayson rounded on him, reminding him how low his rent was in comparison with those off the moor, of their generous summer grazing rights and of the abundance of cheap labour that was still available. Jack had no answer; he knew he was beaten and, a week later, the letter came through.

"*Three* hundred pounds…ye gods." Jack closed his eyes and lowered his head, pinching the bridge of his nose. "And where's *that* coming from?" He rested his chin on his hands. Charlotte looked aghast. They had expected something…but not this? It had come as a blow and nobody moved.

"Can't you go and see Wilmot? P'raps 'e could help." His sister lent across the table. "Go on, Jack. 'E's got the money…'e's our brother. You'd do it for him…we all would. Look at the luck he had earlier on. 'Tis only for a year or two, 'til things get straight."

"No." Jack held up his hand and shook his head. "It'd be business within the family. Just wouldn't be right."

"Then what about going to see Frederic, dear?" Katherine took his hand. "I know he's got problems. He's told us about the mines but he…he always listens and it's not as though you've asked before."

Jack thought for a moment, chewing on the inside of his cheek. "I can't." He looked up and saw their faces. "No. Honest…I could never do that. There's no way I could." He got to his feet. "Call me stubborn, call me what yer will but we took on this place to make a go of it and I could never go cap in hand like that. Never. He know's what this rise means to us…and he knows that it'll hurt, hurt bad." He looked at the two women. "If he's gone and done this to us then he's in right sore trouble himself and I could never go begging if he's down like that. This is our business an' we'll have to get along, same as all the others'll be doing."

✳

Wilmot moved as soon as the size of his share dividends had been confirmed. The figures amazed him. On top of that just a week earlier he had been appointed to the board of the Bristol Steamship Company, having turned down an offer to move to Peninsula and Oriental a month earlier. Piers Deveraux had adjusted his salary and allowance package accordingly.

Wilmot Tucker had always wanted to be a landowner and now was his chance. The money was there in abundance and he bought three farms, two outside North Molton and one from Frederic Knight. It was then that Sherdon changed hands.

212

Chapter Fourteen

It had taken him just seconds to see there was little hope. Gillan Rawle's body was riddled and it now had to be a question of time: a year if the man was lucky. Collyns was surprised that he had kept working for so long. He could not have achieved much these last few months, certainly done nothing demanding since the summer. The doctor checked the pulse once more. "It's not good, I'm afraid." He shook the wrist gently, no more than a gesture of encouragement, and looked at the man lying propped against the head of the narrow cot. Gillan Rawle knew the verdict; the eyes said it.

"How long, doctor?" He coughed harshly then lay back breathless, opening his eyes only after regaining his composure.

"It's always difficult to say. We must never give up but it appears as though it's got to your lungs…and we know about the tumours further down, don't we." Collyns bit on his lip and glanced through the window to the hillside beyond the garden. The high slope opposite faced north and the frost, untouched by the winter sun, lay on the dead bracken like flour on the mill floor. He had to be careful for the man would be clinging to his every word.

"I can never be sure, not even after thirty years and more, but I'd say you've got around a year or so…a bit more perhaps." Collyns moved his head from side to side, weighing his thoughts. "Trouble is that it's worked its way in deep and I can't see how we're going to clear it."

The young wife, sitting close to the open fire for warmth with her feet tucked under her serge skirt, was waiting as he clumped slowly down the steep stairs. In spite of the worried look on her face, she was pretty in an earthy sort of way, sensuous even. She would cope; there was life and an energy there, he could see that. There were no children to tie her and she would be left with more possessions than most in her position. Once her man had gone she would move away and there would be no shortage of suitors.

"It's bad, isn't it, doctor?" As she rose, she smiled anxiously. "I can see from yer face." Collyns was surprised at her assurance. Kitty tossed her head then reached up to fish the locks of red hair from her collar. "Glad Sexton told me so. Said she used to 'ear 'im coughing an' hawking up at the farm. They'd catch 'im bending over for breath an' that."

The doctor smiled kindly and motioned her towards the door, holding out her black shawl for her to slip around her shoulders. The pale sun, little more than a hazy orb low over the hill, still had enough strength to warm the front porch where he paused, taking in the view before leading her away from the cottage. "You're right Mrs Rawle." Dr Collyns spoke quietly. His voice was low. "Your husband's a very sick man."

213

"Aye." Kitty, her head lowered in thought, fell a pace or two behind. "Aye, I know…we all do, doctor. D'yer think he'll manage…pull through, I mean? He will, wont 'e?" He heard the hope in her voice as she quickened her step to catch up with him.

He stopped by the beech hedge that ran down to the river and took her hands. "Listen, my dear." Her worried expression had suddenly turned to one of fear. "I have to tell you that your husband's not at all well. We call it wasting…it can take people at any age and, once it's there, it's the devil to shift. It's got to him I'm afraid, and it's spreading."

"You're telling me he's going to die…aren't you?" her eyes were searching his. "Gillan's going, isn't he, doctor?" Her voice rose and a hand came up to her face. The other grabbed for his arm. "He is isn't he? Go on then…tell me…I've got t'er be told."

"I'm afraid so…and he knows." Collyns smiled sadly, his voice little more than a whisper. "Before I left him we talked about it." He paused, giving the girl time to take in what he said. "He'll need you, you know, my dear. There's little chance of him going back to work." They walked on in silence, both starting back as a mallard sprang from the water. "He'll be fine for a while and you'll be wondering what all the fuss is about. But then, as time goes on, it'll get back to him again. I'll give you some laudenum…it'll help ease the pain."

The girl had strength and would manage, of that he was sure, but she would need help as her husband began to weaken. Somehow she was going to have to find enough work to keep them both and that meant going out to look for it. But where? He would tell them up at the farm, perhaps they would know.

"Thank you, sir. Thank you kindly." He watched as she forced back tears. It hurt to see her like that, just as it always did, for he had never got used to breaking such news. In a village there were neighbours next door and friends who could be warned and prepared. But out here…and at this time of the year? Suddenly the landscape around him looked bleak and forbidding and it worried him. "I'm away up to Sherdon right now." Both her hands were in his. "Young Charles's not well again…a touch of pneumonia this time. I just wish he could shake it off," he mused, pausing to choose his words. "But listen. I'll warn them about your husband, tell them I've told you what I think. It'll be easier if people know and I'm sure they'll do what they can." Collyns sighed, allowing his shoulders to sag as he glanced up the track, before turning and smiling encouragingly.

✳

Charlotte nodded. "I 'eard it were such." She looked at Katherine. "'Member I told you a month or more back. Gwen Fisher and Mabel Shapcott from Litton both said they'd heard it. Bamber heard about it down at The Royal Oak. Dan an' Winnie Pearce told 'im. Kitty calls in to see 'er at market."

Collyns warmed his hands on the mug. He felt better. Katherine and Charlotte had accepted the news as he hoped they would and young Charles seemed to be on the mend. His fever had subsided and the crisis gone on its way. But the ten year old was still too frail and shouldn't keep going down like this. It was odd, something was amiss but another two weeks should see him back at school.

"Don't see there's much to be done, *can* be done." Jack turned his coat on the rail in front of the fire. "There's precious little work to be had out here, and the two youngsters are still settlin' and feelin' their way. Sounds a bit hard, I know, doctor, but it'll be money going out without much coming back. Things aren't easy, you know." Collyns noticed Charlotte's sharp glance at her brother, as if she knew something. Was there a feud between the farm and the cottage, he wondered, or something that was not quite right?

He was not to know the differences there had been within the Sherdon household when, a week previously, they had heard about the farm changing hands. Jack had been horrified, failing to appreciate how their cause had been helped and had tried to spurn his brother's financial package.

*

For two days he refused to countenance it, then, at lunch, Charlotte's patience snapped. "Oh, fer Heaven's sake, you stupid man." She threw down the empty bowl and rounded on him, making the others jump back in alarm. "He's our *brother*...fer cryin' out loud. Our very own brother and *still* yer go on. What's got into yer, Jack? What's up? Go on...what's so wrong in 'im helping us? Eh? Some stranger could 'ave bought the place, someone who wanted us out...what wanted to take the place over. What then?" For a moment she hesitated and they all felt the silence. "An' that would be all of us, mind, *you* as well...right out in the cold. But 'e didn't, did 'e? Will came all the way out to tell us we could stop worryin'. She paused again. "Anyways," her voice dropped. "He's bought it now so there's no going back."

"There's no need for that." Jack stood and faced his sister, pointing angrily. "'Tis not right workin'..."

"Oh, for *God's sake*," Charlotte leant forward against the table and glared at him. "Honest, Jack, you don't deserve a brother like Will...and this isn't the first time. What's up with yer these days? You jealous of 'im, or summat? He's bin lucky in life and now, fer once, 'tis the same fer us...a bit of luck's come our way and you go on like this." The others watched her breathing heavily. "Count yer blessings in life. Go on, Jack...be 'appy fer once. For God's sake smile at life an' not go grumblin' so. Don't know what's got into yer lately...for ever moonin' around about this an' that. Proper old sour face, so you are."

He had seen it in the end but it had been a difficult time. Neither he nor Charlotte were to know that, two weeks before Frederic told them about the farm, Katherine had sold more of her jewellery. Knowing that negotiations were underway, Frederic had been reluctant to take them. But she had persisted and when he rode out with news of the farm sale, he confirmed that the money from her grandmother's diamond brooch and cross pendant had been banked.

In fact, the two women had been discussing the plight of their young neighbours for some time. They had been considering how best they might help Kitty and had mentioned it to Jack. Both had been surprised at his reluctance to become involved now Gillan was so ill. It was unlike him, the man to whom neighbours knew they could turn, the one who always put the needs of others first. But, in the end he had relented, accepting that they would have to become more involved and it was this sudden reaction to what Collyns had just said today that surprised them.

"Listen, dear." Katherine crossed the kitchen. "Don't let's say no to her…we can't. Things here aren't quite as bad as they were. And just think of the poor girl." She turned to Collyns. "We'll keep watch on them, Charles. We pass their door daily and can see how things go. Lottie and I'll call by and see what we can do."

"Aye, that's right," Charlotte nodded vigorously in an angry show of support for Katherine. "Us could never let the poor maid struggle on her own like that."

Katherine turned to her husband, resting her hand on the back of his chair. "Look. When Gillan gets bad…I mean when things become more difficult, I'm sure we'll find something for Kitty. Heaven knows," she threw her arms wide. "There's enough and more for her to be doing here." Jack's coolness continued and it puzzled her. She found herself worried but she didn't know why. Worried and ashamed that the man she loved could appear so hard on those at the cottage at a time like this.

✳

Once Collyns had gone, Jack left for the sheep on sixty acres, leaving his wife alone with his sister.

"Oh, 'tis nuthin…he's always bin the same." Charlotte added salt to the stew and grunted with effort as she took both hands to the heavy pot. "Ever since 'e was a boy 'tis bin nuthin' but worry, worry, worry…money usually." Katherine watched the sturdy frame of her sister-in-law bending over the fire. "*There.*" Charlotte eased the iron maid across the fire until the pot hung directly over the embers then steadied it with a log while she replaced the lid.

"There we are." She picked a fold in her frock to wipe her hands. "No, 'tis nuthin' reelly…he'll come round to the idea." A cry from Anna took Katherine from the room and she never saw the look on Charlotte's face as she set about the cutlery in the sink.

She had barely started but stopped suddenly, her hands still deep in the tepid water. It was as though she had seen the face of a ghoul staring at her through the window, staring in that dreadful way they were supposed to do. Lottie stood

216

motionless. Perhaps Bamber *had* been right after all. At the time she had dismissed what he had said but he had been worried and that concerned her. It was the second time, he told her, that he had picked up word. First, Wally Sexton had told him that Jack had been calling on the Rawles, then his own Edgar had asked why such an interest was being shown at the cottage. His lad had heard from the Gillards at Sandyway. Bamber had puzzled over the matter and the more he puzzled the less he liked it.

Charlotte had chided him when he told her but then Rex Fisher heard word at the Exford lamb sales and he, like the others, had mentioned it to Bamber. Word was that something at Sherdon was amiss. Perhaps she should not have agreed so readily to have Kitty working in the house. It could mean trouble, bad trouble for them all. Perhaps, if the whispers were true, Jack was fighting temptation. She continued to stare out of the scullery window but the face had gone; only the steady drip from the draining board disturbed the water.

2

"Heavens, Gaile. That's far too much." Katherine eased the stone jar across the kitchen table. "Honestly, dear, one would be more than enough."

"No. We won't have none of that." The young woman lowered the second honey jar. "I reckoned it should have been three but Dad said two's fair. Mother agreed, so that's that." She turned, eyebrows raised and laughed. "So there."

"Well, it's more than enough and the children'll love it. Thank you...come here." She hugged the slim figure and smiled warmly. Gaile Fisher was fun, a happy little soul and her presence lightened the day. "I hear that the business is going really well. Ralph brings me news of you all."

It was the beginning of the new season for the bees and the Fishers had been out looking for swarms almost as soon as the first lambs appeared in the fields. Gaile, she knew, had been making straw skeps and now had more than a dozen ready for the new arrivals. Honeycombs were the children's favourite but they had long since gone. The honey in the stone jars Gaile had brought was pure, having been strained through butter muslin and it was going to have to see them through until high summer.

"Oh aye. Us 'ave had a bit of luck. Winstons, the new chandlers in Dulverton 'ave bought last year's wax, all of it...right off in one go. Said he'll take all we've got this year an' all." She paused, catching her breath before changing the subject. "'Ave yer finished it, Katherine?" she looked at her expectantly. "You know...did yer get the lace on and do they other bits?"

"Let's see what you think." Katherine led the way to Alice and Anna's room. The dress she had been making for her young neighbour, hung from a beam, covered carefully by a cotton sheet. She knew from the moment she had seen the scarlet satin that the colour would suit the black hair and sallow complexion. All it needed was some fine lace edging to the bodice and skirt and this had come from Honiton. She had brought the waistline up under the bodice, keeping the material close to the trim figure before flaring it into the wider skirt.

Gaile's hands smoothed the material against the flat of her stomach; it had taken her no time at all to slip from her farm clothes. "Oh my…'tis beautiful, Katherine…reelly, reelly beautiful." She turned slowly, her eyes never leaving the mirror. "D'yer think he'll like it?" Katherine looked up and took the pins from her mouth.

"He's a very lucky young man, so he is." She looked at the slim, youthful figure. The young girl's face was radiant. "Oh yes, indeed…Mr Ralph Rudd can count his good fortune." Then their eyes met. "But then, he's a grand young man as well," she went on. "And you've not done so badly yourself, you know."

"Mmm, I know. He's a lovely lad. Quiet mind, not like…."

"Declan?" Without thinking the name had slipped out.

Gaile laughed. "Oh aye. He was a one. Never stopped pratlin' an' chatterin' away, did 'e now. Used to make us chuckle but Dad said 'e were not right." She pulled a face at the memory of the confrontation with her father. "Too much away with the fairies, he said." This time they both laughed.

"Clever though…and so very quick." Katherine struggled to her feet, pulling out the skirt of the unfinished dress, then stood back with her head to one side regarding her handiwork. "Used to read like mad. Read everything I'd got then pester me for more…I just couldn't stop him." She looked at the young woman. She was beautiful, of that there was no doubt; just where those fine, chiselled features came from she had no idea. Not from her father that was for sure and, as for the figure, poor, dear Gwen could never have been like that. Little wonder the Irishman had been attracted.

Gaile saw her look and smiled back then shrugged shyly. Katherine caught her breath. Had little Harriet lived she would have been thirteen this month, just beginning to flower, moving on from childhood and worrying about what people would make of her and how she should dress. If only this girl in front of her was her own; one she could dress and spoil, love and fuss over. What fun it would be for them to talk together like this, to share those little secrets and laugh about life. If *only* it could have been like this. But no, she would have to wait. Their own little ones were still tiny and it would be an age before they were like Gaile; years and years of waiting out here at Sherdon…and for what? What would they be like at the end of it all? Could it be that they would be as pretty as her? For a moment her heart sank but she caught the other's smile.

"Your father was right, you know. Declan lived life from the cuff of his sleeve. We all loved him dearly but he'd be a devil to live with…did he ever tell you about the mine – Ralph, I mean?" Katherine hung the dress on the hook under the beam and smoothed the satin gently before stretching up to replace the sheet. "D'you remember you were going to ask him?"

"He never said much." Gaile pulled the cord tight around her cotton working dress then bent down to lace up her boots. "Can't get much out of 'im about himself, what he's been up to or where he's been. He's a quiet lad...never says nuthin' much when 'e's working neither."

✳

Earlier, before bringing the honey into the house, she had watched him in the lambing shed. Only the night before a ewe had lost her lamb while another had given birth to triplets. He had motioned her to stand quietly as he decided which of the three lambs to take. Knowing what was to come, he settled for the largest and strongest.

He worked swiftly, removing the head and feet of the dead lamb then carefully skinning the little corpse, pulling the legs through the skin to leave small trousers. The live lamb, too young to fear, stood tottering and shivering at his feet, calling plaintively for its mother. He took it gently, smeared it with the dead lamb's blood then fitted the skin like a second coat, pulling the leggings over the feet as breeches might be fitted to a doll. Her eyes never left him and, as she watched, she could hear him talking quietly, soothing the helpless mite as he worked. Still he did not speak, simply beckoned her to follow him to where the ewe that had lost her lamb, was calling.

He bent over the wooden hurdle, placed the fresh lamb down carefully in the straw and stood back. As the tiny newcomer struggled towards the ewe, dragging its second coat, she stopped calling and looked down. The lamb, lost and confused, called out and stumbled on. The ewe lowered her head, sniffed, then butted the lamb to the ground. Time and again it got up and shuffled towards her but the old ewe knew instinctively that it was not her own. "We'll use the dogs." He took the lamb from the pen, smeared more blood onto the coat then fetched the two collies. He then replaced the lamb with the ewe, this time leaving the pen open.

"Pssshhhhhew. *Gid on...hey up.* Pssshhhew." The ewe battered the first dog into the straw then stood over the lamb as the collies tried to reach them, snarling and barking, darting forward and jumping quickly back to avoid the horns. Several times one or the other was butted, sometimes yelping in pain but always returning for more, their attacks getting ever bolder. The lamb, frightened and confused, struggled towards its foster-mother, searching desperately for warmth and protection. The ewe was cornered but she did not flinch. Now standing right over the lamb she faced the dogs with her head lowered and stamped her feet defiantly.

"There look." Ralph caught her arm. "Her'll take the lamb. See that, her's feeding 'it now. *Gid over...gi'back.*" He nudged the dogs away with his feet and closed the pen. They watched in silence as the ewe let the newborn lamb feed at last, its tail wriggling in pleasure. The shepherd backed away carefully, still watching them both least the ewe should change her mind. "There'e be." He turned and grinned, his face shining. "She'll take the littl'un now…wunnerful, that is."

She could see he was tired. His face was creased and lined and his hair was a tangled mess. But she could feel a warmth in him, a glow of satisfaction at what had been done. He was a gentle man, and had always been so, but in that gentleness lay a strength. There was something reassuring about him, something comforting and protective. Suddenly, as they stood together, she felt a surge of happiness and took his arm before resting her head against his shoulder.

3

Wilmot was in a pensive mood. He loved the ride from Heasley up to Simonsbath where the track rose above Lyddicombe to Fyldon then on to Kinsford Gate. But today he saw little of the countryside and only half heard the birds around him. Even the soft, sad cry of the curlew, his favourite, failed to make him look up.

His son, Lionel, was three now and in December Jessica would be two. The staff at Court Hall would have to be increased. That was no problem and already Rebecca had taken to Mrs Lock. The aimiable woman had come to them from Dunster Castle and they would be making her position as housekeeper permanent at the end of the month. But he needed more, especially now the children were getting mobile, and he would have to put word about. The second brougham he had ordered from Martin's of Oxford would be delivered shortly and Bulled, the gamekeeper, had asked for an assistant. The household was certainly growing.

*

"Wilmot, my dear good man, how splendid to see you." The study was still as dark as he remembered it, masking Frederic's features into little more than an outline against the window. The two shook hands. "Look, let's go through to the front drawing room…come on. Florence is away up in town, I'm afraid, but sends her apologies…and best wishes to you all, of course." Young Knight turned and smiled warmly at his visitor before turning to the butler who had Wilmot's cloak over his arm. "Thank you, Tarr. Bring the drinks through, would you please…and best to check the logs I've put on the fire."

Wilmot followed the taller man. Perhaps it was a good thing that they were on their own. He knew that his host was worried, for he had told him so himself when he had asked him to come and talk about the mines. But, as far as he was concerned the subject was dead in the water. For more than a week he had put out feelers among his old contacts but the verdict was always the same. Had old John Knight been gambling on the fact that Exmoor was sitting on top of a great mound of iron or copper then he had lost out, and lost badly. It was *not* and the project was no longer viable; simple as that. They would have to close, yet even now Freddy could put up a fight. It might just get difficult over lunch and the last thing he wanted was a woman hovering and twittering away as harsh realities were faced.

Frederic told him everything, or enough at least for his position to be clear, then sat and heard him out. He listened carefully, frowning or nodding sombrely, sometimes picking at the creases in his trousers. "And that's about the sum of it, Freddy," Wilmot concluded eventually, by now hunched deep in the armchair with one arm along each rest and a glass of madeira in his right hand.

"I thought that'd be your verdict." Frederic sounded dejected. He stood bathed in the late sunlight looking down to the Barle that was in spate, both hands behind his frock coat. Wilmot watched his head shaking slowly. "And it ties in exactly with what the banks have been telling me. But it's *maddening*," he exploded, turning and raising his arms. "Abso*lutely maddening*." Here we are, sitting on top of God knows what...every report says so, yet the damned stuff's as elusive as the Holy Grail."

"Diminishing returns are always dangerous, y'know." Wilmot rose and joined him. "The whole business is a gamble, nothing less...and will always be so," he added hurriedly least the truth should be taken as a cruel jibe. "You know it's out there somewhere...rather you *think* you do, and you go on and on pouring in the money, ever more desperate for the big one." He lifted his head to flick back a lock of hair. "And a sniff here or a touch there only adds to the temptation...draws you back yet again and forces you on. Honestly, my advice is to call a halt...for the time being anyway."

He perched on the window seat where he could see Knight's face. "Look, Freddy...seriously, just hold your horses for a year or two. They're making fantastic technological strides the whole time and, who knows, once you've got the rest of your affairs in order you might feel inclined to have another go...it'll still be out there, waiting for you. Think about it." He leant back, his eyes on Frederic's fingers as they toyed impatiently with his watch chain.

"You've got the land, so hang on to that," he continued. "Each season it's improving...as will the returns, given half a chance. You can renegotiate the exploration rights easily enough and you've got time on your hands. Look upon the potential as some sort of...what shall I say, some sort of long term investment. Why rush at the mines now when the funds are so low?" He gave a short laugh at the idea. "*Why*, for God's sake?"

"Hmmph," Frederic sighed angrily, scratching at his wave of dark curls. "You're right, Wilmot. Damn it...yes, it all makes sense. And yet," he paused, held momentarily by a flicker of determination then made up his mind. "Ugh...no, that's it. I'll call a halt." There was a note of finality in his voice. "I had a mind to...but no, I've got precious little option and what you've said puts a cap on it all. Damn you, Will," Frederic laughed and clapped the other's shoulder.

*

There was half an hour to lunch and the two, now close friends, sat happily together. Frederic asked him about his new farms. Wilmot questioned the Member for West Worcestershire about the affairs of state and Lord Aberdeen's new ministry. Word was that Palmerston's Liberals were making life difficult for the Peelites.

It was when Tarr had just announced that lunch was ready that they turned their attention to matters closer to home. "And what news from Sherdon?" The question was simple enough.

"Not bad. No...not bad at all." Wilmot pulled a wry face. "The two lads are up and away serving Queen and country and the new littl'uns are settling in well enough. Jack's fine. Still works every hour he can, though. Flogs himself...too hard, *far* too hard. I just wish he'd take a bit of time off with the family...but he won't. To be honest I don't think he'd know what to do with himself."

"And Katherine?" Frederic held the door. "We often wonder how she's faring."

"Mmm," Wilmot raised his eyebrows. "Don't we all...don't we all. You know...I can't imagine how she must feel shut away out there like that. I'd go mad. As it is I take her books. They keep her going, takes her mind off the price of turnips and fat lambs for a bit." They walked across the hall in silence.

"Florence is worried as well." Frederic lifted his tails then sat as Tarr pushed his chair forward. "And the Aclands, too. We all think dear Katherine lives, exists rather, just for your brother. She's eyes for him only, dotes on him...lucky man." The two laughed. Wilmot toyed with the fruit knife on his napkin; it was difficult enough for him when he went to the farm as the new owner but for Frederic it must be worse. A certain coolness had crept between his host and Katherine, he had sensed it the last time they had all been there together. It was nobody's fault, rather that Florence's appearance on the scene had made the complicated tangle even worse.

It was as though Katherine had distanced herself even further. Frederic had noticed it too, asking him later if he had detected anything untoward. Yes he had, he replied, for there had been no choice in his answer. Throughout their visit, she had barely spoken of the Knight family or asked Frederic about their friends and had made no mention at all of his new wife, not even a polite enquiry. Florence, poor girl, had barely got to know Exmoor and it was not as though there was anything wrong with her, far from it, but he had detected Katherine's resentment at such an intrusion.

Perhaps she had been trying to force from her mind all links with the past, to cut herself away from those who had anything to do with her earlier days. Florence, so it seemed to him, had become the catalyst for her emotions and her unhappiness. If Frederic had discovered this also then he, Wilmot, could see no end to it all. "Anyhow," he took a deep breath, inching his glass forward to be filled, "all's not lost yet." He tried to sound cheerful but considered it fell some way short. "I've got Alfred Tennyson coming down again in the autumn. He loves it there...adores Katherine and she him. They sit chatting for hours on end so Heaven knows when he's going to do all this writing he's promised himself. Won't be at Sherdon."

Frederic rang the bell and the two men, lunching alone, talked on while sixty miles away bands were playing and crowds were cheering.

4

The cavalrymen were hot as they marched in squadrons along The Hoe at Plymouth yet their chargers became hotter still as, later, they waited patiently in the afternoon sun. One by one they were lifted from St Bede's dock, their legs hanging limply either side of the canvas cradle as they were swung high in the air then lowered deep into the hold of the *S.S. Simla*. For many of the soldiers and for most of the horses it was to be their last glimpse of England.

✳

"All troopers and grooms to the hold...all troopers and grooms to the hold." The midshipman of the watch ran between the lines of hammocks.

The *Simla* was three days out and for the last twenty-four hours the captain had watched the barometer falling. He had taken her as close as he dared to Ile d'Ouessant hoping to make the run through the Bay of Biscay before the storm broke. He would have done so had he not been ordered to wait for the frigate from Spithead. She had been late and Captain Dokes cursed his luck.

Now the seas were rising and the *Simla*, beam on to the swell, began to roll. In an hour it would be dark. His new course, sou' sou' west to Cape Finisterre, would take him into the teeth of whatever the Atlantic had in store and he cursed again.

Billy had been sick even as they left port. More and more soldiers succumbed to the steady rise and fall of the ship so that, before they had cleared the Western Approaches, the floor beneath the three tiers of closely packed hammocks on the lower deck was running with vomit. The plight of the NCOs and the Officers was just as bad, leaving only Davey and a few others to check the hundred and twenty horses. The main hold, dark and foul smelling, was lit by two lanterns that swayed with the movement of the ship. Each time she rolled the horses on the lower side slithered forward, crashing into their mangers, while those opposite, and higher due to the list, slipped back until their hindquarters pressed up against the railings. It was a giant macabre dance. First one side rose then the other, then the first again. Then the whole ship shuddered, struck hard by a wave. As it grew darker so the swaying and rolling, the heaving and lurching, the rising and crashing increased.

The wretched animals, tethered in lines just a few feet apart and with barely enough room to lie down, strained at their head collars, their eyes rolling in fear. The first one went down just before dusk. The little mare slipped on the wooden decking, already awash with a thin, green soup of dung and urine. She panicked, her legs trapped under the railings separating her from the horse in the next stall.

Their legs became entangled and he, a black gelding, kicked out and stamped on her before collapsing himself.

By the time it was dark, seawater was crashing through the hatches left open for air. The water, with nowhere else to go, sloshed around the legs of men and animals, soaking everything, the lower decking now as treacherous as ice. More and more horses slipped and fell. Some bore it stoically in silence but most thrashed about calling loudly, the noise in the hold like a host of terrified children. Sometimes men had to jump for their lives as a horse lashed out. One broke free, plunging and kicking madly before he, too, fell and skidded into the woodwork. The farriers, unable to swing their axes, sat on the heads of those with broken limbs and cut their throats, the red blood mixing with the green sludge as the whole evil mess swashed to and fro.

*

"*Get up…get up. Damn yer eyes, yer goddamned, idle swabs.*" The bosun's rope fell on the figures lying helpless with seasickness. Some staggered to their feet, some collapsed on the greasy deck or lurched about helplessly as the ship rolled. Others simply lay prostrate, incapable of moving anywhere. "*Get up…get up, yer lazy swine. Get to yer 'orses. Sort 'em out…sort 'em out.*" Those who could, made their way down to join those already struggling desperately in the hold below.

On deck the night was wild, the wind whipping the crests from each huge wave as it shuddered into the ship when the green, foaming water poured across the deck and down into every hatch and stairway. It crashed through a bulkhead, cascading into the engine room. The stokers, too late to close the boilers, watched helplessly as first one then the others were flooded. Great sheets of hot steam escaped across the ship before vanishing into the night. High above the deck whatever sails had not been furled tore themselves free from the rigging. The canvas flapped wildly until it was ripped into shreds and blown to the heavens. Everyone on deck was soaked by the rain as it lashed down, driven on by the howling gale. The night was as black as black could be.

"'Tis a madhouse down below, sir." The first mate hung on to the balustrade with one hand, the other cupped round his mouth. "The animals are going mad. *Mad, sir…mad with fright,*" he yelled, pointing to the hatch.

"Shorten sail…top gallants only." The captain swayed uneasily. "We'll bear away before Finisterre to give ourselves more sea room then run with the storm…under bare poles…all the way to Gascony Bay, if needs be. "A looped warp astern, if you please. *Number One,*" Captain Dokes bellowed into the gale. "My compliments to the Commanding Officer…would he be pleased to come to the bridge…*now.*"

Lieutenant Colonel The Lord Paget listened aghast. The engines had flooded and they were coming about to run before the storm. As they spoke, both men wiped at the spray on their faces. Too many horses had broken free and were endangering the lives of his men and the crew. "I can give it thirty minutes, Colonel. Just half an hour and no more," he roared. As the ship plunged and bucked, the two men clung to each other. "Thirty minutes from when we begin our run and unless this abates we'll have to get rid of the animals...overboard, dead or alive, I don't care which. It's either them or my crew and the ship herself.

"It's hell down below," the first mate shouted. "Sheer hell, sir."

*

"Sit on his head...keep him down."   "Watch out for the legs."   "Close the hatch...that one up there."   "Bring a lamp, someone."   "*Farrier*...over here." "Get that bay secured...quick."   "Look out!"   "*Help*, somebody. Give a hand." "Loose horse...and she's down."   "*Watch out.*"

Davey leapt at the animal's head and hung on. He could feel the strength in the neck as the charger tried to rear up, the head collar jarring cruelly as the double rope snapped tight. "Whoa, whoa...steady. Steady...steady." Two men next to him fell into the bilge swilling across the deck, another crashed screaming, kicked by a deranged horse. He looked around desperately.

'Cover the eyes, so you must.' Declan's voice came quietly. *'Cover the head too...if you can, that is. The poor thing's mad for what it can see and hear. Think's the divil hi'self's behind him.'* He remembered how the Irishman had done it at Sherdon when breaking young horses and again with the cattle when they were cutting the bull calves. He tore at his shirt and threw it over the animal's head. Others were doing the same. Everywhere, soldiers, some in uniform, some half dressed were holding or sitting on horses. But the ship had turned and gradually, as she ran with the gale, the terrible battering and flooding eased.

Slowly, throughout that dreadful night, The Fourth Light Dragoons brought their chargers to hand. Many were injured, seven had to be destroyed but the battle had been won.

*

A week later, they were praying for the return of wind and rain. The *S.S Simla*, like long lines of other ships, lay waiting to pass through the Bosphorous.

The Sea of Marmara, flat calm and glistening, reflected the sun's glare as blindingly as any mirror. Every hatch had been opened while sails had been set as awnings above the companionways to catch what little breeze might be coming from the land. The sun blazed down. Metal was hot to the touch and men lay listless in the heat but it was the horses that fared worst of all.

Below, deep in the hold, the heat was burning off what little air was left, now rancid and foul with the stench from the bilges. Movement was an effort and breathing difficult. The horses stood listlessly in lines, their heads low, moving occasionally from one leg to another to adjust the weight of their bodies but no more than that.

They were spent, exhausted and beaten. The troopers, despairing at their discomfort, spent hour after hour bathing their chargers with seawater and washing their eyes and nostrils with vinegar. Drinking water, luke warm and rancid, was in short supply. Fodder, ruined by seawater, lay uneaten.

One at a time the weakest and those injured in the storm, were hoisted onto the main deck. For a few glorious minutes they were able to ease their cramped limbs, walking stiffly and gingerly along the crowded deck before they were turned to walk back again, too tired to even care what might happen next.

"Billy...Billy, listen. It's the boilers. We're moving." Davey looked though the porthole. "Come on, let's check below."

"Another three days, yeah?" Trooper Granby looked across the horse lines. "That's what Cap'n Smedley said. Three sodding days to a poxy place called Varna or summat. Then ashore...off this bastard, stinkin' hell hole, thank Christ."

5

"Davey...no!" Charlotte shook her head. "No, I can't believe it. Just can't." Wally and Glad Sexton stood next to her in the parlour at Sherdon.

"Well...what can we say?" Katherine looked from one to the other then down at the bundle in the crib, before easing back the woollen blanket and leaning forward to peer more closely. She stood, smiling and looked once more at the visitors, still smiling kindly. "What can any of us say other than welcome the little soul...welcome him into the family?"

"Oh, Wally. What's to do now?" Charlotte buried her head in her hands. "Never would 'ave thought nuthin' like this would 'appen. Never."

"Ssshhh. There, there, maid...'tis harmless enough." The farmer from Barkham looked from one to the other. "Us'll manage t'il the lad's back home again." For three months they had managed to keep the secret but now it was time for the world to know.

Arthur David Tucker had been born at Darlick, just half a mile from Barkham. Gladys Sexton, his grandmother, had been there at the confinement along with her own mother, the old lady who lived alone in the shepherd's cottage. The two of them had coped and the young mother had not wanted for anything.

"So, 'tis reelly my Davey?" Charlotte looked at her. "He's the one is he...the father?"

Jade Sexton nodded with her head lowered. "Yes," she whispered then glanced up fearfully. "'Tis Davey, Lottie...he's the father. There's nobody else."

Katherine, one arm around her shoulder, pulled the girl towards her.

Chapter Fifteen

Gaile got as far as the bridge and waited. Eventually she saw him emerge from the wood. "The sheep're breaking across," Ralph cried. "Further up…there look. Lambs I 'spect." He trotted up to her and rode close before turning his horse alongside hers. Reaching over to catch hold of the back of her saddle he pointed out the gap in the hedge. "By that fallen tree…up there. To the left of the Rawles, just beyond the cottage. I'll come down later."

She leant back against his arm and smiled. "I reckon about a dozen've broken through," he confirmed. From the bridge, the lane to Sherdon skirted to the left, around the worst of the high ground, but here the two riders parted. He took the track up to the farm while she turned downstream and followed the river home.

He had almost passed the cottage when his horse whinnied softly. One of the collies from the farm ran towards him and he stopped, looking around uncertainly. The dog had come from the gap in the hedge that sheltered the cottage. Then he saw the horse, tied up and almost out of sight. It was Jack's. Ralph stood in his stirrups looking for Gaile but she had gone. He craned his neck, biting his lip as he did so, but she was nowhere to be seen. He turned back to where he could get a better view of the garden but there was no sign of movement. Dismounting quietly, he bent to fondle the dog then led his horse onto the grass verge, moving silently until he was clear of the building.

Jack had to be there and it saddened him. The rumours and gossip must be true, there could be no other explanation. Jack Tucker, a man for whom he had so much admiration, had to be involved with Gillan's wife. Katherine knew nothing. He had been watching her since he had first heard word and was certain she had no idea. Living at Sherdon from now on, even talking to them, was going to be difficult.

*

Jack sat on the edge of the cot. For the last ten minutes they had been together, but time was running out. She had helped him off with his coat and hung it behind the door, but it was still too warm and he wiped his mouth pensively.

Kitty smiled. It was the same friendly smile he remembered. As she did so, her face lit up, her worries seemingly forgotten. "You *are* hot, aren't you." Her voice was low. She had left her shawl and shoes downstairs and padded across the room to where he was sitting. He let her mop his brow then stood quietly. "Are you sure you've time?" she whispered.

He took her hand, nodded and smiled encouragingly. "Yes, he murmured. "Come on."

"Be gentle though, won't you?" She turned back the top sheet and looked up at him. "Please be gentle." He smiled again then bent down, easing his arms under the body.

"All right, Gillan...'tis only me, Jack. Come on, old lad...try to move onto my arms so we can get you up." For a moment the man's eyes stared vacantly. "Once you'm on your feet, we can get you down...I'll see yer down the stairs."

He was shocked by his lightness. The body had gone: simply disappeared. Where he had expected to find strong thighs, there was nothing while his back felt more like an empty cage than that of a man in his prime. The farmhand had wasted away. As Gillan was lifted, he gasped then cleared his throat, forcing Jack to wince at the stench of rotting flesh. Even as it struggled for life, the body was decaying. The end could not be far away.

"There, lad. We've put yer in the light by the window." Gillan lay back with his knees raised. The short move had exhausted him and Jack covered the wasted frame, unable to ignore the claw-like hands and feet or the two knees, perched like white stones on top of the flesh-covered bones.

"Thanks, Jack. Bless yer for that." The thin face smiled up at him but the eyes, sunk deep into their hollows, stared intently. Jack waited until the rattling cough had finished. "Thanks," Gillan whispered, closing his eyes.

"I'll help you with his things." Jack could see she was near to breaking. Even as he followed her back up the stairs he could sense the despair. He looked at the crumpled sheet where Gillan had been lying then down at the few belongings scattered on the floor. Inside the room it was warm and even as he breathed he detected the smell of death and the foul, soiled clothes. She could see he had.

"Sorry," she whispered, hurrying to throw open the window. "Not very nice, I'm afraid. Is it?" Kitty picked a sweat-soaked vest from his cot. "The poor lad...the poor, dear lad..." She turned away with her mouth clenched tight, first one hand then the other covering her face. As she started to weep her whole body shook. All control was lost as she drew in deep lungfuls of air to fuel her sobs. Then, suddenly, she was quiet again. Her hands were half hidden in her red hair, one still holding her husband's vest. Jack stood, silent and undecided, yet longing to take the helpless young woman into his arms.

It was when she looked up, her face streaked with tears, that his hand reached out. "Come, Kitty...don't cry now." She half fell against him, buried her face in his shirt and began to weep again. One hand held her close while his other reached up to stroke the locks of dark, red hair that shook with her sobs.

"Ssshhh...you've got to be strong, my love...got to be strong. Ssshhh, there now." His hand caressed her face, half turned as she rested against his chest with one fist pressed tightly to her mouth. "Gillan needs you now...more'n ever. Needs yer to be strong." He could feel her nodding as she listened.

"It's so difficult," she whispered, her voice shrill between the tears. "I try, Jack...dear God, I try. But, here...on my own." Her head shook again. "It's just that sometimes...sometimes, I need help. I do my best...reelly I do, " she sighed. Slowly one hand moved up to the back of his neck. Her fingers stroked his ear then twined in his hair. "Thanks, Jack," she whispered. "Thanks." Both hands reached for his face. Her lips, soft at first, crushed against his mouth. His arms drew her in. For a moment their bodies came together, then slowly and gently he pulled away.

"Oh, I'm sorry." Kitty forced a smile. "I didn't mean it like that. It's just that...well...I just needed someone...something. But I'm fine now...fine."

"I know, dear. Yes, I know." Jack could feel his heart pounding. Had he not pulled back, he would still be in her arms and she in his, desperate for his support and his love. Her warm, soft body had pressed its curves against him. He had felt her trembling as she cried, yearning for the love she was so cruelly denied. He reached for her again, determined to make it brief. "I'll not let yer down, Kitty. Honestly, no matter what."

Even as he held her face between his hands and kissed the mouth, he could see her eyes pleading for him to stay. "I'll come and see how he is...so hold on, hold on tight," he whispered, squeezing her hand. "I'll be back." With that he turned and hurried down the stairs, not daring to look behind him.

*

"I need to see yer, Jack."

"Oh, aye?" He slipped the saddle from the horse and wiped his hand across the warm, damp withers. Surprised that Charlotte had come out to the stables, he paused with the saddle over his arm. "Summat's up?" His sister glanced behind her, then lifted her skirt and picked her way over the cobbled entrance. He could see she was worried. "What's up, then? No one's hurt or nuthin' are they?"

"Jack...it's you." The words tumbled out. "Listen." She checked behind her again then hurriedly closed both halves of the stable door before turning and facing him. "There's talk, Jack. Talk about you an' that Kitty Rawle. 'Tis everywhere." Jack folded the girth over the saddle and eased it slowly onto the rack. Then he paused, hands still holding the saddle before turning and staring at his sister. His face was blank.

"*Talk*, Lottie? *Talk?* Who's talking, and what am I s'posed to have done?" He could feel the anger rising. "Well...come on. You're here to tell me...what's it all about?"

"You an' Kitty, Jack. They say you've been seein' each other. Callin' in at the cottage an' that." Charlotte stared back, determined yet wary of her elder brother. "'Tis true, Jack. True...ain't it?"

"*Yes.*" The boldness of his reply made her step back. "Yes, 'tis quite right…I have bin seein' her. Like today, just now. An' yer know what I was doin' Lottie? Know why I was '*seein' her*' as they say? I was moving her poor, wretched man down the stairs. Nuthin' more than a livin' skeleton he is, Gillan, poor devil. She an' I moved his bed down so he needn't go climbin' the stairs no more." She could see his face was flushed with anger. "An' yes, I took her in my arms, I did, when her heart broke and she stood there weeping for him." By now he was having to breathe heavily to control himself. "So…who's doin' all this talking then? People out there with nuthin' better to do, I s'pose. Eh?"

"Dunno, Jack. Just dunno." So, it had been true but not in the way they said. "But you know what word's like…once things start."

"Aye. I know right enough." His face was set hard. "Well, just put word back that Jack Tucker *is* seein' Kitty Rawle. Sees her often too, like any good neighbour would. People can't have it both ways, you know…one minute go asking me to help, then getting back at me for callin' in and doing just that." He paused. "Does Katherine know about all this? 'Ave any of this lot bin up chatterin' away and whisperin' in her ear?"

"No…not that I knows anyway." Charlotte shook her head. "No one's said nuthin to 'er. Oh, I'm sorry, Jack. Sorry but pleased, too. Well…you'm…so nuthin's amiss, like. Nuthin' that could 'urt."

"Well *I'm* hurt, Lottie. Hurt and angry that folks go thinking like that. Kitty's there on her own and can't say nort to anyone. She can't talk back, can't defend herself or anything. She's stuck there nursin' her man. You just go back and tell 'em that…that I am seein' her and that's all there is to it."

*

Jack circled the ewes on sixty acres then dropped down to the river. The cattle should have been there but he did not care. His mind was in turmoil and he had to walk, walk until his head cleared. Who was it who had noticed him first and what was it he could have done or said that gave away his thoughts? Somebody, somehow had read his mind. And, whoever it was, was watching…damn them.

He knew he was being drawn towards her, lured helplessly and that he was powerless to stop. He could feel it and someone had seen it in him. He had wanted to help her and he had: but it was more than that, far more. And somebody had seen that too. And now, after this morning, he wanted her more than ever. But *why? Why*, for God's sake? Why, when a man's blessed with a loving and beautiful wife, does he start longing for another, and some little frippit of a girl like that? Were other men like that or was it just him?

He had heard others boast about what they'd supposed to have done but they were nothing. The braggarts were always just mouth and no more than that.

Others would be tempted but would be able to hold themselves back, honouring their vows. It was just him: he was different. He was weak and could feel it, and now others could see it as well What strange quirk of fate had brought him and this woman together like this, he wondered. What was it that had turned his head that day and, why, oh why, had he ever gone into the cottage?

If it had been hard up to now, it was going to be harder still. When she had clung to him, he had felt the animal in her, sensed the raw passion fuelled by her grief. And he had responded; she would have sensed that. He knew he would not be able to resist her for much longer and that sooner or later he would return. And she would be waiting.

So, let them know - all of them, Katherine, Lottie and the others. Perhaps the prying and whispering would stop and perhaps, once he knew that they all knew, he would be able to resist…but it would only be for a time. Someone would know that in the end he would succumb and whoever it was would be waiting for them to come together. Dear God it was madness, but he was caught and there was no way out.

2

Dorcas Venner pulled his cottage door shut behind him. Fifty yards away the bridge over the Mole was bathed in moonlight.

In front of him, across North Molton's lower square, lamps glowed in the windows of the long row of cottages. He would try again. For the last three nights he had been up to the Miners' Arms but there had been no sign of the man. Dorcas had promised to keep checking for the whole week and today was Friday. Brack Fanshawe had asked him to keep looking, and if Brack Fanshawe's soldiers were waiting out in the hills for the man, then he would keep his word.

Lantern in hand, he limped as he walked up through the village. The legacy of the half-spent French musket ball still hurt and had done so since eighteen-fourteen. He and Brack had charged together at Toulouse with the Old Second. When the day was won, Brack had helped him from his horse. That had been the end for him but Brack was still there soldiering on. Regimental Sergeant Major Fanshawe had done well for himself, very well, and Dorcas had been delighted when a detachment of The Royal North Devons, his old crowd, had called two weeks ago.

The tavern was crowded. Dorcas rubbed the windowpane and peered inside. Pay night it was and the place was as full as ever. "Dirty, heavin' brutes," he cursed, mumbling to himself. "Drink themselves stupid, chase the womenfolk all about the place and foul the streets. A touch o' the rod an' the lash like back in the Squadron. That'd shift 'em." He moved on to look through another then another. At the fourth window he saw him.

Jasper Harper was just where Brack Fanshawe said he would be. It had to be him: smart claret coat, the thigh boots and the lace at his chin. Two pistols, they told him. He could see one but there was his rapier. No more than a toy it was, nuthing like the old cavalry sabre.

He limped into the road and swung the lantern to let them know. Three times he swung it high then waited. Far away across the bridge, just beneath High Bullen, a lantern replied. Brack Fanshawe had asked him to warn his men when the highwayman would be on his way and now his job was half done. It was too far for him to hear the sound of hooves as the rider left, galloping hard for the moor.

*

"Aye, that's me, old man. Jasper Harper none the less." The coat was undone, his boots up on the table and both legs outstretched. No customs men or Redcoats could get near him in here, and he knew it. Dorcas caught the arrogance of the insolent young pup. Harper, for what it was worth, frowned, annoyed at the old soldier's presence. There was better company about and he glanced away as if to tell him so. "And what d'you want of me, sir?" Harper looked back at him, wrinkling his nose. "Hurry now, then be on yer way."

Dorcas bent forward and whispered briefly. One leg came off the table and the beer spilled as Jasper grabbed him. "Who told yer that? Eh?" The dark eyes narrowed menacingly. "Quick...be out with it. Who told yer? Answer me, yer old dolt."

"Came through from Exford, so they did. The troop watered their 'orses under the bridge." Dorcas repeated what he had said. "They said she was bad," he growled. "Mazed they said and locked 'er up, so they did. Said 'er wouldn't last long. Hardy Cockram, her Dad, brought in the minister, so 'e did. Never done nort like that afore."

"You speakin' the truth, old man? Eh? The truth?" Harper was on his feet buttoning his coat. "If 'tis a trap or false word why I'll...."

"Could be, my boy. Could well be." A finger went up for Dorcas Venner had long ago learned to cover himself. "But that's the word what was passed. Said young Bess Cockram were bad and for to tell yer to get up there fast...afore she goes. Be on yer guard, lad...but be on yer way afore it's too late." Dorcas followed Harper into the yard, holding the lantern as the rider checked his horse.

"My thanks." The words came back over the clatter of hooves. Dorcas held the lantern higher still, dropping it and raising it three times. A second horse left High Bullen, kicking out as the spurs dug deep. The highwayman would be riding fast and the trooper on the hill had but five minutes start to where they had set the trap. His job now done, Dorcas Venner turned for home.

*

"Stay down...right down." Sergeant Hector Coward hissed to the men around him. "Get down and *stay* down, damn yer eyes." The second horseman had come and gone. His message about the highwayman had been delivered and there was little time left. "I'll challenge him once, in the name of the Queen, and we'll take him there an' then." He looked at the bodies lying waiting in the gorse. "Go for the man not the horse. Right...everyone keep down."

The road was a ribbon of moonlight, the sky a mass of stars, and the ditches around Sandyway Cross were cold and wet. Hector Coward's eight men lay hidden, well back from the hollow where the four tracks met. Behind them, back up towards the ridge, his party of Redcoats lay hidden in the gorse. The high-wayman, RSM Fanshawe had demanded, was to be taken, one way or the other, and the soldiers lay ready.

They saw him long before he reached the cross tracks as his figure was outlined clearly by the full moon. Those closest might have seen him rein in his horse, bend forward and search the track. There were many sets of prints in the soft earth but two caught his eye, both scored freshly with mud and sand flung back. They were the marks of galloping hooves so he pulled up and moved off the track, waiting patiently and listening to the sounds of the night. Then, slowly and carefully he moved back again, crossing over to the high ground and circling cautiously. Sergeant Coward and the others watched him pick his way warily through the heather.

The ragged volley was far too early, just as Sergeant Coward reckoned it would be. Even as the sound of the shots echoed down the valley behind them, they heard the hooves drumming. *"Stand up...Fire at will."* He knew they were too slow, too late and the rider far too quick. Harper, his hat lost and his hair streaming behind, swung down from his saddle and clung to his horse's neck as he sped away. '*Diddly-dum...diddly–dum...diddly-dum.   Diddly-dum...diddly-dum...diddly-dum,*' the hoof beats drummed into the night. It was over. The quarry had escaped and, one by one, the soldiers rose to their feet.

✻

"You did what?" Regimental Sergeant Major Fanshawe glared at the sergeant in front of his desk.

"Tried for him in the open, sir. 'Twas the only way."

"What'ya mean the only way? We told you to get into the place an' to take hold of the wench hostage. Use 'er as bait. Lock 'er up and let 'im come to you. What were you thinking about?"

"Couldn't 'ave done that, sir." Hector Coward swallowed hard. "The place was packed out...drinkin' night, sir. Me an' Corporal Webber checked it out. There would 'ave bin hell to pay, sir...the place would 'ave gone mad." They had indeed checked out The Sportsmans Inn. There were but two lonely souls in the parlour and it was on the way back to the horses that Dan Webber had put his hand on his friend's arm.

"You know this Harper fellow…this highwayman? He's one of our Luke's…one of *Luke* Harper's lot, his nephew or summat. Did yer know that?"

Coward slowed and stopped. "*Luke* Harper? Jack's old pal from Lynmouth, you mean?"

"Aye, that's the one." The two men stood in silence. "Summat else as well. Remember, Jack's lad Davey…him and the Westcott boy what's gone off to join the Fourth?" Hector nodded. "They talked about this Jasper Harper…said he was a right good friend of Jack's as well. Done a smugglin' run out to the farm or summat."

Hector Coward said nothing. The ambush, like every night before it, had been right slap on the cross tracks where nobody in their right mind, certainly not a Gentleman of the Road, would have come blundering through. But tonight he had moved them back. The soldiers were hidden away well enough but they were far too far away for any damage to be done and far too spread out, Sergeant Coward had seen to that as well. Jack's friend, any friend of Jack Tucker, he vowed, would live to ride again.

3

The gentle breeze off the Black Sea felt cold and the effect of the hot tea from the cook's wagon had long since worn off. Davey and Billy, like the rest of the squadron, swung their arms and stamped their feet as they waited for the sun to rise beyond the Tchernaya valley.

"That Exquisite's a beautiful animal." Davey rubbed his hands in the dawn chill as the burly figure of Sam Parkes led Lord Paget's charger to the officer's tent. "Looks a bit different now to when 'e was on board…eh *Parksey?*"

"Off to wake 'is nibs then, are ye, Parksey boy?" one of the troopers jeered. "Got 'is nibs's potty all ready 'ave yer?" Trooper Wood wiggled his backside obscenely. "And 'is nice clean panty-woos as well?" Those nearest sniggered. One belched loudly.

"Up yours," the tall manservant growled. "And keep yer arse to yerself, Woodsie. It's big enough."

The soldiers paused, their minds drifting back to what they had been talking about earlier. "Aye…they reckon it's going to be today all right. I 'eard that Mr Martyn talking to Major Lowe last night." Trooper Bobby Hamlyn spat out his wad of tobacco. "Never stops yatterin' on 'e don't. Never bloody stops but that's wot they were sayin'. Them Turks 'ave legged it an' left the door wide open for the Ruskies. That's wot they reckon."

"'Ow many of 'em?" Tommy Wood hawked and adjusted his belt.

"Coupla thousand, so they reckon…summat like that. Nuthin' we can't hack." The news was digested in silence. The Fourth Light Dragoons, along with the rest of The Light Brigade, had been standing at their horses' heads since the ice-cold hour before dawn. The Russians were making for Balaklava and the British cavalry was going to stop them. The troopers, neither aware nor interested in the grand design of things, waited impassively to do whatever their masters required of them.

*

Two hours later the Fourth were drawn up alongside the Eighth Hussars, the two regiments in line together behind the Eleventh, the Seventeenth Lancers and the Thirteenth. The Light Brigade stood patiently but, over to their right, the battle had already begun. They watched quietly as the Heavy Brigade engaged the enemy on the high ground beyond the valley. Billy Westcott stood on Crimond's rump to get a better view. Davy and Trooper Archie Braund also stood on their mounts, leaning against one another for balance.

"Them Heavies are bloody pullin' up, look," Jimmy Ellis, swarthy and unkempt even in his uniform, guffawed loudly. "'Ere…bleedin' chickin, that lot. They're stoppin'. Ain't got the stuffin' fer it."

"'Oo said two bleedin' thousand? You, was it?" Tommy Wood rounded on the troopers behind him. "You bloody blind or summat? Look at all that lot in front of the 'Eavies'…an' that lot up there on the left. Up there for Chis'sake." He pointed to the slopes on the other side of the valley then turned and scanned the valley itself. "Then there's all that lot…right down the far end. Way off down there, look. *Two…bleedin…thousand.* What's 'e on about? More like twenty thousand, mate."

"Leave it all to the Light boys, eh…usual bloody story." Trooper White, his huge red nose protruding from under his battered busby, offered his opinion. "Send for the Light Brigade, my man," he mocked. "Give 'em all the shitty work…they'll sort it out for yer an' Tally Ho to that."

They ate as they waited. Eggs, biscuits and thin rashers of ham were chewed as they watched the Heavy Brigade on the high ground. Some smoked while others passed canteens of rum up and down the line; others dismounted to ease their chargers. Few cared what their officers were doing or saying. "Usual bloody game…eh?" Archie Braund snorted. "Up in the middle o' the bloody night…then hang around all 'effin' day. Then what? Eh? No one says nuthin 'til the last minute then there's hell to pay…right old panic. Couldn't give a stuff, them lot…champagne charlies, the lot of 'em."

But all of a sudden people began to care and to care a very great deal. Suddenly life sprang into the line of cavalrymen in front of them. Trumpets sounded, men scrambled back onto their mounts. As the lines of horses shuffled and pranced, uniforms were adjusted hastily. One charger kicked out and another bucked as orders were barked along the line.

"The Brigade will advance...Walk, march...trot!"

"That's where we're headin'. Up there, look...up onto the high ground over there, just past the Heavies." Bert Perkins, riding between Billy and Davey pointed with his sabre. "Them's the ones we're goin' for...those Ruskies, look...just up there."

"Bloody hell."

Sssscccchhheeew...........sssscccchhheeew. Sometimes the shells whistled, sometimes they moaned. The musket balls, almost spent, hissed and pinged among them. Two horses in the Eleventh went down. One tried to rise but fell back again. Somewhere behind them a man started screaming.

"Steady, lads, steady there...keep up the pace...an' keep it steady." Sergeant Bell looked down the line. Bridles clinked and accoutrements flapped. Horses heads nodded and shook as they moved. Some blew impatiently. *"Keep up there...oi...you...bloody White...keep it there."* But they never wheeled, they never turned, they just kept on going.

"Jesus...we're not going to wheel to the right." Tommy Wood on Billy's left rose to see better.

"No, we're not for Chris' sake. Look at that, will yer. The Seventeenth and Thirteenth are goin' straight on and we're going after 'em. Right be'ind...straight down the valley." As the Russian guns on the high ground to their left and right began firing at them, the Fourth followed obediently.

"Hey, Sarge...where we going?"   "We can't be going straight on."   "Hell's teeth, bloody can't be...not between all that lot."   *"Shit* ...three down, no four." "Sod the bastards,"   "Where' we goin' then?"   "The guns at the end of the valley."   "Right at the end?"   "Christ Almighty, it's a bloody mile an' more." "Effin orficers."   "Those guns there, look...right down at the far end." *"Jesus* wept."

"Leave that man...close in on the centre."   "Shut yer noise."   "Keep up there...close the gap."   "Steady B Squadron...steady as we go."   "Get that loose horse away...get it away!"   "Leave those two...keep yer dressing...watch the gap." Then the trumpets. *"Canter...steady...steady...steady as she goes...steady.........wait for it.........sabres ready......... wait for it.........chaaaaaaaarge!!"*

✳

Billy remembered little of the next ten minutes or so save when the first line reached the guns. Huge gouts of smoke and flame tore through the ranks as the whole Russian battery fired point blank.

Pieces of men and horses whirled through the air. Blood and entrails flew. Arms waved, legs kicked out, sabres flashed and lances plunged. Men cursed and horses screamed, rising up and falling down again, twisting and rolling, bellies split open, legs in the air. More blood, more flesh. Helmets and busbies here and there. Bitter, filthy smoke all around them. Then they were amongst the guns…

Swords clashed and men cursed. Others yelled, shouted and swore. Many fell, screaming and moaning. More thick, stinging smoke. Horses reared up, cried out, whinnied and shrieked. The line bunched, broke then bunched again. Loose horses, many with flesh gashed wide and blood streaming, crashed terrified here and there, running wild in the awful melee.

Yet still they cut, still they slashed and still they drove on against the line until, suddenly, they were through. They were *there…through…*past the guns at last. *"Rally…rally. Halt front…about."*

"Billy…Billy. You all right." Davey, headdress gone and sweat streaming down his red cheeks, reined in. "Bloody hell…what a do, what a fight. Look at yer arm, Bill." The sleeve was almost torn through yet the arm itself was untouched. "Close…eh?" He turned, caught his breath and shouted. *"Hey…Bert. Tommy. Here…over here. All right, pal? Not hurt are you?"* Billy heard him laugh.

Then came the order to withdraw. *"What?* They cried. Back again?" They stood in their saddles, mouths agape in horror, not believing the command they had just heard. *"What? Back?* Where we came from? Right back down that same bloody valley? And the same bleedin' way…Christ alive." But the guns had been taken and the Russians pushed back…yet now the order came to withdraw.

✳

As they rode back, men continued to fall from shot and ball, others came down when their horses stumbled or fell exhausted. Some were running, some limping, some crawling even. Horses in every position of agony struggled to rise; some floundered back with just their heads rising in anguish. Some riders stayed with their mounts tending their wounds. Slowly, painfully, the proud Light Brigade limped wearily home.

"Billy, quick." It was Tommy Wood who saw Davey fall. "Davey Tucker's down…there look. Behind the grey over there." Tommy reached him first.

"Get on back…get back d'yer hear," Davey gasped. "Get away from here or they'll have yer as well." Billy knelt beside him. "My back, Bill. Got me in the back." Davey clutched at his friend's sleeve. "Hell, Billy. Hell an' damn…an' after all that." He bent forward coughing blood.

"I'll take him, Tommy. You go on." Wood hesitated. "Honest, Tommy. Just go...I'll bring the lad in. Leave 'im to me."

"Get on, Bill...you as well." Davey shook his head, coughing up more blood. "I'm done for...I can feel it...no pain nor nuthin'....just feels weak, like."

"No, Davey. Come on, pal...up yer come. Crimond'll take yer, cross the saddle, like." They struggled to their feet. "Did yer think I would leave yer lyin' there...no way, never. Come on...*hup*, heave now...*up* yer get. One more...that's it. We'll get back together...you an' me."

After Davey had fallen twice, Billy dismounted, lifted him up and held him in the saddle. Like this, they trudged on, horse, handler and rider together, along with the others as the guns continued to roar and muskets to crackle around them. "I'm goin', Bill. Goin' ever so slowly." Davey's voice croaked then he coughed more blood. Now dark and frothy, it was spilling from his mouth down the front of his tunic.

"Hey, come on, lad...not far now." Billy took more of his weight. "Listen, Davey, I'll tell yer summat. Remember the Barle? The river at home? On the way to school that day? The stag...remember? When he went for me. 'Twas you then, wasn't it...you came to pick me up. Picked me up, yer did. Remember?"

The laugh turned into a cough and Davey slipped again. Billy pushed him back. "Tell 'em we did it, Billy." His voice was weaker. He was snatching for breath as the blood in his lungs was slowly choking him. "Tell Mum...an' Jack...an Ralph. Tell 'em we got there, Billy. You, me and the lads." Billy held him in place. "Tell Jade, Billy...yes, tell Jade an' all. Tell 'er I missed 'er but I'll be waitin'." His head slumped forward. "Look after 'er," he whispered. "Look after the lass, Bill." Then he slipped again.

Billy pushed him back. He slipped once more and fell to the ground, where he died in his friend's arms with the lines and the tents but yards away.

✳

Some of the men sat silently, hollow-eyed, filthy and exhausted. Some talked non-stop. Some walked off by themselves, others chatted and laughed as though nothing was amiss. Several got blind drunk on anything they could find. All that night they brought them in, the dead and the dying. Loose horses were caught, the wounded ones tended and nursed by the cavalrymen. Those badly hurt were shot where they lay, the troopers weeping by their sides.

✳

"Billy…Billy Westcott?" The squadron orderly opened the tent flap. "S'arnt Major wants you…over at the horse lines. Straight away…so on yer way, lad." Billy ran.

"You helped Parkes look after Exquisite on the journey out…right?"

"Sort of, sir. Sometimes I gave an 'and. When I could, like." Billy stood to attention. Sergeant Major Hawkes, crop-haired and menacing, looked him up and down, his face half hidden by the bushy red muttonchops.

"At ease, lad, at ease. Parkes 'as gone…killed or captured, we dunno which. The Colonel's for home tomorrow with the despatches. Asked fer you to go as 'is man. Get yer kit together and up to the office tent…right." Billy half turned then stopped and looked back.

"What's up, lad. What's up?" The face had softened.

"Beg pardon, sir but it's Tucker…Trooper Tucker, sir. We were close, we were. Very close and…"

"I know, I know. We'll see to 'im, lad. See to 'im proper, we will. There's nuthin more to be done…yer did all yer possibly could, my boy…all yer could."

"And his kit, sir?" Billy could feel the tears welling. "His things?"

"Oh, aye, his things." Hawkes's hand was on Billy's shoulder. "Right then…came from down your way, didn't 'e? Down the Westcountry?" Billy nodded. "Know his people, d'yer not? Then take his things, lad…take 'em to 'is folks and pass 'em on." Hawkes paused. The two men looked at each other. "An' when you see 'em, tell 'em…tell 'em the boy did well…a good lad 'e was an' all…an' a damned good soldier at that.

"Tell 'em…" The hand pressed hard. Hawkes blinked and looked away, then sighed heavily. "Tell 'em he was there at the guns." He turned back, almost shouting. "Right up there at the guns so 'e was… an' yer could never do better than that."

4

Katherine wrapped the shawl around her shoulders and opened the garden gate. She had not been to the cottage before and stepped carefully along the narrow pathway. As she passed the first window she saw movement but went on to the door. It opened at her second knock. "Hullo Kitty." The frightened look shook her. The girl, she thought, looked wary, fearful of what might come next as though she had come with bad news. "Kitty, I'd like to talk…is it possible to come in?"

"Why yes...yes, of course, ma'am." Kitty held the door. "Afraid 'tis a bit rough in 'ere. Gillan's downstairs now, find's things more easy."

"Yes, yes I know. Jack told me he helped you." She paused to choose her words. "Listen, Kitty...it's time we spoke. Is there somewhere...?" Katherine felt her stomach turn at the smell; it was all she could do to refrain from holding her shawl to her face.

"Oh yes, ma'am...yes, the kitchen." Kitty half tripped and ran to the door then turned and looked at Katherine, searching her face anxiously, still worried. "This way, but 'tis a mite untidy, I'm afraid."

Katherine closed the door. "Kitty, listen. I know how things are." It would have been easier had the younger woman not kept looking away. "I've heard about your husband, you know." She paused, wondering how to go on. "We've all seen you struggling. Things must be difficult."

"Not bin easy, ma'am." Their eyes met at last. "Gillan's too poorly to walk far now and things're a bit tight, one way or t'other."

"Exactly." Katherine smiled sympathetically. "And that's why I've come. We were wondering if you might care for a bit of work...a few days a week up at the house, perhaps. The money might help, and it'd do you good to get out...as long as Gillan's safe on his own."

Kitty moved away from the fire then stopped with her head hung low before she turned and stared at Katherine. "Thank you, ma'am," she whispered. "'Tis very, very kind." The words came quickly. "Us needs it bad...ain't nuthin left. Just dunno which way to turn." She covered her eyes. "'Tis hard right now, ma'am. Very hard, it is." Katherine put her arms on the girl's shoulders.

"Listen. Start as soon as you can, will you. There's plenty to do and you can take whatever meals you like with us. And Kitty...one more thing."

"Yes, ma'am." The worried look again.

"Everyone calls me Katherine. None of this madam or ma'am. Please, Kitty. I hate it and I won't have it. Honestly, even the little boys say Katherine...and that's for you too."

Kitty's eyes shut tightly, both hands went to her face. "Oh God," she sobbed, falling against Katherine's shoulder. "You're so kind, ma'am. All of you, reelly...you're all so kind."

Chapter Sixteen

Katherine lowered the wicker basket onto the top stair, stood slowly and eased her back. Everywhere outside was damp. The raw late October mist had seen to that. The fires in the kitchen and parlour were surrounded with wet clothes yet still she needed more room. She paused then wearily picked up the washing again and made her way to the girls' room where she found space by the window. Behind her, in the attic beyond the stairs, she could hear the two boys.

They had settled well, and Ernie's high, piping voice was already a source of amusement. As bad as Declan's flute, Jack had joked. He was tall for his thirteen years, half a head higher than the older Stan Bawden. The youngest of eight, he had had to fight his corner at home and had tried it at Sherdon until Charlotte calmed him. At first he had resisted, scowling fiercely with his eyes glaring pugnaciously from under his dark, beetle brows. Stan was the opposite. Short, red faced and tubby, he beamed quietly at the world, inclining his good ear so he could hear better. He had been born partially deaf and would sit silently at the table, grinning benignly and looking on while the ones around him chatted away.

Katherine smiled at the memory of how Ernie had tried to tease the older boy. She and Jack had watched carefully lest the jibes should hurt but Stanley, jovial and placid, had simply ignored the hooting taunts. Ernie had been puzzled, then angry but finally he had tired. Now, the two boys, like Billy and Davey before them, were inseparable.

She hummed to herself. Sunday would be All Saints Day and she had agreed to decorate a window in the church. Before that Wilmot was coming with Tennyson and already they were making preparations for the visit. Wilmot would be bringing more books and Alfred would surely be his usual bright, amusing self. It would be lovely to see him again. Having left her wet shoes by the back door, she padded quietly towards the attic steps in her bare feet. Above her she could hear Ernie, his voice raised as usual. Still smiling she climbed the first few steps to listen.

"I tell yer, Stan, Ralph says so. Jack an' Kitty's been seein' one another." Katherine inched closer. "Charles an' Harry knows about it an' all. Everyone does...'cept Katherine that is."

"What do them do?" Stan's voice crackled and he cleared his throat. "D'yer think they...you know, at it, like?"

"Yeah, course they are. Rex Fisher reckons so. Ralph says Rex saw 'em. Says they must 'ave been. Just up from Ferny Ball, on the riverbank they were. Reckons that Kitty's real swell, 'e does. Reckons Jack reelly fancies 'er, an' all.

Yeah...course they'm at it."

"I dunno." Stan sounded unconvinced. "All talk it is. Nobody seen nuthin'."

"Get away. Ralph's seen 'em, *an'* Edgar Heard's seen 'em...honest, Stan. They're doin' it, all right...Jack an' Kitty. You watch 'im...an' watch 'er when they'm together. 'Tis true enough."

*

Katherine managed to hold on to the empty basket but she was gasping heavily. Then, stopping only to glance blindly up and down the landing, she stumbled down the stairs. Dropping the basket by the fire, she hurried into the scullery, pulled on her shoes and staggered outside.

She ran, arms pumping and hips swinging, past the shippon and stables before stopping to catch her breath. Her eyes stared, pained and desperate, first at the mist around her then down at her hands clasped tightly together. Slowly she sank back against the wet stone wall, her eyes shutting tight as if to close out the awful vision in her mind. It was impossible, it *could* not be true....it *had* to be made up, it *had* to be. Her stomach churned making her heart thump wildly as it tried to keep pace.

Yet how could a boy like that make it up? And why should he? Why should he lie like that? How could Ernie, a simple young farm boy, dream up such a tale? And Ralph, and Rex and Edgar? Charles and Harry? *Little Harry*...a child of just eight years. How could they all have been drawn into this? And what about Lottie? What did she know, what had she heard? Dear God, who else? What more was there? Her head sank into her hands.

And Kitty...*Kitty*, who she had held in her arms as she wept and to whom she had offered work in the house. *Kitty*...and *Jack*...her very own Jack. Wait a minute...wait a minute...think, think. Stop and think...stop. Slowly her hands ran through her hair. As the mad jumble of thoughts tumbled and whirled through her head, she could feel her heart pounding heavily. She had to be calm...to stop panicking...to think. Think carefully. Where should she start? She closed her eyes then opened them wide and breathed in the cold, damp air. Her whole body was trembling.

An hour later she returned to the house, changed and began to prepare supper. She was surprised at how calm she felt. Her mind had steadied and she had begun to think coherently. Her hands were shaking and her heart still fluttered in shock but her mind had cleared. She would have to watch, watch and listen for those tiny tell-tale signs. A glance here, a quick smile, a gesture from the body, the movement of a finger...she would watch. Until then she could do nothing: she would have to be patient. Tomorrow she would be gathering greenery for the church and the day after the visitors would be arriving. It would be a busy time she told them at the table before excusing herself and retiring early. Once alone in bed she lay like a stone, silent and still, her eyes searching the darkness above her.

Later Jack joined her, sliding quietly between the rough, cold sheets. She felt one hand on her thigh then the other closed gently around her breast. She waited, tensing for his kiss with her fists clenched to keep her body still, and made no response. Only when he turned away heavily, the soles of his feet like ice against her legs, did she relax and continue her long vigil through the night. By lunchtime the next day she knew beyond doubt.

*

She had not expected to see Bamber at Landacre Bridge but recognised at once the stout frame leaning over the parapet. She approached quietly, her arms full of dead bracken fronds and rushes from the water's edge but her foot scuffed a stone and he turned, lurching and swaying to spare his hip.

"'Ello, my dear." His smile was as broad as ever and his arms were held wide. "An' pretty a picture as ever a man would want. 'Tis either for the church or young Wilmot tomorrow. Eh?" He nodded at the reeds in her arms. "Well, me dear, you've caught the guard nappin' proper, you 'ave. Good job you weren't they ponies." Bamber chuckled and rubbed his hands.

"Ponies, Bamber? What brings you here?" She tried to respond to his warmth but her voice sounded thin. If it was anyone but him she would have had no desire for company. Her mind was full enough and she sought peace on her own where she could think, but his presence was comforting. "And all alone at a spot like this?"

"'Tis pony time, m'dear. Drifting time they calls it. Yer 'e be." Bamber picked up two sacks and folded them into a cushion. "There you are, 'ave yourself a seat." He patted his handiwork, motioning her to sit on the parapet. "You can watch…'elp me too if yer want. Up there look." Bamber pointed to three riders on Withypool Hill. "They'm driftin' the ponies down to the village where they fence 'em in and take off the yearlings…for Bampton Pony Fair. Now's the time."

"And what's your part?"

"We-ll." He lifted his felt hat and scratched, then chuckled, his face now more like that of an excited child. "Well, us older ones…ones what can't go gallopin' about no more, they puts us out as stops, for to turn back the herd." Bamber looked at her and wiped his mouth, then looked closer. The smile drained from his face and he caught her hand. "'Ere…you'm not seeming yerself today, m'dear, that's fer sure. Don't sound too cheery, neither. Now then, us can't 'ave yer all glum like that. Summat's up."

For several minutes she parried his questions but it was no use. If she said nothing in response he would assume she knew and would then surely tell Charlotte. But, if she confided in him, he might help, and she needed help. She hung her head. "There's talk, Bamber," she whispered, bending to pick up a frond of bracken she had dropped.

"Oh ah." The farmer didn't move.

"You've heard no doubt. Even *I've* heard that everyone's talking." Now she looked at him, her eyes questioning his. "You know what I mean, Bamber? Know what I'm talking about, don't you...what they're all saying?"

"Ah...I've 'eard talk." His blue eyes stared straight into hers. "Not much mind...but words...just now and then, like."

"And...what d'you think?" For a moment she glanced away. "Oh, Bamber...it's dreadful, really dreadful and I don't know what to believe. Just don't know what to do."

"Well now." Bamber took her arm gently and she put a hand over his, reassured by the strong warmth. "Words 'ave bin said, that's fer sure, dear...but...*I* don't know. There's for ever talk 'bout summat or other. Countryfolks're like that...not much else to talk about. But...here...Jack an' Kitty? *I'm* not so sure."

"But I've got to know, Bamber. I have to." Her words tumbled out. She noticed then, just for a moment, that the softness in his eyes had gone. "It's impossible to live like this...I can't bear it. It's awful." She could feel the tears coming again yet couldn't help herself and she shivered. "What am I going to *do*, Bamber?" she muttered. "What's going on?"

The farmer studied his hands then looked away, across to the high moor. His mouth was drawn tightly down. Eventually he spoke. "My...advice," the words came very slowly. "My advice is to do *nort*...do nothing until you're *sure*. 'Tisn't never worth goin' rushin' around 'til you're sure...an' you're not, are you? So, bide yer time, m'dear."

"But it's likely to be true, isn't it? I mean, *all* this talk...everyone seems to know and they can't *all* be wrong. There must be *some*thing going on."

"There's always a chance, dear. Always a chance...I have to say that." Bamber was smiling again but the merriment had gone from his face. The eyes regarding her now were filled with compassion. She knew he would never lie to her, but he would never be able to tell her either. It was his eyes, his wise, blue eyes; they were telling her what she feared. He, too, had heard and it was then that she knew.

2

"Wait, wait...hold everything." Wilmot chortled at the sheer exhilaration in the voice and watched fascinated as Tennyson fumbled with his spectacles. "Now...oh, for goodness sake...let's see. Let...us...see." He adjusted the second of the two pairs and peered into the distance.

Sherdon, now bathed in the late autumn sunshine and less than half a mile away, beckoned warmly. "There you are, Tucker…just look at that. *Wonderful*…a *most* wonderful sight. And the *peace*. Ye gods what solitude. Listen to that silence…roaring and thundering away out there."

"Come Alfred, we're late already and my sister-in-law'll be vexed."

"Huh! Yes, yes…never keep 'em waiting…'tis dangerous, ye know," he wagged a finger mischievously. "That's their prerogative, Will. Now listen, *you* tell them about the baby." Wilmot frowned. "My young 'un, Will. Our little Lionel. *You* tell 'em we've called him Lionel…and when they've guessed why, we'll drink to it. Here…see this." The poet tapped his saddlebag. "I've brought enough good claret for us all."

Katherine had to admit that their arrival broke the spell. One of the leather boxes on the packhorse was filled with books, new and old together. There was months of reading for her. Wilmot walked alone with Jack, the two returning an hour later, flushed and happy. At last he seemed convinced that his younger brother wanted him to farm Sherdon as he knew best. Alfred took over the window space in the drawing room. Letters, books and newspapers lay scattered across the table and window seat. More spilled onto the floor.

✳

"It's all quite mad." Tennyson threw his arms into the air, knife and fork in his hands. "This world of ours…these terrible, terrible wars." He peered from face to face, his eyes searching clumsily. Then he shrugged expansively. "Why on earth can't man learn to live together, side by side…there's room enough for all of us. I don't know…I just don't know." He stared hard at his plate then addressed himself to the slices of beef, cutting vigorously and urgently. The youngsters perched silent and wide-eyed, looking from one to another in wonderment then warily at the tall figure, crouched and bearded. Jack, Ralph, Kitty and Katherine waited patiently, only Wilmot remained unconcerned.

Katherine reached for his hand. "D'you think we're going to have to wait long, Alfred? For news, I mean. News of what happened and that they're safe?"

"I know, I know…of course. I'm so sorry…just can't get it off my mind," he was still chewing hungrily, politely behind his napkin. "It shouldn't be long now until we know. Goodness me…and to think they were just two little boys when I saw them last, two young lads…and now this." He swallowed noisily and reached for his glass. "Lottie, my dear…it must be dreadful for you…poor you," he gasped. "Oh dear, it's all so cruel."

"Well, we *think* they were there and we're all anxious to hear but not even the hussars in Barnstaple have heard." Katherine smiled across to Charlotte. "It'll be wonderful just to know they're safe."

"I know, my dear, I know," Tennyson took her hand. "I understand…let's pray hard for glad tidings. 'Twill be just like that, I'm sure. They're fine. But you must be proud, all of you…so very proud."

✳

The news came next morning. Harry saw the horseman first, then Francis. *"Mama, mama, quick.* Look, a soldier. *Quick*…he's coming up the lane. Look everybody…"

"'Tis a Barnstaple man," Jack shaded his eyes. "One of The Royal North Devons. And he knows we're here by the way he's kickin' on, that's for sure." Charlotte and Katherine were at the door, Tennyson by the open window as the rider slowed before reining in. The two boys held on to their father's hands as they watched the hussar salute.

"Mrs Tucker, sir?" he queried. "Mrs Charlotte Tucker?"

Jack nodded, studying the man closely. "Aye," he replied. "This is her home an' she's here in the house right now."

"A despatch from London, sir." The soldier glanced at the writing. "Came through Exeter last night. Through Higher Barracks." He leant forward and handed the envelope to the waiting hand. "Be kind enough to see 'er gets it, sir. Straight away, like, if yer don't mind." He sat back in the saddle and was about to salute. "Oh, and beggin' yer pardon, sir." Jack glanced up: he knew already. "Very sorry to hear the news, sir. All of us was…all the lads at Ebberley Lawn. Thank you, sir."

Jack never saw the salute, neither did he hear his two boys asking him what was happening. He only looked up at his sister as he climbed the last of the front steps. He glanced at Tennyson, then up at Kitty watching from an upstairs window. Charlotte's face was impassive. "'Tis Davey?"

Jack swallowed. "Shall I open it, love?" She nodded. Katherine put an arm round her as Tennyson came to the door. The first few terrible words were enough but he finished reading before looking at his sister. "Aye," he murmured. "'Tis the lad. 'Tis our Davey…he fell in the battle."

✳

Nobody saw the second horseman as he rode towards the farm late that afternoon. It was unusual for a uniformed trooper to be leading a pack animal but that's who crossed the bridge by Sherdon cottage.

246

Trooper Westcott had been given one week's furlough. Lord Paget had dismissed him as soon as they reached London. The ten guineas he had pressed into his hand on Horseguards' Parade was more than enough. "Take a week, Westcott. My thanks; you've served me well, very well. After that, get back to Exeter and they'll see to you there."

He had longed to get home but knew Sherdon would be waiting to hear news of the one who would not be coming back. He had to see them; he owed them that. He had to tell them about Davey, to deliver his things and to tell them what his friend had said as he died. It was Kitty's shout that made him stop, just as he led the packhorse through the gate. *"Billy,"* she shouted, running from the garden. "Billy…oh, Billy, you're safe. Thank God, thank God you're all right." She ran to his horse and stared up at him with both hands on his boot.

"Aye, I'm fine…fine as can be, thanks Kitty." He paused, frowning momentarily, for it was more than a year since he had seen her last. "Have you heard anything yet? The news…about Davey?"

"Yes," she replied, suddenly ashamed at her own excitement. "Yes, we heard this morning." She paused uncertainly. "'Twas awful bad, Billy. You'll be wanting to see Lottie, of course."

"Aye," he replied. "I had to come…had to make sure she heard." She watched as he dismounted and tied the animals to the wall rings in the yard.

"She's with Katherine." Kitty gestured towards the house. "There're visitors, Billy. With her now so they are. She's being brave, ever so brave but I know she'll love to see yer. Oh, Billy…it's so sad…so sad." Kitty threw her arms round him then left him to walk in alone.

*

He walked slowly, unafraid of confronting them yet burdened down with guilt. Guilt that he had survived and survived untouched when so many others, like Davey, had fallen. They had all felt the same after the battle; ashamed that fate had spared *them* rather than their comrades, the ones they had left in the three long lines at the bottom of the olive grove. They had been happy enough with their own company afterwards but chose to hide away from the rest of the world, from their kin who could never understand. It had been easy in London where nobody knew him and on the train, too; but now he had to face those who knew what had happened, those who would see that he had been spared while their own had not.

Bamber met him at the door. Jack had sent the boys for him earlier, as soon as they heard the news. Charlotte, he knew, would need her man. The old farmer beamed warmly and his arms opened wide, then fell to his side. His smile vanished and his head shook in disbelief as Billy climbed the steps.

As he entered the hallway he felt uncomfortable in his uniform. It was somehow making the point about Davey's absence yet, one by one, they clasped him. As she hugged him, Charlotte laughed, her tears wetting his face. When he grasped hold of Billy's hand, Tennyson stared wild-eyed. He, too, shook his head in wonder but had nothing to say. Nobody could understand why just the one had come back. They asked each other and they asked themselves but no one was any the wiser. Later, they listened at the table as he told them what they wanted to know. Sometimes a question was asked, sometimes an eye dabbed but they listened until they knew; then, one by one, they took their leave.

Billy stayed on until just he and Tennyson were left together. He did not feel like sleep and was happy to talk. "Tell me again, Billy," the Poet Laureate pleaded, his tall frame hunched under the beams as he moved his chair. "Come over here. Pull yourself up a chair...next to the fire. Now, let me hear it again, if you will...all of it, all of it. It's the very stuff of legend and, by the very devil himself, it's something to hear from one who was there."

He waited until Billy filled his glass and the two of them were sitting side by side, their faces lit by the flames that jumped suddenly from a fresh log. "How far did you have to go, for Heaven's sake?" Tennyson swept back his shock of unkempt hair, peering closely at the young soldier.

"Nigh on half a league or more, sir...a good mile an 'alf, anyways." Billy thought for a moment. "Aye, must've bin all of that."

"That's a terrible long way," Tennyson muttered. "Too far...far, far too far. Heavens, yes. And the guns...both sides, you said earlier? Eh?"

"Aye, both sides of the valley we were going down...and right up above us, they were. Firing down on us, like." Billy stared at the fire. "And more right down at the far end. They was the ones we were sent after. Ordered us off after that lot, so they did." He paused, prodding the log further into the fire with his foot. 'Twas a mighty long way, an' all, sir." He paused. "Too far, it was...too far for anyone." He shook his head, remembering it all so well.

Tennyson caught him by the shoulder. "All round you, eh? Just as the reports said...left, right and to the front. *Madness*...dear God what madness." He gestured wildly at the futility of it then sat back. The two men regarded each other in silence; the tall, spare poet alone with the young cavalryman. First one smiled weakly then the other, the older man muttered to himself and picked at his ear. "And then back again? Eh? The same way? All that long way back down the valley? Why...in the name of all that's merciful, why? *Why*, for God's sake!"

"Dunno." Billy shrugged and turned the wine in his glass. "That's what they said, sir, so us just got on an' done it. That's when they got Davey...got 'im in the back." There was silence again as one remembered while the other imagined.

"Thank you, Billy." After what seemed an age, Tennyson leant forward staring into the embers. "Thank you most kindly." He spoke slowly, nodding reflectively. "There's something awful about it all, yet there's something…how d'you say, something heroic…majestic even. Something I would never've known." It was as though he was talking to himself. "I've read it all, of course…the reports. William Russell…he described it all so well and I've tried to understand, tried to feel like those who were *there* must have felt." He sat back again now staring in awe at the figure next to him.

"But it's the soldiers' tale that brings it all to life, y'know. How the trooper himself saw it that day…and now I know. Now I can see it all." He laughed suddenly, as if surprised at himself. "And to think, Billy…to think that you must be the only man in England right now who could have told it like that, for the others'll be weeks away yet. It's a tale that'll be told down the ages…a wonderful, terrible tale and to think young Davey's still out there." He sighed heavily. "Oh dear, oh dear…I don't know."

*

Charlotte handed the silver spur back to Billy the next morning when she told him about Jade. "Tell 'er, I'll be up directly, Billy. She'll be there fer certain, bound to be. The babe, young Arthur's more'n three months now. Just like his dad 'e is." She forced a smile. "She'll love the spur an' what you told me they said about Davey. She's missed 'im, has Jade. Just as Davey missed her." Billy could see she was struggling.

"'Tis all right, Lottie. I'll tell 'er everything an' er mum an' dad as well. Part of Davey's there now at Barkham, an' they can all be proud of 'im."

Billy spent more than an hour at the farm. She had cried quietly when he told her, rocking the baby sleeping beside them. Then he left at dusk. As he bent down to kiss her farewell, Jade pleaded with him to return. He looked at her, then at the babe in her arms. He knew he would be back and promised her so. Just as the front door shut behind them, he bent forward and kissed her again, more tenderly than before.

3

Storm after storm beat up Sherdon valley. Winter, so it seemed, had come early, bearing down heavily on those living together at the farm.

They all knew that it would be difficult living and working together but none had any idea how life would press in on them all. Everyone found themselves watching the others, listening carefully to whatever was said, none daring to speak freely or joke too quickly for fear of catching the eye. Gillan grew weaker, Kitty more despondent. Her world had become a nightmare. Bamber, sensing Charlotte's unhappiness, asked her to move out but she refused, electing to remain at the farm with Katherine.

✳

Kitty went back to work after lunch, the others listening in silence to her feet on the stairs. Jack, his legs outstretched in front of the fire, sat brooding. The roots, he had explained at lunch, breaking the silence when only knives and forks were scraping across plates, the roots were late and that meant difficulties at lambing if the weather was bad. Ralph's rejoinder that there was little enough hay served only to deepen the gloom.

The rain threw itself down, swashed against the windows by an angry wind that moaned in the eaves and lifted the sack under the scullery door. Smoke billowed out from the fires, preferring to remain in the shelter of the rooms and maddening those trying to keep warm. Jack knew he had work to do for the lambs needed to be sorted yet he sat on, only bothering to move his legs out of the way when they cleared the table around him. For a while he was silent and morose; his wet clothes still clammy and uncomfortable, his spirits as black as the day outside.

Then suddenly he stood. "Ayeeeuh…*right*". As he stretched and yawned, so his arms punched the air. There was work to be done and his place was outside not by the fire. "Gotta change first," he muttered, unbuttoning his shirt roughly, lifting it from around his belt and throwing it down before striding from the room.

"Cuh…just look at that, will yer now." Charlotte nodded towards the damp shirt on the table. "Moody as an old ram these days 'e is. More'n a drop of rain out there and he's worse than any of 'em. Forever changing his things, he is."

Katherine, her hair streaked with moisture from the steam, took the last of the washing from the tub. She shook out the clothes, flinching back to avoid the spray as she did so, then began to ring them out. Charlotte helped her, the two women turning the mangle together before shaking them again to fold and put in the basket. Neither spoke. Both wanted to but chose to wait until they knew they were on their own.

✳

Jack threw open the bedroom door and stopped. Kitty spun round, shocked at the sudden intrusion and stood like a frightened child with one hand to her mouth. He could see she had been in tears again but he hesitated. Perhaps she wanted to be on her own. "What's up, Kitty…why now…and why in here?" She gave no reply, just turned her back and stood with her head bowed and shoulders hunched.

"Come on, dear. What's this about?" Even as he came up to her she made no reply. His hand on her neck toyed with her curls. "Why the tears this time?" he whispered gently. "Why? Come on…tell me."

"I can't go on…can't go on like this." Even now she looked down. "It's no good staying on here, Jack…'tis not possible. I can't. It's the looks I'm getting…the silences when I walk in…the whispers and things. I can't, Jack…can't take it no more. I'd rather be at home, back at the cottage sittin' with Gillan. Better on me own down there."

He cursed silently. For almost a month he had steered clear, watching his ways and avoiding the cottage. Ralph had gone to help them whenever she asked; Lottie had taken her to the market, Katherine to the church. What more could he have done? "Listen…come here." She turned and moved towards him, then closer still until she was up against him. "Bide yer time, dear. Don't go running off anywhere. Just stay the same old Kitty and it'll pass. 'Tis the same for me and we've to see this through." She stood quietly, now tucked between his arms with her head against his chest where she felt secure.

"Jack." She pulled back and looked up at him. "Y'know, I don't know what I'd 'ave done without yer." Her eyes were searching his face. One hand crept up to his cheek. "You've saved me, Jack…saved me from…I dunno…from goin' mad, I s'pose. Dunno reelly, but your'e a wunnerful man."

Suddenly she laughed, her eyes once again sparkling and her locks of red hair dancing in the light. "You're a wunnerful man, Jack Tucker…truly, truly wunner-ful. You'll never be mine but I love you dearly." As she lifted her face to his, she felt his two arms pulling her into his body.

*

Katherine left the washing basket on the top stair and paused, both hands running down the small of her back. A draught of wind caught a bedroom door and it knocked suddenly, unable to close itself. She stepped round the basket and crossed the landing in her bare feet to try her own room first, opening the door to check.

And there she froze, one hand still on the catch. They had not seen her but she watched, transfixed and horrified as his bare arms closed around her, one hand moving to hold her head, her own two arms reaching around and up his naked back.

Katherine stood unmoving, as still as death itself with only her chest heaving and her heart pounding. Then, as she backed away across the landing, so her hands crept to her mouth. Her eyes were staring wildly through the open doorway between them and it was the wicker basket she had left on the top step that caught her foot.

Her scream, piercing and long, came as she tumbled backwards and plunged down. As she fell so her feet kicked high in the air. Her hands grabbed wildly before she crashed deep into the stairwell where her cry was cut short and her neck was broken.

4

The funeral was five days later.

Wilmot and Bamber between them saw to the arrangements. Arthur Fisher and Edgar Heard helped Ralph run the farm. Twice Jack rode out to Simonsbath to see William Thornton. He tried to find the courage to talk to the parson, to ask him why, but he never brought himself to do so, choosing instead to burden himself with his guilt and his secrets.

The day before they buried her he rode back down the Barle, past Wheal Eliza, past the hill fort and on as far as Ferny Ball. Before he turned up Sherdon Water he stopped. The Great Deep had not changed. He stared long and hard across the bog to where the water lay innocently amongst the moss and grasses. It was there it had all begun. For a moment he saw the white hand stretched out in terror, the desperation on her face and her pleading eyes.

He crossed the river at the ford, rode upstream then turned and looked again. In the deep pool beyond the bridge, he saw her reflection. This time it was Badgeworthy. He saw the half smile as she lay back under the tree in the dappled sunlight; the day the buzzards wheeled and called above them. Without thinking he reached up to stroke his neck where he had first felt her hand.

He saw again her anguish when Harriet had not lived, the love in her eyes when Charles and Harry, and Frank, and Alice, and little Anna had first cried. And he looked down at his hands, staring in disbelief. Only yesterday, these same hands had picked her clothes from her chair then held them to his face as he drank down the fragrance of her body; these same hands that had caressed her soft warmth as she used to lie beside him.

He sat on the high rock above the river, alone in his hour of grief, until the lengthening shadows chilled the day. And as he rode on so his mind cleared. He knew what had to be done and would see to it. He would have to for it was the only way. Earlier in the day, the undertakers had brought her back and left her as he had told them, so that all those who wanted could come and pay their respects.

*

Some came in the evening, others came later by lantern light, staying a while to give comfort and support. The Bawdens and Loosemores came from Molland, the Corwens from Lynton. Lizzie, together with her brother Lord Preston, rode down from Simonsbath with the Aclands and Frederic.

But most, and there were many, came early on the day of the funeral itself; the first arriving soon after dawn. More and more came to pause before her coffin in the front parlour. Some just gazed at the peaceful face on which the hair now lay still.

Some crossed themselves and knelt before her body while others wept. He received them all, his black cravat and black frock coat setting off his gaunt features.

At noon Bamber came to him. "Us'll be moving on 'ere long, Jack...as soon as we've closed her down." The old man took his arm. "Said yer wanted to know when."

"Aye, Bamber. My thanks, dear friend." Jack smiled and touched the farmer's cheek. "Collect them all up in the hall and front parlour, will you now. Where they can hear what I've to say. Everyone now...family, friends, friends of friends, young and old...all together."

"You sure, Jack?" Bamber glanced round nervously. "P'raps 'tis not reelly the best time for speeches an' that." The blue eyes, still moist and red rimmed, looked at him sorrowfully. "P'raps after 'tis over, m'dear. Might be better...easier then, like."

"Don't worry, Bamber." Jack nodded reassuringly. "It won't be long...just a word that has to be said before she's laid to rest." Even as he eased his way past those in front of him, the hall and passageways were filling. More squeezed into open doorways. He ran up the stairs, two at a time, and went into his bedroom, then reappeared, keeping one hand behind him as he began his descent.

He chose his place half way down and stood in the deep stairwell at the turn of the stairs, on the cursed spot itself as he had come to call it. Even as he raised his hand, the house fell quiet. He paused, looking around, until he knew they were all waiting for him to begin. "From the bottom of my heart, I thank you all for being with us today." He stood with one hand holding his lapel, glancing down at the faces. Some smiled affectionately but most were anxious and expectant. "'Tis unusual for an address to be given at such a time but I wanted to be sure that *all* of you, *all* who loved dear Katherine, should hear me before we bid her farewell." He cleared his throat then paused, choosing his words with care.

"These last few months have been difficult...there has been rumour and gossip, talk in such volumes that it has reached our own ears out here at Sherdon." Some looked down confused, others turned away now afraid to catch his eye. That apart there was not a movement, not a sound. "I believe I owe it to those closest to me, and to Katherine, my dear, departed wife, that I should speak honestly and freely, here and now and before you all, so that this vexed matter can be laid to rest forever." He withdrew his right hand from behind his back and raised it high, the black leather-bound Bible plain for all to see. Several gasped. One or two cried out aloud. Hands flew to mouths. Once more he paused, this time until all who had moved to cross themselves had become still again.

"I beg you all listen to what I have to say," he continued. "Mark my words with care". He glanced up at the Bible then down at those below. "I do solemnly swear before all of you here present, and before Almighty God, that I have never, since taking my darling Katherine to be my wedded wife, that I have never known the body of any other woman." He could see the pain on the drawn upturned faces. "Of any…other…woman, neither here, nor anywhere else and that is the truth upon this Good Book. So help me God."

Even from where he stood, Jack could feel the tension. The air was tight and thin yet laden with expectation. Those who knew nothing about it were stunned, looking round to seek an explanation. But the ones who thought they did know, now knew better. No man would have dared to swear such a solemn oath before God, in front of his wife's coffin and before so many, had his conscience not been clear.

5

Jack bade farewell at the graveside. One by one the mourners filed past. Many took his hand and whispered that they were glad he had been so brave. Few, if any, realised that what they said only grieved him the more. He felt like turning away and running for home but he saw them all through, leaving only when the sextons returned to do their business.

He rode fast. Bamber had asked the others back so he rode home alone, determined to get back before nightfall. Although not yet dark, the soft glow of lanterns shone from the windows as he rode up the lane. It would be strange in the house, very strange, but he was glad to be back. It was the sanctuary he had been yearning for, the peace he craved.

✳

The knock on the door came as he was reaching for his farm jacket. There was a second knock, louder, then a third, louder still. He ran in his stockinged feet and waistcoat and pulled the door open. The figure in the porch swung round to face him, hands on hips and with his cloak swept back. The high top hat was still on his head. Behind him a groom held two horses. "Ah, Tucker…Mr Tucker, so it is."

"Lord Preston …we met very briefly earlier but it's been a long time, I do believe. Pray, step inside, sir." He was tired to the bone but smiled nonetheless for it was good of him to call.

"That I will not do. Not now, nor ever." Jack stared uncomprehending. "I'm here to make sure you know how mortified and outraged I am at the death of my dear sister." The hat came off and was jabbed at him. Jack stepped back. " If ever…"

"But, sir…" Jack interjected. He stood bewildered, his eyes searching the other for an explanation.

"Stay quiet and, for once in your life, keep your place." The voice was hard and cutting. "You are nothing more than a vile, self-opinionated devil of a man who stole our beloved Katherine and imprisoned her out here in this foul and barren land. You are a parasite who took her from us purely for your own wretched advantage...simply to use our family name." Herbert Preston's chest was heaving, his breath now coming in gasps.

"You...you worked her like a chattel until she was fit to drop, even when she was heavy with child. And then...and then you sullied her good name with your carnal dalliances among your own kind. You are *terrible*...you are an *awful* man and it gives me what little satisfaction I can muster at this time to tell you so to your face." He faltered, shaking: his eyes were staring madly.

"God damn you, Tucker." He paused, this time to fill his lungs. "That's what I and the family have to say." Now he was shouting. "Damn you, man...damn you in hell and damn you for ever more." Lord Preston turned on his heels. Once mounted he rode off into the autumn twilight, never once looking back.

*

Jack supported himself against the doorway. He could not think. He did not know how to think. He was speechless and helpless, unable to act and unable to move. But at the sound of footsteps on the stairs, he managed to turn, slowly and clumsily. It was Kitty who had remained behind. Now she came up to him.

"It's Charles, Jack. The fever's back again and it's bad this time, very bad. We must send for..." She saw his face and stopped. "Oh Jack...what's happened?" she breathed. "What was all that about?" As he looked at her, his whole body sagged, exhausted. "Oh...Jack, what is it? Tell me."

"Kitty," he whispered. "I need you. Dear God, how I need you." As he fell forward, her hands caught him and cradled his head against her shoulder.

THE END.

Bibliography.

The following books, magazines and pamphlets were all sources of information, either read avidly from cover to cover or dipped into whenever the need arose. To them all and, in particular their patient and trusting owners, I owe an immense debt of gratitude.

History.

Devon and Somerset Staghounds. The,
  Macdermot. E.T.
Exmoor. A little History of, Bourne. Hope. L.
Exmoor. The Heritage of, Burton. Roger. A.
Exmoor. Portrait of, Peel. J.H.B.
Exmoor. Yesterday's, Eardley-Wilmot. Hazel.
Exmoor. Sporting and otherwise, Marshall. H.J.

Exmoor Forest. The Reclamation of,
  Orwin, Sellick and Bonham-Carter.
Exmoor. Murder and Mystery on, Hurley.J.
Exmoor in the 1850s. A filthy barren ground.
  Bonham-Carter. V.
Exmoor Review – various.
Westcountry mysteries. Wilson. C.

Mapping.

Ordnance Survey of England and Wales. First Edition 1809. Sheets 74,75,82 and 83.

People and places.

Alfred Lord Tennyson. A brief biography.
  Everett. G.
Arlington Court The National Trust
Barnstaple. Exploring, Bradbeer. J.
Devon Family. A, Acland. A.
Devon Families. Lauder. R.

Dunster Castle The National Trust
Glenthorne, A most romantic place. Halliday. U.
Luttrell Family. The, Victoria to Elizabeth II. Lee. T.
Lynton and Lynmouth. An illustrated history of,
  Travis. J.

Living England.

Below stairs in the great country houses.
  Hartcup. A.
British farming. 150 years of, Patterson. A.
Crime and Society. Fitzgerald,
  McLennan and Lawson.
The English. A social history. 1066-1945. Hibbert. C.
Farming Times. Dixon. M.
Fashion in the western world. Yarwood. D
Furniture. The observer's book of, Woodforde. J.
Georgian house style. Cranfield.I.
Highwaymen. Ash. R.
Horsedrawn vehicles. Discovering, Smith D.J.
How much is that worth? Munby. L.
Irish in Britain. The, 1815-1914.
Living Sword. The, Nadi. A.

Making of the English working class.
  Thompson. E.P
Miller's Antiques. 1993.
Mines and miners of Cornwall.
  Hamilton Jenkin. A.K.
The Newgate calendar. Reflections on,
  Heppenstall. R.
On Fencing. Nadi. A.
Poor relief in Devon. Wheeleker and Eyles.
Rural life in Victorian England. Mingay. G.E.
Rural Rides. Cobbett. William.
Victorian England. Reader. W.J.
Wild Flowers. Field guide to, Reader's Digest.
Within living memory. Bate.M.

Military.

British Army. The, Talbot-Booyh.
Near Run Thing. A, Howarth. D.
Waterloo. The Hundred Days, Chandler. D.G.
Waterloo 1815. Wootten. G.
Crimean War. The, Sweetman. J.

Reason Why. The, Woodham Smith. C.
The 4th Queen's Own Hussars. 1685-1958.
  The story of, Scott Daniel. D.
North Devon Yeomanry, The. Rowe. J.